# THE
# SEED
# GATHERERS

# The Seed Gatherers

## INGE MELDGAARD

## A Novel

Published by Inge Meldgaard
18 Colby Drive, Belgrave Heights
Victoria, Australia 3160

**Australian distributor:**

Digital Print Australia
135 Gilles Street, Adelaide
South Australia, Australia 5000
www.digitalprintaustralia.com
books@digitalprintaustralia.com

National Library of Australia Cataloguing-in-Publication entry:

Author: Inge Meldgaard
Title: The Seed Gatherers
ISBN: 978-0-646-91168-7
Dewey Number: A823.4

Cover design and artwork by Inge Meldgaard
Website: redmatilda.daportfolio.com

Thanks are due to my sister Tove
for her generous assistance with
editing this manuscript.

Maintaining genetic diversity, or biodiversity, is one of the most fundamentally important concepts relating to life on Earth. It is both the cornerstone and the culmination of evolution.

# DEDICATION

This book is dedicated to the memory of Nikolai Vavilov and to the staff of the historic Pavlovsk Research Station in Saint Petersburg, Russia. Established by Vavilov, a botanist, in 1926, this research station was the first seed bank of its kind in the world. It is one of a number created across the former Soviet Union to house a vast collection of seeds and tubers from both wild and cultivated crops, collected over decades, and from many different countries.

The collection at the Pavlovsk Research Station is also a botanical garden of trees and plants, spread over some twelve hundred acres. This collection is harvested to replace ageing stock, while seedlings and cuttings are sent to other parts of the world. There are, for example, around six hundred varieties of apple, collected from thirty-five different countries.

Vavilov and his staff had the foresight to realise these old food crop varieties and wild plants had both the potential to enhance our diets and to save us from starvation should existing crops fail...and fail they do. Industrialisation of agriculture has reduced the number of crops grown worldwide to a very low number, often requiring the use of expensive pesticides and fertilisers to maintain their health. As the climate and geography of the world changes, crops that were once viable may no longer be so, either due to changes in the weather, increased vulnerability to pests and diseases, or simply because in some regions suitable agricultural land is no longer available. Climate change is also forecast to decrease the protein content and increase the natural toxins in many crop varieties due to higher carbon dioxide levels in the atmosphere.

While genetic engineering may solve some problems, reintroduction of, or cross-breeding with, older varieties of food plants is frequently a far more productive, less expensive, more reliable, less dangerous and faster method of obtaining results. However, since the collapse of the Soviet Union in 1991 the Pavlovsk Research Station has been critically short of funds and so struggles to maintain its vital work.

The history of this priceless seed bank is both tragic and ironic. Vavilov was imprisoned by Stalin and subsequently died of starvation in 1943. Also during World War II, when Saint Petersburg, or Leningrad as it was then named, was under siege[1], twelve of the scientists working at

---

[1] The Siege of Leningrad by the German army and their Finnish allies began on the 8th September 1941 and was lifted on the 27th January 1944. Hitler's expressed aim was to utterly destroy the city. This battle alone cost millions of lives, civilian and military, in both the city and throughout the region, from starvation and the direct effects of war.

the research station chose to die of starvation rather than eat the seeds and tubers in their collection.

The future of the station was again under threat in 2010 when the Russian Government decided to use twenty percent of the research station's fields for a housing development. An international campaign succeeded in temporarily preventing this from going ahead, gaining the attention of Prime Minister Medvedev, who undertook to look into the matter.

The Royal Botanic Gardens (RBG) at Kew, in England, now also house a vast collection of seeds and are part of the Millennium Seed Bank Partnership, which comprises organisations across some fifty countries. The RBG targets plants and regions most at risk from climate change and the ever-increasing impact of human activities. In 2012, ten percent of the world's wild plant species were represented in their seed bank. Another important organisation within the international network of biodiversity conservationists is the Global Crop Diversity Trust. The Trust is actively involved with the Government of Norway in the operation of the Svalbard Global Seed Vault, a 'fail-safe' facility established by the Norwegian Government and opened in 2008. This facility provides a safety backup for existing gene bank collections.

In Melbourne, Victoria, the Royal Botanic Gardens, established in 1846, play a vital role in the conservation of plants, through biodiversity research, programs to protect rare and threatened plants, and the study of habitats. The organisation encompasses two large sites in Melbourne and includes the National Herbarium of Victoria, the State Botanical Collection and the Australian Research Centre for Urban Ecology. The National Herbarium of Victoria was established in 1853, and houses a collection of approximately 1.2 million dried plant, algae and fungi specimens. The majority of the collection is Australian, with an emphasis on the flora of Victoria. The Herbarium is responsible for the Victorian Conservation Seedbank, which is part of the Millennium Seed Bank Partnership (MSBP). The seed bank collects seeds from native species within Victoria for long-term storage, research and restoration programs. Over the first five years of the project (2005–2010) seed collections from over 500 Victorian plant species were incorporated into the Victorian Conservation Seedbank, and duplicated within the MSBP. Of the approximately 3,200 native species in Victoria, nearly 800 are considered to be in danger of becoming extinct within the next few decades. Developing techniques for seed germination and seedling growth are critical if plants are to be returned to the wild, and work related to this issue is routinely undertaken for all species collected. [2]

---

[2] Reference: www.rbg.vic.gov.au

# CHAPTER ONE

The flooded streetscape of the central city and the brown waters of the Yarra River, snaking its way toward Port Phillip Bay, greeted Yngwie as he peered out the window of the interstate airjet circling high over Melbourne's Tullamarine airport. The bright, early autumn sky had turned the glass of the landmark Rialto tower into a gleaming finger of blue light, soaring upwards in a gesture that to him seemed appropriate, considering what he had come here to do. Yngwie chuckled, then stretched and yawned. The trip from Western Australia had taken most of the day, travelling from the north of the state, where, amongst other things, he had taken a tourist flight over the Bungle Bungle range, located in the vast Purnululu reserve. At this time of year, during the wet season, the heat and humidity were in stark contrast to Norway, still in the grip of the same icy sub-zero temperatures of two months ago, when he left his home town of Rjukan.

Yngwie was not due back until mid-June, ready to begin university in Oslo in July, where he intended to study information technology. Eventually, he wanted to specialise in the challenging new field of large-scale holographics. Meanwhile, there were still three months left to enjoy, so he hoped Melbourne would prove more interesting than he anticipated. There was one place, though, he wanted to see, and this was the old forest on the northeastern boundary of the city. The forests here were altogether different from those of Europe and elsewhere, and were home to a remarkable variety of unique creatures and colourful birds.

His thoughts were interrupted by the voice of the airjet's captain announcing that they had landed and passengers were now free to disembark. Although nowhere near as hot as Western Australia, the heat outside still held Yngwie in its fierce grip as he walked the short distance from the main airport building to the waiting railcar that would take him to Ferntree Gully, located on the outer edge of Melbourne, at the foot of the Dandenong Ranges. He entered his Federation identity number into the transport's terminal, together with his destination, then found a seat and watched while the other passengers from the latest flights settled into theirs. A little over an hour later, Yngwie was standing outside the communal house, in the centre of Ferntree Gully, where he had booked a room.

The entrance to the communal house consisted of a plastiglass-enclosed foyer, surrounded on the outside by what appeared to be a large vegetable garden and a small fruit orchard. Dusk was falling and Yngwie was more than ready for his evening meal, so instead of exploring the area as he might otherwise have done, he approached the foyer door and asked to speak to the manager. When the door slid aside, he didn't have long to wait before a young woman entered the room, smiled, and introduced herself. As they shook hands, Yngwie said, 'I have a booking for two weeks, which I confirmed yesterday... Oh, and by the way, is the *entire* living area beneath the ground?'

'Yes, it is,' replied the young woman, her eyes crinkling in amusement. 'Most of the buildings outside the older central areas are underground. They have been for a long time... More energy-efficient, and safer too. It also frees up the land. Did you notice our garden outside?'

'I did. It's a unique approach, and gives an air of mystery.' Yngwie grinned. 'I like it, and I like the gardens I saw on the way here from the airport.'

'Well, there should be plenty for you to enjoy then, especially our forests. Do you intend to do any walking?'

'Oh yes. The big trees...the mountain ash...are one of the main reasons I came here. I understand there aren't many left?'

'No, sadly, but we look after the ones we still have. Now, we need to complete your booking, so if you could just place your right hand on the identification pad of the computer here... Thank you... And we also have an old-fashioned custom of asking our guests to sign and date our guest book. Do you mind?'

'Not at all.' Yngwie signed his name with a flourish then wrote the date: Saturday, the third of March 2457.


After the evening meal, rather than socialising with the other guests, Yngwie returned to his room. He took his hand reader from his backpack, checked the time, had a shower, then got into bed and set the alarm to wake him at 04:30. Five years of painstaking research, testing and probing had gone into the software he and his friend Torleif had built, and tonight, they would see the results of their work. For their plan to succeed, they each needed to be precisely where they were now: Torleif was still in Rjukan, Norway, and Yngwie was here in Ferntree Gully, Melbourne. At 04:56 Melbourne time, the software would be activated, and two minutes later, when the sun set in Rjukan at 18:58, local time, Torleif would see whether the first step in their plan had succeeded. If not, he would contact Yngwie, and if Yngwie heard nothing, he would find out for himself what happened next, when the sun set tomorrow, here in Melbourne, at 19:53. The final step, when the cascade was programmed to begin worldwide, would occur at 21:46 Melbourne time, which was when the sun went down in Perth, at 19:46, their time. Yngwie smiled; he was sure of their success. Afterwards, well...that was another matter.

The next morning, in nearby Berwick, Shahid rose from his bed, laid out the mat his mother had so lovingly embroidered, then knelt to pray. When he had finished, and after carefully rolling up the mat and putting it away, the young man made his preparations for the day, with his usual calm, precise movements and attention to detail.

Today, his morning would be spent travelling from his home to the forests of Sherbrooke, in the Dandenong Ranges, thirty-five kilometres from the centre of Melbourne. Once there, he intended to make his way up the hillsides on foot until he found the mature mountain ash for which he was responsible. Due to environmental degradation and changes in climate, *Eucalyptus regnans* was now a rare and increasingly endangered species in the State of Victoria, so the regions where it grew were divided into segments, each with its own seed gatherers and team of forest guardians. As a seed gatherer, Shahid's work contributed to the survival of the species and to the rehabilitation of areas where the trees could be reintroduced.

Outside, the day was already too warm and, despite the air-conditioned comfort of his landjet, Shahid looked forward to the cooler temperatures within the forest. He had brought food for his midsun meal plus an ample supply of water because once he reached his destination, there would be nowhere convenient to obtain any. All private dwellings had long since disappeared from the Dandenong Ranges, and the closest township, Ferntree Gully, was located on the plains of the western side, with Gembrook twenty kilometres away on the eastern plain.

When he arrived at the base of the mountain, Shahid secured his landjet and put on his backpack. The dry forest of mixed trees – messmate, narrow-leaved peppermint, mountain grey gum and blackwood – grew far up onto the hillsides, replacing the mountain ash that once lived there. As he walked, Shahid listened to the birds calling to each other, some loud and raucous, others melodic and sweet to his ears. He recognised the song of a grey butcherbird, which was followed by the screech of a white cockatoo, and then the keening cry of a currawong. The sound he longed to hear was missing: the call of the lyrebird. Common in this area before white settlement, they became increasingly rare as the forests were cut down and introduced animals preyed upon them. Now, they were all gone, their glorious dance a distant memory.

After walking for some time, Shahid located the tree he was seeking: a three-hundred-and-fifty-year-old mountain ash, some ninety metres in height. Straight and tall, with white bark and brown peeling layers, it was, to him, a wonderful sight. The old tree was in flower and the coming season promised to be bountiful. Scientists from the Willsmere Research Centre in Kew, here in Melbourne, had almost finished their aerial survey of the mountain to establish how many of the eucalypts were in flower, and the results so far were encouraging. For the past three years, very few had flowered sufficiently for a good harvest. With luck, however, this year, he would collect the seeds in mid-winter and send some to both the Global Seed Vault in Svalbard, Norway, and to the Federation Herbarium in Oslo. It was time to replenish their stock.

Shahid inspected the tree closely to make sure it still appeared to be in good health, then continued on towards the next mountain ash listed on the survey map. The dry forest floor crackled underfoot and small insects scurried away as he walked. The danger of fire was ever-present, and too frequent bushfires in the past were one of the reasons the mountain ash were now rare, but today the risk was low, there being only a light breeze. Nevertheless, should the worst happen, he had memorised the locations of the well-provisioned underground fire bunkers liberally dotted throughout the hills.

One of these bunkers provided a cool and restful place for Shahid to first pray and then eat his somewhat elaborate midsun meal, prepared by his mother that morning. Although he was twenty-eight years of age, he saw no reason to live elsewhere than with his parents, particularly as he thoroughly enjoyed their company. His father worked as a medical practitioner at the Ferntree Gully medcentre, while his mother was a psychologist with the Melbourne Peacekeeping Force. Both were proud of their son's work and glad he had chosen to remain at home until, perhaps, the day came when he found a bondmate, although this was not something they discussed.

The early afternoon passed pleasantly, despite the breeze having become stronger, ruffling Shahid's soft, black hair. He wore it shoulder length, which suited his oval face, with its large, expressive brown eyes. Of a slight build, he was nevertheless extremely fit, and strong enough to easily climb to the tops of the mountain ash to collect their seeds. Perched in the treetops, Shahid felt even closer to his spiritual centre, as well as to the forest he helped protect. Today, though, was a day of remaining close to the ground, looking for signs of ill health in the understorey plants and the soil surrounding the trees. Noticing a young blackberry seedling – a noxious and rampant weed if left to grow – he knelt to remove it, and then collapsed to the ground, writhing in agony. His leg felt as if it had been stabbed to the bone and he had only enough time to pull his comlink from his pocket, desperately hoping to activate its emergency signal, when he lost consciousness.

With a wet scarf wrapped around his nose and mouth, Yngwie watched the flames for as long as he dared. The reality was far more frightening than he had ever imagined, the noise and smoke almost overwhelming. Turning aside at last, he moved away from the fire and walked as quickly as he could safely manage in the direction of Ferntree Gully. Running was out of the question – the terrain was far too dangerous and stumbling could cost him his life. With still almost two and a half kilometres to go before he reached the edge of the forest, Yngwie noticed someone lying motionless on the ground, near the base of a small eucalypt. He cautiously approached then knelt down to feel for a pulse. Although weak, it was there. As he reached for his comlink to call the nearest medcentre, he noticed, about one and a half metres away, a large, dark spider, hiding in the leaf litter. He instinctively flinched, but the startled spider soon scuttled away. Relieved, although still wary in case there were others nearby, Yngwie spoke with the medtech who answered his call.

'A large, dark spider, you say,' said the medtech, eyebrows raised. 'Were its legs thin, or thick-looking?'

'Definitely thick,' answered Yngwie, 'and it was one of those fat, ugly things everyone thinks of when they talk about scary spiders.'

'Hmm... We're not aware of any large, venomous spiders in this part of Victoria, but we'll send some anti-venom with the ambutechs anyway. They should be there in about twenty minutes at the most. Keep him still in case he wakes up, and don't move him.'

'What if the fire comes closer? The smoke is getting worse.'

'If all else fails, you'll have to carry him out, but in the process, if he *has* been bitten by the spider, he might die. You need to be prepared for the possibility.'

'Damnation!' muttered Yngwie. 'Well, I hope the ambutechs get here quickly. Can you stay with me while we wait, in case something happens and I don't know what to do?'

'Yes, no problem... Where are you from, if you don't mind my asking? Your accent is a little unusual.' The medtech smiled in an effort to reduce the tension.

'I'm from Norway...on holiday. I want to stay for at least a few weeks. This is a fascinating country, but harsh.'

'Yes, it can be, but yours can be unkind as well, can't it?'

'Oh yes... The winters are long and it's easy enough to die, but we're used to it, so manage fairly well.'

'How are you finding the heat?' The medtech had noticed Yngwie was beginning to perspire.

'The heat is fine. Our summers can be just as hot, though not for long.' Yngwie wiped his face with the scarf he had taken off to make his call to the medcentre. He was beginning to feel ill from breathing in so much smoke.

'Do you have any water with you?' asked the medtech.

'Yes. Why?'

'I suggest you drink some and then cool your face and wrists with as much as you can spare.'

Yngwie did as the medtech suggested, feeling slightly better as a result, but not much. 'Oh hell!' he exclaimed. 'The fire's too close. The wind has sprung up and changed direction. Sorry... I need to get us out of here. You can keep track of my comlink, can't you?'

'Yes, we'll keep a close eye on you, don't worry. Do you know which direction to go?'

'I do...' replied Yngwie, before shoving the comlink into his shirt pocket and then manoeuvring Shahid onto his shoulders. Holding him tightly, he began walking, trying hard not to think about what would happen if the approaching fire caught them. After almost a kilometre, Yngwie was close to collapse. He stumbled, regained his balance, and as he did, saw two ambutechs approaching. One of them gripped his shoulder to reassure him, then helped each other lift Shahid onto the hoverbed they had brought with them. A quick, but meticulous, examination showed that Shahid had indeed been bitten by a spider, which in all likelihood sounded like some species of funnel-web, even though they were not normally found in the region, other than an innocuous, relatively small variety.

'Right,' said the taller of the two ambutechs as he administered the antivenom, 'this should do it, though I don't imagine he'll wake up for a while.'

'With all these trees and so much undergrowth, I think it'd be best if we carry him, rather than try to use the hoverbed, don't you?' suggested the second ambutech.

'Yes, I do, so let's get going. We don't have much time. Can you manage to walk, young fellow?' he said, addressing Yngwie.

Yngwie stood up from where he had been sitting, resting his back against a tree. 'Yes, I can manage. It's not far.' He staggered slightly, then straightened his shoulders and tried to smile.

'Good man. I'll go first, you follow, and my mate here can follow on after you. Okay?' and with that, the ambutech, who was now carrying Shahid over his shoulders, walked on at a brisk pace, with the others close behind.

Once they reached the waiting ambulance, Yngwie looked back and saw the firefighters were already tackling the flames, which, fortunately, hadn't reached into the treetops. However, this was no time to linger, so when Shahid was safely strapped in and everyone was inside, the ambulance lifted off and shortly afterwards landed outside the main entrance to the Ferntree Gully medcentre.

'There, you should be feeling better now,' announced the practitioner treating Yngwie. 'Your nose, throat and lungs don't seem to have sustained any lasting damage. Your blood pressure is normal now too, so you're ready to go home.'

'Thank you,' replied Yngwie, standing up. 'Are you able to tell me whether the man I came in with is recovering?'

'Ah, yes... It seems I have you to thank for saving my son's life. It's his Namingday today, too. It would have been doubly tragic if it had also been the day he died.' The practitioner hesitated, making an effort to control his voice. After taking a deep breath, he managed to say, 'We intended to celebrate this evening, but will need to do it another day. My bondmate and I would be glad if you could join us when Shahid has recovered.' He put his head to one side and smiled, holding out his hand.

'I did what anyone would do,' replied Yngwie, raising his eyebrows in surprise, but returning the smile and taking the offered hand in a firm grip.

'Perhaps, but not everyone would have the strength to carry him so far. It's just as well the spider bit him through his clothing. Otherwise he might have died immediately, or else soon afterwards from having to be moved before pressure bandaging could be applied. We'll need to investigate though, because I've never heard of this type of thing happening here in Melbourne. People are sometimes bitten by other spiders, but none as venomous as this one.'

'What do you think it was?'

'We agree with the ambutechs that it was most likely some type of funnel-web...possibly a male. Apparently at this time of year they tend to wander around during the night searching for a mate, and if they haven't managed to return to their burrows by morning, hide somewhere dark and damp. Shahid must have knelt down just where the spider was hiding.' The practitioner looked away for a moment, frowning, then shook his head and said, 'Would you like to visit him tomorrow, when he'll no doubt be in better shape to thank you himself?'

'Why, yes, that sounds fine,' said Yngwie. 'Could you tell him I'll come back at around 14:00?' By then he and Torleif would know how their 'experiment' was progressing, although it would take a full twenty-four hours to complete.

'Good, good... Thank you again, and we'll look forward to your visiting us when Shahid is home, which we anticipate will be in a few days time...assuming you intend to stay in Melbourne that long?'

'Oh yes, I have places I want to see and the communal house is very comfortable.' Yngwie smiled, and then the practitioner left to see to his other patients. After he had gone, Yngwie checked his comlink: 16:42. Excellent... There was enough time for a brief nap before the evening meal, which would be followed by a long sleepless night tracking the cascade.

## CHAPTER TWO

Despite the lack of sleep, Yngwie revelled in his sense of achievement. So far, the cascade was working perfectly, and unless the Federation managed to block the software, it would continue to do so for the full twenty-four hours of its operation. Afterwards, he was certain this security glitch in the lattice communications network would be resolved, and no one in future would ever be able to repeat his and Torleif's actions...which was precisely what they wanted. Their artwork, as they regarded it, would be unique, unable ever to be reproduced by anyone else.

He paused to enjoy the warmth of the sun against his skin and to breathe in the delicate, fresh fragrance of the living carpet of tiny red flowers that made up the surface of the trafficway. The distance from the communal house to the Ferntree Gully medcentre was only about one and a half kilometres, so, for Yngwie, used to the mountainsides of Norway, this was a pleasant little stroll. A few minutes further walking brought him to the building, which consisted of two towers, one rising fifteen storeys high and the other eight. Yngwie wondered why the building needed to be so large... Presumably the Federation limited the birth rate here to one child per family as they did everywhere else? And surely Australians were no more accident prone than other people? Perhaps the medcentre housed research facilities?

Dismissing the question from his mind as being of little importance, Yngwie concentrated instead on simply enjoying this exhilarating day. The doors of the main entrance – which was located at the base of the smaller of the two towers – slid aside for him as he approached. He went to the reception area and waited until someone in attendance noticed him.

'May I help you?' asked a middle-aged woman, looking up from her computer screen.

'I hope so,' replied Yngwie pleasantly. 'I came in yesterday afternoon with a young man named Shahid, who, as it turns out, was bitten by a spider. His father works here as a practitioner and suggested I might want to visit – if Shahid is well enough by now?'

'Oh yes! I heard about it. You're quite the hero, rescuing him from the fire, too.' The woman grinned. 'He's doing fine, so if you go to the fifth

11

floor of this tower and look for room 504, you'll soon find him. I'm sure he'll be glad to thank you in person.'

Yngwie, embarrassed by the praise, nevertheless returned the grin and thanked her, then found the lift to the fifth floor. A short while later, he was standing outside room 504 and wondering if he should have brought a gift of some type, particularly as Shahid had missed out on his Namingday celebration. Oh well, he didn't know him, so it'd be difficult to guess what he might like. Still, perhaps he could bring him something when he visited the family for the promised dinner? Yngwie knocked on the door, waited a moment, and went inside.

'Hello,' he said, standing by the foot of the bed and smiling. 'You're feeling better, I see. My name is Yngwie. I'm the one who found you when you were unconscious...in the forest yesterday.'

Shahid gazed at him, the dark smudges beneath his eyes showing the stress of his ordeal. He held out a slim hand and Yngwie moved closer to take it in his own. They looked at each other for a few seconds, brown eyes meeting grey, before Yngwie gently released Shahid's hand and sat down on the chair conveniently placed by the bed. 'I met your father yesterday,' he said. 'He treated me for smoke inhalation. I'm fine today, though. I understand the firefighters managed to put out the blaze fairly quickly, and that very little damage was done.'

Smiling, Shahid nodded.

'Do they know yet how the fire began?' continued Yngwie, wondering why Shahid hadn't yet spoken.

Shahid nodded again, but held up a hand, as if to say, 'Wait a moment.' Yngwie then watched while he leaned over to his bedside table and picked up his hand reader.

As Shahid used the keypad in an extraordinary display of speed and dexterity, Yngwie was startled to hear a soft, mellow voice answer his question: 'Yes, two people were camping in the forest and lit a fire at midsun, even though it's illegal to do so. The fire spread into nearby grass, then into the undergrowth. They contacted the forest guardians almost immediately, but even with only a slight breeze, fire can spread quickly in hot, dry weather. We were lucky to escape.'

'Aren't you able to speak without using your hand reader?' asked Yngwie, intrigued by this use of the technology, which he knew existed but had never before witnessed.

Shaking his head, Shahid touched a single icon on the hand reader's screen: 'No. I have a rare genetic disorder and have never been able to speak.' Clearly, he answered the question quite often and had programmed the icon to give this explanation.

'I'm sorry,' said Yngwie. It wasn't often he came across anyone with a serious disability. Not only did the Federation limit families to one child in most circumstances, they also required prospective parents to undergo genetic screening before granting them fertility rights.

Shahid touched a different icon on his hand reader: 'Don't worry, I'm used to it. My work doesn't require me to speak with many people, so it isn't a big problem.'

Yngwie laughed, while Shahid grinned. Obviously, the conversation was proceeding along familiar lines.

'Okay,' said Yngwie, 'one more standard question. What is your profession?'

Shahid waggled his eyebrows, touched the screen again, and the hand reader's 'voice' said, 'I'm a seed gatherer, and I look after the forest as well. Seeds from rare species are stored here in Melbourne and samples are sent to the Federation Herbarium in Oslo and to the seed vault at Svalbard as backup, to make sure we have stock for the future. We also use some to rehabilitate degraded areas.'

'Were you collecting seeds yesterday?' Yngwie knew of the Svalbard facility, and like most Norwegians, was proud of his country's contribution to its establishment during the twentieth century.

'No, we do that in pairs, or teams. It's too dangerous to do alone. I was assessing the trees' health, as well as that of the surrounding areas. The mountain ash are flowering well this year, so we want to collect as many seeds as we can in mid-winter, when they ripen. We were lucky there was little wind yesterday and the fire didn't get into the treetops. They usually die if they're burnt.'

'What about the spider that bit you? What if there are more? Won't they make it harder to do your work?' Yngwie repressed a shudder at the memory.

'I'm sure the Federation will send someone out to do a survey, and afterwards, we'll decide what to do. If it's a ground-dwelling species it may not be so difficult to deal with, but if it's a tree dweller, that may not be so good.' Shahid made a face, then, using the hand reader, searched for an image to show Yngwie. 'Is this anything like the spider you saw?' he 'asked'.

'It ran away very quickly, so it's hard to say, but, yes, it did look something like that. Your father said it was most likely a funnel-web. Is that one?'

'Yes, it is. I'm amazed some people actually like these things and enjoy studying them. Ugh!' answered Shahid, after closing the image.

'When you're well again, may I come with you on one of your surveys? One of the reasons I came to this part of Melbourne was to see the old forest. It's so unlike those we have in Norway. There's much more variety, and the birds are wonderful.'

'Yes,' agreed Shahid, pleased. 'I'd enjoy the company. Do you take photographs?'

'Not often, unless I want something special. I'm interested in art though, especially holographics. I intend to go to university this year and eventually specialise in that field. It's another reason I wanted to come to Melbourne. The person who succeeded in creating the first true, moving, life-sized holographic image came from Melbourne. Unfortunately, they died soon afterwards, but the woman's son continued her work. I'd like to meet him, if possible, and see some of his performances. Have you ever seen any?'

'No, but I've heard of the woman, and her son, Zarik. I work in collaboration with the Willsmere Research Centre here in Melbourne, and some of the scientists were involved in a case some years back when someone tried to steal their research and sabotage their work. The woman, Marika, worked as an information technologist at the central computer site in Clayton and almost certainly engineered the security breach that allowed those responsible to break in and attack one of the researchers. He wasn't seriously hurt, but during the investigation, she was murdered.'

'What! Murdered?' exclaimed Yngwie.

'Yes, and then the person who killed her was murdered as well, the same day. The case was a complex one that went on for a long time. I had only just begun working at Willsmere, so it was all extremely upsetting. If you come to visit again tomorrow, you could meet one of the scientists involved in the case. Her name's Karla. I think you'd like her.' Shahid smiled. He and Karla had a great deal in common. She had spent many years collecting samples of rare plants from all over Australia for a reference collection and so could fully appreciate the work Shahid did.

'What time does she intend to visit?'

'She promised to be here at 14:30. Would that be convenient for you too?' answered Shahid.

'Yes, I think so... Tell me, are you allowed to leave your room yet? I could take you for a tour of the hospital if you wanted a change of scenery. I see you have a comfortable-looking wheelchair here.'

'Thank you, Yngwie, but only for a while; I'm still very tired. We could go to the roof garden. It's not far.'

The roof garden provided a pleasant environment for staff, patients and visitors alike, and also helped keep the building cool. Shahid breathed a sigh of relief once they were outside. He hated to be cooped up for long, so remaining in hospital for even a few days seemed almost like being in a prison, albeit a comfortable one. Still, at least his father popped in to see him as often as his work allowed, and his mother had spent most of the morning with him...and he wasn't dead!

'Great view,' remarked Yngwie, peering out over the safety railing. 'Forest on three sides, and a wonderful vista across the valley towards the older city areas. My home is in a valley too, but the mountainsides are steep. We like to think trolls still inhabit them.' He chuckled, then turned around, saying, 'Do you know what trolls are?' Shahid shook his head. 'They are part of our Norse mythology from thousands of years ago. Giants, they were the children of the first living being and grew in wisdom until even the gods consulted them, but in more modern times they are described as hideous and an enemy of humankind. It's hard to know the truth of the legends. Do you want to hear their story?'

Shahid nodded, and then listened, entranced, as Yngwie suddenly began to sing, his voice strong and pure. There was no one else in the garden to hear this saga of the old Norse gods, their lands and their battles. When it was finished, the silence was complete. Not a bird called, not a tree whispered, no mechanical sounds interrupted the peace. Yngwie stared out across the land, lost in thought.

'Thank you,' said Shahid, after almost a minute had passed. 'Will you sing again for me one day and allow me to record your song?'

Yngwie turned to him and said, 'Yes, why not... But it's time for me to go and for you to return to your bed and rest. You must get well enough to show me your trees!' Laughing, he wheeled Shahid back to his room, then said goodbye and left.

Once back in his own room in the communal house, Yngwie returned to the task of checking the progress of his and Torleif's artwork. Satisfied, he allowed himself a few hours sleep before the evening meal. Afterwards, at sunset, it would be time for the cascade to reach Melbourne.

In Luzern, Switzerland, Federation investigators were putting all their resources into dealing with the mass of reports coming in from all over the world of an event generally regarded as virtually impossible. By 19:16, as the sun set and the cascade reached them, they had already begun their investigations, yet even now, were no closer to either stopping the event or discovering where it originated. All they knew at this stage was that it began at sunset in Perth, Australia, on the fourth of March, and was making its way around the world to coincide with the sun setting at every point on the globe where someone with a comlink was located. This meant that nearly everyone over the age of seven would potentially receive the message – or image, to be precise.

Unless for some reason they were unable to use one, the Federation required its citizens to carry a comlink, using their Federation identity number as their contact code. The safety benefits were considerable and it made physically locating people relatively simple. Official messages could also be broadcast to any target audience required, and it was this facility the perpetrator of the outrage had taken advantage of.

As the reports came in, Morag MacIain, the Coordinator of the Federation Special Investigation Unit, sat with arms folded, staring at her computer screen. How long the event would continue was anyone's guess. The best theory to date suggested that once initiated, the software was self-perpetuating, using the comlinks it infected as servers. Morag knew that whoever had done this needed to be highly sophisticated, since the programming skills required were considerable. The cascade had even been so well managed that once the incoming message was retrieved and the image had displayed for five seconds, the message deleted itself, leaving no record other than the time of deletion. To date, all attempts to capture and trace these messages had failed. However, other than the shock factor, at least the event was doing no real harm...so far.

Communications and computing devices used by libraries, medcentres, training centres, transportation systems, financial systems, private homes, commercial and government buildings, and individuals, were all connected to the intricate global network referred to as the 'lattice'. Overall responsibility for maintaining the lattice lay with the Federation, but each country had its own section to manage, and where there were semi-autonomous states, or where the country was particularly large, some tasks were delegated to regional centres.

In theory, the lattice and its communications layers were secure enough to prevent misuse of the messaging system, even if an employee of the Federation's Special Investigation Unit, for example, chose to run amok and use their high-level access to make the attempt. Therefore, someone had evidently found an obscure security loophole, or had used their connections to create one. Either possibility was a potential nightmare.

The messaging system had been developed in Luzern one hundred and forty years ago and required constant maintenance to ensure all its routines were up to date and that there was no possibility of mistakes being made, such as sending a message to the wrong target audience. Periodic testing and maintenance involved one or more information technologists in each country, and therefore the number of people who could potentially either create or directly exploit a security loophole numbered in their hundreds. Other than senior members of the FSIU, there were also numerous people worldwide with the authority to use the system – senior peacekeepers and environmental guardians, for example, as well as various government officials. However, very few held the necessary authority to send a message to every comlink on the planet. Morag herself was one of these few, but had never had reason to use the facility.

Investigating each and every one of these people within a relatively short period of time would be a logistical headache of gigantic proportions, requiring more resources than the FSIU could readily employ. So, was this the real purpose behind the cascade: to tie up their investigators while something even worse was being put into place?

Naturally, it would be a comparatively easy matter to scan the lattice storage areas of everyone authorised to work on or use the system, together with their comlinks, hand readers, back-up drives and computers, but it seemed unlikely anything suspicious would be found, and there was always the possibility there were storage devices of which the FSIU would be unaware.

Nevertheless, the process was already underway, and at the same time, all their storage and other devices would be examined for faults that could potentially have compromised security. Morag expected to receive the initial set of results first thing in the morning. Meanwhile, they had at least determined that none of these people's individual identities appeared to have been used to initiate the cascade – or to be more accurate, there was no record of their having done so. And to make matters even more difficult, there was no record of *anyone* having initiated it, although this was hardly surprising.

Morag stood up to make herself another cup of strong coffee. It was nearing midnight, yet she needed to deal with one last issue before she could allow herself to go home and sleep. The thought of her bed in her beautiful house on the steep mountainsides of The Rigi, overlooking Luzern, was almost too enticing, but she knew that without thinking this through, it would be almost impossible to sleep. Sighing, she stretched, making a conscious effort to relax her neck and shoulders, then sat down to drink some of the hot, aromatic liquid, and began putting her ideas together.


The minutes ticked by, then the seconds as Yngwie stared at the screen of his comlink, almost holding his breath as he waited for the sun to set. 19:49, 19:50...19:51... Yes! There it was! The flames burned, writhing in their five-second display of ecstasy and passing on to the next wave of comlinks, moving with the sun in perfect concordance. He had almost two hours to wait before the fire reached the end of its twenty-four-hour journey around the world, after which he and Torleif would go down in history...anonymously, of course.


The news broadcaster paused, then said, 'I have just been informed by Federation authorities that the worldwide breach of our communications network, which showed an image of flames burning the Statue of Liberty in Paris, appears to have ended.' Yngwie grinned as an image of the statue was briefly displayed on his hand reader. 'However, peacekeepers are on alert in case it is a prelude to a further attack on the Federation, or even a warning of some type. Morag MacIain, Coordinator of the Federation Special Investigation Unit, is here with me... Coordinator MacIain, has the FSIU determined how this breach occurred, or who is responsible?'

'So far, we are reasonably certain that no one with the authority to send out messages on behalf of the Federation or any other government body is responsible for the security breach, either inadvertently or on purpose. We have yet to determine how it was accomplished, but are putting all available resources into finding out. Fortunately, no actual harm seems to have been done by the message, but we will be on alert for any further occurrences or other interference with our communications systems.' Morag smiled grimly. 'If the person or persons responsible for this event are now watching, which I assume they are, please be assured that your actions are regarded as being of a criminal nature and are subject to severe penalties.'

As Morag's green eyes seemed to gaze directly into his own, Yngwie looked away, suddenly unsure, although not afraid. Instead, he felt drained, exhausted. 'I need to sleep,' he thought, then realised what he needed even more was company. He couldn't call Torleif; that would be far too dangerous. They would have to wait at least a week or more for the FSIU to find the security loophole and close it. Once that was done, they could celebrate, even if only to raise a glass of schnapps to each other over the lattice.

After a long, satisfying shower, Yngwie began to feel a great deal better. He looked at himself in the mirror, ran a hand over his cropped blonde hair, even though it didn't need it, then carefully chose what to wear. It was still warm outside, even though it was now late in the evening, so he put on a loose-fitting sleeveless black top that showed off his finely muscled arms, followed by matching trousers and a pair of lightweight, comfortable shoes. With luck, there might be someone in the common room of the communal house to meet and to get to know, and perhaps go out with – at least for a walk, but preferably somewhere more interesting where there was music.

His luck seemed to be holding because the first person he saw in the common room was a young woman sitting alone, reading. She looked up when he entered and smiled...grinned, actually, as she was dressed in black as well, also with a sleeveless top. Her dark, curly hair fell around her shoulders in a luxuriant mass, and as Yngwie approached, he noticed her eyes were dark brown – quite beautiful. A long, straight nose, well-defined mouth and high cheekbones lent character to her face. She stood up, held out a hand, and introduced herself. 'Hello. I haven't seen you here before. My name is Laurita.'

18

Yngwie shook the outstretched hand and almost winced. Her grip was remarkably strong, matching her overall build, although she was slightly below average height, while Yngwie, at one hundred and ninety centimetres, was ten centimetres above average. He held her hand a fraction longer than normal for two strangers meeting for the first time, then said, 'Hi, mine's Yngwie, and no, I haven't been to Melbourne before. I'm here on holiday and to do some research before I begin university in Oslo, at the beginning of July. What about you?'

'You are Norwegian?'

'Yes, and you?'

'I am Spanish, but travel so much I begin to see myself as a kaleidoscope of nationalities.' Laughing, she sat down, patting the chair next to her, inviting Yngwie to sit as well, which he did.

'Where have you come from this time?' he asked her.

'The Independent Democratic Republic of Tibet. Fascinating place... Such an old culture, although it's remarkable they still have so much left, considering how long they had to struggle to retain it.'

Yngwie nodded. The country was high on his list of priorities as one he wanted to visit, although he had to admit, more for the mountains than for the culture. 'And why have *you* come to Melbourne?' he said.

'I work as a seed gatherer. I was in Tibet to locate certain ancient strains of barley and bring them to the seed vault in Svalbard, then afterwards, to take some to the Federation research facility here in Melbourne. You see, I am familiar with your country...or at least, part of it.' At Yngwie's obvious surprise, Laurita smiled and added, 'Have you never heard of seed gatherers?'

'As a matter of fact, I have. I met one only the other day. How strange. His name is Shahid. Perhaps you know him?'

'No, but I hope to meet him tomorrow. My friend, Karla, who works with the research facility, mentioned a seed gatherer had met with an accident and was in the medcentre in Ferntree Gully. She suggested he might like some company while he recovers and thought that if I stayed here, it would be easier than if I stayed with her at the communal house in Kew, which is near the Willsmere Research Centre. I'll be visiting him tomorrow with Karla... You're grinning! Why, what is so funny?' Laurita grinned as well, liking this young man, although he seemed quite a few years younger than herself.

Yngwie shook his head, chuckling. The old gods, it seemed, had a sense of humour. 'I've arranged to visit Shahid tomorrow as well, while this mutual friend of yours, Karla, is there. He suggested I'd like to meet her.'

'What a coincidence! Not only do we dress alike, we already have friends in common!' Laurita stared at Yngwie. 'It is rather odd, you know. You even remind me of Karla... How did you meet Shahid?'

'I'll let *him* tell you. I wouldn't want to spoil his story. Does he know you'll be there?' Yngwie looked down at his hands for a moment, wondering how Shahid would manage with so many people visiting at once.

'Yes, Karla did tell him, though he may have forgotten. It seems the accident was serious.'

'I doubt he forgot, even if he didn't mention your visit. No, I think he just wanted to leave all the introductions to Karla. We had a lot to talk about already, and he was still very tired, so I didn't stay long.'

'I understand. Speaking of tired, I see you are dressed to go out. Would you like some company?'

Yngwie could hardly believe what he had heard. 'I would,' he replied, as nonchalantly as he could. Laurita stood up, took him by the hand and said, 'In that case, let us find the closest leisure centre, where, with luck, there will be a dance floor and some decent music!' She laughed when Yngwie answered, 'Precisely what I was hoping for myself.'

Outside, the silence was broken only by the sound of an occasional owl or the screech of possums fighting, as well as the chirruping chorus of frogs, which seemed to be unusually abundant here. They walked to the nearest callstation, entered a request for a leisure centre into its terminal, and were given the choice of one a few kilometres away in Ferntree Gully itself, or in Berwick. When Laurita glanced at Yngwie for his opinion, he selected the one in Ferntree Gully. No need to spend time travelling further than necessary. The terminal confirmed that their transport would arrive in twelve minutes, so they sat down to wait.

'How long do you intend to remain in Melbourne?' asked Yngwie.

'Only a few weeks. My next trip will be to Peru. The Federation has a special gene bank in Lima for potatoes, sweet potatoes, and a number of other edible roots and tubers from the Andes. It was started in the second half of the twentieth century by people who recognised how dangerous it would be to let the old varieties die out. There are thousands of different types, and I am to bring a selection to a new agricultural project in Ethiopia which will make use of some particularly poor soils.'

'Why doesn't the Federation simply use the postal service? They're usually very reliable.'

'We prefer to make these deliveries ourselves because the stocks are so valuable and it also gives a personal touch to the project. If there are any issues, I can help resolve them. I am a type of ambassador for the Federation, if you like.' Laurita smiled. 'Using the lattice to communicate is easy, but nothing can replace dealing directly with people.'

'No, that's true.' Yngwie smiled as well, then laughed. 'It's so peaceful here, it reminds me of home.'

'Well, we'll find some noise for you to enjoy. Here comes our transport!' Laurita stood up, and after boarding the light railcar, a few minutes later, they were walking towards the entrance to the brightly lit leisure centre.

Inside, it almost seemed as if the entire population of the outer southeastern region of Melbourne was determined on having a night out. There were people everywhere! Surprised, Yngwie and Laurita mingled with the crowd, content for a while to simply wander around, taking in the atmosphere. There were live performances here and there: musicians playing, artists of various types exhibiting their works and their skills, mini-theatrical events, singers with their original creations, and people reading their poetry or other written pieces. Fortunately, the acoustics of the centre were excellent, otherwise the noise level would have been unbearable. They stopped to listen to one particular performer, whose voice was heartbreakingly pure and entrancing. She sang of the time when, long ago, the mountain was home to thousands of people, living in small towns – Kallista, Olinda, Sassafras, Ferny Creek, Belgrave, Emerald, Cockatoo, and many others with names still alive in memory only. All were gone now, abandoned as the fires became more frequent and more fierce each dreaded summer; abandoned as the need to conserve the few remaining natural forests and other wild places became a priority for the newly formed World Federation of Nations as it struggled to deal with the devastation created by hundreds of years of war, over-population and environmental degradation.

Laurita wept. She knew all too well how difficult the ongoing struggle was to rehabilitate the forests, the open plains, the oceans and rivers, and how hard it had been, and still was, to restore the farmlands. Yngwie took her hand in his and gently pressed it. Listening to the singer, he had picked up the melody as well as the refrain, and as she reached what seemed to be the last one, joined in, harmonising perfectly. The singer nodded slightly, while Laurita stood on tiptoe to kiss Yngwie on the cheek. The other listeners applauded when the song finished. Smiling, Yngwie shook hands with the woman, exchanged a few words, then together, he and Laurita continued on in search of their dance venue.

By the time they reached an open doorway leading to a large, high-ceilinged room full of dancing couples and groups, Laurita had recovered her earlier good humour and was eager to join in. The walls of the room were covered in moving images of people and places from all over the world, which almost gave the illusion of being part of an even larger space, full of colour and life. The music was a fusion of modern with the current interest in early nineteenth-century western European and English dance melodies. Yngwie grinned. He was familiar with both the style and the dancing itself. One of its most attractive features, at least for him, was the close contact it allowed between the dancers.

They moved around the perimeter of the dance floor and, as the next arrangement was about to begin, joined in. Laurita, it seemed, was also familiar with this style of dancing and accepted Yngwie's hand as he offered it to her, then circled gracefully, ready for the moment when he held her by the waist, lifted her high into the air, then set her down, before bowing and leading her on towards the next movement. As they held each other before moving apart and then closing in again, Yngwie found himself wishing their time together need not be so brief. Yet brief it would be, and nothing could change that. Best to focus on enjoying the evening.

By midnight, the full effect of a sleepless night and the aftershock of the forest fire began to take their toll – Yngwie felt dizzy and even a bit weak. Shaking his head when Laurita noticed his expression and asked if he was alright, he crouched down, putting his head in his hands. Concerned, Laurita knelt down beside him. 'Do you want me to call the medcentre?' she said, putting a hand on his shoulder.

'No, I'm just exhausted. I didn't sleep last night and I think it's finally caught up with me. I'll be fine, honestly, though perhaps you could get me some water?'

'Of course. I won't be long,' and Laurita walked swiftly over to the servery, where various refreshments, as well as iced water, were available. When she returned with the water, it was to find Yngwie where she left him, but standing up and staring at the display wall in horror. She turned to look, and saw the same image that briefly showed itself on her comlink at sunset, but this time, it was huge and the flames seemed to burn even more fiercely, eventually melting the Statue of Liberty. As it dissolved, the onlookers gasped, then gazed at each other, confused. Someone took out his comlink to call the peacekeepers. One joke was moderately funny, if no harm had actually been done, but this seemed to be taking the prank too far, particularly if it meant there was more to follow.

'Perhaps we should return to the communal house,' suggested Laurita, taking hold of Yngwie's arm. 'I don't feel like dealing with this.'

'Yes, let's get out of here,' murmured Yngwie, after taking a deep breath to steady himself. 'I'd like to walk back, if you don't mind? It would help clear my head.'

# CHAPTER THREE

The following morning, Yngwie and Laurita sat opposite each other at one of the dining room tables, having breakfast. After a sound night's sleep, Yngwie felt like himself again, despite the shock of the image they saw the previous evening. Thinking it through, it was blindingly obvious that someone might anticipate the arrival of his and Torleif's cascade and be ready to record their imagery, then modify it, or do whatever else they wanted. Annoying as this might be, there was no way of preventing it, and all that could be hoped was that no one used the concept for anything worse than harmless copycat stunts like the one last night... Well, it wasn't entirely harmless, as no doubt the peacekeepers would have their time taken up hunting for the person who did it, on the assumption there might be a link to the cascade.

Laurita nudged him with her foot, interrupting his train of thought. His mouth full, Yngwie couldn't say anything – at least, not politely – so nudged her back. She grinned and said, 'I hope you slept well.'

He swallowed the last of his black rye bread and honey. 'Yes, did you?'

'Wonderfully well. There's nothing like dancing to calm the spirit, although we could have done without the final event. Do you think there was a direct connection with the message sent out earlier, at sunset?'

Neither of them had wanted to talk much on their walk home from the leisure centre, and definitely not about this. Instead, they had focused on the simple pleasure of being outside on a still, warm evening, with a cloudless sky full of stars, and the scents and sounds of the surrounding bushland to keep them company.

'No,' replied Yngwie, 'I don't. I think someone borrowed the idea, and it's quite possible others will as well.'

'In my opinion, it is all silly and such a waste of time.' Laurita frowned as she held her cup of jasmine tea with both hands, her elbows on the table. 'Surely there are more important things in life than playing ridiculous jokes.'

Yngwie raised his eyebrows and paused before saying, 'I suppose so...but don't you see art as important?'

'Art?' You consider this to be art?'

'Yes, of a type. It's designed to bring out an emotional reaction, to make people think. That's a valid form of art.'

'And what is it they'll be thinking about? Freedom?' Laurita finished her tea, then stood up to go to the servery to fetch another piece of pineapple from the selection of fresh fruit available. Yngwie watched as she walked, admiring her self-contained air and the way her body moved, graceful and confident. He quickly looked away as she came back, carrying two plates instead of only her own. 'Here, try this,' she said, placing one of the plates in front of him.

'What is it?' He stared at the brown object sitting in a small pool of slightly thickened sauce.

'Taste it,' said Laurita, still standing.

Yngwie cut a piece and sniffed it, then tentatively put it into his mouth. 'Excellent!' he exclaimed a moment later, and ate another piece. 'The sauce is made with maple syrup, isn't it? But I can't make out what the other thing is...fairly sweet, but not like anything I've come across before.'

'It is one of friend Karla's experiments,' explained Laurita, sitting down to eat her own serving.

'An experiment...' Yngwie hesitated, looking doubtfully at his plate.

Laurita laughed. 'Yes, indeed, and a very successful one too. It has become popular in this country and will soon be exported to others. One of her main interests, you see, is to genetically engineer fruits and vegetables to contain complete protein, in the same way meat does. It is more efficient and far more humane to grow protein this way than to farm and kill animals.'

'Oh... Yes... Well, I do see...' He tried another mouthful, and then finished it all. 'I must congratulate her when we meet this afternoon. Does it have a name?'

'Yes, Oak Apple.'

'The scent did remind me of apple, with faint overtones of something like cardamom, though not quite as pungent... Hmm... A good name.' Yngwie stood up and carried their dishes back to the servery, then stacked them in the washer. 'What would you like to do this morning?' he asked when he returned to their table. 'Assuming, of course, that you'd like some company?'

'How about a stroll over to Berwick? It *is* only twenty kilometres, so we could be there by midsun if we catch a transport for part of the way. We could bring food for a picnic, stay a while and still be back in time to visit Shahid. On the way, I'd like to visit Willsmere's research farm in Narre Warren, if you wouldn't mind? They have recently planted a new strain of high protein rye in their test fields. Very exciting... At least, to us!' Laurita laughed at Yngwie's expression. 'It will not take long, I promise.'

'What is there to see in Berwick?'

'Something that *I* would call art,' replied Laurita, smiling.

'What do you think, Yngwie? Aren't they amazing?' Laurita spoke quietly while she admired another of the botanical drawings from the extensive collection held by the National Herbarium of Victoria. The Herbarium was housed in a large complex that had at its centre one of the few remaining twentieth-century buildings in Berwick: 'Edrington', the former home of Lord Casey, who, according to the historical notes they were reading, was appointed Governor-General of Australia in 1965.

'It's amazing the oldest have survived for so long,' replied Yngwie, studying the fine detail of a coloured line engraving of *Banksia serrata*. It was based on the original 1770 illustration by Sydney Parkinson, one of the botanists on board the *Endeavour* during its first scientific voyage of discovery, lead by Captain James Cook. The Herbarium held copies of all the illustrations still in existence that were produced during the voyage. Each exquisite work in the display was accompanied by a specimen of the plant.

'It says here,' Yngwie continued, 'that the Herbarium was originally located in the oldest part of Melbourne, but was moved because of the rising sea levels that eventually flooded the entire area... This place is certainly far enough from the sea to be safe! It's a fair distance from the forests too, so I don't imagine it's in any danger of burning down, either.'

'No, they seem to have made sure of that!' replied Laurita. 'Oh, the poor man! It seems Sydney Parkinson died of fever while he was with the *Endeavour.*'

'Oh yes, so he did... Apparently lots of people died on those old sailing ships.'

'Millions...often from scurvy, which could so easily have been prevented. The Chinese took food ships with them on *their* voyages throughout the fifteenth century, and, I gather, grew mung beans sprouts to prevent Vitamin C deficiency. Clever people!'

Yngwie nodded, then glanced at his comlink and said, 'I think it's time we went.'

Laurita sighed. 'Yes, we should... I'll come back when I'm next in Melbourne. I always make time to come here when I can.' As they walked towards the main entranceway, she added, 'One of the things I like most about the Herbarium is its potential for new life. Do you realise that in the last few years we've been able to use some of the material here to bring back extinct species?'

'Why, no!' replied Yngwie, stopping to look at her. 'Really?'

'Yes. The pioneering work was done by a woman named Meng Jarrah, who is a friend of Karla's. She shared her techniques with Willsmere, and then she and Karla began working with a few of the plants from this collection. They chose some of the species critical to the overall health of degraded forests and grasslands, here in Victoria.'

'I can see why this place is so important to you, Laurita, though I've never really thought about all this before.'

'No, most people don't. It is so easy for everyone to become complacent, even if we did come close to losing everything. Memories are short.' Laurita frowned, but then took Yngwie's hand as they walked on towards the nearest callstation. Some thirty minutes later, they arrived back in Ferntree Gully, in time for their visit to Shahid.

Reports were arriving from all over the Federation of events that had 'borrowed' the image from the cascade. They all needed to be followed up, which wasted valuable time because so far all of them had turned out to be innocuous – simply pranks and practical jokes. The only potentially serious occurrence, this morning, was when someone doused the real Statue of Liberty with kerosene and set fire to it, intending to record their act of vandalism before anyone could prevent them. Fortunately, the fire went out quickly and a passer-by called the Parisian peacekeepers, who promptly apprehended the offender. The subsequent interview convinced them that this same person was not responsible for the cascade; they simply did not appear to have the skills or contacts required to have pulled off a stunt of that magnitude.

In the meantime, everyone with authority to work on or use the messaging system, or its associated databases, was undergoing another background check to ensure nothing suspicious had developed in either their personal or professional lives. Also, the scan of their lattice storage areas, together with their communications and other devices, had so far produced no result other than the usual relatively insignificant human foibles, which were no cause for alarm. Information technologists who no longer worked on the system, but who had done so within the last five years, were being scrutinised as well. The FSIU was casting its net as widely as possible before they began interviewing anyone, or taking further measures to discover if any of these people were involved in creating the cascade.

However, Morag MacIain was becoming increasingly frustrated with their lack of progress. The software used by the Federation's messaging system was being tested, and re-tested, against all their access routines, the Federation population database, and the application used to locate citizens at any given time, assuming their comlinks and other communications devices weren't all turned off or malfunctioning. Furthermore, every permutation and combination of authorisation codes was being tested to ensure some freak array of Federation identification numbers, for example, hadn't allowed access to the messaging system: a determined person could, in theory, find out who had authority to use the system, then collect their Federation IDs. Naturally, anyone accessing the messaging system would require a great deal more than their identity number to do so, but the investigators needed to consider every possibility, no matter how improbable it seemed.

'Blast and damnation!' Morag glared at her computer screen, almost as if it would somehow give her the answer to the puzzle if she only stared at it long enough. One possibility was that someone had stolen and replicated the entire set of identification routines required to access the messaging system, then worked out how to erase all trace of both their activities and the identity itself. This implied that someone with legitimate authority had either been careless or had been spied upon, or that the thief already had access and was therefore in a good position to understand what was required and then steal what they needed.

Alternatively, perhaps the security systems controlling access were faulty? Or...what about a hidden piece of code, inserted some time ago, waiting for precisely the right circumstances to activate itself, piggybacking on a legitimate message? A 'trojan' was the term used in previous centuries, when such things were commonplace.

Morag felt almost certain that one of these scenarios provided the answer, but sighed at the thought of how long it might take to work out which one...and to find the culprit. She leaned her elbows on the desk and rubbed her forehead, then asked her computer to contact her bondmate, Chiu Liow Jones, a senior peacekeeper in Melbourne who had used the messaging system some years ago. Speaking with him might help her see the way forward more clearly.

The practitioner tending to Shahid stepped back, smiling. 'One more day, and you should be fine, young man. The spider will have to wait for someone else's life to claim. Yours is safe, and I'm sure your parents will be glad to see you back home.'

Shahid returned the smile, and as the practitioner left, lay down on his bed. He was indeed feeling fine, but impatient to be back in the forest. His trees were waiting for him! The spiders, well, he would need to be more observant, that was all. Still, he had been warned that after one bite, another might kill him almost immediately. He pushed the possibility aside... A soft tap at the door interrupted his thoughts. Sitting up, Shahid saw that Karla had arrived, and grinned, waving a welcome.

'Hello, you,' she said. 'I hear you've been battling tarantulas. Rather silly, don't you think?'

Shaking his head, Shahid picked up his hand reader, quickly found an image of a Sydney funnel-web spider, and showed it to her.

'I damned well hope not!' said Karla. Looking closely at the picture, she shuddered. 'Any other possibilities?'

Shahid showed her a male Southern Tree-dwelling Funnel-web, *Hadronyche cerberea*. 'According to the literature, this one's the most likely,' he 'said'. 'It's been gradually moving south for some time.'

'Ugh! We'll need to have a survey done,' replied Karla, running a hand through her short, blonde hair. 'I know just the person, if he'll agree. It's ages since he's been here, and he might like a break from the weather in Greenland. Søren Thorup... Do you remember him?' When Shahid smiled and nodded, Karla picked up a nearby chair and set it down close to the bed. 'Now, tell me everything. What happened?'

Another knock at the door interrupted them and Karla turned around to see Yngwie and Laurita waiting to come into the room.

'Laurita!' exclaimed Karla, rising to walk swiftly over to her friend. They hugged, then still with an arm around each other's waist, Laurita introduced Yngwie, explaining how they met at the communal house.

Although Yngwie was taller than Karla, so alike were they in appearance and overall build, they could easily have passed for mother and son, had Karla been a few years older. However, whereas Yngwie's eyes were grey, Karla's were blue, and whereas Yngwie preferred to wear dark colours, Karla loved all the bright ones. She shook his hand firmly, saying, 'I think our ancestors are from the same part of the world!'

Yngwie grinned. 'Yes, I was born in Norway and still live there. What about you?'

'Oh, I'm second generation Australian, but my grandparents on one side came from Norway and the other two from the northern part of Germany.' She laughed and added, 'Hence my name. It was my grandmother's.'

'Perhaps we *are* related,' replied Yngwie, also noticing the resemblance between them.

'We'll have to chase it up,' said Karla, moving over towards Shahid, who had been listening to every word and studying Laurita. Unlike Yngwie and Karla, she was darker in appearance, similar to himself. She held out her hand to him and Shahid shook it, holding on for a little longer than one normally would.

Laurita smiled, instantly liking this fellow seed gatherer. 'Hello,' she said, gently releasing her hand. Karla had already told her of Shahid's inability to speak, so she wasn't surprised when he answered using his hand reader.

Meanwhile, Karla fetched chairs for both Laurita and Yngwie. 'Shahid, have you and Yngwie already met?' she asked, having noticed they looked at each other in a way that seemed to indicate they didn't need to be introduced.

Shahid nodded, so Karla returned to her earlier question: 'Good... Now, do you want to tell us exactly what happened to you?'

'Maybe Yngwie should tell you,' replied Shahid, waggling his eyebrows.

Yngwie shook his head.

'A shy hero,' teased Shahid. 'Very well then... He rescued me, not only after I was bitten by a spider, but from a fire. I was unconscious, and after calling the medcentre, he carried me down the hillside, then once the ambutechs brought us here, he needed treatment for smoke inhalation.'

Laurita and Karla stared at Yngwie, astonished. He merely shrugged his shoulders.

'The peacekeepers notified Willsmere about a forest fire, but I didn't realise it was so close to Ferntree Gully!' exclaimed Karla. 'I gather a pair of campers lit a fire to toast bread, even though they should have known better?'

'Yes,' answered Yngwie, 'they did. It seems a piece of wood exploded and set fire to the undergrowth, which was too close to the campfire, and then the flames moved into the loose bark of a tree. They tried to put it out, but when it escaped, did the right thing and called the forest guardians. The firefighters arrived in time to extinguish the fire before much damage was done.'

'I heard on a news broadcast that the matter was dealt with quickly and the campers were sentenced to two months community service at the Healesville Wildlife Rehabilitation Centre. That to me seems just,' said Shahid. 'I know the fire didn't get into the canopy, but I'll need to check our trees once they let me out of here. I want to be sure none of them were damaged.'

'Would you allow me to come with you?' asked Laurita. She wanted to see the forest too, and was more than a little curious about Shahid. 'You could come along as well, Yngwie, couldn't you?' she added, turning to him and smiling.

'Shahid has already promised to take me with him on one of his surveys, so it would be an excellent idea if we both went, to make sure he's well enough to do his work.'

'In that case, you'd better see what might be living in the forest,' said Karla, half-joking, half-serious. 'Do you want to show them the picture of the spider, Shahid?'

When they saw the image of the Tree-dwelling Funnel-web, Yngwie let out a yelp, while Laurita immediately turned away. Although they were both seasoned travellers, particularly Laurita, neither had a fondness for arachnids, and neither had ever met anything quite like this ferocious-looking beastie.

'They're not really native to this area,' explained Karla, 'but there's a good chance they've migrated this far south over the past few hundred years. The climate has changed so much, as have the forests, and now there are lots of plants and animals that have taken up new habitats. I'll be calling one of my former colleagues this evening to see if he'll pay us a visit and do a survey...work out how many we're potentially looking at, then make some recommendations to do with public safety. People will have to be warned. It might take a while, but he's good at his job, so we'll get a thorough understanding of the situation.'

'Who's that?' asked Laurita.

'Søren Thorup, a zoologist from Greenland, but he's also an expert on Australian spiders. He's spent a great deal of time here over the years, and a while ago worked with me at Willsmere when we were searching for potential plant-animal combinations to enhance protein levels in food crops.'

'Oh, yes! I tasted the Oak Apple this morning!' said Yngwie, with a broad grin. 'It was good. Congratulations, Karla. It's an honour to have met you.'

Karla laughed, but was pleased by the compliment. Not everyone was happy with their genetic engineering efforts, especially this particular approach.

'We stopped by your test plots at Narre Warren this morning,' said Laurita. 'We were on our way to Berwick because I wanted to show Yngwie the Herbarium and the botanical drawings. How is the rye progressing?'

'Good. The new crop will go in once the rains begin in April, and we're analysing the harvest from last summer now. We hope to release some of the grain for taste testing before too long. There's a local baker who'll turn it into rye bread once it's milled, and there's a group of locals who have volunteered to try it.'

Laurita turned to Yngwie to explain: 'I brought the rye here last year for them to use. It's an ancient strain with higher protein levels than those normally grown. The team at Willsmere also want to test for how well the seeds are retained, as rye tends to drop its grain too readily.'

'Ah, I see,' answered Yngwie, but he had to be honest and add that this was not something he knew much about.

Karla smiled. 'No, very few people seem to realise how important all this is, but thankfully, the Federation does. So much of our land is still badly degraded, and crops like rye are good because it tolerates cold, drought and waterlogging far better than wheat, for example. Also, its roots bind the soil, which helps keep it in better shape. We leave the tough stubble after harvest to protect the next season's crop, whether it's rye or something else, like barley.'

'What about pests?' asked Yngwie, vaguely recalling something to do with rye and a form of poisoning.

'Oh yes, testing for pest resistance is vital too. While the crop's growing, we have a quarantine field over the entire area, and keep each test plot separate from the others, using internal quarantine domes. That way, we can be sure nothing gets in to contaminate the plants, and that they can't cross-contaminate each other. Some of the test plots are deliberately infected with various pests, one of which is the ergot fungus and that's nasty if it takes hold.'

'Ah, yes, that's what I remember!' Yngwie recalled how ergotamine poisoning had broken out quite frequently in Europe, particularly during the Middle Ages, causing a wide range of symptoms, in some cases thought to be the result of witchcraft.

'There's an article here,' said Shahid, consulting the lattice, 'that says the poison, ergotamine, was used during the twentieth century to treat migraine headaches. Earlier on, in 1938, it was also used to produce Lysergic acid diethylamide, or LSD, which is, it seems, a non-addictive, non-toxic, psychedelic hallucinogen. LSD was used as a drug for various psychiatric uses from 1947, until it was eventually discontinued, in part due to potentially dangerous side effects, such as panic attacks and severe anxiety.'

'Yes, I came across it when I studied the effects of ergot poisoning,' said Karla. 'Anyway, let's go find something to eat, then take it outside. I believe there's a roof garden here, and the weather's gorgeous.'

Everyone agreed, and they were soon munching their way through an assortment of sweet cakes and glacé fruits, while seated in the shade of one of the garden's trees.

'Yngwie brought me up here yesterday and then sang for me,' said Shahid, after carefully scooping up the last piece of an exceptionally luscious apricot pie.

'Did he, indeed!' exclaimed Laurita. 'Will you sing for us now, Yngwie?' she added, grinning.

Yngwie pulled a face and hesitated, but Karla immediately suggested they sing together. 'My grandmother used to sing wonderful lullabies, and there's one in particular I remember: *Gjendines Bånlåt*. My accent's probably dreadful, but I'd love to try singing it with you.'

'I didn't know you could sing!' said Laurita, and Shahid too gazed at Karla with new appreciation.

'Well, I'm not good enough to do it for an audience, but for friends, it's fine,' replied Karla, with a smile.

'Okay,' said Yngwie, 'let us try. If you sing the first verse, I'll join in and find the harmony.'

Karla stood, took a breath, and began. The others listened, entranced, and when Yngwie joined in, it was impossible not to be moved by the sight and sound of these two people, so alike, so much literally in tune with each other, despite having only just met. When they finished, for a few moments the silence was profound, except for the slight rustling of the trees. Applause from someone nearby startled them all, and they turned to see Shahid's father standing several metres away.

'Beautiful!' he said, walking towards them. He held out his hand to Karla, and then to Laurita, introducing himself. 'My name is Shafiqur. I work as a practitioner here and this is my son, Shahid. It is good to see he has company today, and it's good to see you again, Yngwie.' Shafiqur clasped Yngwie's hand before greeting his son with a kiss. 'How are you feeling, Shahid? Are you ready to go home tomorrow?' When Shahid nodded, his father said, 'In that case, Yngwie, would you like to come to our house on Thursday for the dinner we promised? Perhaps you would like to bring your two friends as well?' Shafiqur glanced at Laurita and Karla as he spoke.

'Why, yes, that sounds fine,' answered Yngwie, turning to the two women for their answer.

Surprised, neither Karla nor Laurita could see any reason to refuse, so quickly agreed.

Shafiqur smiled. 'It's settled then. It is a late celebration of Shahid's Namingday. The spider bite prevented us from having it on the correct date.'

'Oh, that's awful!' exclaimed Karla, but Shahid simply shrugged and made a face.

'Well, I must get back to work, so I'll leave my son in your good hands,' said Shafiqur, giving everyone another smile. 'See you all on Thursday!'

'When my mother will spend all day cooking,' said Shahid, grinning. 'With three guests to feed, she'll put on a banquet.'

'Is that a problem?' asked Karla, laughing.

'Oh no... I just want you to be prepared, that's all. Look, do you mind if we go back inside? I'm getting rather tired.'

With one last admiring glance at the view, they took Shahid to his room, then stayed a while longer to make sure he was comfortable. Eventually, Laurita and Yngwie went back to the communal house, while Karla returned to Willsmere to finish off the work she had begun that morning.

# CHAPTER FOUR

Søren Thorup felt hungry, and when Søren felt hungry, he also felt irritable...very irritable! His cat, Dandelion, jumped onto the wide windowsill to rub her head against his cheek, her soft, thick white fur matching the deep snow outside. For three weeks now, there had been no deliveries to the city. The weather, unseasonable for this time of year, had prevented the normal pattern of life here in the south of Greenland from continuing in its pleasant, predictable manner. Blizzards were hindering normal air traffic and the snowploughs were struggling to keep the trafficways clear. As a result, Søren and Dandelion were forced to make do with the barest of essentials.

'Drat and damn!' exclaimed Søren, startling the cat, whose bright blue eyes opened even wider. Deciding he was beyond help, she jumped off the sill and did what all cats do when nothing else appears to be worth doing – she went to sleep, dreaming of her last substantial meal, two days ago: mashed pumpkin with yoghurt and grated cheese.

Poking around in the kitchen cupboards improved Søren's state of mind. He found a small bag of buckwheat flour, sugar, salt, oil, some maple syrup, and one precious egg – enough to make pancakes if he used water instead of soymilk. Being a meticulous man with a strong sense of aesthetics, he spent the next twenty minutes enjoying making the pancakes as beautifully as he could manage. The smell of cooking woke Dandelion, and when she sent a polite inquiry to the cook, she received a highly satisfactory response. The first pancake, which had cooled by now, was rolled up and placed into her food bowl on the floor by the window.

As Dandelion ate, a bright ray of sunshine broke through the overcast sky, forming a pool of warm light around her. When Søren stopped to watch, his mood improved even further, so he decided to allow himself a small pot of Yunan tea from his fast-dwindling supply. He sipped the tea slowly to prolong the satisfaction, and just as he was finishing his breakfast, the household computer chimed an incoming call: it was Karla, his Australian friend and colleague from Melbourne.

'Karla! You are the very person I would have wished to speak with,' said Søren, smiling broadly.

'Why? What have you done to upset the authorities this time?' replied Karla, remembering the incident he told her about the last time they spoke.

'I've done nothing at all, dear Karla,' answered Søren, shaking his head and still smiling. 'It isn't my fault if there are those who fail to enjoy having their errors pointed out to them, is it?'

'No, it's never your fault, Søren, but you could keep in mind that being perfect in every way sometimes annoys people.'

'Ah well, that is their problem, not mine, and in any case, I am not perfect.'

Perfect Søren might not be, thought Karla, but despite being twelve years older than her, he was still the same elfin, beautiful creature he had been a decade ago, when they first met. His mass of golden curls hadn't faded, and his delicate classic features had hardly changed at all. Even his grey eyes were the same, without any telltale signs of age at their corners when he smiled. Still, he was only in his early fifties, so perhaps this was understandable.

'No, I suppose you aren't,' said Karla, with a grin. 'However, I've called because we need your help.'

'Oh, good! What do you want me to do? If it's something that can get me away from this accursed weather, I will forever be in your debt. Do you know, we have barely anything to eat in the house? Even Dandelion is beginning to suffer!'

Knowing Søren's tendency to both obsess about food and to exaggerate, Karla wondered if he was joking, but his expression seemed to indicate something was seriously wrong. 'What do you mean?' she said, frowning slightly.

'We have been snowed in for three weeks, listening to the howling wind. Only occasional airlifts are possible, and even then, only in certain areas. Priority is given to essential services, naturally, so private individuals like myself and Dandelion are forced to make do with what they have. Still, we have just eaten some delicious buckwheat pancakes, and I have enough potatoes left to make something for midsun, but Karla, after that, there's almost nothing left!'

'Truly?' Karla gaped at him.

'Yes, Karla, truly!' Søren grimaced, then turned to Dandelion, who had meowed, wanting to be part of the conversation.

At a signal from her companion, the cat jumped up and placed one paw on the screen. Karla replied by blowing her a kiss, then said, 'Dandelion's looking lovely, and we don't want her to go hungry, so how would you both like to come to Melbourne for a month or so? I can promise you plenty of good food!'

'If I could hug you, I would!' replied Søren, hugging Dandelion instead. 'So how will you get me out of here?'

'I believe the job's important enough for the Federation to arrange special transport, so an airlift should be possible. Is there somewhere nearby where an airjet can land, and are you even able to get out of your house?'

'Yes to both questions, although I cannot go far; the snow is too deep. Still, I'm sure everything can be managed if you just send someone to rescue us.' Søren grinned, and Dandelion, having listened to every word, understood that their enforced isolation would soon be over. She purred and rubbed her head against Søren's forehead, smooching until he gave her a kiss on the nose. Laughing, he said, 'Dandelion has given me an image of pasta with cheese and tomato sauce, followed by a bowl of yoghurt. Stop it, cat, you are making me hungry!'

Karla laughed too. 'Right, I'm sure we can manage that. I'll make some calls and get back to you, hopefully within the next hour or so. Now, before I do, I'd better tell you exactly what we need you for.'

Staring at the information before her, Morag tried to find anything at all that made a pattern, no matter how nonsensical it might seem, and noticed something peculiar. She had been thinking about the main requirements for a message to be sent to a particular target population. Coordinates were needed if the target was based on geography; Federation identification numbers were needed if the message was aimed at specific people, irrespective of geography; and in either case, the timing of the message was usually important.

Their investigations had managed to establish that the cascade began at 19:46, on the fourth of March, in Perth, Australia, at a latitude and longitude of 31° 57' South and 115° 51' East. If the date was put into numerical form, 04-03-2457, and then the time and date put together, the resulting number was 194604032457. This twelve-digit number happened to be the same as the Federation ID allocated to a certain child on their first Namingday, something which typically occurred three months after they were born. The cascade began, therefore, at precisely the same time as when the identification number was presumably issued, and originated at the coordinates of the child's birthplace, as entered into the Federation population database.

'Bizarre, but so what?!' muttered Morag to herself. Was there some meaning associated with this numerical coincidence, or was the person responsible simply fond of practical jokes and thought this would add to the humour? Based on records of applications for fertility rights and subsequent births, someone with access to the population database could, with reasonable accuracy, predict the date when a specific ID would be issued...although not necessarily the time. She was left with yet another question without an answer. Nevertheless, the pattern was something for them to work with once they had more information.

Their scrutiny of information technologists and others associated with the messaging system was progressing according to schedule. It was now taking into account personality and usual behaviour in the hope of giving some clue as to why someone might want to initiate the cascade, and therefore, who that person might be. However, they still had no leads. Instead, Morag was partially pinning her hopes on the analysis of all the messages sent out over the past five years, which numbered only six hundred and twenty-two. Unfortunately, the scope of the task was still considerable, due to the complex security measures surrounding access to the system and to the creation of the messages themselves. Also, if a trojan was in fact attached to any of them, it would need to have been so well encrypted and disguised that detecting it would almost certainly involve the development of completely new heuristics.

Sighing inwardly, she asked her computer to contact Welcome, one of the psychologists working with the Melbourne Peacekeeping Force. They knew each other well and had worked together in the past, so Morag felt confident that if anyone could assist with personality profiling, Welcome could.

A few moments later, his homely face, with its warm brown eyes, button nose and double chin, appeared on her screen. 'Hello,' he said, smiling. 'Is this a social call, or do you need some help with this case of yours?'

'My bondmate's been discussing it with him already,' thought Morag, returning the smile. 'Hello,' she replied, 'and yes, we do need some help, if you're not too busy?'

'No, no, I can always fit in a case like this. Rather unusual, to say the least, eh?' Small crinkles formed at the corners of Welcome's eyes and around his mouth as he chuckled. 'What do you want me to do?'

'To begin with, I'd like some insight into the reasons why someone would spend time and energy creating this event, and what the likelihood is of this not being a one-off. Could this be a prelude to something else? Also, we're just over halfway through double-checking everyone who could have accessed our messaging system, either directly or indirectly, so if there's anything you could tell us that might describe the personality associated with this behaviour, we can add it to the traits we're already looking for. If necessary, the information we've collected so far can always be re-analysed.'

'I assume it's out of the question that any of them are either sociopaths or psychopaths?' replied Welcome, with a grin. 'No...of course not. Needless to say, they would've been weeded out by now. Similarly, I suspect that other major psychiatric disorders can be ruled out, which leaves us with the more run-of-the-mill personality disorders that are far more difficult to detect – such as a massive ego; abnormal craving for attention; a wish to punish others due to some feeling of being slighted or otherwise treated unfairly; a desire to have the upper hand and therefore to feel superior, or merely to have a good laugh at others' expense.' He paused, waiting for Morag to comment.

'Yes, all that fits in with what we thought,' she answered 'but what about people who are perfectly sane and rational? What would their motives be?'

'The most common is the challenge of doing something others believe is virtually impossible. It's a bit like the thrill of gambling against massive odds. However, if they're sane, whoever did this didn't think it through in terms of the possible repercussions, which means they're either young and inexperienced, or remarkably naive.' Welcome scratched his chin in thought, then said, 'The next most common reason is a wish to make a symbolic attack on authority. If no further actions are planned, again, this would be typical of the young and the naive. Naturally, this event may also be the beginning of a campaign designed to make people question our well-ordered society, with its world government and emphasis on social responsibility and self-restraint. Not everyone believes we have enough freedom in our lives...which can apply to people of any age. We've met the type before, of course.'

'Yes, we certainly have!' replied Morag, remembering all too clearly the case they dealt with seven years ago when a rogue corporation resorted to murder and sabotage in order to challenge the Federation. 'I hope we're not dealing with an organisation this time, and that all this *is* simply a one-off, dreamed up by some young person with more time on their hands than they know what to do with. Unfortunately, though, the repercussions are already annoying us. Investigating all the copycat events cropping up is taking up far too much of our time. I suppose you've already heard about some of them?'

'Oh yes, though nothing too serious, thank goodness. Now, I suggest you pay particular attention to anyone who seems relatively asocial, tends to spend a great deal of time at home, has a higher than usual ability to persevere with a task, and who is highly independent in their behaviour and attitudes. Also, there's a similar but fundamentally different type, and that's someone who, rather than being asocial, is outgoing and adventurous, highly creative and somewhat of a thrill seeker. Is that any help?' Welcome turned aside to speak to someone. Turning back, he said, 'I have to go, Morag. We have a presentation to make to the Judge, and I've just been reminded it's time for us to leave. Call me if anything turns up that you want to discuss, won't you?'

'I will, and thanks. You've reassured me that we're on the right track.' Morag grinned, then closed the connection, in a far better mood than before.

\*

Karla had been as good as her word and the arrangements for Søren and Dandelion's 'rescue' proceeded without drama, other than a minor mishap when the airjet sent to pick them up was about to leave. The snow accumulating on the roof of the house slipped, covering the front entrance. At first Søren wanted to make arrangements for it to be cleared, if possible, but soon realised it might well happen again and that it was unlikely any real damage had been done. Shrugging, he finally decided they could depart and heaved a sigh of relief as the airjet took off, lifting high above the stricken city.

'Warmth,' he thought, 'and no snow. Even better, plenty to eat!' Dandelion silently agreed, gazing down at the icy landscape as they sped towards their rendezvous with a flight from Quebec to Melbourne.

Once on the international airjet, and after two generous servings of lasagne each, followed by a dessert of delicious apple strudel, accompanied by coffee and a piece of fine chocolate for Søren, the two travellers slept. Dandelion snuggled next to her companion, purring as she dozed, her stomach full and satisfied for the first time in days. Her paws twitched as she fell fully asleep and dreamt of bright, sunlit days without snow covering the ground. After a short while she gave a huge sigh and began to snore. The other passengers were nearly all awake, but took little notice, cats now having the right to travel in the main cabin rather than being consigned to the cargo hold, as they were until relatively recently. However, Dandelion's general mood of profound contentment affected them, and for no apparent reason, everyone felt far happier than usual. They chattered to each other and looked out the windows, admiring the cloud formations below, while even the hosts serving them were noticeably more cheerful.

The airjet finally touched down at Melbourne's Tullamarine airport at 06:15 the next morning. Two hours later, Dandelion sat patiently waiting while Søren spoke with the manager of the Ferntree Gully communal house.

'Yes,' he said, 'we would like breakfast for two. My cat is as hungry as I am, and given she has very good manners, I doubt whether any of the other guests would mind if she has her food in the dining room.' He smiled angelically when Dandelion told him the manager was about to object to the idea of cats eating at the table. 'Not at the table, of course!' he added quickly. 'No, no, a bowl on the floor will be perfectly fine.'

With somewhat of an effort, the manager returned the smile, and after a gentle prompt from the cat, agreed that, yes, it would indeed be perfectly acceptable. She led the way to their room, showed them the facilities, and left Søren to unpack their few belongings, not least of which was Dandelion's brush and comb. Her thick fur needed attention every day, or otherwise everything would be covered in white cat hair, which was not something Søren was prepared to put up with. While Dandelion rolled around in delight, he gave her a thorough combing, followed by a brushing as well. Afterwards, he took a shower, changed into fresh clothes, and went to the dining room. Dandelion walked by his side, tail in the air, picking up on the thoughts of the other guests eating their breakfast.

As Søren deliberated whether to begin with the sweetened yoghurt with fresh peaches or the tomato and mushroom omelette, two other guests entered the dining room and instantly caught his eye. They were both dressed in black and were chattering to each other as if they were old friends sharing a good joke. A striking pair in terms of physical appearance, the younger of the two, a young man, put his arm around the woman's shoulders and gave her a brief hug. She responded by kissing him lightly on the cheek and then taking him by the arm. They sat down at the one of the tables and studied their menu.

At this point, Søren's attention was brought back to his own choice of breakfast, as well as Dandelion's, by her asking him to hurry up. She was hungry! Søren mentally apologised, chose the yoghurt and peaches for himself and the omelette for Dandelion, then went to the servery to collect it. While he was there, the young man was collecting a tray of food as well and glanced his way. Søren smiled, inclining his head politely before going back to his table and serving Dandelion her breakfast. Some of the guests watched, surprised but amused, and both the young man and woman seemed particularly interested. Søren grinned at them, then thought no more about it, instead concentrating on the luxury of having as much to eat as he could possibly want. Meanwhile, Dandelion finished her omelette and sat contentedly at his feet, cleaning herself.

The long and luxurious breakfast over, Søren took out his comlink and called Karla. 'Good morning,' he said, when she answered. 'I cannot thank you enough for bringing me here to this wonderful land of warmth and plenty!'

Karla laughed. 'Oh, I'm sure we'll all be grateful if you can track down the spiders and confirm what they are and how far they've spread. When do you want to begin?'

'I think tomorrow should be fine, don't you? We intend to spend part of today resting, and later, exploring the area. That will allow me to begin well before dawn to see if I can spot anything unusual moving about. The traps can be set once the sun is up. Do you have the pheromones ready for me to use?'

'Yes, and the motion detectors with infrared cameras. It's nice and warm at the moment, so they should be easy enough to spot if they're out and about. I can meet you at the communal house whenever you like. It'll only take about forty minutes or so to get there once you call me.'

'Good. Do you want to say hello to Dandelion?' Søren leaned down to hold his comlink in front of the cat's face and she obligingly sniffed, purred, and then yawned hugely. Karla chuckled and said, 'She can meet Aurora tomorrow. I hope they'll like each other.'

'It's hard to say whether they will or not. Dandelion isn't used to other cats, but I can tell she *is* curious, so that's a good start.' Søren yawned as well, quickly apologising. 'Sorry, my dear friend, but I really must go back to bed. A nap before lunch and I'll be a new man. Which reminds me, what are you doing this evening?'

'Didn't you say you wanted to be up well before dawn?' replied Karla, with a grin.

'I did, but I may not be able to sleep for a while because of the time zone difference.'

'I'm going to a dinner party, Søren. Sorry... I wouldn't want to impose on the hosts by asking if I could bring a guest at this late stage, much as I'd like to.'

'Oh, that's quite alright, Karla; I agree, and I'd have to leave early anyway, which would be terribly rude. No, no, it will be a pleasure to dine here at the communal house. From what I've eaten so far, their food seems to be very good.'

Relieved, Karla explained further. 'The party is a Namingday celebration for the young man I told you about who was bitten by the spider...Shahid. It was actually his Namingday when he was bitten, so the party had to be put off. He still lives with his parents, so it's at their house. The person who rescued him will be there too, since the dinner's in his honour as well. He'll be bringing one of our seed gatherers with him. They both happened to be staying at the Ferntree Gully communal house and liked each other when they met. You might bump into them while you're there. His name's Yngwie, and hers is Laurita.'

'Ah,' replied Søren, 'how fascinating! "Yngwie", that's an anglicised version of a Scandinavian name. Where is he from?'

'Norway, and is here on holiday before he starts university in July. Laurita's here on business, but I suggested she stay in Ferntree Gully because Shahid was taken to the medcentre there, and I thought she might visit him. Cheer him up a bit.'

'Always looking after everyone, eh?' Søren grinned, then yawned again and stood up, saying, 'Now I *must* get some sleep, so see you tomorrow morning sometime. Enjoy your dinner party!'

'I will, I'm sure, and yes, see you tomorrow.' Karla put away her comlink and bent down to stroke Aurora's soft fur. The cat had been waiting for the call to finish and her golden eyes almost seemed to glow as she looked up at Karla, purring. 'Want to go for a run, puddums?' said Karla, smiling when Aurora replied by enthusiastically rubbing against her legs and purring even more loudly. 'Great. Wait while I change and then we can go.'

Before long, they were outside in the bright, warm sunshine, and soon afterwards, down by the riverside. The Yarra River snaked its way past Willsmere, in Kew, and on towards the old centre of Melbourne, finally reaching the mouth of Port Phillip Bay. The path along which Karla and Aurora ran was flanked by bushland, so the fresh, clean air was scented by the mature gum trees dotted throughout. Occasionally magpies warbled, and when the two companions heard the screech of pink and white galahs as a flock flew overhead, they stopped for a short while to watch.

Half an hour later, exhilarated and ready for a cool shower before resuming work, Karla paused by Willsmere's heavy wrought iron gates to glance at the security scanner and to wave and smile at their Gatekeeper, who returned the greeting. Moments later, after the gates opened, Karla and Aurora walked along the gravel pathway towards the main entrance. Aurora pressed her nose to the newly installed identification panel, and once her unique skin pattern and Karla's second retina scan were recognised, the massive wooden doors swung open for them.

After her shower, the first task was to call the baker in Narre Warren who would be testing their most recent batch of rye for palatability and ease of use. Karla had already verified that the grain would be milled on the following Monday.

'Hi, Phil,' she said. 'Are you ready to begin as soon as we deliver the flour?'

'Yep, we're ready and waiting,' he replied, a friendly smile on his sun-browned, earnest features. 'Just one final question, for peace of mind... What's your system for making sure the crop you used to test for ergot resistance can't be mixed up with the one you're giving me?'

'That's a fair question,' said Karla, with an understanding smile. 'We use a quarantine field while the plots are growing, both between each test plot and around the entire area, which means no contamination is possible, either from outside or within. The harvesting is then done in batches, one plot at time, using colour-coded equipment, and the grain is stored in bags with the same colour code. The bags containing the grain that isn't to be eaten are marked 'Not for consumption', and are stored in an entirely separate area, also colour-coded. As you know, the building is underground, with only the main entrance aboveground, so it's very safe in terms of anyone getting in and doing something they shouldn't.' Karla paused in case Phil had any other questions, but as he didn't, finished off by saying, 'Do you want a tour?'

'No, that's fine. I'm sure you know what you're doing – I'll take your word for it. When will the delivery arrive?'

'About 13:00 on Monday. Is that okay?'

'Absolutely fine. I'll begin the first batch of bread immediately and then the second on Tuesday morning, so if you have your volunteers ready to receive their loaves during the afternoon, or evening if that's more convenient, we should be able to hear back from them by either Wednesday or Thursday.'

'Yes, that sounds great, and thanks. I'll confirm the delivery time for you on Monday morning, and afterwards, we can all hope for good results.'

'Excellent... I'll look forward to hearing from you.'

Karla nodded, and then, the call over, decided it was time for morning tea. All this talk of bread had made her hungry!

Despite the overcast sky and the rain clouds looming on the horizon, Shahid revelled in once again being outdoors. He straightened his back and stretched, then went back to work, planting vegetable seedlings in the family's produce garden. When his mother, Wania, called him to come and give his approval to the final preparations for his Namingday dinner, he tenderly pressed the soil around the last of the silverbeet plants, then went inside.

Wania gently stroked her son's cheek, then stood on tiptoe to kiss him as well, before leading him into their dining room, where the table was set to perfection. Silver candelabra stood at each end, ready for their cream-coloured beeswax candles to be lit once the meal commenced, while a heavy, hand-woven, pure silk cloth in shades of blue, red and gold covered the table surface, hanging generously over the sides. An heirloom used only for special occasions, the cloth brought a smile to Shahid's face. He had seen it every year on his Namingday, and also on those of his parents, and never failed to appreciate its beauty. The arrangement of roses at the centre of the table, with their subtle colours and delicate shapes, completed the effect. His mother had picked them that morning, just after sunrise prayers, to make sure they were at their best.

In the kitchen, more than a dozen different varieties of food awaited their final touch before being presented in their serving dishes. The blue and white porcelain dishes to be used tonight were part of a collection Shahid had gradually obtained each year as Namingday gifts for his mother, and so held singular meaning for them all. Of the finest quality, they were hand decorated in traditional geometric and floral patterns, used throughout the Middle East and China for a thousand years.

Shahid hugged his mother, kissed her on both cheeks, and held her hand for a moment, then returned outside to finish planting the vegetable seedlings, ready for when the rain began. Afterwards, when his father came home from work, it would be time for sunset prayers before their guests arrived.

# CHAPTER FIVE

The stench of burnt wood met Søren's nostrils as he entered the forest. Dandelion wrinkled her nose and stared up at him, her blue eyes wide, her mind full of questions. Placing one dainty paw upon his knee, she asked if they could leave this place.

'No, not yet, my love, we need to learn more about the damage the fire has done and also what lives here.' He bent down and took her paw in his hand, stroking it tenderly, then walked on, with the cat following close behind. Her paws became blacker and blacker from the ash on the ground, and at one point, she stopped, examined them, mentally shrugged, and went on, deciding Søren would no doubt wash them when they returned to the communal house. He turned to look at her and laughed, but agreed, then knelt on the blackened earth to closely examine a small hole at the base of one of the old eucalypts.

Taking an optical probe from his kit, he slowly extended it into the hole and about half a metre down, saw a smallish black spider, which seemed to be the harmless, local variety of funnel-web. It moved away as he touched it lightly with the probe. Satisfied, Søren took some images containing location information, added a few notes after uploading them to the lattice, then continued on through the forest.

After about a kilometre, they had found eleven local funnel-web tunnels; a wide variety of other spiders hiding under rocks, unburnt logs and debris; and even a few new webs strung between half-burnt twigs. The area was quickly being recolonised, and as far as Søren could see, none of the older trees were severely damaged. Moving into the unburnt areas, he began searching for the irregular silk trip-lines that radiate out from the burrow entrance of most species of funnel-web native to Sydney and more northern regions. Eyesight alone would have been sufficient if he'd had time to crawl around on hands and knees, but instead he had specialised equipment with him to scan the area. It was programmed to search for the silk-lined retreats commonly created within holes and crevices in a variety of rough-barked trees by the Southern Tree-dwelling Funnel-web Spider, *Hadronyche cerberea*. The exposed surface of the tunnel tended to be disguised by a covering of bark or wood particles, with trip-lines running out across the bark. Being daytime, he didn't expect to see any of the spiders themselves, which Dandelion thought was just as well!

So far, during this brief initial survey, Søren hadn't seen any unusual spiderwebs or burrows, but at least he now had a feel for the area and a better idea of where to begin setting traps for the intruders. Eventually, as the sky began to darken with the gathering rain clouds, they returned to the communal house. Once inside, and as they were making their way past the manager's workstation, she looked up, saw Dandelion's dirty paws and frowned.

'We have been out walking in your forest and passed through the recently burnt area,' explained Søren, smiling as sweetly as he could. 'I'll attend to her feet...immediately.' While he spoke, Dandelion hid herself behind him, looking at her paws, embarrassed.

'Good,' replied the manager, politely returning the smile. 'We wouldn't want black pawprints everywhere, especially not in the dining room.'

'No,' agreed Søren. 'We'll be going out again early tomorrow morning, before dawn, so she will most likely come back filthy. I do hope you won't mind too much?'

'Oh no, as long as you clean her up as quickly as you can.'

Søren gave her a small bow and Dandelion came out from her hiding place to sit by his feet, purring. The manager stood up and walked over to them, putting out a hand for the cat to sniff. Patting her on the head, she said, 'You're a real sweetie, aren't you.' Dandelion responded by rubbing her head into the manager's hand and trilling softly. The woman was completely won over and even knelt down to give her a cuddle, ignoring the dust on the cat's coat. Dandelion fluffed out her whiskers and stood up, arching her back in pleasure as the manager stroked her beautiful thick fur.

At that moment the door opened and the two young people Søren had noticed at breakfast walked in. 'Hello,' he said, grinning. 'You are just in time to be properly introduced. My name in Søren Thorup, and this is Dandelion.'

The young man held out his hand, saying, 'Hello. I'm Yngwie, and this is Laurita.'

'Oh, is that so!' replied Søren, shaking first his hand and then Laurita's. 'I believe we have a friend in common – Karla, from Willsmere.'

Yngwie looked up from stroking Dandelion. 'Really! Yes, we've met and are going to a dinner this evening where we'll meet her again. How extraordinary!' He hadn't remembered the name of the scientist Karla mentioned would be brought out to study the spider situation.

'You must be the arachnologist she spoke about,' said Laurita, accurately recalling who Søren was. 'She was at the medcentre here in

Ferntree Gully when we were visiting the seed gatherer who was bitten by a spider while they were out working in the forest. Karla said you were from Greenland?'

'Yes, and we have been rescued from near starvation after being snowed in for weeks. It is only Karla's connection with the Federation that brought us to this wonderful warm country, with its plentiful food.'

Yngwie stared, intrigued by this unusual man, who was significantly shorter than average, of slight build, but of extraordinarily beautiful appearance. His accent was accounted for by his being from Greenland, where Danish and the local Inuit dialects were still the main languages spoken, rather than English.

Equally fascinated, Laurita gazed at him and said, 'Snowed in for weeks? Isn't that a little out of the ordinary?'

'Yes, and no. It doesn't happen often these days, but when it does, it's usually severe. I keep stock enough for two weeks, but this was longer than I, or anyone else for that matter, anticipated. Even Dandelion didn't have enough to eat for the last two days we were there, which is simply not to be tolerated.'

Dandelion looked up at him and then at Laurita. She giggled when the cat showed her a mental image of Søren ransacking his cupboards for something to eat and afterwards carefully preparing his pancakes. 'Your cat just 'spoke' to me, which is a bit strange as well, isn't it?'

'She sometimes likes to laugh at me, don't you, eh?' Søren nudged Dandelion with his foot and added, 'But yes, not all cats like to speak with anyone other their companion. This one gets bored, so occasionally likes to have a chat with someone new.'

'Seriously?' asked Yngwie, not having had much to do with cats before.

'Yes, seriously. I often spend time away in places she cannot go, so my little darling has learnt to entertain herself with other people, and now, even when we are together, occasionally wants someone else to talk to. Quite understandable, when it comes down to it. I do at times become lost in my work.'

Dandelion pressed herself against his legs, then sat down to wait for them to finish talking, tail draped across his feet.

'Ah, which reminds me,' said Søren. 'I have assured the good manager here that I would wash Dandelion's paws. We have been out walking in the forest and the ash from the burnt area has made them filthy.'

The manager had returned to her workstation, but smiled when she heard what Søren was saying, glad he remembered his promise.

'Well, we'll see you later, probably tomorrow,' said Laurita. 'We need to get ready for our dinner party anyway, so goodbye for now.'

She took Yngwie by the arm as he also said goodbye, then, as they turned away to go to their rooms to shower and change, Søren and

Dandelion went to theirs – not exactly to do likewise in the cat's case, but at least to be clean in time for dinner.

The coincidence of the cascade having been initiated at the exact time recorded in a newly issued Federation identity number still bothered Morag MacIain. Frustrated and annoyed at lying awake dwelling on this problem instead of sleeping, she rolled onto her other side. This was not like her! After so many years working as an investigator before taking on the role of FSIU Coordinator, she had trained herself not to obsess about her cases. What was it about this one that was different? The enormity of the act, the sheer cheek, and the reckless disregard for the consequences. Stupid! Stupid, stupid, stupid person! Unless of course they were plotting something evil. Oddly enough, this thought calmed her. Morag understood evil, but stupidity was somehow harder to deal with – less predictable, less manageable.

She switched on the light, then got out of bed and put on her dressing gown and slippers. A trip to the kitchen for a piece of chocolate cake and Morag felt more like herself. 'I'll give it half an hour, and if I can't work out what it is that's rolling around in my brain, wanting to pop out, I'll go back to sleep,' she thought, staring at the vase of yellow daisies on the kitchen sideboard without really seeing them.

On any given day, she reasoned, there would always be at least one baby born, and, having checked the Federation population database for the past five years, she knew there was always at least one identity number issued each day for Perth, typically a great many more. So, if it isn't just coincidence, then perhaps whoever created the cascade set the population database software to issue an ID at a specific time and on a specific day for a certain baby they knew was born in Perth three months earlier, and coordinated the messaging system to begin the cascade at the same time, or...what other possibilities were there? Morag ate a little more of the cake, then fetched a glass of ice-cold water and drank a few mouthfuls.

Considering the question from the opposite angle, what if a flaw in the messaging system was able to track the IDs as they were issued and managed to create a message to coincide with one of them? The flaw could even be in the population database software, allowing the messaging system to be notified when certain IDs were allocated, triggering a response as required.

In either case, there would need to be an obscure coding mistake that someone had exploited, or a piece of malicious code. Theoretically, aside from the routines used to select who to send messages to, the only direct interaction between the messaging system and the Federation population database were entries in a table indicating which message had been sent to whom, where, and when. This table had already been checked and the requisite vast number of entries were there, recording the fact that the cascade had been sent around the world to, as it turned out, everyone over the age of fifteen who possessed a comlink.

Specialist FSIU information technologists were still searching for trojans and as yet had found nothing, but that didn't mean there wasn't one, and it didn't mean there wasn't a security loophole that no one had yet thought to look for.

Morag checked the time and to her disgust realised she might as well give up the idea of any further sleep since it was almost time to get up anyway. Still, at least she now had something specific to hunt down.

Amongst others in their target group, several dozen infotechs with access to either the messaging system, the population database software, or both, were found to have the personality types and behavioural traits regarded as being consistent with the descriptions Welcome had given Morag. Four of them were currently working in Australia, and one of them now faced the psychologist. With a halo of blonde curls, bright blue eyes, purple lipstick and matching nail varnish, the young woman was dressed in a dark grey, two-piece body suit, with a very short, pleated crimson skirt and a crimson and grey plaid waistcoat. Tall, slender, and with an air of extreme confidence, she most definitely fell into their more outgoing and creative category.

'I would never have used that particular image,' she said, referring to the cascade. 'It's too obvious and what does it say? Fight for liberty? We want more freedom? Or is it just for the shock value? A prized icon burning... As far as I'm concerned, we have enough freedom and the Federation does a great job. No, the whole thing's ridiculous and it's taking up far too much valuable time looking for faults in our systems. True, for all we know there *might* be a security flaw we've missed, but *I* think it's an inside job, and I even think I can give you a name: Wentworth-Smith. He's a total bastard! Arrogant, a loud-mouth, knows everything about everything, but when it comes down to it, leaves all the hard work to someone else. Little shit!' The young woman lowered her eyes to study her nails, mouth pursed in a moue of disgust.

Welcome stared at her. This wasn't at all what he expected. 'Really?' he answered, rather weakly.

'Yes, really. He also sees himself as an artist – produces crap, if you ask me. Anyway, a lot of people can't tell crap from the real thing, so why should I be worried? Now *my* work, *it's* different. *I* produce stuff that says something...something worth saying.' She took out her comlink and showed Welcome a series of images: subtle, beautiful, and disturbing. He handed back the comlink and with sudden insight understood what the young woman was suggesting.

'You think this is an artwork? An event?' He continued staring at her as she replied.

'Yes, I do. Whether it's the first of a series, I couldn't say, but yes, it has all the hallmarks of someone who wants a lot of attention, and at the same time, wants to be able to laugh at everyone else.'

This was so close to one of their own theories that Welcome's eyes widened a fraction as he paused, taking stock of the situation. 'Wentworth-Smith, you say? Do you think he has the technical ability to pull this off, without leaving a trace?'

'Oh yes, he has the ability, I'll give him that, and he's patient. He's probably been working on this for years, just waiting for the right time...and trust me, there'll be a trace somewhere. There always is.'

'Well, thank you. I'll discuss the information you've given me with my colleagues. If you have any more thoughts on the matter, or any ideas as to what type of trace this fellow, if he is our man, may have left, then please, let me know.' Welcome gave her his comlink code, then stood up and, before escorting her from the interview room, shook the young woman's hand.

'We'll be watching you, young lady, that's for sure,' he thought. 'Very, very clever... But who knows, she might just be right and be quite innocent herself.'

A few minutes later, Morag viewed the recording of the interview and came to the same conclusion as Welcome. What better way to throw someone off your own trail than to implicate someone else? However, this Wentworth-Smith was already one of the four Australians on their list, which meant the information provided was potentially highly useful, as was the idea of the cascade being some form of extremist artwork.

With all the guests seated at the dining table, and Karla's cat, Aurora, curled up by her feet, Shahid's mother, Wania, began serving the dishes she had prepared with so much care. Meanwhile, Shahid's father, Shafiqur, sat at one end of the table, beaming with pride for his bondmate's achievement and with the simple joy of being present at his son's Namingday dinner. The candlelight brought an atmosphere of cosy comfort to this colourful, elegant, and yet homely, room, with its abundance of tapestry wall hangings, silk cushions, and photographs of family members in silver frames, arranged on an ancient cedar sideboard. Shahid noticed Karla looking at them while she waited for Wania to finish serving a particularly delicious-looking baked salmon.

'That's my grandfather,' he said, using the hand reader which rarely left his side. 'He migrated from southern India, where many Bangladeshi people moved when our homeland was flooded by rising sea levels, centuries ago.'

'You still regard Bangladesh as your ancestral homeland?' asked Karla, her voice gentle, yet with a hint of surprise in it.

'We all do,' replied Wania, giving Yngwie more of the fish. 'Ancestry and culture are important. Aren't they to you?'

'Yes and no,' replied Karla, smiling. 'I'm glad I know where my family came from and who they were, and still are, but I see a constant ebb and flow, changing patterns and new beginnings, stemming from our interactions with each other over time. I like to keep what is good from the past and take up what is better from the present.'

'How do you know what to leave behind and what to adopt?' asked Shafiqur, after tasting the fish and saluting his bondmate. The flavour was superb, perfectly complementing the saffron rice already on their plates.

Karla served herself some of the cucumber, tomato and carrot salad, all the ingredients freshly picked that afternoon from the family's garden. 'I try to think about what's best for everyone; the planet included,' she said, then realising this sounded a touch pompous, looked at her food and began eating.

Both Wania and Shafiqur nodded in approval. 'Good,' they remarked at the same time, then laughed at each other. Shahid grinned and said, 'So do we, but the question is, how do we know what's in everyone's best interest, as well as the planet's?'

At this point, Laurita, who had been paying more attention to the food than to the conversation, looked up and said, 'It all depends upon how much we care and how much we understand, doesn't it?'

'Yes, and how well we can divorce ourselves from our own selfish needs to truly understand what is best in the long term,' answered Wania. 'Perhaps we are beginning to learn from our past mistakes. I hope so.'

'I do too,' said Laurita, 'but even now, after everything we have done to this poor planet of ours, there are many who do not see how important it is to support the Federation and not think only of their own national interest. I see so much petty squabbling as I travel around the world.' She lowered her eyes for a moment, then glanced at Shahid, sorry to have introduced such a gloomy note to the celebration. He smiled, fully understanding. Relieved, Laurita continued by saying, 'There's also a great deal of wonderful work being done, thank the Sun, and the cooperation I generally receive is amazing. Without the assistance and knowledge of local people, much of the work we do gathering seeds and plant stock from ancient food sources and promising wild species would be impossible.' For a short while, she was back in other lands, remembering, but then collected herself, shook her head, and said, 'You know what I mean, don't you, Shahid?'

Reaching for the salad dish, Shahid simply nodded, but gave her another brilliant smile. For the first time he noticed just how beautiful Laurita looked this evening, in her long black gown, with its swirls of light grey and hints of blue. He blushed, but no one could see the colour in his dark cheeks, so his momentary embarrassment went unheeded.

'Would you like more iced water?' offered Wania, reaching for the carafe and offering it to Yngwie, who so far had said very little.

'Thank you,' he replied, holding out his glass. 'You are so generous,' he added, indicating the table with his hand.

'How can we ever be generous enough to thank you for saving our son's life?' replied Shafiqur, his head to one side, his expression now serious.

This time it was Yngwie's turn to blush. Shafiqur leaned over and patted him on the shoulder. 'No, no, please do not be embarrassed. I mean what I say, but you are no doubt right – enough is enough.' He grinned and patted Yngwie's shoulder again, then applied himself to his food.

Yngwie did likewise and for a time the room was silent, except for Aurora's soft snoring. Karla had made sure to feed her before they left home, uncertain whether her hosts would be prepared to provide for a cat. Consequently, Aurora was at peace with the world and thoroughly enjoying both the new company and the chance to snooze. Every now and again, she woke up to check all was well, then went back to sleep, bushy tail well tucked in, out of harm's way.

Before the next course was served, Shafiqur and Shahid stood up and left the room, explaining that it was time for their evening prayers. Wania remained behind to care for her guests. When they returned, she brought in a variety of fragrantly spiced dishes, including one containing meat, which was relatively unusual. 'From the annual kangaroo cull,' she explained, hoping no one would be offended. 'We always have it for our special occasions. Some of our traditional recipes can't do without meat, but I understand if you prefer not to eat it.'

Karla, who never ate meat, smiled, shaking her head slightly. Yngwie, on the other hand, was used to eating venison from similar culls in neighbouring Sweden, and said he'd be glad to taste some, while Laurita appeared uncertain. However, when Yngwie gave his approval, she tentatively accepted a small serving. After tasting it, she looked at Wania in amazement. 'It's delicious!' she exclaimed.

Pleased, Wania laughed. 'Yes, it is, but it's not for every day. The land can't support much in the way of livestock, and the cull has to follow scientific and humane guidelines, or the kangaroo population will suffer, which would be totally unacceptable.'

'Mmm...' answered Yngwie, chewing. He swallowed his mouthful, then asked, 'What about rabbits? Aren't there still plenty of them?'

'Not really. We're optimistic the problem is finally under control. Mind you, that's been thought before...many times...over the past five hundred years! At least there aren't many around here, so the garden is reasonably safe, as long as we keep it well fenced and with a mesh roof as well to keep out the possums and birds. In some respects, it's just as well there aren't many wombats around either to cause a problem... *They're* master burrowers!'

'Cute though,' said Karla, with a chuckle.

'I suppose so,' replied Wania, smiling. 'Speaking of meat, Shahid has told me your research is aimed at creating plants with complete protein, and also increasing the protein content of various grains.'

'Yes, that's right. We've had a fair amount of success, and next week we'll be trialling our latest batch of bread from the rye plots in Narre Warren. Have you heard about them, too?'

'Oh yes,' said Shafiqur. 'Perhaps we should volunteer to try the bread this time. When will it be baked?'

'Next Monday afternoon, and if all goes to plan, a second batch on Tuesday morning. I need to make sure all the volunteers are ready by then to take delivery. If you want, I can add you to the list. Let's hope it's tasty!'

'I'm sure it will be. Phil's a wonderful baker. We usually buy some of his flatbread each week, and a few loaves of the speciality pasta dura. At the end of Ramadan each year we treat ourselves to one of his banana and passionfruit pavlovas too!' Shafiqur grinned and they all laughed. Pavlova was such a popular dessert, and had been for hundreds of years, that it was hardly surprising it might cross into almost any of the hundred or so cultural groups in the country. 'What do you think, Wania? Do you want to try the new bread?'

'Why not. Yes, let's.' She looked at Shahid, who nodded, pleased. It would be good to help in this small way.

Karla took out her comlink and added their names to her list of volunteers, then put it away and said, 'Done!' She turned to Laurita and Yngwie, who seemed about to say something, and with a smile, added, 'Local residents only... Sorry.'

They each pretended to frown, but laughed instead. 'There's plenty of other food here, so we won't go hungry,' said Yngwie. 'Speaking of which, I must have more of this wonderful feast!' He helped himself to a soft flatbread roll filled with thin strips of spring onion, fresh coriander, and various other vegetables, cooked to perfection.

## Chapter Five

The evening continued pleasantly, and when Wania placed a large bowl on the table containing dessert, her guests looked at it curiously, not quite sure what it was. A jug of dark red sauce soon sat next to it. 'This sauce is made from sweetened and cooked pitted black cherries, and this,' explained Wania, indicating the bowl, 'is *ris á l'amande*, made with white rice, sugar, vanilla, milk, cream, and finely chopped blanched almonds. It has been served on special occasions in Denmark for many centuries, and as it's very similar in concept to a traditional sweet of ours, I thought to make it in honour of Yngwie's Norwegian background, although I'm not sure if it's part of his country's cuisine nowadays. We love it! Please, have as much as you like.'

The bowl of *ris á l'amande* was passed around the table, and afterwards, the jug of cherry sauce. Karla tasted her serving first and raised her eyes in delight. The light texture and delicate taste of the rice dish was beautifully balanced by the stronger flavour and mild acidity of the cherries. Despite this, having already eaten more than usual, she wasn't able to finish it all, and apologised.

'Don't worry, my dear,' said Wania, smiling. 'Your cat may like to have it. She's awake.'

Aurora had indeed woken up and was eyeing the table. The sense of intense enjoyment while they were eating had filtered through to her and she had begun dreaming of food.

'I'll take it to the kitchen,' continued Wania, picking up the bowl containing the remainder of Karla's dessert. Aurora scampered after her, tail in the air. She ate her treat by the kitchen sink, even gobbling down the few cherries that remained with relish. Afterwards, she sat in the doorway, cleaning her face while Wania made coffee. The aromatic smell soon wafted into the dining room, pervading the house with an atmosphere of wellbeing and contentment.

Shahid left them for a few moments, returning with his lute, which he had long since mastered. The instrument was his real 'voice', an inner connection that lent his music a tender poignancy which rarely failed to touch his audience. Tonight, everyone listened, entranced, and when Yngwie began to sing the words to a piece he knew, Laurita began to weep, covering her eyes with one hand. She couldn't have said why, but the sheer beauty of the song and the sight of these two young men, so contrasted in appearance and yet so deeply in harmony with their music, affected her deeply.

Concerned, Aurora crept to her knee and, with a soft meow, asked her why she seemed so sad. Astonished to 'hear' the cat's voice in her mind, Laurita looked into Aurora's eyes, whispering, 'You spoke to *me*?' She caressed the cat's head, tentatively at first, and then, as Aurora began to purr, more confidently.

When Karla turned to see what was happening, Aurora told her that she didn't want their friend to be unhappy, particularly not when everyone was having such a wonderful evening. Waiting until the song finished, Karla stood and moved over to Laurita. 'They don't tend to speak with anyone other than their companion,' she said, stroking the cat's golden fur, 'but Aurora's very fond of you.'

'I see!' replied Laurita, smiling now. Aurora licked her hand, then padded over to where Shahid sat and rubbed her head against his leg. Karla laughed, saying, 'I think Aurora feels it's time *she* had some attention as well!'

Shahid ran his hand along Aurora's back, and to his astonishment, she also 'spoke' to him. He glanced at Karla, and was startled to 'hear' Aurora relay what he was about to say.

Karla raised an eyebrow, also surprised, as this was something Aurora had never done before, although she knew other cats sometimes chose to communicate this way.

The others, not knowing what had happened, looked puzzled, and when Karla explained, stared at Aurora, wondering what else the cat was about to do. Were no one's thoughts truly private with these creatures nearby? As if in answer, Aurora yawned and padded over to Yngwie, then sat down to thoroughly clean herself all over.

'Most of what runs through our heads doesn't really seem to interest them,' said Karla, then laughed when Yngwie replied that this was probably just as well!

Shahid, however, watched Aurora and wondered. Did she understand that he couldn't speak in the usual way, so had chosen to speak for him? Aurora turned to him, her eyes glowing in the candlelight. 'Yes,' she 'said'. 'You need someone like me – a grimalkin of your own.'

The next morning, a fine mist covered the entire mountain as Yngwie, Laurita and Shahid set out to search for the area of recently burnt forest. According to the weather forecast, the mist would lift within the hour, after which the day promised to be fine and mild; perfect for checking the mountain ash weren't unduly damaged and whether the area would soon recover from the fire. When they found the site, tiny new green shoots were already lifting their heads above the blackened earth, while a pair of kookaburras were perched in an old wattle tree, eyeing the ground for anything that moved. One swooped down to catch a small lizard, which soon disappeared down its throat, but the birds flew off when it became clear the human intruders intended to stay.

Bellbirds had moved into the area a long time ago, and their high, echoing call resonated throughout the grey-green forest as they searched for insects and nectar-bearing flowers. Yngwie used his comlink to record the sounds and to capture some footage of their surroundings. After a while he said, 'Seeing and hearing the forest today has made coming here worthwhile. It's magical... Old and mysterious, like our mountains and fjords. Pity about the horrible smell though!'

'It'll be better further up the mountain,' replied Shahid, before bending over to examine the base of the nearest, massive mountain ash. He poked around in the blackened soil for a while, then straightened up and said, 'It all seems fine here. Let's move on.'

The atmosphere of the forest seemed to call for silence, not chatter, so they walked in single file, Yngwie and Laurita following Shahid. Eventually, as the mist finally receded, the burnt area gave way to the freshness of healthy growth, the heady scent of eucalyptus, and clean, life-giving earth. This time, a pair of magpies greeted them, carolling their extraordinary song before flying off further up the mountain.

Shahid turned to smile at his companions, who had stopped to listen. 'Other than the kookaburras,' he said, 'there's nothing so Australian as a magpie call.'

While Yngwie peered into the treetops to see if he could spot more birds, Laurita warmly returned Shahid's smile. 'I agree,' she said. 'It's one of the sounds I look forward to every time I come here. Karla loves the call so much she even has a recording as her wake-up alarm.'

'A wonderful idea,' said Yngwie, who had just taken an image of a lone crimson rosella perched on the lower branches of one of the gum trees. He examined it critically and then, satisfied, put his comlink away.

They walked on until Shahid located one of the mature trees that were in flower. 'Ready to climb?' he asked Laurita.

While Yngwie watched, fascinated, the two seed gatherers used their combination of ropes and pulleys to take them into the canopy. Although Laurita was an expert tree climber, it was some time since she had ventured this high up and the experience was exhilarating beyond almost anything she had ever before felt. These trees were, after all, the tallest flowering plant in the world, and without someone to accompany her, they were far too unsafe to climb. With a chuckle of sheer pleasure, she secured herself to one of the tree's sturdy limbs, then turned to gaze at the view, listening to the gentle buzz of a swarm of honeybees gathering nectar.

As well as the wonderful view, the scent of the eucalypt's flowers filled Laurita with joy, and she called out to Shahid, 'Thank you!' He waved to her, then concentrated on the task at hand. This tree was old, and some of its branches were beginning to fail; negotiating the climb had taken considerable care and getting down again would take even more. Nevertheless, he too relaxed for a few minutes, sharing the pleasure of being here – with Laurita. In this sea of green, they were virtually alone.

When a light breeze ruffled his hair, he glanced at her. She met his eyes and smiled, also enjoying the soft caress of the warm air.

'One more sample and we're done,' signalled Shahid, using the universal sign language taught to all who worked in dangerous conditions.

Laurita nodded, then helped by packing the sprays of flowers and young leaves into their sealed container for later analysis. 'It's a pity it isn't spring,' she said, 'Wurundjeri time, time of the brown butterfly. How marvellous if there was a flight of butterflies up here with us!'

Shahid paused, made sure he was secure, took his comlink from his pocket, and quickly typed: "Silver wattle blooms, orchids spring from the soft earth, the rains of September fall."

They were just close enough together for him to hand Laurita the comlink, rather than have it speak the words. Somehow this seemed more fitting. She laughed, delighted with the poetic phrase, so precisely complementing her words, then typed: "Black swans on a lake, proud heads on their long, curved necks, wings furled as they glide." After reading the haiku, Shahid added, "Ripples of light following ~ silence with the setting sun."

'One more,' said Laurita, when he handed her the comlink again. Shahid smiled, studying her intently as she concentrated for a short while, before writing: "Perfectly silent, the moments before sunrise ~ hold your breath, waiting."

With his head to one side, considering, Shahid suddenly grinned, finishing the poem with: "The day begins with laughter; the sound of kookaburras."

'Oh, that's perfect!' exclaimed Laurita, handing back the comlink. 'So many times, when I've been out in the forest, or searching for plants along a river, I've heard them at dawn. Do you miss their laughter, living underground?'

Shahid shook his head. 'No. They're awfully loud!'

'I expect you hear them here almost every day, as well as all the other wonderful birds.'

'Yes, they're rarely silent, thank God. They're the life of the forest... Although, speaking of loud, the cockatoos are a bit much when a flock flies overhead, particularly when I'm up this high!'

Laurita made a face and grinned. 'True...but they're gorgeous all the same.'

Shahid agreed, then put away his comlink and signalled it was time to make their descent.

Meanwhile, Yngwie had set about capturing as many worthwhile images as he could, having missed the chance on the day of the fire. He waved at his two companions when they were halfway down, excited by his success.

'How did it go?' he asked, when both the seed gatherers were safely on the ground.

'Incredible!' replied Laurita, as she began packing their gear away. 'It's a pity you couldn't come with us. You would have loved it!'

Yngwie chuckled. 'Yes, I'm sure I would, but I imagine it takes a long time to learn how to climb these giants.'

With a smile, Shahid nodded, then carefully loaded their samples into the cool storage unit they had brought with them, indicating they should go on to the next tree. They planned to work until mid-afternoon, after which time the flowers and leaves needed to be taken to Willsmere, where their health would be assessed.

Some ten minutes later, as they stood near the base of another gigantic mountain ash, Yngwie noticed something unusual and pointed it out to Shahid. 'Do you think this might be a spider's burrow?' he asked.

Shahid looked closely at the web before capturing an image with his comlink. 'Yes,' he said, 'this looks like one of the funnel-webs. We *should* be safe enough during the day, but from my last experience, I suggest we move on. I'll forward this to Karla first.'

He was about to do so when Laurita said, 'Why not send it directly to Søren Thorup? He's probably prowling around the forest now, too.'

'Oh, yes, of course!' replied Shahid, and entered Søren's name into his comlink. A few moments later, he had sent the image with a brief message, and shortly afterwards received an effusive thank you and a promise to examine the burrow later in the day. Søren was indeed "prowling" the forest, but was almost five kilometres away, so sent his regrets that he could not meet up with them. "Perhaps this evening, at the communal house in Ferntree Gully?" his message continued.

Shahid showed the message to Yngwie and Laurita, who quickly agreed, and arrangements were made to meet at 20:30, after dinner.

The base and lower trunk of the next mountain ash appeared to be free of venomous spiders, so the two climbers were able to ascend into the canopy without worrying about being bitten, although the swarming bees certainly kept them on alert. As the sun rose in the sky, the scent of the flowers became stronger, almost intoxicating, and by mid-afternoon, both Shahid and Laurita were relieved to be at ground level again, where it was a great deal cooler as well.

'May I come to Willsmere with you?' asked Laurita, as she put the last of their samples into the cool storage unit.

Surprised, Shahid looked up from fastening their backpacks, then nodded, and immediately looked down again. 'Does she want to see Karla, or does she want to spend more time with me?' he thought, as his pulse quickened in a sudden burst of self-consciousness. When he raised his eyes, it was to see Yngwie glancing at Laurita with an odd expression on his face. 'Jealousy?' wondered Shahid, even more surprised. 'Surely not?' But he saw that Laurita avoided Yngwie's gaze.

Feeling distinctly uncomfortable, Shahid led the way back to Ferntree Gully, wishing he hadn't agreed to meet up with them after dinner.

# CHAPTER SIX

The morning mist covering the mountain had prevented Søren from setting his funnel-web traps as early as he intended, which suited Karla for it meant she could sleep in, after having gone to bed later than normal the previous evening. When she did eventually meet Søren at the communal house, it was already mid-morning.

While Dandelion and Aurora cautiously sniffed each other, Karla asked her colleague what he had discovered so far in the way of roaming spiders.

'Enough... In fact, more than enough,' he answered, pulling a wry face. 'I found one male funnel-web and two burrows in an area approximately one hundred by one hundred metres. If this is indicative of the entire forest, we will have to issue a public safety statement and ensure the medcentre has ample anti-venom on hand.'

Karla also made a face – of disgust. She found it difficult to comprehend how Søren could actually like spiders and wasn't in the least afraid of them, even the largest, which in northern parts of Australia meant huge, and extremely dangerous. She handed him a bag containing the traps, cameras and pheromones, saying, 'Well, we'll soon find out, won't we. Two weeks should be enough, I suppose, as long as the equipment isn't disturbed.'

'That *is* unlikely, isn't it?' replied Søren, examining the contents of the bag.

'Yes, but one never knows. Still, let's not worry about that. It's time we got going if we want to be finished by evening.' Knowing Søren couldn't go long without thinking of food, she added, 'Have you arranged for something to bring with you for midsun and afternoon tea?'

'Oh yes!' he replied, with a mischievous grin. 'See here...' and he picked up his backpack and opened it. Inside was a cooler, which he told her contained a delectable sauvignon blanc – low alcohol, given they were working – fresh, ripe peaches, carefully wrapped in plastifoam to prevent them bruising; an assortment of aromatic cheeses, already cut into convenient portions; a variety of small, beautifully prepared vegetable quiche; and for afternoon tea, marzipan chocolates, macadamia shortbread, and coffee in a separate, self-heating container.

Karla laughed and held up her contribution: a flask of iced water and two freshly prepared salads...plus food and water for the cats.

'Good,' said Søren, 'we are ready!' Followed by a subdued Dandelion, he marched off towards the exit, with Karla and Aurora close behind.

In the past, the law required cats to be kept on leashes when in public, but only three months ago, this changed and they were now free to walk unhindered, as long as they were accompanied by a human and kept close to their companion. Aurora wanted to walk with Dandelion, but the other cat preferred to keep her distance. Disappointed, Aurora fell back and padded along by Karla's side. She was used to other cats, and had three friends, whom she first met six years ago. They were companions to two of Karla's colleagues, Mik Theophanous and Tamara Solanum, who were currently in Queensland, following up on progress with reforestation trials at the Lamington research centre.

By coincidence, Søren happened to be thinking about his Australian friends. Turning to Karla, he said, 'How are Mik and Tamara? I was hoping to spend some time with them, and thought I could come back to Willsmere with you this evening.'

'Oh!' replied Karla, embarrassed. She had forgotten to tell him they wouldn't be there. 'They're away, in Queensland, and won't be back for about a month... Sorry!'

'I am too,' he answered. It was many years since he had seen them in person, although they often called each other.

'They've applied for fertility rights, would you believe,' added Karla. 'If they don't do it now, they never will. Tamara will be too old to have children if they wait much longer.' At Søren's stunned expression, she said, 'Yes, I know. It was a bit of a shock for me too. Let's hope the cats like babies!'

'Assuming they succeed with their application,' said Søren. 'Not everyone does, of course. Still, I cannot recall them mentioning any genetic disorders in their families that might prevent it, and I'm sure they would make excellent parents.'

'I agree, and feel certain they'll be allowed to go ahead.' Karla herself had never entertained the idea of having children. Her nurturing instincts simply didn't include having babies...besides which, she had no intention of giving up fulltime work for ten years to care for a child, as the law required both parents to do.

'It will be an immense change in their lives, and you will miss them at Willsmere,' remarked Søren, saying nothing further for some time, which was fairly unusual for him.

When they reached the edge of the forest, they climbed the hill to the place where Søren had done his sample survey. He soon found the two burrows he mentioned earlier and showed them to Karla, who decided a close inspection was the last thing she wanted to attempt – and even more so when Søren showed her the images he received when he used his optical probe to locate the resident female funnel-web. Karla shuddered and took a step back, then sat down on a nearby log, waiting for him to finish. Aurora kept close by her side, not at all happy at the prospect of meeting one of the spiders. Dandelion, used to her companion's ways, seemed unperturbed, and was amusing herself inspecting the gap between the log and the ground below, searching for something to chase. There was no intention to harm any small creatures she found, but a little gentle prodding to send them scurrying away always intrigued her. So far, she had remained unhurt by this pastime, but a sudden thought occurred to Karla: 'Søren, I'm not sure Dandelion should fiddle about in here. She might find more than she bargained for.'

Søren turned around, looked at the cat and said, 'Yes, you are right. I didn't realise. Dandelion, come here, and don't hunt in this forest. There are too many things that might bite you.'

Dandelion stopped what she was doing, sat down, and studied him closely. When Aurora, who had once seen a highly venomous tiger snake in the bushland surrounding Willsmere, sent this image to Dandelion, the cat turned to face her, and without any warning, leapt. Aurora, used to mock fighting with Mik and Tamara's three cats, was not in the least alarmed and grabbed Dandelion with her paws, deftly rolling her over. Pleasure turned to alarm, however, when Dandelion twisted around and sank long teeth into her opponent's neck. Aurora screamed in pain and shock, then, when she tried to get away, howled in fury as Dandelion threw herself on top, knocking her over and viciously clawing her with both back feet. Managing to get away, Aurora, with hackles raised and back arched, spat furiously at the other cat. Dandelion, ears laid flat, her eyes narrowed and shoulders hunched, yowled and struck Aurora across the face, drawing blood. After only a moment's hesitation, Aurora launched herself forward, and while Søren and Karla watched in horror, too shocked to react, the two cats became a screaming, whirling mass of flying fur and unleashed rage.

Karla moved towards them, but Søren yelled out to stop her: 'No!' Instead, he grabbed her backpack, took out the flask of iced water, quickly poured it into its cooler container and flung it over the cats. They parted, panting, tails lashing to and fro. Dandelion made as if to attack again, but this time Søren did the only thing he could. He smacked her, hard, on the rear end. Never in his life had he ever so much as threatened to hit her, or even shouted at her, yet now there was no choice. She immediately slunk to his feet, crouching, shoulders still hunched, the tip of her tail twitching. Meanwhile, Aurora crept over to Karla and also crouched down, but stared up at her, confused, the pupils of her eyes fully dilated, huge and black. Karla knelt beside her, staring back, hardly knowing what to say. She slowly put out a hand for Aurora to sniff, and when the cat gently rubbed her head against it, Karla stroked her, then used her kerchief to wipe away the blood from her face. The scratch had missed Aurora's eyes, thank the Sun, but ran across her nose, making a small tear in its tip.

'It hurts,' Aurora 'told' her. Karla stood up to fetch the first aid kit she always carried on outings such as this and applied a soothing antiseptic cream, then examined the cat as well as she could, searching through the thick fur to see if there were any other wounds in need of attention. There were: other than small puncture wounds in her neck, Karla found several deep scratches that had raked across Aurora's shoulders and one on her left leg as well. 'Damn!' she thought. Having never heard of cats fighting like this before, she wondered what on Earth was going on?

When Søren examined Dandelion, he also found several marks, although none as deep as the ones she inflicted on Aurora. He told her to stay where she was and walked over to Karla to borrow the antiseptic. Frowning, she handed it to him. 'What are we going to do? We can't just keep working and hope they behave, and we can't leave one of them here alone. Blasted cat!' She cast a look of disgust at Dandelion, who whimpered and crawled a few centimetres towards her, but Karla would have none of it. Instead, she turned away to stroke Aurora, who was still confused, but no longer angry.

'I am so sorry, Aurora,' said Søren, kneeling beside her. He didn't attempt to touch her, but stayed where he was, concentrating on making her aware of the full extent of his apology. She stood up at last and bumped her head against his, purring. Relieved, Søren ran a soothing hand over her fur, smoothing it down, then stood up and went back to Dandelion. He crouched down to apply the antiseptic, at the same time asking her to 'explain' why she had attacked Karla's companion. When she failed to respond, other than to relax slightly, he said, 'I *had* to hit you. There was no choice. I didn't *want* to hurt you, just stop you fighting with Aurora. You can't do things like that...you just can't!' Tears ran down his face as he said this. Dandelion was his dearest friend and companion and they had been together for so many years. Nothing like this had ever happened before. He put the antiseptic away and sat down on the ground, holding a hand over his eyes. Dandelion crept to his side and leaned against him, meowing softly. As he put an arm around her, holding her close, Søren wept, more from shock than anything else. The sight and sound of the two cats fighting, together with the cloud of fur that enveloped them, was something he would never forget!

Karla kept her distance, unsure of what to do and unwilling to leave Aurora for a second in case Dandelion decided to attack again. At last Søren wiped his eyes, heaved a sigh and stood up. 'Karla,' he said, with a tremor in his voice, 'do you have a leash with you? I don't, but Dandelion needs to be taken back to the communal house. Will *you* do it? Aurora could stay with me while I continue working.'

Without a word, Karla rummaged around in her backpack, took out the leash she still kept with her in case of emergencies, and handed it to him. Dandelion kept perfectly still while he attached it to her collar, then meekly went with Karla back down the hillside, while Aurora watched, unhappy and wondering what would happen next.

The young man sitting across the table from Welcome stuttered a few times, then managed to say, 'I haven't the least idea what you're talking about.'

Welcome could tell Wentworth-Smith was stalling, so simply waited. Not many people could stay silent for long.

'Just because I have access to the population database *and* the messaging system, and I happened to be working on the night when all the comlinks were hacked into, doesn't mean I had anything to do with it!' Wentworth-Smith folded his arms and stared at the psychologist, frowning. His earlier nervous reaction to being interviewed was apparently wearing off.

'You were in Perth, too, when the cascade was initiated. Don't you think this is all a bit too much of a coincidence?' replied Welcome, returning the stare.

'It's irrelevant,' answered Wentworth-Smith. 'With the right authority, the systems can be accessed from anywhere in the world.'

'Very well,' said Welcome, with a friendly smile. 'Perhaps you can help us then. Recently, when we examined a table of message records created during the cascade, we found one entry containing the Federation ID of a three-month-old baby, born in Perth, together with the comment "message failed, no comlink", which, under the circumstances, is hardly surprising.' He paused to see if Wentworth-Smith wanted to say anything, but the young man merely shook his head. 'In your opinion, what would cause the messaging system to even attempt to send a message to someone who clearly would not possess a comlink?'

This time, Wentworth-Smith leaned forward eagerly and said, 'That's easy! There's a manual override that allows messages to be sent out in cases when they may seem a bit illogical. The software would always query the request and require additional authority, but if the second authority is given, it'd allow the request to go ahead. You see, it's impossible to predict every single type of message that might need to be sent out, so there has to be some form of manual override. Though I must say, this *is* an odd one. I can't recall anything like it before.' He sat back in his chair, thinking, then added, 'Was there anything else unusual about the table?'

'Yes, there was,' said Welcome, pleased Wentworth-Smith was able to confirm something they had already discovered for themselves. It seemed to indicate he might not be directly involved. Still, best not to assume anything... 'The messages were only sent to people over fifteen years of age,' he continued. 'Remarkably considerate, don't you think?'

Wentworth-Smith gave a snort of laughter and ran a hand through his abundant mop of curly black hair. 'Bloody peculiar, I'd say. Still, maybe they didn't want to upset the little kiddies with their ridiculous image!'

'You think it was ridiculous?' asked Welcome.

'Of course it was! What a waste of an opportunity. If they wanted to freak everyone out, and I mean, *really* freak them out, why leave out the kids? And why use such a cliché? If it were me, I'd have sent it to the whole world and used something that said no one's safe – ever!' He gazed earnestly at Welcome, one hand raised to emphasise his point. 'No one *is* safe, you realise? The Federation might've fooled most people into thinking they are, but it only takes one total nut job to put everyone at risk. If they're good enough, they can work away for years without anyone noticing, and then – bang! The whole bloody system falls apart.'

Welcome regarded him steadily for a few moments before saying, 'Wouldn't our security systems prevent someone from being able to do that much damage?'

'Theoretically, yes, I guess so, but there's always a loophole, even if it's not a technical one. People always let you down eventually. There's always someone who's careless, or greedy, or stupid, or has some crazy idea they want to force everyone to listen to. People! I tell you, they're all bloody mad!'

'Except you, and possibly even me.' Welcome waved a hand to make it clear he was joking. 'Is there anyone you can think of who might have done this? Some nutter, as you say.'

'Oh yes! There's this guy who sits by himself all day mumbling away about how everyone needs to be given a big wake-up call, and if he could have his way, they'd all be made to recognise that if it wasn't for people like us, the whole world would grind to a halt. In his opinion, we're not even paid enough and our shifts are far too long. Silly bugger! We only work the same hours as everybody else, and our pay's no worse than anyone else's. Don't know what he's complaining about, but then, we *are* talking about someone who isn't quite right in the head.'

'What's his name?' asked Welcome, suppressing the urge to laugh. It appeared the blame game was catching on.

'Kaj Jonsson... Swedish, hasn't been here long, just a few months, and hates it, but he's on contract so has to stay another nine.' Wentworth-

Smith grimaced. 'Don't know how we're going to put up with him for that long. Still, I must admit, he's good at what he does.'

'And what does he do, and why do you think he had a hand in all this?' Welcome was genuinely curious as they had already come to the conclusion Jonsson was unlikely to be their culprit. He did, of course, already know that the Swede was a systems technologist of the highest calibre, brought to Australia to overhaul the various encryption keys used for satellite communications associated with the messaging system, a painstaking and lengthy process requiring even greater attention to detail than usual.

'He's a code-maker and breaker,' replied Wentworth-Smith glibly, 'and responsible for making the necessary periodic changes to the codes used when the messaging system interacts with certain geosynchronous satellites. Can't keep the same encryption keys forever, so every now and then they have to be changed and tested. Dreadful job! It takes someone with a screw loose to do it, come to think of it. What I mean, though, is that he's in the perfect position to initiate the cascade; he'd know how to overcome satellite security.'

'I see. You may be right, and we'll take what you've told me into consideration,' said Welcome, standing up and holding out a hand to indicate the interview was over.

The information technologist stood up as well, shaking Welcome's hand with a vice-like grip – he only just managed to avoid wincing. 'Little shit, indeed!' Welcome thought, as he closed the door behind him. 'Still, perhaps we should have a chat with this Kaj Jonsson after all.'

After his trip to the forest with Shahid and Laurita, the instant Yngwie entered the communal house he heard a keening wail and stopped in his tracks, unable to make out where it was coming from. He wasn't even sure it was an actual sound, rather than being only in his mind; it was the most peculiar sensation he had ever experienced. Holding a hand to his forehead, he glanced at the manager and saw she had apparently noticed nothing. The wailing grew louder, to the point where he needed to sit down. Stumbling over to the nearest chair, Yngwie collapsed into it, then realised the manager was staring at him.

'Do you hear anything?' he shouted, trying to overcome the din inside his head.

The manager's jaw dropped in astonishment. She stood up, then hesitated, but finally came over to him. 'What do you mean? I can't hear anything unusual.'

'Has anything weird happened here?' shouted Yngwie, now holding his hands over his ears in a vain attempt to drown out the sound.

'No. Why? What's wrong?' The manager was beginning to wonder if Yngwie was having some form of migraine attack, which was the only thing she could think of to account for his strange behaviour.

'I can hear a loud wailing inside my head. It's awful, like some animal in pain, screaming for help.'

'Oh, I think I know what's wrong!' exclaimed the manager. 'It might be the Greenlander's cat. She came back a while ago in a dreadful state, and she wasn't with *him* – she was with a friend of his called Karla. I don't know exactly what happened, but it looked as if the cat had been in a fight and needed to be kept locked up for some reason. She's been in their room ever since.'

Yngwie stood up, grasped the manager by the elbow and shouted, 'Could you let me into the room? If this doesn't stop soon, I'll go crazy!'

The manager didn't hesitate, and together they went to Søren and Dandelion's room. When they reached the door, the wailing subsided, to be replaced by a mournful howl, which was even worse. Yngwie slid to the floor, his back against the wall, head in both hands. Meanwhile, the manager opened the door, then leapt aside as the distraught cat bolted out to make her escape. Once Dandelion was gone, the noise inside Yngwie's head stopped.

'Thank the Sun!' he muttered and stood up. 'Where has she gone?' he asked. The manager shook her head, but pointed down the corridor towards the entranceway. 'Damn!' exclaimed Yngwie. 'Can she get out?'

'I don't know,' replied the manager. 'I hope not!' She took a brief look inside the room, saw the bedding had been shredded to pieces, gave one horrified yelp, and ran after Yngwie, who was following the cat.

Unfortunately, Dandelion was nowhere to be seen, and a quick inspection of the nearby rooms showed she was no longer in the building. Yngwie pulled out his comlink and called Søren. 'I'm sorry to have to tell you this,' he said, when the call was answered, 'but your cat has escaped and is now running around loose somewhere.'

Søren's eyes widened and he gaped at Yngwie, too shocked to answer. 'What do you mean, she's escaped?' he managed to say at last.

'For some reason I don't at all understand, after I came into the communal house, I could hear her wailing, inside my mind, and the manager realised it was your cat I must have been hearing. We went to your room and she bolted as soon as we opened the door. What should we do?'

'There *is* nothing you can do,' answered Søren, beginning to think more clearly and making an effort to remain calm. 'If she doesn't want to be found, she won't let anyone remember they have seen her. They can do that. They can hide themselves from us if they want to – or at least, some of them can. I must come back and look for her. She was in a fight with Karla's cat, which is why my friend brought her back to the communal house... Nothing like this has ever happened before and I have no idea why Dandelion attacked Aurora, and neither does she. I have them both here with me now, so thank you for letting me know and please do not call the peacekeepers. It would only make everything worse.'

It hadn't occurred to Yngwie to call the peacekeepers, so he wondered why Søren had even mentioned the possibility, but this wasn't the time to ask questions. Instead, he quickly agreed, and Søren abruptly ended the call. Turning to the manager, Yngwie shook his head, shrugged, and said, 'He's coming back to search for his cat. It seems she *was* in a fight...with Karla's cat, Aurora.'

Having had little to do with cats, the manager could only look mystified and say she hoped Dandelion would be all right and that her guest would soon find her. Shaking her head, she went back to their room to take a closer look at the damage and to begin tidying up, while Yngwie stayed where he was in case Søren needed him for anything.

About forty minutes later, Søren came in, tired and distressed. He walked up to Yngwie and, without preamble, said, 'I think you could hear Dandelion because you were the only person in the building, other than the manager, to whom she has been properly introduced. Could you please help me find her?'

'Of course I will,' replied Yngwie, placing a hand on his shoulder. 'Do you want to put your equipment away first?'

'Yes,' said Søren, absent-mindedly handing Yngwie everything he was carrying.

To save time, Yngwie ran back up the corridor to Søren's room, told the manager the Greenlander was back and that they would be going out to look for Dandelion, then piled the equipment and belongings into the closest convenient corner, and left.

Once outside, they both hesitated, hardly knowing where to begin. 'Why did you think I might call the peacekeepers?' asked Yngwie.

'It was just a thought that occurred to me, that is all. Cats can be dangerous to people if they want to be, although it's virtually unheard of, except in self-defence or in defence of their companion...but attacking another cat, this is something I have never before come across. Either way, it's against the law for her to be outside, alone, like this. If someone does see her and decides to call the peacekeepers, it could turn ugly. At the very least, we might be required to put leashes on them again. Worse, they might stun her and take her into custody. I have seen it happen...being taken into custody, I mean.'

'I see,' said Yngwie, frowning. 'How far can she hear us, if we tried calling her, using our minds?'

'A few kilometres... Maybe more if we both call at the same time.'

'Well, we'd better try, but let's move away from the building and find somewhere to sit, where we won't feel conspicuous. I imagine the harder we concentrate, the better.'

'Yes, you are right... Thank you,' and Søren touched Yngwie's arm, pleasantly surprised by his understanding and readiness to assist. After all, they had only met the once, and briefly at that.

They walked on until they found a convenient bench, unobtrusively located beneath the canopy of an old English oak tree, one of the few still left in the area. Sitting quite still, they focused as hard as they could on sending comforting words to Dandelion and asking her to return. Five minutes went by and nothing, then ten, and still nothing. It was all Søren could do to control himself. Feelings of panic began to almost overwhelm him, but then he suddenly realised it was her panic, not his own. He jumped up and ran as fast as he could towards the trafficway, with Yngwie only a few steps behind him. They could hear her!

## CHAPTER SEVEN

The black, longhaired cat facing Dandelion sat perfectly still, without moving even a whisker, utterly bemused by this snarling, frightened, miserable creature, whose thick white fur still showed the marks of the earlier fight with Aurora. The elderly man accompanying the black cat also kept still, totally bemused. What was an unaccompanied cat doing loose in the neighbourhood? Despite the new laws, he preferred to use a leash when he took his own cat for walks, which in this instance was probably just as well. After all, who knew what his cat might do if the other one's mood was infectious? Taking one cautious step backwards, he securely fastened the leash to a nearby sapling then slowly approached Dandelion with his hand held out for her to sniff. 'Are you lost, little one?' he said softly. 'Do you need help? I won't hurt you, and neither will my cat, so you needn't be upset.'

Dandelion spat at him, so he retreated slightly and crouched down as well as his somewhat stiff knees allowed. 'It's alright, don't worry, we won't hurt you. Now aren't you a beautiful creature. Where have you come from? Are you from around here? Has something happened to your companion while you've been out for a walk? Can you tell me who they are? I'll do my best to help.'

As his soft, soothing tones and gentle thoughts began to calm Dandelion, she settled into a more relaxed pose, although her blue eyes narrowed with suspicion while she tried to focus on him, tried to clear her mind, tried to decide whether to trust him...and his grimalkin. Switching her gaze to the cat, Dandelion asked who they were, but was met with silence... Nothing, not the slightest attempt to answer, only a fixed stare from the yellow eyes. The black cat sat with her feet together and tail curled tightly around her body, ears fully erect. She shifted her weight a little but chose to remain silent.

The elderly man moved closer again, with hand still outstretched. This time Dandelion stood up, walked slowly towards him and touched his hand with her nose, then waited to see what he would do next. As she did, Søren and Yngwie appeared in the distance, running towards them at full speed. The black cat saw them, gave a hiss of surprise, and crouched down, thoroughly confused. Sensing the cat's alarm, her companion turned around and also saw the two men. Not knowing whether they were responsible for the white cat's dreadful state of mind, he pulled out his comlink and engaged its emergency signal. Next, he went back to his own cat and unfastened her leash, wondering what the men intended, yet sure that if they meant him or the white cat any harm, his own darling would defend them both, even if she *was* confused and alarmed by the situation. As if to confirm this, the cat planted herself squarely in the path of the oncoming strangers and braced herself to attack.

Søren and Yngwie slowed down to a walk once they were close enough to see that Dandelion didn't appear to be in any danger. 'Hello!' Søren called out. 'You've found my cat, I see. She's had a fright and ran away from us not long ago.' Yngwie in the meantime stayed where he was, rather than make the situation worse by coming any closer.

At that moment, a Melbourne Peacekeeping Force patrol car landed several metres away from the small group and a blue-uniformed peacekeeper climbed out from the airjet. 'Oh no!' groaned Søren. 'Just what we didn't need!'

Doing his best to remain calm, he walked up to the elderly man, held out his hand and, with a brilliant smile, introduced himself. 'Søren Thorup, pleased to meet you.' Turning to the peacekeeper, who was about to ask why the emergency signal had been activated, Søren added, 'Pleased to meet you too, Peacekeeper. My cat, Dandelion, was badly frightened a little earlier and ran off. It seems she may have given this man and his cat a scare, but believe me, everything is under control now. My friend Yngwie and I were about to take her back with us to the communal house, where we are staying.'

Yngwie, with more presence of mind than Søren would have expected, approached, then introduced himself to both the peacekeeper and the elderly man, shook their hands, and bent down to greet his cat. She sniffed Yngwie's fingers and gave him a friendly nudge with her head.

'Hmm,' said the peacekeeper, looking dubious. 'What do *you* say happened?' he asked the elderly man.

Clearing his throat, he replied that they had found the white cat in a highly distressed state and when these two gentlemen came running towards them, thought they might be the cause, but he now felt sure this wasn't the case.

By this time, Søren had moved away and was sitting on the ground next to Dandelion, speaking quietly to her. She leaned against him and began purring, very softly.

'She is sorry to have upset you,' said Søren, addressing both the black cat and her companion.

'It's quite alright,' answered the elderly man. 'These things can happen to anyone, I'm sure.' The black cat rubbed herself against his legs, tail in the air and purring, making it plain to the peacekeeper there was no reason to stay.

'Well,' said the peacekeeper, 'if there's no actual emergency, I'll be on my way. You'd better take your cat home, hadn't you,' he added, giving Søren a stern look.

Søren smiled sweetly and stood up, saying, 'Yes, we will...immediately...and thank you. It may be best if we keep her inside for a few days.'

'Sounds like a good plan,' replied the peacekeeper, before taking images of them all for his records, including the cats, and climbing back into the patrol car. They all watched as it lifted off, soon disappearing from sight.

'My goodness, what an adventure!' said the elderly man to his cat. 'Still, not one we'd want very often,' he concluded, holding out his hand to Søren, and then to Yngwie. 'We'll be off, and good luck with the rest of your evening.'

After he was well out of hearing distance, Yngwie said, 'What's going on?'

'I don't know,' answered Søren. 'I'm as confused by all this as you are. The only one who can explain, is Dandelion.'

They both turned to her, questions in their minds. She stared at them and sighed. 'Horrible spiders... Snakes... Want to go home!' they heard in their minds.

Søren could sense there was more, and suddenly understood: Dandelion was jealous of his relationship with Karla, and by extension, of his friendship with Aurora. They had never actually met before this trip, only seen each other on computer screens. He held a hand to his mouth. This was a problem he hadn't foreseen! 'Damn!' he exclaimed.

'She doesn't have to go out on field trips with you,' said Yngwie, with a grin. 'She can stay with me, if she wants. I'll be here for a while. How long will your work take?'

Søren gazed at him in relief. 'It should only take two or three weeks. What do you say, Dandelion?' He stroked her head, fondling the cat's ears. 'Do you want to stay with this wonderful young man while I'm out in the forest? Once our work finishes, we can go home, I promise.'

Dandelion sighed again, yet saw there was little choice if she wanted to avoid the forest...and Karla. She knew her companion's work was important. Still, if she didn't actually have to *see* Karla, and *feel* the bond between them, then once they were home, everything would return to normal.

'She agrees,' said Søren, crouching down and taking Dandelion's paw in his hand. 'Thank you,' he whispered. 'I am so sorry.'

Dandelion licked his nose, then stood up and led the way back to the communal house. 'Perhaps you should avoid other cats when you have her with you,' remarked Søren.

Yngwie nodded. He was looking forward to getting to know this exotic creature. To some extent, it would make up for seeing less of Laurita, as he was almost certain would be the case. One didn't have to be a telepathic cat to see she had far more in common with Shahid than she did with him!

'How is she?' asked Karla when Søren called, after making a fuss of Dandelion and ensuring she was given her favourite food for dinner.

'Much better, although she may need to remain here while I work in the forest, and quite possibly when you and I meet. My little Dandelion appears to think there are far too many nasty beasties here...and I'm sorry to say this, Karla, but she is jealous of our friendship.' He raised his eyebrows and turned down the corners of his mouth.

'What! You're joking?' replied Karla, eyes wide. Sitting next to her, Aurora was listening intently and her eyes also widened as she began to understand why Dandelion had attacked.

'No, I'm not,' and Søren told her what happened after he returned to the communal house, and the part Yngwie would play. 'She will need to be on a leash if he takes her outside,' he concluded, 'so may we borrow yours a while longer?'

'Yes, of course, but this is incredible! What would you have done if Yngwie hadn't been there, or wasn't popular with Dandelion?'

'I don't know. Perhaps I'd have asked the Breeding Centre to take her. Do you think they would have agreed?'

'Yes, I do, Søren, and if anything else goes wrong, I think it'd be a good idea; they could help sort her out – psychologically, I mean.'

'True... Still, let's hope nothing further happens and we can both go home when my survey is finished... That is, if there is any food to go home to. I've not had time to check the weather report. Have you?'

'No...but looking at it now, it says Greenland is still unusually cold, and that your region is still snowed in. Hmm... If this keeps up, you might have to stay here longer than planned.'

'I don't think Dandelion would find that acceptable. I promised we'd return home when my work here is finished.' Søren frowned as he tried to think of an alternative.

'You couldn't even risk paying Mik and Tamara a visit in Queensland because of their cats,' said Karla, also trying to think of somewhere for them to go.

'We could simply take a holiday!' said Søren, grinning.

'Well, there's an idea, but let's wait and see,' answered Karla, relieved to hear the lighter note in Søren's voice, but still annoyed at the complication created by Dandelion's attitude.

'Yes, and in the meantime, I shall take advantage of Yngwie's kind offer and assume Dandelion will manage. Which reminds me... I arranged to meet with Shahid, Yngwie and Laurita at 20:30, and it's almost time. I'll call you tomorrow morning after I've checked our traps, and then, if you like, we could spend the rest of the day together, catching up.'

'Good... And yes, that'd be great. Well, take care of yourself when you're out and about, won't you. It's supposed to be hot tomorrow, so watch out for fires and make sure you have enough water with you.'

'Yes, Karla, I promise to look after myself. I always do, and you don't need to worry.'

Karla laughed. 'I know. It's just that today was awful, and I'm being silly. I think the spiders have set me on edge, too. I hate the thought of them being here. There's no way I could live in Sydney, for example, where they're everywhere!'

It was Søren's turn to laugh. 'So I gather, but they don't, as a rule, jump out and bite people. In reality, very few do get bitten, and as far as I know, no one in recent history has died from a bite. They do hurt, of course.' He looked thoughtful for a moment. He was lucky in only having been bitten a few times and was never seriously affected, mainly because he knew how to deal with the situation.

'Yes, poor Shahid! I'm glad he recovered so well. Say hello to him for me, will you?'

'I will, and I must go, so until tomorrow.' Søren closed the connection, turned to Dandelion, who was asleep on the bed, and gently prodded her, saying, 'Come on, let's go see your new friend.'

Dandelion opened her eyes a fraction and yawned, then jumped off the bed and padded to the door, waiting. 'Leash first,' said Søren, fetching it.

After Dandelion reluctantly allowed him to attach it to her collar, they walked the short distance to the common room, where the others were waiting for them to arrive.

Shahid and Laurita both stood up to shake hands with Søren. 'This is Dandelion,' he said pleasantly, indicating the cat, who waited by his side, looking up at them, expecting to be introduced. 'No doubt Yngwie has told you about our adventures this afternoon?'

'Yes, he has,' replied Laurita, bending down to stroke Dandelion, who pushed her head into Laurita's hand, smooching. Shahid hesitated, then crouched down beside the cat and told her his name, using his mind, not his hand reader. Puzzled at first, Dandelion soon sensed he couldn't speak like other wights, so studied him curiously, her tail curling back and forth as she touched his thoughts. Shahid felt her touch and realised she was quite different from Aurora, even if his interaction with the other cat had been brief. This one seemed less certain, more wary. She sat down and placed a paw on his knee, but when he took the paw in his hand, stroking it with his thumb, Dandelion withdrew it. However, she stroked herself against him, tail in the air, back arched in pleasure.

Shahid stood up and said, 'She seems to have settled down, but she's not as relaxed as Karla's cat was last night.'

'Yes, fortunately she *is* feeling much better now,' replied Søren, reaching down to pat Dandelion's head, 'and has promised not to misbehave again, haven't you, eh?'

Enjoying being the centre of attention, Dandelion purred loudly, then walked over to Yngwie to curl up by his feet. 'I don't think she has forgiven you yet for bringing her here, Søren,' he remarked, laughing.

'Possibly not, but as long as she doesn't attack anyone, we'll manage, I'm sure,' said Søren, with a grin. Dandelion half-opened an eye to look at him, then with a small 'huff', settled back down to sleep. 'Well,' he continued, 'does anyone want coffee and cake? I do.' When everyone agreed, he went to the servery to see what was available and ordered a selection of pastries and sweet biscuits. Before long, they were all seated comfortably, sipping their coffee and enjoying their early supper.

'Søren,' said Shahid, 'there's something I've wanted to ask. I could just as easily have asked Karla, but I needed to think about it a bit longer.' As Søren nodded, he continued, 'Aurora suggested to me last night that I get a cat...to help me communicate. What do you think?'

Yngwie and Laurita looked at him in surprise, but quickly realised there was no reason why the option shouldn't at least be explored.

'You seem to communicate perfectly well without one,' said Søren, smiling. 'I can't say the idea would ever have occurred to me, but I could go with you to the Breeding Centre in Werribee, if you like. They know me well there, you see.'

Shahid's expression brightened and he leaned forward eagerly, saying, 'When would you have time?'

'It depends upon the spiders and how willing they are to wander into our traps! I need to check them every morning for the next two weeks at least, but assuming nothing untoward comes up, we could send in an application this evening and go there on Sunday afternoon, if that would suit you?'

Casting a glance at Laurita, Shahid agreed to the plan, even though he and Laurita had tentatively arranged to take a trip around Port Phillip Bay on one of the replica eighteenth-century sailing ships that regularly took passengers on short cruises. Smiling, Laurita shrugged. Another day would do just as well, or so she hoped. Yngwie, noticing both the glance and the response, realised something was being put off, but decided not to let it spoil his evening. He shifted his left foot slightly because Dandelion was resting her head upon it, and being a heavy cat, Yngwie's foot was becoming uncomfortable. With a small snuffle, Dandelion rolled onto her back, paws raised to her chest, and continued dreaming of her home in Greenland.

Yngwie chuckled and leaned over to stroke the soft fur of her stomach, then left her to sleep in peace. However, when he touched her, part of her dream filtered into his mind and a wave of homesickness washed over him. 'How odd,' he thought, 'I've never felt like this before.' Aloud he said, 'She's dreaming of home, Søren, and now I'm feeling like I should go back to Norway!'

Søren stared at both Yngwie and Dandelion. 'As far as I know, she has never affected anyone else this much. You seem to have formed a strong connection with her!'

'You don't mind, do you?' asked Yngwie.

'No, no, not at all. After all these years, I am quite certain she won't desert me. It's probably the shock of today still affecting her... I'm glad, really. I'll feel less guilty leaving her with you when I go to the forest, or when I visit Karla, which I intend to do tomorrow afternoon, if it's convenient for you? There will be Sunday as well, since it wouldn't be wise to take her to the Breeding Centre. It would be too much of a risk – unless we were taking her there for treatment, of course. Karla and I discussed the possibility, if her behaviour doesn't completely return to normal within the next few days.'

'It's all fine with me,' replied Yngwie, looking forward to having the cat's company. She looked so sweet, lying like that, on her back.

'How long do cats live?' asked Shahid, suddenly worried.

'At least forty to forty-five years,' replied Søren, understanding how important this question was.

'And how old is Dandelion?' asked Yngwie.

'Twenty-four. We have been together since she was about two.'

'You said the Breeding Centre staff know you well?'

'Yes, they do. Seven years ago, I was involved in a case that affected Willsmere, as well as the three cats who are companions to two of the researchers – Mik Theophanous, and his bondmate, Tamara Solanum. They are friends of mine and still work with Karla. One of the cats actually killed someone to prevent Tamara from being murdered. The cat was put on trial, and since background information was needed by the Judge, I did some of the research into their behaviour. The Breeding Centre helped with her defence, too, and as a result, I had a great deal of interaction with the staff there.'

'What happened to the cat?!' exclaimed Laurita, putting a hand to her mouth in astonishment. Although she had met Mik and Tamara several times, and was vaguely aware they had three cats, Karla had never told her this story. Perhaps it was something she preferred to leave in the past.

'Acquitted, thank the Sun, since she did what any human would have done in the same circumstances, if they were capable of it, but she was kept under house arrest until the trial.' Søren frowned, remembering how ghastly the whole situation had been.

'How extraordinary! Still, I am glad she was treated properly,' said Laurita. 'Was this the first time the Judge had dealt with a cat?'

'Yes, and our work became the basis for them to gain the legal status they have now. In recent years, when certain cases were being prepared for human trials, they have even provided the Judge with evidence, via an official Witness. Naturally, it must be corroborated by other evidence; their 'word' alone is not enough, as it generally isn't for a human.'

Fascinated, Shahid asked whether any of these cases were available for the public to read.

'They certainly are. Last year, there was a complex one in Queensland, which ended up in Argentina, and involved three cats giving some of the evidence that led to the Judge convicting the accused, of whom there were three, charged with different crimes. If you do a search on the name 'Rhianna O'Connor', you will soon find the public transcripts. It was a murder case, amongst other things, and by strange coincidence, the peacekeeper involved is a friend of ours too, and so is her bondmate, who helped with the forensic investigation. They live in Brisbane, and their cat, Shela, provided some of the evidence that brought Rhianna's killer to justice. The whole situation was all very tragic though.' Søren lowered his head for a moment, musing over the details he had read after Karla told him about the case, once their friends returned to Australia.

Shahid, who had already been busy entering search queries into his hand reader, held it up in triumph. He had located the transcripts without trouble. 'It says here that this cat, Shela, helped prove the case against the person who murdered Rhianna O'Connor by frightening them into a confession!'

'Sounds a bit drastic,' remarked Yngwie, frowning.

'That's for sure!' replied Shahid, looking up. 'It seems she combined her telepathic powers with those of two humans and created a lifelike image of the dead woman, tricking the killer into believing she was really seeing her. I didn't even know there were human telepaths!'

Søren raised his elegant eyebrows and smiled, while Yngwie and Laurita both turned to look at him, eyes wide, mouths open. Obviously, they didn't know either. 'Yes,' said Søren, 'there are. We don't yet know how many, but I first heard about them six years ago when someone who was a suspect in the Willsmere investigation suddenly developed somewhat unusual abilities! Fortunately, she turned out to be innocent and eventually took on a role helping the staff at the Werribee Breeding Centre with their research into cat behaviour. Her abilities were critical in helping solve both the Willsmere and the Rhianna O'Connor case.'

'Gwenllian?' asked Shahid, consulting his hand reader.

'Yes, Gwenllian, who is now a close friend as well – an astonishing woman, who chose to remain in Queensland once the case was over. Rhianna had a cousin, Robert O'Connor, and he and Gwenllian fell in love.' Søren sighed. He adored romantic stories.

'Oh my!' exclaimed Shahid. 'According to this, Robert O'Connor is a telepath too. What a relationship they must have!' He grinned, and the others joined him.

'If you read on,' said Søren, laughing, 'you'll find there was a third telepath as well.'

'Margrethe,' said Shahid at last. 'How incredible! And a very courageous person, too. She provided a home for the young woman who killed Rhianna, on condition she received regular counselling and remained under virtual house arrest until she could be trusted again. I'm amazed, truly.'

'Yes, it is rather extraordinary. However, the Judge decided this young woman acted out of desperation while in a state of extreme anxiety and after she herself had been deeply wronged.'

'What happened to her?' asked Laurita.

'She still lives with Margrethe in the small town where Rhianna was born and grew up, and is still undergoing counselling. It's difficult to know how it will all turn out, but as far as Gwenllian understands, she has made progress. As an added layer of security, you see, Gwenllian keeps in contact with both the young woman and Margrethe, just in case things don't go as well as expected.' Søren paused, wondering.

'I've never heard of anything like this before,' said Yngwie, shaking his head. How trivial his and Torleif's actions seemed in comparison!

'No, nor have I,' agreed Laurita. 'I'll make sure to read the transcript myself, and will now begin to wonder how many other human telepaths there are! I'm not entirely certain I like the idea. Cats are somehow not an issue as far as I can see, but humans? What if one of them used their abilities to do harm?'

'Yes, this was one of the questions we had in our minds when we were researching cat behaviour, but Robert, Margrethe and Gwenllian all say they feel totally incapable of even contemplating using their powers to harm anyone, and so far, we have never heard of a cat doing so to any significant extent, except under circumstances similar to those I've already mentioned.'

'Let's hope it remains the case,' said Yngwie, nudging Dandelion with his toe. She twitched, but didn't wake up.

'Does anyone know how either cats or humans developed these abilities?' asked Shahid.

'No, but there are myths and legends, which you may have heard of or read about. So far, though, there are no known human telepaths who didn't originate in Australia, which is very interesting,' answered Søren, with a grin.

'And peculiar,' said Yngwie. 'We have so many legends and creatures of fantasy in Scandinavia, I almost feel as if *we* should have some.'

'Not that we know of,' said Søren, smiling. 'Still, time will tell, now their abilities have been recognised by the Judge as having legal status. Some, like Gwenllian, are even registered and able to act in an official capacity when a particularly difficult situation arises and the peacekeepers need their specialised skills.'

'I must keep all this in mind,' replied Yngwie, also smiling, 'if I ever decide to break the law.'

'Oh yes, do, because during an interview the peacekeepers are under no obligation to inform a suspect that they have a telepath present, or even if they are using a cat to find out more about the person's activities and state of mind.' Søren looked serious for a moment, but then smiled again.

'Oh, I see,' said Yngwie, glancing at Dandelion, wondering if she knew what he had done and whether she would 'tell' anyone if she did. He took a deep breath. The risk was worth it. After all, why would anyone ask Dandelion about *him*, and why would she choose to volunteer to tell anyone even if she *did* know?


Before contacting Morag MacIain, Welcome checked the time in Luzern to make sure it was a civilised hour to call. When she answered, he was surprised to see her looking frazzled, a highly unusual state for her to be in. 'What's wrong?' he asked, his head to one side and a sympathetic expression in his warm, brown eyes.

'No matter how hard we look, we can't find anything resembling a trojan in either the messaging system software or the population database! Also, there aren't any peculiar combinations of Federation identity numbers or other authorisation methods which somehow managed to give access to the applications, and we can't find any mistakes in our code that could explain how this person managed to bypass our security. As a result, I feel like an idiot, which isn't pleasant! The only concrete thing we *have* found wrong is that the Federation ID of a three-month-old baby born in Perth, which the messaging system tried to include in the cascade, was created at 00:00:01 on the fourth of March, and not at 19:46 as the ID itself would indicate. The problem is, as far as we can see there's no record of a request to create this ID at the 'wrong' time, although I appreciate it's theoretically possible to do so because of a manual override designed to allow unusual requests – for example, people occasionally ask for a specific ID for their baby.'

'I sympathise, Morag, and may have something for you. The interview with Kaj Jonsson has given us a lead. He examined the satellite used to distribute the cascade, and it seems it has a flaw.' Welcome grinned, waiting for a reaction.

'What!' shouted Morag, gaping at him.

He laughed. 'Yes, indeed. Ghastly, eh? Ultimately, he'll track down the how, why and wherefore of the flaw itself, but at this stage, we thought the most important thing was to determine how it was exploited. Wouldn't you agree?'

Welcome liked teasing Morag now and then, but also knew when to stop, so after she glared at him, he explained further: 'Kaj discovered that a message can be initiated without authority via a signal to this particular satellite, *if* simultaneous signals are sent from a pair of latitudes and longitudes that form a certain angle relative to the satellite and which is also related to the birthplace selected. The angle required is coincidental, but specific. The difficulty is, though, there are vast numbers of latitude and longitude pairs that could be used.'

'How utterly bizarre!' exclaimed Morag. 'I wonder if the same flaw could be used to create the baby's ID? That is, make the initial request, then provide the override by simulating the second authorisation that'd be required because of the nonsensical nature of the request. Yet why did they need to create the ID? What purpose does it serve?'

'We don't yet know, but our good Swedish friend will continue working on it, and I feel confident he'll find the answer. He has the necessary persistence, and I must say, I'm impressed with his technical ability. I have to handle him carefully, though. He's a real *prima donna*.' Welcome grimaced. Still, this was his job, and he could put up with almost anyone if he needed to.

'Well, I'm sure you'll manage, and in the meantime, I'll keep thinking, now that you've given me something to chew on!' Morag grinned. Talking this over with Welcome was a relief, and she began to feel optimistic that the answer to the puzzle was now within reach.

# CHAPTER EIGHT

On this beautiful Saturday morning, two days after arriving in Melbourne, Søren left for the forest at dawn to check his spider traps, leaving Dandelion in Yngwie's care – once the manager of the communal house let her out from their securely locked room, several hours later. Yngwie, with the cat on her leash, now stood outside Laurita's door, hesitating over whether to disturb her or not. Deciding he might as well, he tapped on the door and waited. When Laurita answered, it was with a vague smile, and not the welcoming one he had hoped for.

'Hello,' he said, 'I thought we could take a trip to the Bay and do some sight-seeing along the shoreline. It's too good a day to spend indoors.'

Laurita shook her head. 'No, not now, Yngwie. I'm sorry... I want to keep reading. I have already read the transcript of the first trial Søren talked about last night, about the cat who killed someone during the Willsmere attacks, which began seven years ago. Absolutely amazing! This was well before cats had any real legal status, so it's a miracle she wasn't put down straight away. Her name is Possum. How cute!' Laurita grinned, then became serious again. 'I'm almost halfway through the second trial and up to the part where the Australian peacekeeper and her bondmate have gone to Argentina to follow up on their main leads. It's quite a story! I can't wait to find out exactly what role their cat, Shela, played in convicting Rhianna O'Connor's killer.'

'I see,' answered Yngwie, managing a smile. 'I'd have expected trial transcripts would make dry reading. Apparently not.'

'Oh no! Whoever puts these things together has made them read extremely well. I expect it's because they're for public consumption, so they can't be too legalistic. Mind you, the language is still fairly formal and they're a bit repetitive, but I'm used to reading scientific papers, so it doesn't worry me.'

'Well, perhaps I'll see you later. Dandelion and I will go out anyway, but I plan to be back in time for dinner. Will you be in?'

'I'm not sure. Shahid mentioned something about calling. He intends to read the trial notes too and wants to discuss them with me. He's very excited about going to the Breeding Centre tomorrow with Søren, so before they go, wants to know as much about cats as possible, including how powerful they are.'

*Chapter Eight*

Dandelion was finding the images in Laurita's mind fascinating and the conversation interesting, but she was eager to go for a walk, particularly by the sea, which, strangely enough, was something she had never done before. Purring, the cat rubbed herself against Yngwie's legs, but resisted the temptation to give him more than a gentle reminder. Instead, she sat down patiently to wait.

The conversation soon came to an end and before long they were on their way to Black Rock, where they could look out over the bay from the cliffs. When they arrived, a light breeze was blowing in off the water, which Dandelion sniffed eagerly, taking in this entirely new scent. Although the original sandy beach had long since been submerged by rising sea levels, the cliff tops, with their surrounding bushland, gave them an uninterrupted vista of the sea and the furthest reaches of the bay. A small flock of noisy seagulls squawked and quarrelled over a few scraps of food, while overhead, fluffy white clouds gathered here and there, confirming the weather report that there might be rain during the night. At the base of the cliff, small waves curled and frothed, their barely detectable sound reminding Yngwie of all the other seascapes he had seen. It was always the sounds of places that stayed with him the longest. For most, it was the sights, and even the scents, but to him, new sounds and old formed part of his interior landscape: his view of the world. The opposite, the absence of sound – silence – was equally important, and one of the reasons he would always want to go home: to experience the profound silence of a Norwegian winter, interrupted only by the soft, and sometimes sudden, movement of snow, and of course, the storms – the howling fury of the old gods at being forgotten and ignored.

He thought of Torleif, waiting for him to call. Tomorrow, maybe tomorrow the Federation investigators would find their answer. Meanwhile, he wanted to forget the cascade and simply enjoy being here – free, young, and with all the time in the world to do what he wanted.

'Come on, cat, let's walk until we find a way down to the ocean. Have you ever been swimming? No? Well, there's a first time for all things, so perhaps it's time you tried. I've heard cats know how to swim even if they've never encountered water before.'

When they saw a path leading down to the sea, where a small, shell-strewn beach had formed, Dandelion hesitated, then went first, wary, yet eager. Yngwie laughed softly, picking up on her feelings. Not being in the mood to share this experience with anyone, he was glad no one else was there. He took off his sandals, rolled up the legs of his loose, comfortable trousers, and stepped into the water, looking back at Dandelion, who tentatively sniffed the seawater, then sneezed when the saltiness tickled her nose. Yngwie grinned and tugged gently on her leash. Could he take it off? No, better not... At least, not yet. Dandelion put one paw into the water, promptly drew back when she felt how cold it was, then licked her paw and gazed at Yngwie, disgusted by the taste. Finally, she sat down on the beach, refusing to budge.

'Oh come on, Dandelion, it's not so bad. Just don't get the water into your mouth.' He tugged on the leash again, and this time the cat gingerly walked through the shallow water towards him, holding her tail upright to make sure it stayed dry. A small wave sent the seawater up to the base of her chest, and she retreated again, sneezing and shaking her head. Yngwie chuckled and waited, and sure enough, Dandelion slowly came towards him, this time, without protesting, allowing the water to reach almost to her shoulders.

'Do you want to see if you can swim?' asked Yngwie. 'Here, watch me!' He removed her leash, wound it up, and put it into his trouser pocket, then walked out far enough to lower himself into the water, where he swam a few strokes. 'See,' he said, laughing, 'it's easy!'

Dandelion moved further out into the sea until the water reached her chin, then took one more step and instinct did the rest. She could indeed swim. Paws splayed, the cat paddled over to Yngwie and, when he stood up, found she could also stand on her hind legs and place her wet paws on his midriff. He gave her a hug, then burst out laughing at the sight she made, with her fur all wet and sleek against her body, but her head still fluffy and dry. Bracing herself, Dandelion leapt up, forcing Yngwie to catch her, then because of the weight, he fell into the water. Splashing about, they were soon completely soaked. Seeing Dandelion's whiskers and long eyebrows sticking straight out from her wet face, Yngwie giggled, and then gasped as she pounced on him, forcing him under. Recovering, he grabbed her around the middle and they mock-wrestled for a few minutes, until a shout from the beach caught their attention.

'Are you alright?' called the onlooker, who had never seen a cat in water before, let alone one behaving in this manner.

Yngwie stood up, and Dandelion paddled around as he waved and answered, 'Yes, we're fine. Just enjoying the water!'

'Okay, that's good then. I'll leave you to it,' said the woman, who could hardly help but smile at the sight of the two of them, soaking wet, and with Dandelion's white fur contrasting so markedly with Yngwie's black clothing.

Once she had gone, Yngwie watched Dandelion while she practiced swimming a little further out. Then, feeling hungry, he decided it was time to find something to eat, so called her and together they waded back to the beach. The bag Yngwie had brought with him contained a large towel, which he used to rub Dandelion dry. She wriggled and purred with pleasure, but when he stood up to shake out the towel, in the faint hope all the white hair would come off, he heard a mental 'Ugh!' when she tried to lick herself. 'Salty!' 'said' Dandelion. 'Awful!'

Yngwie made a face. 'Yes, I imagine it wouldn't taste too good. You'll need a bath once we get back to the communal house. You won't mind, will you?'

Dandelion agreed that a bath would be acceptable, now she was used to the idea of water, and while Yngwie took off his shirt to wring it out, she sat down to watch the ocean, intrigued by the waves and far off horizon, where the clouds were now becoming heavier. The breeze had picked up too, and before long they were both reasonably dry, so it was time to head off towards the café-restaurant Yngwie had located and which sounded promising. He picked up Dandelion's leash from where it was drying on the sand, but she flinched away when he tried to put it on.

'I gave my word,' he said, reaching for her. She sighed, then let him attach it to her collar, but was subdued while they climbed the path back to the cliff top. 'Don't sulk, Dandelion,' said Yngwie. 'You know why it's necessary. Hopefully, it won't be for much longer. All you have to do is promise Søren you'll never lose your temper again, then make sure you don't, even if you meet other cats.'

Dandelion didn't answer, so they both walked on in silence until they reached the café, where a few patrons sat outside, enjoying the sunshine. Yngwie scanned the area for cats, but fortunately, there weren't any. Unsure whether they were allowed onto the premises, he tied Dandelion's leash to a railing, beneath a small tree so she could be in the shade if she wanted, then told her he wouldn't be long, and went inside.

The proprietor looked up from where he was sitting, working on the day's accounts, and smiled. 'Hello, how can I help you?' he asked.

Remembering Søren's precise instructions about what to feed Dandelion, Yngwie grinned and said, 'I need a bowl of water for my cat, as well as something for her to eat. Do you have anything made from potato, or even rice and vegetables?'

'Yes, we do, and what about yourself. What would you like?'

'Expresso coffee, white, with sugar, and some toasted cheese sandwiches, with a slice of watermelon afterwards, please,' said Yngwie, after quickly reading the menu.

'Certainly. Shall I bring it outside for you?'

'Yes please, that would be good,' and Yngwie went outside to find a table, before fetching Dandelion.

While they were waiting to be served, Yngwie's comlink chimed, and when he answered, Søren's smiling face appeared on the small screen. 'Hello,' he said, 'how is Dandelion?'

'Excellent!' said Yngwie, grinning. 'We've had a swim in the sea here at Black Rock, and we're just sitting down to have something to eat.' He leaned forward and held the comlink in front of Dandelion's face. 'Say hello to Søren, Dandelion. He's been worrying about you.'

Dandelion sniffed the screen, then sat back, purring as she listened to Søren speak, although since he wasn't actually nearby, she couldn't understand a word he was saying. When Yngwie brought the comlink back up to continue his conversation, he was surprised to hear the disapproval in Søren's voice: 'She looks very peculiar with her fur sticking out all over the place. What if she hadn't been able to swim? She has never been to the sea before, either. I presume you let her off the leash?'

'Well, yes, but only while we were in the water. She loved it, Søren! I'll give her a bath when we get back to the house and she'll look like herself again.'

'Very well, but she has never had a bath before. There has never been any need. I hope you are prepared to be scratched from head to foot!'

'Honestly, I doubt it. We've discussed it, so to speak, and she's promised to be good. I think she'll even like it. Yes, she's purring. She knows what we're talking about. Anyway, must go, our food's arrived and I want it while it's hot. What time will you be back at the house?'

'I'll be back before 22:00, and in the meantime will assume you and Dandelion will behave yourselves.' Søren had recovered from his momentary ill humour and smiled before closing the connection.

Meanwhile, Dandelion had tried to clean herself again, but the taste of the salt on her fur was disgusting, so she spat out the little she had in her mouth and then eagerly greeted the café proprietor as he brought their order. The seawater had made her thirsty, and when the bowl was placed on the ground in front of her, she greedily lapped up the fresh water.

'She needed that!' exclaimed the proprietor. Noticing the damp fur and its rough appearance, he asked, 'Has she been in the water?'

'Yes,' replied Yngwie, reaching up to take the coffee.

'Unusual cat, liking water,' remarked the proprietor, putting the plate of toasted sandwiches onto the table and Dandelion's bowl of food on the ground.

'She's never been in it before, so this was a bit of an experiment, but it didn't take long before she was paddling around like an expert. The only problem is, she can't clean herself; the saltwater tastes dreadful.'

'Yes, I suppose it would. She'll have to take a bath when you get her home. Good luck!' and he left them to their food.

The coffee and toasted sandwiches were excellent, and Dandelion enjoyed her own meal of steamed rice mixed with a variety of chopped vegetables. Once Yngwie had finished his slice of watermelon and washed his hands, they were ready to continue their exploration of the waterfront...that is, almost: Dandelion's skin was beginning to itch. After a few minutes of frantic scratching, something clearly needed to be done, so Yngwie fastened her leash to the leg of the table and went back inside.

'Do you happen to have somewhere I could wash the cat?' he asked. 'She's beginning to itch. I didn't realise this could happen.'

'Ah,' replied the proprietor, considering the options. 'I have a hose; would that do? No, maybe not. How about sponging her down if I give you a bucket of water?' When Yngwie appeared dubious, he finally said, 'Well, bring her inside. There's a large trough out the back that we use for rinsing off the bigger cooking equipment. It should do the job, though I'm not too sure what the health regulators would think. Still, it's not like it happens every day! Just be quick about it, and don't tell anyone I let you do this. Alright?'

Yngwie smiled his thanks and brought Dandelion inside, then out the back as the proprietor led the way. He pointed to the trough, ran water into it, and fetched some detergent, saying, 'Here, use this. If you don't use much, it shouldn't hurt her skin. We have our hands in it all the time.'

Dandelion looked at him, then looked at Yngwie, made an effort to remain calm, and allowed herself to be lifted into the warm, sudsy water.

'Um, you don't happen to have a spare towel, do you?' said Yngwie, turning to the proprietor, who was watching, fascinated by the ridiculous sight of the soaked cat, who had both dainty paws on the side of the trough while Yngwie washed her lower half. She seemed nowhere near as big, with her fur saturated and flattened down. The proprietor held a hand to his mouth, suppressing a chuckle. It wouldn't do to upset her!

'Yes, yes,' he replied, 'I'll get one now,' and as he left the room, began laughing. It was all he could do to control his expression when he returned with the towel and handed it to Yngwie. By this time, he had finished washing Dandelion's face and was letting the water drain away so the trough could be refilled with fresh, rinsing water. Dandelion's wet tail began waving to and fro as she picked up on the image in the proprietor's mind. He was laughing at her! She growled softly, then remembered her promise not to lose her temper, so turned her back on him instead.

'She's angry,' said Yngwie, taking the towel and placing it on the drainage area beside the trough. 'I think she's embarrassed, so it might be best if you leave us to it. I'm very grateful for your help, though. I'm sure she'll be happy enough once I've rubbed her down and smoothed out her fur a bit. You don't happen to have a brush handy, do you?'

The proprietor shook his head, then took Yngwie's advice and left them to sort it out.

'How's that, Dandelion? Do you feel better now?' asked Yngwie, stroking her head and then running his fingers along her back and sides to flatten down her fur. 'Just as well you don't have long hair, eh?'

Dandelion agreed, and tentatively gave herself a lick. Satisfied there was no longer any salty taste, she settled down to clean herself all over, which looked as if it would take longer than Yngwie preferred, but he accepted that it was better to let her do it rather than risk her becoming uncomfortable again. After a few minutes, the proprietor checked in on them, quickly understood the situation, and went back to his customers.

While Yngwie waited for Dandelion to finish, he made himself comfortable on the floor, with his back against the wall, then gave in to temptation and checked the news broadcasts on his comlink. He sat bolt upright and stared at the screen as he listened to the statement being issued by FSIU Coordinator Morag MacIain:

'We have identified a security flaw in our satellite system, which gave access to the people responsible for sending an unauthorised message to comlinks worldwide on the fourth of March. It is regrettable that this flaw existed, and the Federation Government will issue a formal apology later today, but on a more positive note, we can now close the loophole and assure everyone it is highly unlikely ever to occur again. Furthermore, we are close to locating the perpetrators and within the next few days expect to detain them for questioning.' Morag MacIain smiled briefly, then went on to say, 'In the meantime, if anyone has any questions, concerns, or information related to this matter, please feel free to contact the FSIU via your local peacekeeping force. We will treat all contacts as confidential.'

The news statement finished with the presenter thanking the Coordinator and congratulating the FSIU on their speedy resolution of the matter.

'Well,' thought Yngwie, 'I wonder who will be interviewing us?' He chuckled, then put the comlink away and turned his attention back to Dandelion. The cat gave herself one last lick, then stood up, ready to leave and ready for more adventures...although not any involving seawater!

Kaj Jonsson gave a rare smile, shrugging his shoulders as Morag MacIain said, 'This is wonderful work, Kaj, and a major breakthrough. I can't thank you enough for all the extra time you've put in to solve this problem. Will you be able to help us by following through on the changes needed to make sure this can never happen again?'

The tall, lanky Swede nodded, then realised that perhaps for once he should be more forthcoming, and said, 'Yes, Coordinator MacIain, I can easily fit in the extra work, and if you like, I can supervise the checking of all the other satellite systems to make sure they are in perfect condition.'

'Thank you, yes, I think that would be best. We can put together a team fairly quickly and you can report directly to me.'

Raising his dark eyebrows, Kaj gazed down at Morag, who, although of average height, was almost short compared to him. Morag smiled. 'I have an extensive background in security systems myself, so don't worry, I'm sure we'll understand each other.' She glanced at Welcome, who was poring over the results Kaj had given them. Although he was no technical expert, the information was so clear and well presented, he could easily understand it.

Turning back to Kaj, Morag said, 'Now, I must be frank and speak to you about your approach when dealing with your new team members. I gather you haven't supervised others very often and aren't used to coordinating a project of this level of importance. We have also been told that you tend to isolate yourself from others and can be rather prickly to deal with.' Morag paused as Kaj seemed about to say something, but when he didn't, she continued: 'The team must function properly, so once we finish here, Welcome will go over these issues with you. He'll suggest some approaches you might care to take. If necessary, he can also be present at team meetings.' Morag looked straight into Kaj's eyes and finished by saying, 'We can't have *prima donnas* working for us. There's no place for ego in this job!'

Kaj flushed, looked at his feet, then at Morag. 'I understand, Coordinator MacIain. I will make every effort to ensure this project is a success, and I will value Welcome's input.' He straightened his shoulders, took a deep breath, and held out his hand, which Morag firmly shook.

'Good,' she said. 'Now let's see the rest of what you have.' She sat down, then used her hand reader to access Kaj's presentation. 'At 17:00, on the twenty-eighth of February, local time, there was an anonymous signal sent from a location slightly east and north of a small town named Mihalıççık, in Turkey, which is one hundred and seventy-two kilometres from Ankara and so within easy travel distance if the signal was sent by anyone other than a local. Have I summarised correctly?'

'You have,' confirmed Kaj, sitting down next to her. 'The coordinates the signal was sent from are 39 degrees 51 seconds North and 31 degrees 29 seconds East.'

'Thank you,' said Morag. 'There was another signal, also anonymous, sent from Broome, in Western Australia, at 23:00 local time, on the first of March, which corresponds to the exact time of the first signal, in Turkey. You've established that the second signal carried the actual command sent to the satellite?'

'Yes, Coordinator MacIain. The command reads "Commence Federation identification number creation, in birth order sequence, at 00:00:01 on 04-03-2457 for all persons born on 04-12-2456 at coordinates 31° 57' South, 115° 51' East, beginning with identification number 194604032457". These particular coordinates are in Perth, Western Australia.'

'Clever little buggers, weren't they!' remarked Welcome, as he handed Morag a strong coffee and a serving plate of small, sweet cakes. He knew her preferences well, and since she had taken the first available flight to Melbourne after he gave her the news of their breakthrough, he also knew she would appreciate a little 'nurturing'. He sat down after Morag, with a chuckle, accepted his offering, then listened as the discussion continued.

Morag offered the plate of cakes to Kaj, who shook his head, but then remembered to smile. 'This command ensured the ID they wanted would be created, without fail,' said Morag, 'and although the software queried this piece of nonsense, it could be overridden by the same flaw in the satellite system that allowed the cascade to be initiated.'

'Again, this is correct, Coordinator MacIain. There were two simultaneous signals sent from the same locations six seconds later. The ability to initiate this command via one of the satellites, without authority, requires simultaneous signals from a specific pair of latitudes and longitudes related to a child's birthplace, but there are vast numbers of pairs possible. Also, the angles required are purely coincidental.'

Morag raised an eyebrow in acknowledgement, then drank the rest of her coffee and ate another cake. Eventually she said, 'You've discovered that the cascade could be initiated at a time and date to coincide with the ID if it belonged to someone too young to carry a comlink, or to someone who doesn't have one for some other reason.'

'Yes,' agreed Kaj, relaxing at last and reaching for one of the cakes. While Welcome looked on in approval, he ate it, then stood up to fetch himself a coffee. 'That's the whole point,' continued Kaj, sitting down again. 'The request is nonsense, and totally unanticipated. Why would anyone want to send a message to someone who didn't have a comlink?'

'So the whole thing is a coincidence, which is why it was so hard to pin down?' remarked Welcome.

Kaj nodded, his mouth full of cake. To his own surprise, he was beginning to enjoy himself and to think the project they had given him might be enjoyable too. He quickly finished his coffee and explained: 'If you look at the next page of figures, you will see that the cascade was initiated in a similar manner, using two simultaneous signals, and afterwards sending another two to override the software query. However, this time the signals were sent from new locations, although the angles relative to the satellite and the birthplace of the child were the same as before.'

He peered over Morag's shoulder and pointed at the figures: 'Ferntree Gully, in Melbourne, at 37° 53' South, 145° 17' East for the command sequence, and Rjukan, in Norway, for the activation signal: 59° 52' North, 8° 36' East.'

'Hmph!' exclaimed Welcome. 'A highly professional operation, it seems. How long would it have taken for someone to work all this out, assuming it wasn't an inside job?'

'A very long time – years even,' answered Kaj, frowning. 'It takes skill and determination to find a flaw such as this, particularly without direct access to our systems. It's difficult to understand why anyone would bother!'

'Well, let's work out who did this,' said Morag, standing up, 'and then we may also find out why. We have some ideas, but can't yet be sure. I'll put the processes into place to see if we can determine who was at these locations at those times, and hopefully the same two people were at both pairs, otherwise we may be stuck! What do you think, Welcome, should we bring them in if we can find them, or place them under surveillance for a while?'

'I think we have enough to justify questioning them, even though there's little hard evidence to hold them for long.'

'True...' Morag shook hands with Kaj, leaving Welcome to give the promised 'counselling' in interpersonal relationships, while she initiated the search for their culprits.

# CHAPTER NINE

The Werribee Breeding Centre for Cats, on the western outskirts of Melbourne, occupied a site which had been used, in various incarnations, for veterinary research and treatment for about five hundred years. It was one of the most prestigious institutes of its type in the country, and perhaps even the world. The modern cat was the product of extensive selective breeding and genetic modification, and the result of one aspect of a project aimed at reducing the highly problematic and vast population of stray and feral cats in Australia. They were now designed to be exclusively female, sterile, vegetarian, and far larger than their domesticated ancestors, as well as highly intelligent. However, their development of telepathic abilities was an unexpected side effect, and no one to this day knew how this had occurred. Until relatively recently, most people were unaware these abilities even existed, and the full extent of what they could do was still a matter of intense debate within scientific circles and amongst a high proportion of those who came into contact with them.

While Søren, Laurita and Shahid waited in the centre's magnificent sunlit entrance foyer for someone to come out and speak with them, they used the time to look at the extraordinary floor. It was made from multicoloured terracotta tiles and depicted cats of various types in charming poses and playful group scenes. Søren had seen it before, although not for many years, and at the time, had other things than art on his mind, so he used this opportunity to fully appreciate the floor's beauty. All three were studying one particular scene and discussing its merits when a door opened and a short, plump woman strode over to them, held out her hand to Shahid, and introduced herself: 'Hello, pleased to meet you. My name is Genevieve. I gather you'd like to have a cat as a companion and to help you with your inability to speak in the usual way? Yes? Good! Please come with me.' She turned away and began walking towards the nearest corridor, clearly assuming they would all follow without requiring further explanation.

Startled, yet somewhat amused, everyone did indeed follow her, until they reached a small waiting room, which in turn led to an office. Genevieve waved at Søren and Laurita to take a seat, vaguely indicated they were welcome to help themselves from a convenient servery located nearby, then grasped Shahid by the shoulder and virtually propelled him into her office.

'Sit down,' she said, gazing keenly at him, her bright blue eyes taking in every detail of both his appearance and demeanour. 'We've never received a request like this before,' she continued, shaking her head vigorously, 'but I must say, it's a perfectly rational one. So, unless there's some reason why the cats don't like you, or there's some other impediment to your having one as a companion, this could open up all sorts of new opportunities for our charges.' She had, of course, already studied Shahid's application, and as a result, had conditionally granted him the right to meet the cats with a view to choosing one, pending a personal interview.

Shahid opened his mouth as if to say something, then shut it again and blinked. 'What would you like to know?' he said, using his hand reader, while Genevieve watched closely, intrigued by his skill in using it.

'What would you like to tell me?' she replied, smiling for the first time. 'You could, for example, begin by informing me how you intend to care for the cat and how long you think you would want to keep her.'

Again, Shahid gaped. Wouldn't that be obvious? Apparently not, so he said, 'Forever... I'd want to keep her forever...for as long as she lives. I've read all about them, or at least, as much as I could, and I don't think I'd have any problem looking after a cat. She'd come with me wherever I went, and if I was sick or needed to go somewhere she couldn't, I'm sure my parents would help.'

'Have you asked them?' said Genevieve, peering at him closely.

'Yes, and they love the idea. We talked about it for a long time, and they're as keen as I am.'

'Very good. Do you understand they are vegetarian and must never be allowed to roam freely? They must always be either kept indoors or be accompanied outside by someone who can take care of them.' When Shahid nodded, she said, 'They live for a long time, and if you find a bondmate, he or she would need to be prepared to keep the cat, too. Have you considered that?'

Shahid blushed and admitted he hadn't. Genevieve shook her head, saying, 'No, people often forget this point. The cat will not be a pet, and would become so much a part of your life that, to be frank, the chance of forming a bond with anyone who didn't get along with them is remote. Cats can be quite manipulative, you see. They're capable of affecting our emotions, although they tend to be reasonably honest about the whole thing; I've never heard of a case where they did anything to deliberately harm their companion. Do you understand me?'

Hesitating, Shahid hardly knew what to say, so simply raised a hand to acknowledge her point, then took a deep breath, for the first time truly appreciating the commitment he was about to make.

'The hardest thing for anyone is knowing the cat has a shorter lifespan than ours, but from our experience in recent years, the cats somehow prepare their companion for their departure, and before too long the person usually bonds with another cat.' When Shahid stared at her in amazement, Genevieve added softly, 'They care for us to the utmost of their ability. Their love is a treasure few experience. I hope you'll be one of the lucky ones.' She stood up, took Shahid by the shoulder again, more gently this time, then steered him towards the door and out into the waiting room. 'We'll go to the enclosure now... You can't come with us,' she said, as Laurita began to stand. 'We can't risk Shahid's thoughts and feelings being influenced by anyone else's. The cats are used to me, so I'm not a problem, but you would be. Sorry...'

Laurita glanced at Søren, then sat down again. 'Oh, I see. Yes, we'll wait here.' Søren grinned and said, 'With any luck, we'll soon see you with your new companion!'

Slightly bemused, Shahid gave them a small wave and followed Genevieve along a corridor decorated with pictures and drawings of all the various colours and types of cats available. He paused to look at a few, but hurried on when his guide turned around and gestured to him, rather impatiently. Eventually, they came to where the younger cats who were ready to be adopted were kept. The enclosure, which had a plastiglass dome to let in the sunlight, consisted of an elaborate garden room furnished with a wide variety of places for cats to sleep and to entertain themselves. Dozens of cats snoozed, played and walked around in there, but when the door opened and Shahid entered, with Genevieve holding his elbow, they all woke up or stayed still, studying them. Some sat down to continue watching their visitors, with noses sniffing, ears erect, and tails twitching. Others burbled a greeting and came towards them, but soon stopped in their tracks and sat down to wait. A few took one glance before turning their backs and walking away, tails in the air.

Shahid turned to Genevieve and raised his hands in a 'What do I do?' manner, hesitating to use his hand reader to speak, concerned it might worry the cats. Pointing at a comfortable-looking garden bench, Genevieve said, 'Take a seat over there and just watch them for a while. Once you're ready, do whatever seems natural. You can wait and see if one comes to you, or you can take the initiative and introduce yourself to any you like the look of.'

When Shahid put his head to one side, unsure of what she meant, Genevieve explained a little further: 'You can talk to them, or put your hand out for them to sniff; whatever seems best. Don't worry, they'll understand.' She smiled and patted him on the shoulder, then walked a short distance away and sat down.

Shahid did as she suggested and tried to concentrate on the cats, tried to focus not only on their appearance, but on how they behaved. At first, a longhaired black cat with large yellow eyes seemed about to approach, but turned away and began cleaning herself, no longer interested. A slender ginger cat, with white paws and chest, came closer to study him. Her eyes were light green and her expression alert, with large ears that swivelled back and forth, as if listening for anything Shahid might have to say. When he didn't speak, she walked away as well, with a backwards glance and a curl of her tail as if to say, 'Goodbye'. Several more minutes went by and none of the cats approached, although three sat a few metres away, watching his every movement.

Realising they needed to know how he normally communicated, Shahid took out his hand reader from its carry bag, keyed in a few strokes, and 'said', 'I can't speak the way others normally do. This is what I use most often, but I also use sign language.' He showed the cats what he meant, using his hands to say, 'I would like to be friends.' Two of the cats moved closer, so he stood up, then crouched down, with one hand out. One of them, a sleek silver-grey with blue eyes and dainty paws, walked up to him, sniffed his hand and rubbed her head against it, purring. 'Beautiful,' thought Shahid as he stroked her, 'and so soft.' She arched her back in pleasure, tail in the air, then rolled onto her back for a moment, before sitting up and looking straight into his eyes. He met her gaze and imagined her in the forest, walking with him in the fresh air, having the freedom to run and to leap to her heart's content. He imagined what it might be like if she were able to help him share his innermost feelings with those who were closest to him. A tear ran down his cheek as an almost unbearable yearning suddenly overcame him. The cat came closer, put one paw on his knee, and in his mind, Shahid heard her say, 'I will be your voice. My name is Yedda.'


Some hours later, when Søren returned to the communal house in Ferntree Gully, he found Dandelion and Yngwie back from walking around the Ferntree Gully market and ready to listen to his account of their visit to the Breeding Centre. Before sitting down together in the common room, Søren fetched himself some lemonade and a small selection of fresh fruit, as well as coffee for Yngwie and a bowl of water for Dandelion. He patted her head and affectionately ruffled her fur, then told them what had happened at the Breeding Centre.

'I'm quite sure Shahid's life will be completely different now... Much, much better, even though it was perfectly fine already, of course.' He smiled, then ate a few cherries. 'The cat's name is Yedda, which is most appropriate, though I'm not at all sure whether the cat chose her own name or it's a remarkable coincidence, but either way, it *is* wonderful.'

Yngwie checked the name's meaning on his hand reader and chuckled in surprise. 'Yes,' agreed Søren, 'it's so apt, isn't it.'

'It certainly is,' replied Yngwie, 'but go on. What type of cat is she?'

'A silver-grey shorthair with big blue eyes and small paws. She isn't as large as Dandelion here, but big enough, and fully socialised, naturally. That's one of the advantages of having a cat from the modern breeding centres. They are used to living in large groups, so don't often have any issues, unlike our friend here.' He reached out to stroke Dandelion, just to make sure she didn't take offence.

'And where is Shahid now? Did he take Yedda straight home?'

'He and Laurita took her home to meet his parents. They will accept a certain amount of responsibility for her since Shahid won't be able to take her with him on all his trips. An appointment has been made for Shahid and Yedda to meet with one of the trainers from the Breeding Centre tomorrow. The aim will be to make sure they are comfortable with each other, and to see how well Yedda understands what she can and cannot communicate to others with respect to something she sees in Shahid's mind. It will take time, and other training sessions will be arranged as needed, including some with his parents present, if necessary. Still, if this first day is anything to judge by, I think it should all go along very well.' He fell silent, remembering the adoring looks Shahid was already giving Yedda before he left them, and how the cat sat as close to him as she could, although without going so far as to climb onto his lap.

At the mention of Laurita, Yngwie looked away for a moment, but sternly told himself to forget about any romantic involvement – it seemed clear there wouldn't be any. Raising her head to look at him, Dandelion startled him by saying that Laurita was not the right person to be his bondmate; he had never even thought about her in those terms! What could the cat know of such things? She continued to gaze at him for a while, then blinked and turned away, leaving him puzzled and rather confused. *Had* he thought about Laurita that seriously? Well, he definitely liked her a lot... He shook his head slightly in an effort to dismiss the subject. 'I hope Shahid and Yedda do well,' he said. 'It would be a great thing, not only for them, but for others who might need a cat to help them communicate. I don't imagine it would be very common, but there could be others.'

'Yes,' agreed Søren, 'there could be. It isn't impossible.'

As he put his hand reader away, Yngwie came to a decision. Best to tell Søren now, rather than leave him to hear it from someone else. 'Søren, I have a confession to make, if you have time to listen?'

'I have all the time in the world, Yngwie. What terrible crime do you want to tell me about?' There was something in the young man's expression that told Søren this was not a light-hearted request.

'It was me...and a friend in Norway...who sent out the message to all the comlinks last week.' Yngwie waited for a reaction, leaning forward, a strange tingling sensation around his mouth and in his arms. 'I'm actually nervous,' he thought.

'Why?' asked Søren, also leaning forward, his eyes wide. Dandelion glanced at Yngwie, unconcerned. She already knew.

Yngwie briefly looked down, then met Søren's eyes. 'To begin with, for fun, and because of the challenge. As time went by, we saw it as the ultimate artwork. Who else, as a private individual, has ever sent anything worldwide like this? Coordinated and planned down to the last detail, and entirely successful?'

'I see,' said Søren frowning, unconvinced. After a pause, he added, 'I'd call it flagrantly irresponsible, juvenile, idiotic, and completely unjustified. Did you think about the time you would waste...other people's time? Did you think about the copycats? What if someone else tries to do this and sends out something truly ghastly that would seriously shock and upset people?'

'Yes,' answered Yngwie, blushing, his voice hesitant, 'we recognise this now, but the one thing we didn't think of at the time was that so many people would take up the idea and do some incredibly ridiculous stuff. But, Søren, we ended up finding something that needed to be fixed, and now it will be. This goal was ultimately our main justification...honestly. It began with curiosity and the challenge of trying to hack into the communications system. We weren't very old, only fourteen, so for no particular reason, it just seemed like something to do. The problem is, we became extremely good at it and found a serious flaw in the satellite control systems. What were we to do? We didn't think we could *tell* anyone, or we'd be charged. The only thing we saw to do was to *show* it existed, and to leave enough clues for them to find it.' He stopped speaking for a moment, remembering how hard they had worked to make sure the clues would be good enough for the flaw to be discovered without too much delay.

Raising an elegant eyebrow, Søren said, 'Will they realise it was you?'

'Yes, they will. We thought it only fair that we'd be caught. After all, it *is* a fairly serious crime. I imagine the peacekeepers will turn up either later this evening or early tomorrow. First, though, I want to call my friend Torleif and have a little celebration. We did succeed, after all.'

Yngwie grinned, his earlier good humour returning. 'We've kept all our software to show the FSIU, as well as an electronic diary of results and events so they can see we meant this to happen. With luck, the Judge will deal leniently with us and let me begin university in July as I've arranged. Even so, I suppose the worst that will happen is for us to be placed under house arrest without access to the lattice, or fine us – not that we have much in our accounts.' He chuckled, then tried to look serious again, but without much success.

Søren shook his head, and then laughed as he imagined how angry his friend Morag MacIain must be at the moment. Should he talk to her? No... They had made their decision and must now take the consequences. 'What about Shahid and Laurita?' he said. 'Will you tell them?'

'Yes, I'd better, hadn't I. I don't want them to think any worse of me than necessary...'

'Got you!' whispered Morag to herself, with a slight smile. She spoke to her computer and within minutes the peacekeepers in Rjukan and in Melbourne were on their way to bring in their suspects. Meanwhile, Torleif and Yngwie toasted each other over the lattice with a small glass of schnapps. 'Skål!' they said, and drank down the single mouthful, then finally discussed how best to tell their parents. This was perhaps the most difficult part of the entire project, and if they *were* placed under house arrest, they preferred not to have to suffer more than necessary!

# CHAPTER TEN

'Visualise something simple that you'd like Yedda to share with me,' said the gentech, as Shahid and Yedda did their best to follow the Breeding Centre's training exercises. The staff had used their knowledge of the cat's abilities to put together a schedule and were keen to see how well it would all work.

Shahid tried to clear his mind and focus on something definite that Yedda could easily comprehend. The usual clutter of thoughts drifted in and out and seemed almost impossible to drive away, until he remembered the serenity he felt while praying. He relaxed his shoulders, placed his hands loosely in his lap, and closed his eyes. Breathing slowly, the image of his mother wishing him good luck as they left this morning came into his mind. Since Yedda was there at the time, this should be an easy exercise for her to perform.

After a few moments, the gentech said, 'Your mother's name is Wania, she has long black hair, dark brown eyes, is of less than average height, has a lovely smile, and wished you luck before saying goodbye this morning. She also patted Yedda and gave you a kiss on the cheek. Is that right?' He smiled.

'Yes,' said Shahid, 'but I didn't ask Yedda to tell you about the pat or the kiss. Maybe I wasn't specific enough.'

'Possibly not. We need a simple code word. "Stop" is the obvious one. You know what that means, don't you Yedda,' said the gentech, reaching out to stroke her.

Yedda purred and agreed. Yes, she knew what "Stop" meant. This was a word she had learnt when very young!

'Let's try again,' said Shahid, and this time concentrated on what he had given Yedda to eat this morning. He then said 'Stop' in his mind, and visualised what he ate for dinner the night before.

The gentech wrote down the message Yedda relayed to him and gave the hand reader to Shahid.

Smiling, Shahid said, 'Yes, that's what she ate for breakfast, and she didn't pass on something I asked her not to.'

'Excellent!' replied the gentech. 'You've done well, puss. Do you want to try something more difficult?' Yedda purred her agreement. 'Good.

Now, Shahid, try to think of something less immediate to her. Something to do with your work perhaps.'

Shahid thought of the mountain ash trees and the fun he and Laurita had exchanging poems while they were in the treetops together. He tried to capture the joy of being there, with the scent of the flowers and sense of freedom, then told Yedda to 'Stop', and instead began thinking about the trip to Willsmere afterwards. Finally, he looked pointedly at Yedda and nodded. She turned to the gentech and accurately conveyed the scene in the forest, and nothing more.

'How wonderful it must be to see the forest from such a height!' exclaimed the gentech, charmed by the vivid image. He knew Shahid was a seed gatherer, but hadn't thought to ask about the details of his work.

'Did she tell you what we did afterwards?' asked Shahid.

'No... Should she have?'

'No, that was where I told her to stop.'

'This seems to be going exceptionally well,' said the gentech, smiling at Yedda. 'I wonder if we could try an actual message now – exact words. Just a brief message to begin with, I think.' He wrote down his suggestion and handed it to Shahid.

'"I would like some tea",' Shahid silently repeated.

Yedda stared at him for a few seconds, confused, but passed the message to the gentech, who burst out laughing. Patting Yedda's head, he said, 'I know *you* don't want tea, my dear, but you did well, accurately repeating what Shahid told you. So, Yedda, with messages like this, you could also tell me it's Shahid who wants the tea. Do you think you could do that?'

Yedda stood up and rubbed herself against his legs, then sat down again, ready to try another message. When he suggested Shahid give her a similar style of message of his own choosing, the gentech grinned when Yedda told him that Shahid wanted to see where some of the other cats lived. 'We could go to one of the enclosures after we finish, if you really want to,' he said.

Shahid asked Yedda to reply for him: 'Yes, Shahid would particularly like to see the nursing mothers.'

'I'm not sure we can take you in there,' replied the gentech, shaking his head. 'It's best if the cats who look after the young kittens are left in peace. Sorry...'

'Are there others I could see?' asked Shahid silently. Yedda passed on his question.

'Yes, certainly there are. Perhaps I could take you to meet our Guardians, too. They like visitors. It might even be an excellent step in our training program...although not today. We'd better keep it simple for the time being. It might be too confusing for Yedda to direct your thoughts only to me while at the same time keeping them from the other cats, which is what we could ask her to try when we go there. But first, we need to make sure she can send your messages only to the people you choose, and not to others within 'hearing' distance, which can be quite a long way.'

'How far?' asked Shahid, via Yedda.

This time, in her enthusiasm, Yedda lost control. 'A long, long way,' she 'said', 'and with the help of another grimalkin, even further!' Her answer didn't contain these words as such, but this was the meaning she conveyed to them both.

The gentech laughed and gently told her she wasn't supposed to answer the question herself. When Yedda, unperturbed, purred and rolled onto her back, begging to have her stomach stroked, Shahid knelt down beside her, lost in admiration of this treasure that had entered his life. The gentech watched, understanding, but after a few minutes, brought them back to the task at hand.

'Ah, excuse me for interrupting,' he said, 'but we had better continue. We still have some work to do, it seems!'

As Shahid returned to his chair, Yedda sat down next to him, front paws together, eyes wide, focusing as hard as she could on what they wanted her to do. 'Very well,' continued the gentech, 'let's try something similar, but this time, Yedda, let *me* answer.' Yedda blinked, twitched her tail and waited.

'I read something about the Guardians recently,' said Shahid silently. 'Who are they?'

Yedda turned to face him, studying him intently, her ears twitching, but she managed to resist the temptation to answer. Instead, the gentech said, 'Oh, they're very special cats, with an important peacekeeping role. I'll tell you more when we visit them – next week, if Yedda continues to learn as quickly as she's done today.'

Their session continued for another half hour, until the gentech was satisfied they had achieved enough for one day. 'Same time next week?' he suggested.

Shahid agreed, and then stood up as the gentech invited them to walk with him to see the enclosure where the younger cats who had recently received their vaccinations were kept until their immune systems were strong enough for them to join the others in the adoption area. After admiring them for several minutes from outside the plastiglass barrier, Shahid shook hands with the gentech, then left the breeding centre, with Yedda racing along the corridor ahead of him, tail in the air. She turned around to wait until he caught up, and if Shahid could have laughed with glee, he would have, but instead, had to content himself with grinning in delight over how well their training session had gone.

He knelt down to hug Yedda, who smooched and purred, kneading the ground with her paws. 'Yes,' Shahid told her when she asked, 'we can take the long way home and you can stare out the windows as much as you like...but this time, please don't talk to any of the other passengers unless I ask you to. I didn't really want you to tell them all those things you passed on during the trip here. So, from now on, let's keep our thoughts a bit more private, eh?'

Yedda managed to look embarrassed, but spoiled the effect by leaping into the air, doing a somersault, and landing neatly at his feet.

Unlike Shahid and Yedda, Yngwie was having a far less pleasant day. The silence in the room lengthened as Morag and Welcome studied him. He returned their gaze, his expression one of genuine surprise. 'Of course the dates on these files haven't been tampered with,' he said eventually. 'Why would I falsify them?'

'To save you and your friend, Torleif, from being charged with an extremely serious crime,' answered Morag sternly. 'It isn't difficult to change file dates, and for someone with your skills it could be done fairly quickly. I would suggest it's only since my announcement saying we were on your trail that you decided to build this defence.'

Yngwie shook his head. 'No,' he insisted, 'we let you find us on purpose, and kept the files all these years to show you precisely how we managed to penetrate your satellite security systems. Why else would we have kept them? It would have been easy to erase all trace of our actions.'

Morag glanced at Kaj, who sat quietly in the background, there to observe, not to question. He gave a slight nod. 'Very well,' replied Morag, 'I accept you're telling the truth when you say it would have been easy to remove the evidence, but I'm still not convinced these file dates are accurate. Still, the Norwegian FSIU security experts are currently examining the files Torleif has in his possession, and which are, allegedly, exact duplicates of yours. If the timestamps are the same, then I may feel more inclined to believe they're genuine. We expect to hear from them within the hour, so in the meantime, I want you to explain to us, step by step, how you discovered the security flaw and how you worked out your method of exploiting it.'

They listened without interruption while Yngwie went through the electronic diary he and Torleif had kept of their activities, demonstrating how they gradually examined all the various parameters used by the satellites to prevent unauthorised access. He described how, when they first entered the system, they were excited by the possibilities it presented and began to dream of making a worldwide statement that would make history.

'We were only children,' he said, looking up from the screen displaying their first rough draft of the image used for the cascade. 'We thought it would be something exciting, daring, an adventure, but eventually realised we needed to tell someone about the flaw we'd found. The problem was, we didn't see how we could. To tell you the truth, I didn't trust the Federation enough to give them the information. A bit silly, I suppose, but after a while we also realised that if we went the whole way and succeeded, then the Federation couldn't pretend the security issue didn't exist and would have to fix it. I've even developed some of the code needed.' Yngwie showed them the results of his latest work, from five months ago. 'This took the longest. I've had to be so careful not to be detected.' Forgetting himself for a moment, he smiled.

Morag stood up, seemingly outraged. 'You're *still* a child if you think you can sit here and amuse yourself! How *dare* you forget why you've been taken into custody!'

Welcome stared at her, startled by the uncharacteristic outburst. He rather liked Yngwie and his naive charm. The young man might say they didn't have enough confidence in the Federation to tell them about their discoveries, yet nevertheless had built up all this evidence over many years and were now trusting it would be taken at face value. He stood and went to the servery to fetch some coffee, hoping Morag would be distracted and calm down, but she hardly noticed.

'Why did you choose this particular image?' asked Morag, still standing and still glaring at Yngwie.

'It just seemed right for the purpose,' he answered, looking up at her, his expression still one of friendly cooperation. 'Everyone knows the Statue of Liberty and what it stands for. The idea of it burning represents the loss of freedom and justice, which is a constant risk in any society. Look, I know we sound like arrogant idiots, but you have to admit that to some people, the Federation is still a scary concept, with so much power and so much information about everyone. The idea of a flaw of the type we found being used by the wrong people is even scarier. Records in the population database could be falsified and the messaging system could be used to make people do things they shouldn't simply because they thought they were receiving a genuine instruction from someone in authority. The whole planet knows the system is only used when it's important.'

Morag sat down and looked him in the eye. 'You are quite right, and yes, it *has* been possible in the past for records to be falsified. It's been a problem for some time and we've tried very hard to track down how it was done, without much success.' She paused, then said, 'Yngwie, I'm inclined to think you were right after all in doing what you did. There's a large corporation we've spent many years investigating, and missing or falsified identification records keep cropping up. Although we've managed to find out how some of them were erased or altered, there are still quite a few which have eluded us. If your information *had* fallen into the wrong hands, we might never have noticed this flaw, and whoever has been exploiting it – assuming this is what they've been doing – may even have decided you and Torleif were expendable.'

Yngwie paled and opened his mouth to say something, then shut it again, speechless. This was far beyond anything he and his friend had imagined.

'Yes,' said Morag, 'this *isn't* a game for children. Still, at nineteen, you're old enough now to take the consequences of your actions, and so what I propose to do is enter all this into the Judge, then wait to see if it wants you charged. If not, I have a proposal to make, which I suspect you and Torleif will accept.' For the first time since entering the room, Morag smiled, although Yngwie found no comfort in it.

At this point, her comlink chimed, and she left the room to take the call. A few minutes later, she returned and said, 'The Norwegian peacekeepers have confirmed that the files on Torleif's computer and other devices have the same timestamps as yours, Yngwie, and that Torleif's version of events is the same as yours, too. Well, well, it seems almost certain we'll be able to put your talents to good use, but you may be in for a great deal more than you bargained for, young man! However, you're not out of the woods yet – not until the Judge says you are – so in the meantime, I'm afraid we'll need to keep your hand reader and storage drives, and for the time being, confine you to the communal house in Ferntree Gully... You can keep your comlink,' she added, as Yngwie began to say something. 'Don't turn it off, though, as we'll be tracking it, and every twelve hours we expect you to answer our messages to confirm your whereabouts. If you don't, you'll be arrested. Do I make myself clear?'

'Perfectly,' said Yngwie softly.

'Good. You can go now, and I'm sure we'll speak again soon.'

'What do you think, Kaj?' asked Morag, after Yngwie had been escorted from the building. 'Can you use this information to fast-track your team's work?'

'Yes, I believe so,' replied Kaj, looking up from scanning one of Yngwie's files. 'He has been meticulous and thorough.'

'Excellent. Once we've entered all this, I'll look forward to hearing what the Judge has to say. If it agrees with my recommendation, you may have yourself some new team members!'

Kaj nodded, but didn't return Morag's smile. Habitually glum, he would wait and see for himself before deciding whether the young Norwegians would be an asset or a liability.


In Narre Warren, the two twenty-kilogram bags of experimental rye flour arrived at the baker's premises at 13:00 on the Monday afternoon, as agreed with Karla, and the moment he had them safely in his kitchen, Phil eagerly opened one. He scooped out a small handful, examined it carefully, then sniffed – sweet, fresh, and thoroughly delicious! The baker had decided to make a variety of rye loaves, including some of the traditional black breads from Northern Europe. The ingredients were ready and waiting for him to begin, as were his two apprentices, who appreciated this unique opportunity to add to their skills.

Soon, the wonderful aroma of yeast loaves rising filled the warm kitchen, and once they had risen enough, the smell of them baking in the huge ovens was enough to make anyone hungry. When the loaves were ready and cooling on their racks, it was time to clean and tidy the kitchen, then ensure everything was in place for the second batch, early the following morning. The type of bread baked today was too moist and heavy for cutting until the following day, whereas Tuesday's varieties would be a lighter style, best eaten the same day, or frozen for later.

Once the apprentices had gone for the day, Phil wrapped all the loaves and put them safely away in his cool store, checked that the bags of flour and all the other ingredients were secure in their airtight containers, then put out the lights and left, making sure the door was locked behind him.

Early the next morning, he returned and, humming to himself while he worked, tested the bread made the day before to ensure it was ready for cutting, then called out a greeting when his apprentices arrived, ready for work. One of them took on the task of slicing the dark rye loaves, while the other read the recipes they were to use for the lighter breads. Satisfied she understood what needed to be done, the apprentice took out the rye flour from the storeroom then systematically weighed out the proportions of the various ingredients for each of the three varieties to be made. The other apprentice eventually joined her, and Phil looked on for a while until he was sure they had everything under control. Afterwards, he checked that the loaves of sliced black rye bread were properly packed into transparent, airtight bags, each labelled and individually numbered, then put them back into the cool store.

By mid-morning, the second batch of bread was cooling and the kitchen was again filled with the delicious aroma, as well as an atmosphere of satisfaction with their achievement. 'Right,' said Phil, 'let's move on to our usual routine now and deal with the new orders. Once we've finished, we should be ready for something to eat!'

The apprentices grinned, anticipating with pleasure their midsun meal of handmade savoury pastries and fresh fruit. The bakery was well known for its speciality coffee and gourmet chocolates, but they usually managed to leave these treats until the afternoon, just before they finished work. Today, however, Phil took out a box of chocolates from the storeroom, opened it, and offered them one to taste. 'It's a new type. I'd like your opinion,' he said, winking at them and smiling.

The apprentices each selected one of the smooth, dark chocolates, decorated with a piece of sugared orange peel. 'Oh, this is wonderful!' exclaimed the first apprentice. 'Cointreau, isn't it?' Phil grinned, but remained silent, waiting for a reaction from the second apprentice. 'Mmm...' she said. 'No, I think it's Grand Marnier... Yes, I'm sure it is.' She looked at Phil, laughing when he said, 'Yes, you're right. Grand Marnier it is, and still popular after all these years. Expensive though, so I haven't tried it before.' He closed the box and put it away. Shortly afterwards, they were ready to begin their main tasks for the day, content in their work and with each other's company.

With the orders filled and their regular variety of biscuits, cakes, pastries and breads made and placed in the shop for display, Phil fetched his hand reader and checked the list of people volunteering to taste the new rye loaves. Satisfied everything was as it should be, he loaded up his transport, included the additional orders they had prepared, then lifted off and before long, made his first delivery. Shahid and his parents were third on the list, and greeted him with an invitation to come in for tea and a chat, but since he had many more households to visit before he could finish for the night, Phil regretfully refused; for the purposes of the study, it was important all the loaves were delivered the same day.

The door to the eighth house on his list opened almost as soon as he arrived, and a tall, strongly built man named Matthew called out a greeting. 'Hello, Phil! Good to see you. We're looking forward to tasting this new bread.'

He was joined by his bondmate, Marie, who was now in the seventh month of her pregnancy. In their late thirties, they had successfully applied for fertility rights and so were overjoyed when Marie fell pregnant almost immediately. The baby would be a boy, and they already had a name for him: Benjamin, in honour of Matthew's grandfather, a well-known and respected Member of Parliament, although now retired.

'Would you like to come in for a while, Phil?' offered Marie, her hand on her stomach as she tenderly stroked her unborn son. 'It's so hot outside! It must have reached forty by now.'

'No, I won't, but thank you. Maybe next time? I have so many people to see today before I can finish up. Now, could you just press your thumb here to show I've given you the loaf you agreed to? I need to make sure my records are correct, or the experiment won't be right. We don't want any mistakes.'

Marie accepted the light rye he gave her, entered her thumbprint onto his hand reader where he indicated, then stepped back, smiling and examining the bread. 'Oh, this looks good!' she said. 'Well, I'll go back inside now and away from this heat. We'll see you again soon, I'm sure. Bye for now,' and she gave Phil a small wave before leaving Matthew to have one last, quick word with the baker. They were old friends and had gone to school together in Berwick.

'She looks well,' said Phil. 'Is the pregnancy going okay?'

'Yes, everything seems normal and Marie has hardly any discomfort. Benjamin is kicking and moving around like a champion. He'll be a sturdy little fellow when he's born.' Matthew grinned. He was fond of sports and already anticipating the time when his son would be old enough to take an interest.

Phil slapped Matthew lightly on the shoulder, then said goodbye and left to complete his deliveries. By 19:00, he was home and ready for his evening meal, satisfied with his day's work and sure Karla would be as well. After he had eaten something, he called her and sent in the records he had collected of all the people who were participating in the study, which included the identification number of the loaf of bread they were given; Karla already had the list of ingredients used for each type baked. By Thursday, they expected to have heard from all the participants, at which time they would compile their report to the Federation on the results of the trial.

## CHAPTER ELEVEN

Blood streamed down Marie's legs as she doubled over in agony, gasping for breath. 'Oh no, not the baby!' she whispered, then cried out as another wave of pain swept over her. Holding her belly with one hand while groping for her comlink with the other, Marie managed to sink to the ground rather than fall, and then crouched there, waiting for someone to respond to her emergency signal. She was too far out of range of the household security system for it to notice her distress and automatically call the nearest medcentre. *Why* had she decided to go outside in this heat! Harvesting the ripe limes on their small tree could have waited, either until Matthew came home or the weather cooled down...although they tended to drop...

The sun scorched her face as she looked around for some shade. There was a big gum tree about thirty metres away. 'If only I can crawl that far,' she thought, placing both hands on the hot earth and taking a deep breath before slowly inching forward. Twigs scratched her bare knees and small stones bruised her skin. The blood was everywhere...wet and horrible.

Five long minutes went by before Marie made it to the shade of the old tree. Panting, she rolled onto her side and tried to control her breathing; her hands were tingling and becoming numb, most likely from hyperventilating. She mustn't panic; she *must* stay still until someone came to help. Perhaps if she stayed still the pain would ease? Her mouth was dry and she tried not to think about the iced water she'd enjoyed with her midsun meal, two hours ago. Marie tried not to think about Benjamin either, her little baby boy: Matthew's baby boy too. What would he say if Benjamin was dead? Would he blame her for going outside on a day like this? She stared into the distance and began to weep. He was dead; Marie knew he was dead. So much blood – he couldn't have survived. She didn't dare try to look at herself to see what had happened, but felt her stomach... Nothing, no movement, no small kicks to say he was still alive. Despite the heat, Marie began to shiver... *Why am I so cold?*

When her comlink chimed, loud in the stillness, Marie could barely answer. 'Hello?' she whispered. It was Matthew, checking to see if all was well. 'Matthew, I need help. I think I'm having a miscarriage. I'm outside, about two hundred metres from the house, out the back.'

Matthew gasped, but did his best to stay calm. 'Have you called someone?' he asked, keeping his tone even and meanwhile grabbing the few belongings he needed to bring back with him. As he quickly walked towards the gate in the paddock fence, he heard Marie say, 'Yes, my comlink is sending the emergency signal... I hope someone comes soon. I'm starting to feel really ill. I think it's the heat.'

'Stay with me, Marie. I'm not far away. I'll contact the medcentre to see if the signal has come through. Just hold on, my darling, hold on.'

Because of Marie's pregnancy, Matthew knew the call would go straight to the medcentre in Berwick, instead of to the peacekeepers, as would usually be the case. Then, on the assumption that if Marie engaged her emergency signal it meant she was having trouble speaking, the medcentre would send an ambulance immediately, rather than waste time trying to call her. From their point of view, if it turned out not to be a medical emergency, but some other type, the ambutechs would no doubt still manage, since they were trained to deal with a wide variety of situations.

'Marie, are you there?' said Matthew. 'Yes? The call went through. They're on their way. They'll be with you in a few minutes and I won't be far behind them.'

By the time Matthew reached his bondmate, she was being attended to by two briskly competent women who had her pain almost under control and were treating her for dehydration. When Marie reached out to Matthew, he took her hand in his. 'Don't worry,' he said, using the words so many do under the circumstances. 'I'll come with you in the ambulance.' He cast a glance at one of the ambutechs. She nodded, then guided the hoverbed into the waiting vehicle. Once Matthew was safely on board, they lifted off and several minutes later landed outside the Berwick medcentre.

'I'm sorry,' said Marie, her voice beginning to gain some strength. 'I may have lost Benjamin. I shouldn't have gone outside today. I'm so sorry...'

'It's not your fault, Marie; I'm sure it's not your fault. Everything was fine when you had your last check-up a few days ago, and you didn't go outside for long, did you?'

'No, but I probably walked a bit further than I should have in this weather and my blood pressure might have gone up too high... I felt dizzy and sick before the bleeding began, and then the horrible cramps... It was so awful, Matthew. I've never felt anything like it!' Tears began as she tried to sit up, looking earnestly into his face.

One of the ambutechs gently pressed her back down. 'Please, just try to relax. We'll soon have you cleaned up and in a comfy bed where it's lovely and cool. You don't need to worry about anything. We'll take care of you.'

Once inside the building, Marie did her best to relax, allowing the medcentre staff to do what they needed to. Matthew stood nearby, hoping she was wrong, that their baby boy hadn't died before he was even born. Unfortunately, the practitioner who examined Marie confirmed their worst fears: Benjamin was indeed dead, and Marie would need to remain in the medcentre for several days while she recovered from the shock and the substantial loss of blood.

'Why?' asked Matthew, white-faced and anxious. 'Why did Marie lose our baby? It doesn't make sense.'

The practitioner shook her head. 'It's an odd case. We'll perform a genetic study on the baby's tissue once we deliver him, but based on the results from her last visit, there shouldn't be any abnormalities that could explain a miscarriage. She was in perfect health, other than slightly higher blood pressure than we'd like, so unless she ate something that somehow caused a reaction, or did walk too far in the heat and has some condition we haven't yet detected which made it too much for her, then I really can't explain it.' The practitioner wrinkled her brow as she looked at Marie, thinking. 'Has she eaten anything unusual, do you know?' she said at last.

Matthew shrugged his shoulders – and then stared at her. 'Why, yes,' he said, his eyes wide. 'We're taking part in a Federation trial of a new strain of rye. It was grown in Narre Warren and a number of local people volunteered to taste bread made from the grain. It was delivered yesterday and we both ate some last night, also this morning. It's not the usual bread we eat, but it was so good we had more than we normally would... But I'm fine! It couldn't be the bread, could it?'

'It's not impossible,' said the practitioner doubtfully, 'but it doesn't sound likely, either. Still, if it's a new variety, there's always the chance Marie may have reacted to it.' She checked her patient's records. 'There doesn't seem to be any history of food intolerance or allergy. Do you know of any we aren't aware of?'

Matthew shook his head, frowning. 'You could contact the baker, or even the Federation scientists in charge of the trial. They'd know exactly what the bread contained, and even the chemical analysis of the flour.' Eager now to pass on the information, Matthew quickly found Phil and Karla's contact numbers. 'Here,' he said, passing his comlink to the practitioner, 'these are the people you need to speak to.'

'Thank you, I will. We should have the results of the genetic studies by early tomorrow morning at the latest, and keeping Marie under observation may throw some light on the situation as well. In the meantime, Matthew, try to take it easy and don't put any pressure on either yourself or Marie to find out more than you need to. Sometimes these things just happen and there's no actual reason we can find, other than the pregnancy simply wasn't quite right and nature took over and terminated it. There can be so many factors involved, you see.'

Matthew reluctantly went back to sit by Marie's bed. She was almost asleep, having been given a light sedative. He held her hand and waited until a medtech came to take her to the delivery room, where their unborn son would be cared for as tenderly as if he were still alive.

For the next two hours, Matthew sat there, angry, despairing, wondering. Was it the heat? Could it have been the bread? He *had* to know!

His thoughts were interrupted by the sound of the practitioner saying his name: 'Matthew, Marie is awake now. Would you like to come with me? We thought you would both want to see your little boy and tell us what you want done next.'

When Matthew gazed at her blankly, she said, 'There'll be funeral arrangements to make, and you may wish to give him his name beforehand.'

Matthew's face contorted with grief as he forced himself not to weep, but when he stood by Marie's bed and saw her holding the tiny bundle, with Benjamin's little face showing, he could contain himself no longer.

'Oh no!' exclaimed Karla, when the practitioner from the Berwick medcentre called to discuss the rye bread eaten by Matthew and Marie. 'A miscarriage! That's dreadful! I'm so sorry to hear it, and yes, I'll send you the analysis of the flour immediately.' Karla gave her computer a command, and shortly afterwards, the practitioner was reading the relevant tables.

'It seems fine to me,' she said, with a relieved smile. 'I've spoken with your baker, Phil, and he gave me a full list of ingredients. There doesn't seem to be anything Marie could have reacted to, although sensitivities and food intolerances can develop quite suddenly and are sometimes unpredictable, even *with* all the research we've done.'

'I'm almost certain our bread couldn't have affected her,' replied Karla doubtfully, 'unless it *is* a new sensitivity or intolerance that she's developed recently and which is an unusually serious one. 'Also, we have stringent controls in place to make sure nothing can contaminate our test plots, the harvested grain, or the milled flour. Everything is colour-coded throughout the process, and the different strains and test products are kept in separate locked areas within an underground facility. Only authorised personnel can enter, too. In the field, to ensure there isn't any cross-contamination, each test plot is isolated from the others using a quarantine field – although they're down at the moment because the harvest is in and the fields haven't been prepared yet for the next crop.'

The practitioner listened carefully, but insisted, 'Is there any chance whatsoever there could have been a mix-up?'

Karla considered for a moment. 'I don't think so, but to be on the safe side, I suggest we carry out testing of all the bakery ingredients, as well as the premises. We can double check all our storage areas and testing facilities too.'

'Good,' replied the practitioner, relieved at dealing with someone so cooperative, 'though I'd suggest we have an independent person supervise all this...just in case.'

'Yes, you may be right. Are you able to organise it?'

'I should be able to. I'll do some calling around and get back to you as soon as I can. In the meantime, I'll explain the situation to Marie and her bondmate and hope they understand we're doing everything possible to find out if she was exposed to some unknown substance that caused the miscarriage, unlikely as it seems.'

'Thank you,' replied Karla. 'I appreciate your help.'

Two hours later, a Government health and safety inspector called, and made an appointment to meet with Karla at the Narre Warren research facility at 09:00 the following morning. 'We'll inspect your premises and the bakery at the same time. I've made an appointment for one my staff to be at the bakery at 09:00 tomorrow as well. If we place a priority on this, we should have all our results back by late Friday morning. Let's hope for everyone's sake we don't find anything we shouldn't!'

Karla raised her eyebrows and grimaced. 'Yes, let's hope not. We've put too much effort into this project for it to go wrong now.'

'I understand you test your new grain for pest resistance of various types, including ergot?' said the inspector.

'Yes, we do. It's one of the most important aspects of our research, together with the nutritional value of the grain, how well the plants retain the seed when it ripens, and the ability of the crop to grow well without much in the way of added water or fertiliser.' Karla found herself explaining far more than she needed to and forced herself to stop. 'I'm actually nervous,' she thought.

'You do know that ergot poisoning can cause miscarriages?' The inspector leaned forward to emphasise her point.

'Yes, I do,' said Karla, 'but wouldn't the tests the medcentre carried out on Marie have shown up ergot poisoning?'

'Not necessarily. The half-life of ergotamine is relatively short – about two hours – so if she ate the bread in the morning and blood tests were done about six or seven hours later, then it's possible it wouldn't show up. A urine test might not show up anything either, since only trace amounts are ever excreted by the kidneys.'

'I see,' said Karla, frowning. 'The medcentre will take the possibility into account anyway, won't they, and treat her accordingly?'

'Oh yes; they certainly don't want any complications, like gangrene or thrombosis! That would be dreadful. No, no, Marie will be physically fine after a few days rest, but psychologically, that's altogether another matter. It will depend a great deal upon how her bondmate handles the whole thing. Still, let's concentrate on what *we* can do, which is to make sure your flour isn't the culprit.' The inspector smiled grimly, but Karla could hardly return the smile.

Unable to sleep, Matthew got out of bed, went into the study and asked the computer to perform a search based on the symptoms Marie had suffered, together with any links to consumption of rye. When he read the results, he leapt to his feet and swore: 'Damn them! Damn their blasted experiments!'

Everyone in the local area was aware the Federation was testing crops for disease resistance, and they knew that the research facility in Narre Warren was treated as a high-security area, with restricted access, but mistakes could still be made! What if his Marie could never have another child? Their only chance, lost! Benjamin dead! And even if Marie was able to have children again, what if the Federation refused to give them permission? Surely not! Surely they wouldn't refuse? Matthew sat down again and asked the computer to show him the regulations covering miscarriages. They told him that if the cause was genetic, the couple might not be given permission to try again. 'No!' Matthew was almost beside himself with rage. Either way, whether the accursed bread had caused the miscarriage, or something was wrong with the baby, they might never again be given the chance to become parents.

'Take it easy,' he told himself at last, doing his best to control his anger. He would wait until morning to hear what the medcentre's tests had to say. Even so, it would be almost two whole days before they heard back from the Health and Safety Inspectorate about their investigation into the Federation's flour and the bakery's other ingredients. He went back to bed and tried to sleep, but it was impossible. For no apparent reason, the memory of the message sent out recently by some hacker popped into his mind and Matthew knew exactly what needed to be done.

Before putting on his clothes, for one of the few times in his life he turned off his comlink, then went to his toolshed, collected what he wanted and began walking. It wasn't far, and he enjoyed the feel of the breeze as it became stronger, ruffling his hair and cooling his face. The night was still much too warm, but that didn't bother him. He enjoyed walking in the darkness. Even the small sounds of the night were hardly noticed – the occasional squeak of a bat, the sound of a bird protesting at being disturbed, or the rustle of a possum in the trees lining the trafficway. Matthew heard nothing but his own angry thoughts, his own despair. Only the flames would give him peace.

In Ferntree Gully, at almost two in the morning, Jonathon, the forest guardian on duty, was alerted by their satellite system to a hotspot developing in Narre Warren and which was spreading rapidly. He quickly enhanced the thermal image to show the terrain in more detail. The monitoring software gave him further information about the location, telling him that the Federation research station was burning. Or to be more precise, the recently harvested fields of rye, where the thick stubble had been left to protect both the soil and the next crop, due to be sown in April.

With no time to waste, Jonathon did two things: he checked for comlink signals in the immediate area in case a rescue team was needed, and was relieved to see there weren't any, then sent out the order for the firefighters to attend. While the airjets, with their load of fire retardant, were on their way, the final tasks were to double check that no one was present at the Narre Warren facility and to notify Willsmere.

# CHAPTER TWELVE

Karla stared at the blackened fields, shaking her head in dismay. Without the protective stubble from the previous crop, their next one would be far more exposed to the elements than their trials could accept – unless they changed their plans. Doing her best to be optimistic, she thought the additional data might even be useful, although it meant adding an extra twelve months to their project, since they would still need to conduct the trials interrupted by the fire. She decided to contact their research coordinator in Oslo to obtain permission for the change, and while they discussed the idea, Karla continued her walk around the perimeter of the field. As she did, she noticed a tall figure in the distance. The man was dressed in the dark red uniform of a forest guardian and he appeared to be inspecting both the field and its perimeter. She increased her pace, and by the time she reached him, had finished her conversation, with the necessary permission for the change of plan recorded on her comlink.

'Hello,' Karla called out, as she came within hearing distance. The forest guardian looked up, but waited until she was closer before replying.

'Hello, yourself,' he answered, his grey eyes crinkling at their corners as he smiled. Holding out a broad, sun-browned hand, he said, 'My name's Jonathon. You look as if you're here on official business.' His tone and eyes held a question, so Karla explained she was the project coordinator from Willsmere and that the news of the fire had been given to her first thing this morning.

'Was it accidental?' she continued, instantly feeling at ease with him and liking the warmth of his hand as it held hers a few moments earlier.

'I'm not entirely sure yet,' replied Jonathon. He found himself glancing at Karla's left hand and saw there was no fertility ring on it. To his own surprise, he was pleased; it meant there was a good chance she was still unbonded. Slightly embarrassed by his thoughts, he ran his fingers through his hair, then concentrated on what Karla was saying.

Karla noticed the glance, and with a grin, asked, 'How long do you think the investigation will take? We can't clean up the area until we know whether the fire was accidental or not, and I don't want our field trials to be delayed.'

'Oh, of course not! No, no...we'll be as quick as we can. The area isn't large, so I should be in a position to give you the final report by late tomorrow afternoon. Would that help?' Of a similar age to Karla, Jonathon was a highly experienced firefighter and investigator, so the estimate was accurate, and not made in an attempt to please her.

'Yes, that'd be wonderful,' said Karla, smiling. 'Is there anything *we* can do?'

'We have everything under control, thanks, but perhaps you'd join me for dinner this evening? You could give me more background to the work you do at Willsmere, insofar as it relates to this project, and if I've discovered anything at all suspicious by then, maybe you could even think about who might want to harm the Federation by doing this?' Jonathon did his best to make the invitation sound like business rather than pleasure, but the tone of his voice gave him away.

Karla hesitated before replying, 'Well, why not. Where would you like to have dinner?'

'I'm fond of Middle Eastern cooking, so what about the Turkish restaurant in Berwick, or is that too far out of your way?'

'No, it sounds fine. I have enough work here to keep me busy for the rest of the day, so it should actually work out well. Would 19:00 suit you? I tend to be starving by then!'

'It would suit me perfectly,' answered Jonathon, grinning. When he held out his hand, Karla returned his strong grip then left him to his work, humming to herself, despite the fire, and looking forward to seeing him again.

As the temperature outside the forest soared, inside it remained comparatively cool, for which Søren was intensely grateful. The contrast between early spring in Greenland and early autumn here in Australia was massive, and although it felt wonderful to have left the icy cold and early darkness behind, he wished it wasn't *quite* so hot! Besides the heat being uncomfortable, it made his survey of the spider population difficult, since they disliked the heat as much as he did and preferred to stay hidden when the humidity dropped. Nevertheless, his traps were working reasonably well, although his instincts told him he wasn't catching as many as he should. He sat down on a convenient log and took his hand reader from his backpack. After entering the morning's data, he calculated his margin of error and considered what he should do next. As he did, a large, white cockatoo landed on a nearby branch and gazed at him, head to one side, yellow crest half-raised.

'Hello,' said Søren. Loud though these birds were when they chose to be, he adored their antics and their sociable nature. The cockatoo stepped slowly along the branch, raised its crest a little more, nodded a few times, then stood still, as if waiting for Søren to say something else. 'Where are your friends?' he asked. These birds rarely remained solitary for long.

As if in answer, a flock of about two dozen flew overhead, their noise deafening. Søren quickly put his hands over his ears and watched as the bird on the branch took off, huge wings outspread and screeching as it joined them. Smiling, he decided it was time for a mid-morning break and a call to Karla. His backpack held a cooler flask of sparkling apple juice, some fragrant, creamy cheese, two ciabatta bread rolls, and a bunch of sweet sultana grapes. Before beginning his small repast, Søren cleaned his hands with a moist towelette, then moved over to a spot on the log where he could rest his back against a tree trunk. As far as he was concerned, apart from the heat, this was paradise...except that Karla wasn't here, and he had no one else to talk to either, not even Dandelion. Still, he expected to see them both this afternoon...or at least, would speak with Karla if she was too busy to come all the way from Kew to visit him.

Once he had finished eating, and afterwards, tidying everything away, Søren called her, but instead of her usual cheerful greeting, heard a somewhat terse, 'Yes, hello?'

'Karla,' he answered, 'you are upset. What has happened?'

'Well, in addition to having the health and safety inspectors here that I told you about last night, and who are nearly driving me crazy with all their questions, there's been a fire...in our fields!'

'What?! No! How?' exclaimed Søren, mouth agape.

'We don't know *how* yet, but it happened in the middle of the night, and the investigators are examining the area now. They've promised to give me a report by tomorrow afternoon, so at least we won't have to wait long to hear more. Fortunately, the inspectors say they'll have *their* results by tomorrow morning, which leaves only the issue of the genetic testing of Marie's baby... I half expected to have heard the outcome by now, but I suppose the medcentre's busy, and they need to deal with Marie and her bondmate first anyway. Also, Phil, from the bakery, has called and he's extremely upset. The possibility that something he used might have affected the baby is more than he can cope with. Poor fellow! I've told him the chances are remote and to stay calm, but he's still worried Matthew will turn up and accuse him, even though they've known each other for years. I think it's unlikely, but it *could* happen...'

'I sincerely hope not!' replied Søren. He hadn't met Matthew, but from Karla's description, knew he was a tall, strong, outgoing man, and not the quiet, retiring type at all. 'How much damage was there to the fields?' he added.

'The whole area is burned to a cinder, so there's no stubble left to protect our next crop.' Karla held up a hand to forestall Søren's comment.

'It's okay. I've called Oslo and they're happy to authorise a change of plan and to use this as an opportunity to see what happens if we plant the fields as they are. We won't plough, just dry sow in April as we intended. The ash might even be good fertiliser and make up for the lack of cover, although I doubt it, actually. We'll return to our original trial once this next crop is harvested, leaving the stubble, and sow again in April next year.'

'Hmm... Well, the extra data may be useful. Still, what a shame! Do you want to meet for dinner to talk further, or will you need to keep working?'

'No... I won't need to work this evening. At least, I don't think so... Not unless the inspectors turn up something completely unexpected which has to be dealt with straight away. However, I'm actually going out to dinner with one of the forest guardians! I met him this morning while he was inspecting the burnt fields and he suggested we meet over dinner to discuss the situation and how it'll affect our project. Mind you, I suspect it's only an excuse.' Karla laughed, and then abruptly stopped as she noticed Søren's expression. 'I'm sorry,' she said. 'I shouldn't have blurted it out like that.'

'Don't be sorry, dear Karla. We *have* discussed this before, and I know we could never live together, even if we do care deeply for one another. It's just that this is the first time you have specifically told me about someone you were attracted to. If I don't hear about them, I can pretend it isn't happening, you see.' Søren tried to smile, but failed, and turned away for a moment.

'I don't know what to say,' said Karla, thoroughly upset now.

'Don't say anything,' replied Søren. 'Enjoy your dinner and I'll do my best not to be jealous. Seriously, I mean it. What is his name?' While he waited for Karla to answer, he took a deep breath and shook his head slightly, as if to chase away the dreams he had cherished for so many years.

With a catch in her voice, Karla said, 'Jonathon. He was the one who first spotted the fire... Oh, could you hold while I take this other call? It might be the medcentre... Yes, it is. Will you wait? Please?'

Søren waited, thinking. If this Jonathon was a forest guardian, he was probably fit and strong, probably tall, even taller than Karla, and if she'd agreed to go to dinner with him, he must presumably have a sense of humour. He couldn't imagine Karla liking someone who didn't enjoy a good laugh. Damnation! Drat, damn and blast the man! He sighed, then noticed Karla was talking to him. 'What?' he said, glaring at her without realising it.

'You're in a mood now, I can tell,' she answered, trying to make him feel better by adding, 'Aurora might not like him, and that would be the end of it.'

'She won't be there this evening, will she?' asked Søren, with a reasonable attempt at a smile.

'No, true, she won't be, but she nearly always goes everywhere with me. They might meet fairly soon, if there's a need to follow up on the fire... Anyway, the call was from the practitioner who saw Marie yesterday. They want to keep her in for observation a while longer and do a few more tests, but apparently the baby was normal genetically, so they can at least rule that out as the cause of the miscarriage. I must say, I'm relieved. This means there's every chance she and Matthew will be given permission to try again.'

'Assuming Marie is *able* to have another child. Did the practitioner say?'

'Yes, it seems she's fine physically, just tired and depressed. I hope Matthew has been in to see her and is doing his best to be cheerful.'

'So do I, even if I have never met either of them! It's a small community here, so no doubt everyone will be talking about the situation and will be upset on their behalf.'

'I expect so... However, I must go. There's an inspector waving at me. It looks like they want to discuss something. I'll call you tomorrow, and in the meantime, say hello to Laurita and Yngwie for me when you see them. Tell Laurita I'll call her tomorrow as well. I'm sure she'll be worried about the miscarriage too, and once she hears about the fire, she'll be even more worried. This project is as important to her as it is to me, and to the rest of the team.'

'So you have forgiven our young Norwegian friend, have you?' Søren grinned, remembering Karla's reaction when he first told her what Yngwie had done.

'Yes, but you can tell him from me, he's an idiot, even though I understand his motives. He's young, and besides, he doesn't know the Federation and the FSIU the way we do. I think he and his friend realised they could thoroughly enjoy themselves while at the same time do something that would turn out well for everyone. Which reminds me, has he told you how the interview went?'

'No, not yet. He came back to the communal house looking quite chastened and refused to say anything at all. I will see if I can get him to talk later today. Well, you have to go, so enjoy your dinner this evening and we will speak again tomorrow.' Søren blew Karla a kiss and closed the connection.


Silence at the dinner table was normal for Shahid's family, who tended to concentrate on their food for some time before chatting about the day's events. However, this evening, their guest, Laurita, felt uncomfortable because the silence seemed strained. There were two subjects the family appeared to be avoiding, perhaps as a courtesy to her: Yngwie's behaviour, and Marie's miscarriage. In a small community, word travels as quickly as gossiping tongues and comlink messages can carry it, and by mid-afternoon, all those who had volunteered to taste Willsmere's rye bread knew what had happened, as did many others. The whole region was also aware of the fire at Narre Warren during the night and many wondered if there was a connection.

Laurita finally decided to say something, just as Wania was about to go to the kitchen to fetch the last course. She sat down again to listen:

'I've heard that your friend Marie had a placental problem which restricted the blood supply to the baby, and that this was the likely cause of the miscarriage. I've also heard the baby had no genetic abnormalities that would tend to end the pregnancy. Do you know if this is true, Shafiqur? I realise it isn't usually the right thing for a doctor to discuss someone's medical history, but she isn't your patient and the issue is affecting the whole community, as well as Willsmere's reputation and their trials. This is important to me as well. After all, I brought the rye seeds here, and Karla is one of my closest friends.'

Shafiqur looked at his plate, thinking, then raised his eyes to meet Laurita's and said, 'You are right. Everyone seems to have heard these details, so I may as well confirm that, yes, they are true, but nevertheless I would prefer you didn't tell this to anyone else, not even Karla. She will find out for herself before long, through official channels, if she hasn't already.' Without being aware of it, he was frowning and his voice was stern.

'Yes, I expect so, but in the meantime, until the question of the rye bread is resolved, there will continue to be rumours about it being contaminated. It *is* possible, isn't it, that the pregnancy might have continued, and that it *could* be ergot poisoning which caused the blood supply to the baby to be restricted just that little bit too much?'

Wania reached out to lightly touch Laurita's arm, since she was clearly becoming agitated. 'Yes, it is possible,' she said, 'but it's also possible the pregnancy wasn't viable, and that the rye is not contaminated. We haven't heard of anyone else becoming genuinely ill, although a few people have come in to the medcentre with what seem to be psychosomatic symptoms. It's remarkable how hysterical people can become in cases like this.'

Laurita briefly placed her hand over Wania's. 'Yes, you're right. We must wait to hear the answer and not speculate. Still, *someone* seems to have blamed the rye. Someone set fire to the field of stubble on purpose. It *couldn't* have been an accident and even the news reports indicate it was most likely arson.'

'Coincidence?' suggested Shahid. 'A hot, windy night...the perfect opportunity for an arsonist whose main aim was to enjoy the blaze. The fire would spread quickly, without really endangering anyone. There's no forest nearby, and anyone would know it would soon be spotted and easily put out.'

Lying by his feet, Yedda listened to the entire conversation, but due to her limited experience of wights and, to her, their sometimes extremely odd behaviour, it was far beyond her comprehension. She sighed, laid her head on her paws again and fell into a light doze. Something of what she was feeling transmitted itself to Shahid and he leaned down to pat her. Yedda rolled onto her side to look up at him, eyes glinting in the candlelight. Shahid smiled, stroking her for a little while longer before turning his attention back to the conversation.

'It could even have been someone who wanted to make a point and saw this as the perfect opportunity,' said Shafiqur. 'After all, there have been plenty of copycat crimes since Yngwie and his friend decided to play games with the Federation.' He finally raised the subject they had all been avoiding since yesterday, when Shahid told his parents who had initiated the cascade. At the time, after an initial outburst of astonishment and disappointment, Shafiqur had refused to discuss the matter, while Wania, out of respect for her bondmate's feelings, remained silent. She knew he would eventually calm down.

'Is Yngwie himself suspected of lighting the fire?' she now asked, looking at Laurita, assuming she would know.

'Well, yes, the local peacekeepers *did* come to the communal house today, shortly after midsun, asking to see him, but they didn't stay long because Yngwie was able to give them an alibi – me. We were up late, well after the time the fire started. He had a lot on his mind and wanted to talk.'

'Oh, it's no surprise to hear he had a lot on his mind, but I'm relieved you were able to give him an alibi,' replied Wania. The niggling thought had in fact crossed her mind that their young friend was far more reckless than they imagined.

Shahid stared at his mother, amazed, as he suddenly realised she had suspected Yngwie was capable of doing such a thing – although he himself was having trouble coming to terms with what Yngwie *had* done, noble though his motives may, in the end, have been. 'Conveniently noble', was how Shahid tended to see the decision Yngwie and Torleif arrived at.

Accurately guessing what her son was thinking, Wania made an apologetic face, then stood up to fetch the dishes she had intended to a little earlier. When she came back, the atmosphere had improved and so did the evening. After they finished eating, Shahid brought out his lute and played for them, while Yedda lay at the far end of the room with one paw over her face, as if to tell them that she, for one, did not appreciate his music.

'Well,' concluded Shahid, laughing to himself, 'I may be mute, but she's tone deaf!'

'Stop frowning at me, Kaj!' said Yngwie, staring up at him as he stood close by. 'Either the cat stays or I refuse to work with you. Coordinator MacIain knows I have her with me.'

Dandelion gazed first at Yngwie and then at Kaj, but instead of 'enhancing' the situation, decided it was better to leave them to sort it out. There was plenty of time to intervene if needed. She twitched her tail, fluffed out her fur and listened as they continued arguing, which they had been doing since not long after she and Yngwie arrived that morning for the first day of work with Kaj and his team.

'You *can't* refuse to work with me, Yngwie. The Judge has ordered you put in a minimum of twenty-five hours a week, which is precisely what you will do!' Kaj glared at Dandelion and poked her with his toe. She batted his boot with her paw and retreated, but was otherwise unperturbed. Her temper had improved with regular meals and daily exercise outside, as well as constant company.

'Don't do that!' Yngwie stood up, unconsciously adjusting his balance to best effect. He was almost as tall as the Swede, but far broader in the shoulders. Besides which, he rarely felt intimidated by anyone. Like many citizens of the Federation, he had studied Wing Chun kung fu from the age of eight, but unlike most, had continued his studies, so was well on the way to becoming an adept.

'I won't, if you keep her out of my way!' retorted Kaj, lowering his head to look straight into Yngwie's eyes.

'She stays with me. You'll simply have to learn to ignore her,' replied Yngwie. 'Dandelion is quite harmless,' he continued, bending the truth a little and adopting a more conciliatory tone, 'and I don't want her to be lonely. That's why I have her with me. She isn't mine, and I've agreed to take care of her while her companion is working somewhere she can't go... It's a long story, which I'd be happy to tell you if you want to listen,' he added, hoping Kaj would refuse, for otherwise the tale of Dandelion's ferocious behaviour would contradict what he had just said.

'No, and I don't have time for this. Neither do you. I'll discuss the matter with Coordinator MacIain and she can make the final decision. In the meantime, at least tell your cat to keep away from me!' Kaj glowered at both Yngwie and Dandelion then turned his back on them and marched out of the room.

Five minutes later, he came back and handed Yngwie a storage module containing all the data he wanted him to study and analyse. 'Here,' he said, thrusting it towards him, 'do your best with this. It contains the software I have written to check each satellite for the flaw you and your friend discovered, but it will need to be monitored in case there are idiosyncratic faults which haven't yet been discovered, either by you or by us. In addition, we need to perform a comprehensive security overhaul of them all, which will take a long time, even *with* automated processes.' Kaj's tone softened as he added, 'I understand you have in fact done the Federation a favour, and your rather remarkable skills will be of benefit now, but you have still behaved like an irresponsible fool. You could easily have contacted the FSIU and demonstrated how the fault would affect our systems. You didn't have to initiate the cascade.'

Frowning again, Kaj sat down, waiting to hear what Yngwie would say. Yngwie sat down as well and looked at Kaj for several long moments. 'True,' he finally admitted, 'but we didn't dare risk it. I suppose if we'd known exactly who to contact, we would have, but we had no idea how to work our way through all the bureaucratic layers. All it would have taken was for one person to react badly and we could have landed ourselves in even more trouble than we have now. At least this way we could choose how and when we'd be caught. Also, it was a reasonable gamble it would be the people at the top of the organisation who would speak to us...and we were right.'

Kaj shook his head, looked at Yngwie for a short while longer, then stood up and pointed to a workstation. 'You can have that one. If there is anything you require which isn't already there, let me know.' He checked the time and said, 'If you want, we could eat our midsun meal together at 12:30...and the cat can come with us.' He raised an eyebrow as he glanced in Dandelion's direction, but she was now dozing comfortably in a patch of sunlight coming in through the plastiglass dome in the ceiling, and so didn't notice the slight smile on Kaj's face. Yngwie did, though, but made sure Kaj didn't see the grin on his own face as he turned away and connected the storage module to the computer he had been allocated.

# CHAPTER THIRTEEN

'Just as well I'm not vindictive!' thought Jonathon, as he read the results of the forensic examination of the samples collected from the burnt fields in Narre Warren. Whoever set fire to them had used a solvent as an accelerant, so there was no doubting this was arson, particularly if taking into account the absence of comlink signals at the time the fire began – the arsonist appeared to have had sufficient forethought to have turned theirs off. Jonathon knew some people gave in to temptation due to a fascination with fire, but this seemed premeditated, and therefore, far more serious.

'Blasted fool!' he muttered angrily.

The report went on to note that according to local shopping records, no one in the region had bought this particular solvent within the past six months. However, many people kept the solvent on hand for certain types of cleaning, so although it was a long shot, Jonathon called the region's recycling facility and asked them to place a halt on the processing of garbage collections, just in case the container had been thrown away and hadn't yet been processed. They would be able to scan their warehouse for it without too much trouble, even if it was already crushed, although hopefully it wasn't. He also asked them to scan for gloves, on the assumption the arsonist may have protected his or her hands.

Meanwhile, Jonathon contacted the local peacekeeping force for permission to conduct a household search for either the container or the gloves if the scan found nothing. It would be a time-consuming exercise, and one which the local population would most likely resent, but the matter was serious enough for it to be given this level of attention. The problem was, the arsonist might not be a local person, in which case, they might never be caught, unless a future mistake attracted official notice. The other problem was that neither the container nor the gloves, if they turned up, would be proof of arson – only small pieces of evidence to narrow down the field of suspects.

Two and a half hours later, his computer signalled an incoming call from the recycling facility.

'What did you find?' asked Jonathon, assuming the grin on the employee's face meant something had indeed turned up.

'One uncrushed solvent container in yesterday's collection and none in today's. When would you like to collect it?'

'I'll come over now, if it's okay with you?' answered Jonathon, pleased.

'Good oh. I'll set the container aside in the manager's office, where no one will touch it, and we've used gloves to handle it, so if you find any fingerprints, they won't be ours!' The employee held up his hands for Jonathon to see.

'Excellent! See you in about twenty-five minutes, then.'

Jonathon took slightly less than twenty-five minutes to arrive at the Pakenham recycling plant, and was gratified when the solvent container was handed to him in a transparent, sealed bag, labelled with the time and date the item was found and with two employees' signatures as witnesses. 'Thanks,' he said, 'you've done well. You could let your manager know to keep a lookout for the gloves I mentioned. It's not impossible they may still be thrown away... That is, if any were used.'

'Will do,' replied the employee, before turning away as one of his fellow workers called out that it was time for their afternoon break. 'See you later, maybe,' he finished, leaving Jonathon to take his prize to the forensics lab for fingerprint analysis.

An hour and a half later, Jonathon had a name: Matthew Robertson, of Narre Warren.


Marie's face was still far too pale, thought Matthew, as he sat next to the bed, holding her hand. She gripped his tightly and said, 'I know you're not telling me something, Matthew. I can always tell when you're holding something back. What is it? Is it to do with the baby?'

Matthew lowered his face, trying to summon the courage to meet her eyes, to confess what he had done. He looked up, cleared this throat, and said, 'No, Marie, it isn't. I've done something really stupid and I need to tell you before you hear it from the peacekeepers.' He stopped, unable to continue, his face red.

Marie met his eyes, saying, 'Whatever it is, my darling, we'll face it together, like we've always done. It can't be as bad as losing Benjamin, so please, what is it?'

'I lost my temper the other night. I couldn't sleep once I got home, so I checked the Federation's regulations about applying for another chance to have a baby and they said that if a miscarriage happened because something was wrong genetically, then permission might not be given. Then I started thinking that even if Benjamin was perfect, what if you weren't able to have another child, maybe because of the rye bread or the miscarriage hurting you in some way.' He paused. 'Go on,' said Marie. 'What did you do?'

'I set fire to the fields at the Narre Warren research station. I know it was stupid, but I couldn't control myself. I *had* to do something, and I was so sure their bread killed our little boy!'

'But it didn't, Matthew, it didn't. It was just one of those things that sometimes happen. You believe the practitioner, don't you?'

Matthew nodded, then held a hand to his face and wept. The tears trickled down Marie's face as well, and they sat together in silence for a long time, until at last Marie said, 'I think you should tell the peacekeepers what you've done, Matthew. It might save them a lot of trouble, and there's no point putting it off, is there?'

'No, you're right, I should, but I can't bring myself to do it.' Matthew heaved a sigh. 'I feel like such a fool, and I sort of hope that maybe they won't find out it was me and everything will be all right.'

'Oh Matthew, no! I'm sure somehow or other they'll work out who did it. You *must* tell them...today. I wish I could go with you, but I'm still not well enough to get out of bed for long.'

'What if I do it tomorrow? That'd be soon enough, wouldn't it? I'd rather stay here with you for a while, then go back to the farm and do some work on the vineyards. I need to get my head together, and that's the best way I know of. I'll tell them tomorrow, I promise. Will that do, my love?'

Marie shook her head, but said, 'If you promise, but you do realise you're risking they find out before you tell them?'

'Yes, I guess so.' Matthew grimaced. 'It wouldn't be good, would it, if they found out first?'

'No, dear, it wouldn't. Perhaps you'd better do it today...and soon.'

Both looked up as they heard a tap at the door, and saw Phil standing outside, obviously wondering whether to come in. Marie smiled bravely and waved to him.

'Marie and I have been told that her miscarriage didn't have anything to do with your bread,' said Matthew, standing up as Phil entered the room. 'The inspectors contacted the medcentre this morning to tell them they found nothing in either your bakery or at the Narre Warren research station to suggest anything wrong.'

He held out his hand to Phil, who shook it, grasping it hard and holding on for longer than he normally would. 'Thank goodness!' he exclaimed. 'Though it would've been a big surprise to me if there had been something wrong, like ergot, for example; it usually colours the flour slightly, depending upon how much is in there. I always check the ingredients to make sure everything's good. It's just a habit, because in all my long years in this job, there's never been anything wrong. Still, accidents happen, and it's best to be cautious and not take too much for granted.'

Phil rubbed a hand over his face. 'How are you, Marie? I'm so sorry you lost your baby, truly sorry.' He took a seat next to the bed and handed Marie the small gift he had brought – a heavy fruitcake, moist and dark, flavoured with best brandy. 'I know you like these, so I made a batch specially. If they don't let you eat it now, you can take it home. It should keep well if you put it in an airtight container...but you know that. Don't mind me... I'm just babbling with relief, both at being cleared and that you're otherwise okay.'

Marie reached out to touch his hand. 'Yes, I know, Phil, and thank you. I'm sure we'll both enjoy the cake once I get home.' She handed it to Matthew, who set it aside and sat down. 'Has anyone been nasty to you about this, Phil? My miscarriage, I mean... People can gossip a bit too much sometimes and think the worst of people, even if they've known them a long time.'

'Yes, I'm sorry to say that two people came in and cancelled their orders. They could easily have called instead, but chose to come in and make a point of telling me they didn't trust my baking any longer. I'm not sure what I'll do if they come back, wanting to buy from me again.' Phil tried to smile, but it was a poor effort. The customers were particularly rude, but he didn't want to give Marie and Matthew the full details. It would only upset them. A few others had cancelled their orders as well.

'You'd have every right to refuse to deal with them,' answered Matthew, frowning.

'Yes, but then they'd probably keep gossiping. It might be best to tell them that if they're happy to buy what I make, I'm happy to sell it to them. After all, they *were* very good customers, and to be quite honest, I wouldn't want to lose the income.'

Matthew made a face. 'Well, maybe give them one chance and say straight out that you were upset by their behaviour, but are prepared to forgive and forget.'

Phil shrugged. 'That *would* be the best thing to do, I suppose. I appreciate your support.'

Marie glanced at Matthew, who had reddened and was wondering if he should tell Phil what he had done. Still, if he confessed to the peacekeepers, his friend would know soon enough. Taking a deep breath, he decided he could trust Phil to keep it to himself. 'Phil,' he said, 'I've something rather embarrassing to tell you, but I want your word not to tell anyone else, at least for the time being.'

Phil stared at him. 'Why, what is it?'

'I'm the one who set fire to the fields at Narre Warren. I was so upset, and sure the damned bread caused the miscarriage...sorry...and sure too we'd never be given another chance to be parents. I haven't told the peacekeepers yet, but I probably should.'

Phil gaped at Matthew, speechless.

'Yes, I'm a fool, I know,' said Matthew, still blushing. 'The burning Statue of Liberty image sent to everyone's comlink popped into my head and I just couldn't forget it... Not that it's any excuse. If I hadn't set fire to the fields, I might have done something else, equally stupid. It was such a relief, though, when I stood there, watching the flames. I've never felt anything quite like it before.' He shook his head, still amazed at how he could have done it, but also at how much he enjoyed himself. 'Never again, Phil, never again!'

'I should bloody well hope not! Do you want me to come with you...to see the peacekeepers, I mean?' Phil's blue eyes were open wide in concern, and his freckled features, usually full of good humour, showed his dismay at his friend's actions.

'No, but thanks. I'd better face up to this alone. What do you think, Marie?' Matthew turned to her, half hoping she would suggest he take Phil with him.

'I agree. You should do this alone. You can always suggest they speak to Phil later if they want a character witness...though you're well known in the community, so I don't really see that as a problem. Thanks for the offer, Phil,' she added, with a gentle, sad smile. 'It's good of you to want to stand by him, particularly under the circumstances.'

Phil nodded, then stood up. 'I'd better get back to the bakery. My apprentices may have remembered that blasted message too and chosen to accidentally burn the place down! Only kidding! When will you be allowed to go home, Marie?'

'Either tomorrow or the next day,' she replied. 'I'm sure I'll be better soon.'

Phil leant over to kiss her on the cheek, then patted her shoulder and left.

After Jonathon had reported his findings to the local peacekeepers and verified that he intended to search Matthew Robertson's house and outbuildings, he checked Matthew's comlink signal to see where he currently was, which, according to the public transport records, turned out to be on his way home, most likely from the medcentre in Berwick. He decided to meet him at his house and estimated that it should be feasible to arrive five minutes before his suspect did.

'Aaron,' he called out to one of his fellow guardians, 'we should leave. It looks as if Matthew Robertson's been visiting his bondmate, Marie, and is now on his way back to Narre Warren.'

'Sure, I'll be right with you,' replied Aaron, a young man in his early thirties, but already a seasoned firefighter and experienced investigator. He carried his coffee mug to the servery and put it into the washing unit, then picked up three wheatmeal biscuits to eat on the way. Stuffing one unceremoniously into his mouth, he picked up his evidence kit and nodded at Jonathon to say he was ready to go. Ten minutes later, their airjet landed on the trafficway, not far from Matthew and Marie's home. They walked to its greenhouse entrance and waited.

Shortly afterwards, Matthew stepped out from the light railcar as it reached the callstation a hundred metres or so from his property. He was startled to see first the airjet, then the two forest guardians waiting for him. 'Damn!' he muttered to himself. 'They've found out before I could tell them. Damn and blast it!' Biting his lip, he gave a sigh of exasperation, but straightened his broad shoulders and walked up to them, with his hand out.

'Hello,' he said. 'Have you come to arrest me?'

By instinct, Jonathon had shaken Matthew's hand, so felt slightly embarrassed as he answered, 'Quite possibly. We have a warrant to search your premises for a pair of gloves that may have been worn while the person who set fire to the Federation's research fields in Narre Warren was applying solvent as an accelerant.' When Matthew looked away, without saying anything, Jonathon continued: 'We've retrieved an empty container of this particular solvent from the Pakenham recycling plant, and it has your fingerprints on it. Do you have anything to say before we search for the gloves, and do you want a Witness present, other than my colleague, Aaron?' Jonathon gestured at Aaron, who, unsmiling and with a stern expression on his sun-browned face, gazed fixedly at Matthew.

Matthew returned Aaron's gaze, then shook his head. 'No, I assume you'll record everything, which is good enough for the time being, as long as you give me a copy of the recording.' When Jonathon agreed, Matthew said, 'Good. In that case, I'll show you where I keep my gloves, and you might as well know now, it was me. I did it, and I've already told my bondmate, Marie, as well as the baker, Phil, who made the bread I thought caused Marie's miscarriage. That's why I did it, you see. I thought the Federation's bread killed our little boy. You've heard about it, I suppose?' He hunched his shoulders, and without being aware of it, glared at both Jonathon and Aaron.

'Yes,' replied Jonathon, 'we know what happened, but it's no excuse for what you did, is it.'

Matthew shook his head, narrowing his lips and looking down for a moment. 'No, it isn't, but I wasn't myself, and all I could think about was our Benjamin, dead.' Sighing, he ran a work-roughened hand over his face. 'Alright, come on. This way...' He turned and led the two guardians to the toolshed, where he soon found the gloves used to protect his hands while he lit the fire. 'Here, take them. You'll probably find some of the solvent on them... It's hard to use the stuff without spilling a bit,' he added, irrelevantly, but somehow needing to talk.

Aaron held out an evidence bag and Matthew put the gloves into it. 'You can probably smell it,' he said. Aaron sniffed the gloves. 'Yes, I can,' he replied, 'but we'll still need to formally identify it for the records.'

'We want you to come with us to the Ferntree Gully Reconciliation Centre for a formal interview,' said Jonathon, with a certain amount of sympathy in his voice. 'There'll be a Witness present throughout. It's a requirement, and before the interview begins, we'll give you a copy of this recording.'

Matthew nodded, then walked to the airjet, with a guardian at each side and wondering what would happen to him once the charges were laid.


Later that day, thoughts of an entirely unfamiliar kind were running through Karla's mind as she indulged herself in a long, hot bath in the communal house's spa and sauna room. She preferred living in a communal setting, rather than in a house or apartment of her own, because she enjoyed the company of the other residents. It also meant there was virtually no domestic work to be done...which left more time for her research and friends. Sighing with pleasure, she stretched out one long, shapely leg, ran the soapy sponge down its length, then lowered her leg into the wonderfully fragrant water and raised the other to do the same. Holding her breath, she then sank down to wet her hair, sat up again, and massaged in some of the rose petal shampoo Søren had given her, working it into a fluffy head of bubbles and laughing softly as she imagined what it would look like: a pompadour hairstyle! With a giggle, she settled back to let the shampoo work its magic and allowed herself another indulgence: Karla thought about what it might be like if someone was to share her rooms here – Jonathon, for example. Like her, he preferred the lifestyle of a communal house, and his was convenient to his workplace in Ferntree Gully, just as hers was to Willsmere. Perhaps they could compromise and find one they both liked, midway between?

Karla scooped up some bubbles and blew them into the air, watching as they settled back into the water. 'You're getting a little ahead of yourself, my girl,' she murmured. 'You've only had dinner with him, nothing else...so far.'

Her bath was interrupted by the chime of her comlink, lying within easy reach on a small ledge nearby. 'Drat!' thought Karla, but dutifully picked it up and answered, forgetting for a moment where she was. She hastily turned off the visual option just as a startled Jonathon gawked at her from the small screen. 'Sorry,' she spluttered, trying hard not to laugh. 'I didn't mean to give you a fright! I'm having a bath, which I don't do very often...which sounds equally weird, but you know what I mean!'

Jonathon chortled, but managed to say, 'Yes, Karla, I could tell you wash yourself, and if you don't mind me saying so, the bubbles are awfully cute. Do you want me to wait while you rinse them off? I gather shampoo shouldn't be left on too long.' He smothered another chuckle and added, 'I could call back later if you like?'

'No, no, I don't mind if you don't. But you're right; I'd better rinse this off. Won't be long.' Karla placed the comlink back onto its ledge and ducked down beneath the water, then used the flexible shower arm to rinse her hair properly. Smoothing it away from her face, she lay back again and picked up the comlink. 'That's better. I can concentrate now.' Karla grinned, but made sure to leave the comlink on audio only, even though it was tempting not to.

'I'm not sure *I* can,' replied Jonathon, 'though I'll do my best.' He paused while Karla chuckled, then said, 'I know who lit the fire. It was Matthew Robertson, and he's been charged and released on bail. I'll enter all the evidence into the Judge before I go home and then we'll wait and see whether it decides to hold a public trial or simply delivers a determination. The case may be straightforward enough to avoid a trial, though I'm not certain; it depends a bit on the evidence entered by the psychologist who'll be talking to Matthew tomorrow morning. Either way, they'll arrange counselling for him, and also for Marie. It's a bad situation, but with a bit of luck, they may be all right. At least the fire didn't hurt anyone, and Matthew seems to understand how serious the crime was. He did say, though, that it didn't enter his mind to even think about others being harmed, which isn't good.'

Karla listened without interrupting. When Jonathon had finished, she said, 'I'm so sorry to hear it was him. They've gone through enough, losing the baby, without this as well. I hope there isn't a trial. It'd be better for everyone if it was dealt with quietly. Do you think it would help if I put in a recommendation to the Judge along those lines?'

'Yes, I do. It's a good thought. Also, Matthew told us it was that image of the burning Statue of Liberty which put the notion into his head, and the fewer people who hear that, the better, as far as I'm concerned. We don't want anyone else who's in a fragile state of mind getting similar ideas...or for that matter, someone seeing it as a good excuse to try a bit of arson themselves, then plead they were depressed and this was their way of dealing with it!'

'Do you really think that might happen?' asked Karla, shocked, having thought more about saving Matthew and Marie the anxiety of a trial than the possible repercussions. Also, a trial could take up far too much of her and other people's time, given there might be quite a number who were called to give evidence and attend.

'Oh yes. People have all sorts of fixations with fire. Its appeal is very strong...primeval. Until we're out of the fire danger season, I won't be taking time off unless I have to, and most of the other guardians are putting in extra voluntary hours too. It's hot out there, and dry. The forecast is for more of the same as well. All we need is one windy day and the whole mountainside could go up, let alone all the grassfires that might start elsewhere.'

'You're right, unfortunately. It's different for us, here in Kew, where it's a lot safer, although we do have a large area of bushland around Willsmere to maintain. It's well protected, though, and we have additional security over summer, just in case.'

'Yes, the more urbanised regions are a bit easier to deal with compared to these huge areas of forest and grassland. It's one of the reasons no one lives on the mountain any more...too hard to protect. Also, the fewer people out here, the less chance of accidents starting fires.'

'It's a grim subject, for sure,' answered Karla, who was beginning to think it was time to get out of the bath before she turned into a prune! 'Jonathon,' she added, 'would you mind holding again while I get out and dry myself?'

'Yes, I can wait.'

'Thanks.' Karla, put down the comlink and stepped carefully out of the water. She dried herself with a large, fluffy, red towel, luxuriating in its soft warmth despite the topic of their conversation, then hung it neatly on a rack to dry before picking up her comlink. 'Still there? I won't be long. I'll put on some clothes, and we can talk. It's almost dinnertime though.'

'That's fine,' replied Jonathon, enjoying the sound of her voice. It was unusual to have a conversation with visual turned off. Most people in circumstances like this remembered to tell their comlink to announce they were unavailable and to give an estimate for when the caller could try again. Either Karla was being absentminded or unusually conscientious. He guessed the latter, or perhaps even both.

'I'm back,' he heard her say. 'Good,' he replied. 'What's for dinner over there?'

Karla turned her comlink back to visual, smiled, and said, 'I haven't a clue. I just look at the menu when I get to the dining room. Why?'

'Oh, I was wondering if I should come over, have dinner, then come back here and work for a bit longer. It's probably more travel time than I can afford, but it's tempting.'

'You're right, it is, but I promised to call a friend this evening, and besides, you'd never forgive yourself if something happened while you were away. Also, if you came over, I'm not sure how easy it would be to have only a quick dinner.'

'No, I guess not. I'd want to stay on... I know I would.' Jonathon stared at Karla, suddenly aware of just how much he'd want to stay. He felt his face colour and hoped she wouldn't notice.

Karla pretended not to see the change in Jonathon's expression and the blush, but she felt her own face colour and her heart begin to race. In a slightly husky voice, she said, 'I'd want you to stay too... But there's something I haven't told you. I have a cat, and so you need to meet her.' She recovered herself and added, 'I hope you're not allergic to them, or have some weird dislike of cats?'

Surprised not to have heard about the cat already, Jonathon said, 'No, not as far as I'm aware, but I don't know much about them. In fact, I can't remember meeting more than one, and that was a long time ago. What's yours like and why is it so important I meet her?' He was genuinely puzzled and also a little upset by this rather strange, as he saw it, stipulation.

'Cats are extraordinary creatures, Jonathon, and the relationship we have with them is as close as that of a bondmate, although not the same, of course.' Karla hesitated, wondering how much he knew about their powers. When he nodded but didn't comment, she said, 'Did you know they're telepathic? The link with their human companion is extremely close. As far as I'm aware, only a deep trauma could break it.'

'Yes, I've heard they have special abilities, but as I've never experienced the effect, or known anyone who has, I have to admit that I didn't fully appreciate how exceptional they are. How did you come to have one, and what's her name?'

'She's called Aurora, and she came to live with me almost four years ago when a close friend, who had a terminal illness, needed someone to care for her after he died. I had more than a year to get to know Aurora beforehand. Fortunately, she was able to transfer her affections to me, so didn't have to be returned to the Breeding Centre at Werribee. It was still a very difficult time for us all, though.' Karla looked away for a moment, remembering her friend's last hours and how, after he died, Aurora had wailed in deepest sorrow, refusing to eat for several days, sleeping on her dead companion's bed and only drinking a little water now and then, before staggering back to her sanctuary. It was only when they held the funeral and Karla managed to persuade Aurora to leave the apartment to attend it with her that she finally accepted her companion was truly gone.

'Who was your friend?' asked Jonathon, deciding he should do some reading about cats before he met Karla in person again.

'His name was Rohan Maerz. He was the coordinator of the Federation Special Investigation Unit and lived in Switzerland until he moved to Australia shortly before he retired. It's an awfully long story, but we met about six years ago when he was supervising the investigation into the attacks on Willsmere and a number of other sites conducting similar research. Have you heard of the case? It was quite famous.'

'Yes, vaguely, but I must admit we have so much to keep us busy here that I don't have time to read as many of the news reports as I should. You'll have to tell me more about it next time we meet. I gather you were closely involved?'

'Oh yes, I certainly was! The friend I mentioned earlier, who I intend to call this evening, was as well. We were working together on a joint research project. He's a zoologist from Greenland by the name of Søren Thorup and he's here at my request to do some work in your forests. You may have come across his name recently.'

'Yes, I have, actually. We need to be informed of any projects being undertaken here. He's the fellow looking into the spider problem, isn't he? But your name wasn't on the Federation request or I'd have remembered.'

'No, that's true, it wasn't. We needed to get him out of Greenland, where he'd been snowed in for ages, and the only way it could be done was to use my influence within the Federation government to get their help to bring him here. At the same time, to expedite matters, they put through the request.' Karla laughed, remembering the expression on Søren's face when she first called him in his snowbound house. 'He has a cat too,' she added. 'Dandelion. She'd have been on the request form as well, I suppose?'

'She was, and I must admit to being intrigued. Still, one thing I do know about cats is that they're vegetarian and don't go about killing small creatures the way their ancestors did. He wouldn't have been given permission to take her into the forest otherwise.'

'No, but Dandelion isn't going into the forest with him any longer. She took an instant dislike to Aurora when she and I first went in there with them and they had a huge fight. I've never seen anything like it! Fur flying everywhere, screaming and spitting. They were both looking very sorry for themselves by the time we managed to separate them, and since then, we've decided it'd be best for Dandelion to be taken care of by someone else while Søren's working. It seems she was frightened by the idea of meeting the spiders, and also of coming across a snake, which of course is quite possible at this time of year. You see, Aurora made the mistake of telling her about the snakes she'd seen around Willsmere, which is when Dandelion attacked.

'Still, it's dinnertime and I'm getting hungry, so must go...sorry. Perhaps, if you have time, I could meet you for midsun tomorrow? I want to see Marie in the morning and afterwards talk to some people who, once they heard the gossip about her miscarriage, ended up refusing to eat the rye bread sample we gave them for the tasting trial. It's all rather a problem, because it means our results won't be as complete as we'd like. We'll need to use another group from somewhere else for the next trial. The locals might not want to eat our bread again, even if Marie's losing the baby wasn't our fault.' Karla grimaced.

'Right, well, that's a wonderful suggestion about meeting up at midsun, but I'm really sorry to hear about the paranoids. What a pity! Maybe the staff and students at Melbourne University's School of Agriculture could taste your next batch?'

'Excellent suggestion. Thanks! I'll definitely look into the possibility, but now, I really must go. Aurora's hungry too. She's calling me, so see you tomorrow at about 12:00. Let me know where you'd like to meet.' Karla closed the connection, put the comlink into her pocket and walked back to her rooms to fetch Aurora.

In Ferntree Gully, before going home, Jonathon tidied his workstation, all the while grinning as he remembered the sight of Karla in the bath and delighted she wanted to meet again so soon.

## CHAPTER FOURTEEN

After discussing the Swedish team leader's progress with Welcome, Morag MacIain decided to pay Kaj a visit, and at the same time see for herself how Yngwie was managing. By choice, and despite Kaj's earlier complaints about long shifts, the two men were working a twelve-hour day. Joining them for something to eat seemed less intimidating than interrupting their work to ask how they were getting along, and since the dining room for staff and official visitors at Melbourne's Central Computer Site began serving the evening meal at 18:00, this was the time they agreed to meet.

Once Morag's transport arrived at the callstation nearest to the computer site, situated in Clayton, she walked the short distance to its security entrance. There, she was greeted by the gatekeeper, a young woman in her late twenties. Morag was familiar with the centre from the time of the Willsmere investigation, six years ago, and still had personal contacts at the site. She fondly remembered the elderly man who, until recently, held the position of gatekeeper and regretted he was no longer there. However, the new incumbent greeted her with a smile, and when Morag introduced herself, warmly shook hands, saying, 'It's an honour to meet you, Coordinator MacIain. Our systems should all recognise you, but if there are any issues at all, I'll be happy to sort them out.'

'Thank you. I'm sure everything will go smoothly, but it's always good to know we have someone like you on hand.' Morag returned the smile then glanced at the retina scanner. When the gates opened for her, she gave the young woman a farewell grin and went inside.

The dining room was off to one side of the centre's solarium; a place designed to accommodate the entire workforce if social occasions required, but which also had well-furnished alcoves for private pastimes and other forms of entertainment. A small fountain, built as a visual focal point, provided a pleasant background sound, while the solarium's magnificent polished timber floor gave the space an undeniable feeling of luxury. The whole area was lit by natural sunlight coming in through a vast, beautifully designed, plastiglass dome of multicoloured panels, which created an overall effect of warmth and comfort.

Being familiar with the solarium, Morag soon found the dining room, where she scanned the small crowd for Kaj and Yngwie. As it turned out, they were sitting at the same table and appeared to be reading the menu. At least they didn't seem to be avoiding each other, thought Morag, relieved. As she approached, a familiar mental tone made her quicken her stride, and when she was about four metres away, a white form dashed out from beneath the table, almost knocking her over. 'Dandelion!' she exclaimed. 'What are you doing here?'

The cat stood up to place her paws on Morag's midriff, purring excitedly, and was rewarded with a kiss on the forehead. 'Is Søren here as well?' asked Morag, looking around the dining room.

In the meantime, Yngwie had risen to his feet to stare at them in amazement, while Kaj, mouth open and eyes wide, stared too. After answering Morag's question, Dandelion pranced joyfully back and forth, tail high, then capered over to Yngwie, twining herself around his legs.

Morag laughed, and when she was close enough said, 'Hello! Dandelion tells me that Søren is here in Melbourne, and while he's out and about, you're looking after her. What an astonishing coincidence! You told me about the cat, Yngwie, but not that she wasn't yours... Where did you meet Søren? Ah, Dandelion's already informed me... At the communal house in Ferntree Gully, where you're both staying. I must call him after dinner!' Morag quickly looked at Kaj and was relieved to see he had finally stopped staring at her and was doing his best to adjust to the situation.

'I didn't know you knew Søren Thorup,' said Yngwie, sitting down and stroking Dandelion, who now sat by his knee, still purring loudly.

'Oh yes, we've been friends for some time and often visit each other. Well, well... Tell me, Yngwie, does he know what you've done and what you're working on now?' Morag held his gaze while he replied.

'Yes, he does, as a matter of fact, but he didn't tell me he knew you.' Yngwie glanced at Kaj and shrugged. Would he accept this and not hold it against him?

'No, under the circumstances, he *wouldn't* tell you,' replied Morag, with a slight smile. 'Instead, he'd leave you to my mercy, without interfering. Still, he must have confidence in you to allow you to look after Dandelion. It says a great deal about your character. Cats don't generally like people who aren't, what shall we say...'honourable' is as good a word as any.'

Embarrassed, Yngwie blushed, but was nevertheless pleased to hear Morag say something complimentary. However, he chose not to elaborate any further. Best to leave Søren to explain when he and Morag spoke together.

'Perhaps we should order our meal, then talk more while we eat?' suggested Kaj, reasonably enough.

'Yes, good idea,' agreed Morag. 'I came by public transport simply for the enjoyment of the trip,' she added, just to make conversation. 'It's so lovely out here, with all the natural bushland and parks. Such a contrast to my home in Luzern, where everything is so civilised and orderly.' She smiled. 'Still, that has its advantages. I have a house on The Rigi and the view from my greenhouse is superb. Yngwie, you'd understand, coming from Norway. Mountains like ours have soul... And what about you, Kaj? Where's your home?'

Kaj looked up from the menu and said, 'In a small town in southern Sweden...Ljungby. It is a pleasant, quiet place to live.' Standing up, he added, 'If you have chosen what you wish to eat, I can place your orders together with mine, if you like.'

'Thank you,' answered Morag. 'I'll have the cheese omelette with mushrooms, the garden salad, a pot of jasmine tea, and the chocolate cake for dessert.'

'And you?' said Kaj, turning to Yngwie.

'The grilled salmon with steamed carrots and new potatoes in dill sauce sounds good, and I'll have the chocolate cake too...and a mineral water.'

Dandelion looked up from her place by Yngwie's knee and, to Kaj's astonishment, told him she wanted a bowl of water and the cheese omelette.

'She spoke to me!' he gasped.

Morag stifled a giggle, but Yngwie laughed out loud. 'Did she now!' he managed to say at last. 'Well, she must like you.'

Shaking his head, Kaj went to the servery to place their orders, then brought back a plate of assorted nuts and slices of fresh fruit for them to eat while they waited...plus a bowl of water for Dandelion. Thirsty, she lapped eagerly, while Kaj watched, for the first time considering the possibility that cats might not be so out of place here after all. When she finished, he put out a hand to gingerly touch her, then quickly withdrew when she raised her head...and was almost lost for words as he 'heard' her thank him for the water.

'They're like people,' he whispered, more to himself than the others.

'They're not like humans, really,' answered Morag, appreciating what he must feel at this first real encounter with a cat. 'They're very much themselves, but have extraordinary abilities, which we're still learning about. Some of the cats even work with the peacekeepers now. Did you know that, Kaj?'

'No! Do they indeed? What do they do?'

'They help us interview suspects, and sometimes work as guardians when someone needs to be protected. They can be fierce enough if they want to be.'

Yngwie nodded, but still chose not to tell Morag about Dandelion's earlier behaviour. He didn't want Kaj to know, and didn't want to embarrass Dandelion, either. If Søren wanted to tell Morag, that would be his decision.

'I see!' answered Kaj, impressed.

At this point, their food arrived and silence reigned while they began eating. Kaj had chosen a fragrant pumpkin risotto, accompanied by a tomato, onion and cucumber salad and a mineral water. 'Mmm...' he said, with his mouth full. 'This is delicious!'

'I think I'll enjoy working here!' agreed Yngwie, after swallowing a mouthful of the salmon.

'I'm glad to hear it,' said Morag, raising an eyebrow as she poured herself a cup of the green tea. 'We expect you'll benefit from the experience, and possibly even learn something.'

'I hope so,' replied Yngwie, in earnest. 'I know you can't give me full security access to your systems, that would be too much to expect, but working in a professional environment like this will be good, and perhaps, once I finish my degree, I'll be able to earn the trust of the Federation. Otherwise, my future in information technology won't be too bright.'

'No, Yngwie, which you may not have fully understood until now,' replied Morag, serious again. 'You won't be given high enough security clearance to work independently in a centre like this for quite some time. You're under close supervision working with Kaj and the rest of the team, and I suggest you accept the situation.'

'I do, truly.' Yngwie glanced at Kaj. 'I'll do my best. You have my word.'

He sounded so young as he said this, Morag almost felt sorry for him, but only briefly. Young he might be, but he and Torleif had planned the cascade down to the finest detail and with professional expertise. It would be a very long time indeed before either of them would be trusted with access to secure sections of the lattice by anyone, let alone the Federation. The official notation on his Federation record would make sure of that.

'Søren!'

'Morag!'

'You're in Melbourne!'

'Yes I am, and so are you, I see.' Søren smiled, his dark grey eyes crinkling at the corners, his angelic features still as beautiful as when Morag last spoke to him, four months ago. However, she noticed the smile held a hint of sadness, and wondered.

'I've just had dinner with your young Norwegian friend, Yngwie,' she said, 'and I gather you're both staying at the communal house in Ferntree Gully – but why is he looking after Dandelion? I'd have thought Melbourne was a safe enough place for her to be with you when you went out and about. And why are you here, anyway? You haven't been to Melbourne in years!'

'I am hunting spiders for Karla after one of her colleagues, a seed gatherer, was bitten by a species that didn't seem to be the usual type found in the forests here. Karla very kindly rescued us from starvation in Greenland, so I am doing my best to track down the culprit...a funnel-web, we suspect, and a big one. I have already discovered there is almost a plague of them.' Søren grinned as Morag grimaced.

'Truly? Here in Melbourne? I didn't know they lived this far south.'

'No one did, but it appears they have slowly migrated and are now at a level where we will almost certainly issue a public warning. Thankfully, the young man who was bitten has recovered very nicely. Also, the medcentres all carry anti-venom, so, in theory, the spiders pose little danger, unless someone has the misfortune not to get to a medcentre quickly enough or has an allergic reaction. Of course,' Søren added, 'the bite hurts rather a lot.'

'Yes, I can imagine, and luckily I've never been bitten by anything like it. It's one of the advantages of living, at least part of the time, in Switzerland. We don't have nasties like them!'

'No, true, but you don't have these wonderful forests either.'

'You're right, and I wish I could spend a little time in them while I'm here, but unfortunately, I need to get back fairly soon. It's probably for the best; I must admit it's far too hot for me at the moment. Now what's this about your starving in Greenland? Isn't that a bit dramatic?'

'No, we truly were at the point of running out of food, after being snowed in for what seemed like forever. Even Dandelion was becoming hungry, which may account to some extent for her bad temper when we first went into the forest together. Karla and Aurora came with us, and I don't like telling you this, but Dandelion attacked Aurora.' Søren went on to relate the whole story, finishing with Yngwie's offer to take care of the cat. 'So you see, although Yngwie may have done something that caused you and many others quite a lot of bother, he seems to be a remarkably useful young man.'

'I agree on both counts, and he's certainly likeable,' said Morag. 'We've restricted his lattice access, though. I wouldn't risk trusting him yet.'

'No, I suspect that's wise. I don't believe there's any harm in him, when it comes down to it, but who knows what temptation might lead him into? However, there's more to tell, which may help you trust him. Yngwie was the one who rescued the seed gatherer who was bitten by the spider. This was even after a fire began nearby, heading straight for them.'

'Really? Well, he kept that to himself, which I must give him credit for.'

'Yes, you should, because I've noticed he avoids boasting about anything he does.'

'Who was the person bitten?'

'A young fellow named Shahid. He was inspecting the mountain ash and has plans to collect seed in winter; it seems the trees have been flowering well this year. I must say, the forest looks wonderful at the moment, so if you do have the chance after all, you should take a walk. We could even have a picnic, if you wanted?'

'It sounds marvellous, but I'll have to say no. Still, we must catch up. I'm just not sure when.'

'Well, let me know and I shall fit in with your schedule.'

'I will, but now, I'm sorry to say, I'll have to go. It's good to talk to you again, and I hope everything goes well with your project. Before I leave Melbourne, I'll give Karla a call too.' Morag paused, then said, 'Come to think of it, though, perhaps we could meet at Willsmere, for midsun or afternoon tea? I could manage to be there for a little while, I'm sure.'

'What about tomorrow, then, or Sunday?' suggested Søren eagerly.

'Yes, that should work. I'll ask Karla, and call back.' Morag smiled, then closed the connection.


Karla had barely finished speaking with Morag, with an agreement to meet on the Sunday, when Yngwie called, looking apprehensive and slightly red in the face.

'Why hello, Yngwie!' said Karla, putting on a stern expression to tease him. 'I gather you now have a criminal record. Should I even be speaking with you?'

'Probably not,' replied Yngwie, with a shamefaced grin. 'I hope our shared ancestry will help overcome some of the feelings you may have towards me and what I've done.' He opened his eyes wide and gazed earnestly at her.

'I think it'd take more than that, don't you?' said Karla, frowning – then ruined the effect by laughing. 'I...I'm sorry,' she gasped at last. 'You look so funny, trying to win me over. I suppose just about everyone has already told you that you and your friend Torleif are idiots, and presumably Søren has passed on my earlier comment, so I won't add anything further to the chorus. Anyway, oddly enough, I understand why you did it.'

'Seriously? You do?'

'Yes, I do. Some years ago, when one of our scientists here at Willsmere was attacked one night, I and the others working with me, including Søren, became closely involved in what turned out to be a very long and complex investigation. During the investigation, some of the senior members of the FSIU were under suspicion and it became difficult to know whom we could trust and whom we couldn't. I can easily see how it'd be even harder for an outsider, someone like you, to know who to go to and be sure your information didn't fall into the wrong hands, given how sensitive it is. For all you knew, the flaw you found could have been created on purpose.'

Yngwie stared at Karla, then blinked and said, 'That possibility never crossed our minds, I must admit. We just didn't want to run the risk of someone realising they could exploit it...or for that matter, be charged for what we'd done before we had the chance to speak with the most senior people in the FSIU.'

'In that respect, I'm glad your plan worked. I know Morag MacIain well, and so does Søren. She was involved in the Willsmere investigation, and you can be certain that you couldn't be dealing with a better person. Also, her technical expertise in security matters is of the highest order, so any work you do for her will be highly appreciated.'

'Ah, I see! You already know what's happened, don't you.' It was Yngwie's turn to laugh, briefly, and at his own expense.

'Yes, but don't assume either Søren or I put in a good word for you,' said Karla, now solemn, all laughter forgotten. 'We didn't. That would have been dishonest. You needed to stand on your own merits and deal with whatever Morag decided to do. After all, whatever your motives were, it's still a serious crime. We've already suffered one potentially dangerous local incident – the fire at Narre Warren – which to some extent was inspired by your cascade. You've heard about it, haven't you?'

'I have, yes. The peacekeepers came to see if it was me who started it. Luckily, I had Laurita as an alibi. However, that was the main reason I called. I wanted to apologise. Your fields were the ones burnt, weren't they?'

'Yes, and at first I was rather shocked. Luckily, we can adapt our plans and use the fields in the condition they're in...as an additional type of trial for our next crop...but it still puts us behind, and at some point, the person who set the fire has to face the Judge. It turns out he's someone I know well, so I'm not at all happy about the situation. Mind you, I have to be frank and say that he can't lay all the blame at your doorstep. After all, you didn't force him to do what he did. It was his own choice.'

'What do you think will happen to him?' asked Yngwie, grateful for Karla's forgiving attitude.

'I don't know. Arsonists tend to be dealt with quite severely, but the circumstances here are unusual, so the Judge might be relatively lenient. We'll simply have to wait and see.'

'I suppose so. Thank you, Karla. I hope we can still be friends, and I'll do my best to earn Coordinator MacIain's trust and respect over the next few months, before I return to Norway to begin university. I'm fortunate, it seems... They'll let me go home to continue my studies.'

'Yes, you've been incredibly lucky, Yngwie. Someone else may have dealt far more harshly with you. Anyway, keep in touch, and perhaps we can get together again fairly soon. We still have our ancestors to trace.'

Karla smiled and Yngwie returned the smile, liking her even more now than when they first met.

'Agreed,' he said. 'I'll send you a trace of mine so you can compare it with yours, if you have time.'

'I'll make time, but now, I'd best be off. We'll speak again soon.'

'I hope so. Goodnight, Karla.'

Yngwie turned to Dandelion and said, 'Well, puss, do you want to go home? I think we've worked enough for one day, don't you?'

Dandelion yawned, showing her long, sharp teeth, then leapt down from Kaj's workstation, where she had been sleeping since he went home an hour ago. Yngwie noticed the white hair on its surface, but with a grin, left it there. After burbling her approval, Dandelion, with tail in the air, preceded Yngwie down the long corridor and then outside into the night. The temperature had dropped considerably and the sky was clear and filled with stars. It felt wonderful to be outdoors again. Crickets were singing their evening song, while the air was scented with a mix of an almost citrus-like perfume with honeyed overtones, as well as the ever-present eucalyptus. Yngwie breathed it in, savouring the fragrance, and with Dandelion's enthusiastic agreement, chose to walk for several kilometres before stopping at a callstation to request transport for the remainder of the trip back to Ferntree Gully.

'I've written the words for a song, Shahid,' said Laurita, with a soft smile. 'Would you be willing to put it to music for me?' Taking a hand reader from her shoulder bag, Laurita opened the file and passed the reader to him. 'Tell me if you think anything should be changed,' she added, as he took it from her, returning the smile.

While he read, Laurita studied Shahid's profile, noticing again the long eyelashes and the curl of his dark hair as it brushed his cheek. A long, straight nose lent character to his otherwise gentle features, as did the well-defined chin and his beautiful, warm brown eyes. When he looked up, she quickly lowered her gaze for a moment, then said, 'What do you think?'

'It's wonderful! There's a classic, mystical quality in the words and phrasing, and it should be easy to set to music. Leave it with me for tonight and tomorrow, and I'll try to have something for you by Sunday, if you'd like to come here for afternoon tea?'

Yedda was sitting close to Shahid, studying them. Noticing a new tone in their relationship, she purred and settled into a more relaxed pose, one dainty paw over the other, blue eyes half closed in contentment, tail curled around her sleek silver-grey body. Shahid stroked her head, then turned to Laurita and said, 'In the meantime, will you read the song to me? If you don't mind, I'd like to record your voice. It will inspire me.' He tilted his head slightly to one side, smiling.

'Yes, I can read it for you,' replied Laurita, although hesitating, suddenly shy. Shahid returned the hand reader and she sent him a copy of the file, then began the song, her voice uncertain to begin with, but gaining confidence as she continued:

### SONG OF THE RAVEN

A raven's heart of silver
is mine to keep for you.
It dwells alone, in hidden realms
of night and misted vale,
where you and I did meet.

A raven's cry of heartbreak
is mine to give to you.
It cries alone, a song to sing
of starlit shores afar
where you and I once danced.

A raven's coat of darkness
is mine to cloak your dreams.
It flows and shimmers in the light
of dawning sunlight's kiss,
where you and I once lay.

A raven's flight of yearning
is mine to show to you.
It soars above all earthly cares
and flies to seek the place
where you and I once stood.

A raven's life of searching
is mine to share with you.
It has no end or sorrow,
yet finds no rest, nor land
where you and I can dwell.

A raven's heart of silver
is mine to hold for you.
It dwells alone, in hidden realms
of night and misted vale,
where you and I will meet.

142

They were both silent for almost half a minute, Laurita because she almost wished the song had never been written, and Shahid because he wondered who she wrote the song for. Yngwie? Possibly...but instead, was it for him? If so, it contained far more passion and longing than he felt ready to share...with anyone. His work, his parents, his faith, some good friends, and now Yedda, were more than enough for him to feel happy and fulfilled, while music provided sufficient stimulation when he wanted to indulge his creativity.

Puzzled, Yedda watched them both closely, 'listening', but resisting the temptation to probe Laurita's mind, beyond the surface feelings that were all too apparent. She sighed and rolled onto her side, wishing they would speak openly to each other and sort it out! Still, she was fast learning that wights were complex creatures, and, due to her fairly limited experience, were in many ways somewhat beyond her comprehension.

'You read well,' said Shahid, keeping his tone even and ever so slightly impersonal. 'Can you sing too?'

'Yes, but not as well as I would like, and not even as well as Karla. You'll need to keep the melody for the song fairly simple and neither too high nor too low.' Laurita noticed the tone of his voice and tried to moderate her own, although it was remarkably difficult. She slowed her breathing and asked, 'Shahid, have you ever fallen in love with anyone?'

He stared at her, his eyes wide, then shook his head. 'No...only the occasional infatuation, which never lasted long.' He shifted in his chair and looked away, wondering what on Earth she would say next!

'I have,' said Laurita, 'which is why I can write a song like this. So many places in the world hold an attraction and a meaning for me so profound that it has been important to share it with someone else, even if only briefly. Have you travelled much?'

'Not to other countries, though I can understand what you mean. The forests here are deeply important to me and there are other places in Australia equally wonderful and in need of our care. This is the love I value the most...the love I have for this good Earth, harsh though it can be at times.'

'And I share that! Yet I find it difficult always to be alone. My work takes me to strange and even dangerous places, and I rarely see my own parents or the people I knew from when I was still studying. There's no particular reason why – it has just happened that way. For me, there was always somewhere else to go, to explore, to learn from. I am a traveller, a true seed gatherer, but it is lonely. Karla is one of the few real friends I have now and it's a luxury to be here in Melbourne for this long. We often talk, of course, no matter where in the world I happen to be, but all the same, I do long for someone I can truly share my life with – at least, a good part of it. Don't you ever feel that way?'

'Not often,' replied Shahid. 'I still keep in contact with school and university friends, and feel I truly belong *here*. I'm lucky, I know. I've always thought that one day I might meet someone who I could share more with, but it's never been a priority.' He grinned. 'I guess having parents like mine, who I adore being with, has made a big difference. You must admit, our home is comfortable, too!'

Laurita had to smile, and tried to shake off her maudlin mood. Either two people were right for each other, or they weren't, and no amount of forcing the issue could change that. It would only lead to unhappiness. Still, there was also the point that people needed to take time to get to know each other, and sometimes this took work. From time to time, misunderstandings needed to be overcome as well, which was only natural, and sometimes love grew slowly as trust and mutual respect developed and common interests were explored.

'I need to be less impetuous this time,' thought Laurita, and said, 'Yes, I can certainly see why you'd be reluctant to change things! Wania and Shafiqur are marvellous people, and now that you have Yedda, there isn't anything at all you really miss. You are right to enjoy what you have and to let life take its course. If there ever comes a day when you feel differently, I am sure you will find your way.'

Relieved by the change in Laurita's tone and manner of speaking, Shahid changed the subject. 'Would you like to come with us when we visit the Breeding Centre on Tuesday afternoon? I'll have to ask their permission first, but they said we might be allowed to visit the Guardians if Yedda progresses well, which she has, in an incredibly short time. In the morning, if you like, we could go for that trip around the bay we missed.' Shahid turned to Yedda and fondled her ears. She leaned her head into his hand and smooched, while Laurita looked on, almost envious, but she knew, realistically, that her lifestyle did not lend itself to having a cat as a companion.

'Sorry,' said Shahid, as he turned back to her. 'What do you think? Would you like to come along? You could take part in our training. Yedda has to learn to only transmit to other people the thoughts I ask her to, and we had the idea that visiting these cats could be a special exercise; she'd have to make sure they didn't pick up on anything we didn't want them to. It's quite difficult, or so I've been told. It may take more than one session – we'll just have to wait and see.' He leaned eagerly towards Laurita, excited now by the possibility of having her there to add to the training session.

'I would love to be there to help,' she said, smiling broadly for the first time, 'and I'd adore to meet these Guardians. I've never heard of them before. Who are they?'

'I don't know much, but it seems they have something to do with peacekeeping. It's all very mysterious.' Shahid grinned. Yedda, who had laid her head on his lap, raised it to look into his face. 'They can be quite ferocious,' she told him, 'but I have never met them before, either.'

Startled, Shahid stared at her for a long moment, then said, only to her, 'You're not frightened, are you?'

'No,' she replied. 'I know they would never hurt me, or anyone else, unless it was necessary to protect someone.' Yedda sat up and Shahid put his arm around her, holding her close. Watching them, Laurita guessed they had been speaking to each other, and wondered.

Shahid suddenly yawned widely, covering his mouth with a hand, and then apologised. 'Sorry about that! It's getting late, and I need to be up early tomorrow morning to beat the heat, so I'll have to call it a night.' He stood up, and Laurita stood as well. 'We'll walk you to the callstation. It should have cooled off by now.'

They climbed the short flight of stairs leading to the greenhouse, and once outside, breathed in the fragrant night air, which was still warm compared to inside the house. The cicadas had begun another round in their evening chorus and the sound was almost deafening. They both grinned, immediately understanding what the other was thinking, then walked on in companionable silence until they reached the callstation. Taking a seat, Shahid said, 'We'll wait with you until the railcar arrives. It's lovely out here, even if it *is* noisy!'

Laurita sat down next to him. If it had been Yngwie instead of Shahid, she would have linked arms with him, quite naturally, but she now realised that doing so with Shahid was out of the question, at least for the foreseeable future.

## CHAPTER FIFTEEN

Marie held Karla's hand and said, 'I'm so glad your bread didn't kill our little Benjamin, Karla. It would have been dreadfully hard for you to deal with.' She smiled softly, but her lips trembled and she looked down to hide the sudden tears.

Karla, sitting by the bed, put her other hand over Marie's. 'Yes, it would have, but *I'm* glad to hear you and Matthew will apply to try again, and that the practitioner who treated you will endorse the application. You should have every chance of success. I've heard it's not uncommon for someone to have a miscarriage the first time and a perfectly normal pregnancy another time. At least they'll know what to watch for now and everything can be even more closely monitored. Though, Marie, you'll need to avoid becoming paranoid about the whole thing. That wouldn't do at all.'

'No, you're right, Karla, but it'll be awfully hard not to be. Perhaps I should call you if I start behaving like a neurotic! You always seem to make me feel better.' Marie pressed Karla's hand, saying, 'It must be almost time for you to go. Would you like some tea, or anything else, before you do?'

'Yes, thank you, I would.' Karla looked at her comlink to check the time. 'You're right, though, I *will* have to leave soon.'

Marie used her call button and before long an attendant came to take her order, soon returning with two pots of tea, a selection of sweet biscuits, and some fresh apricots. When Marie thanked him, the attendant gave her a quick smile and left them to enjoy their tea. They poured themselves a cup each and for several minutes sipped the hot, fragrant liquid in companionable silence, helping themselves to the juicy, sweet fruit.

'Oh, these are lovely!' exclaimed Marie. 'It's so good to be able to eat normally again. I was feeling rather off-colour before, but now I'm actually hungry!'

'Glad to hear it,' replied Karla, reaching for another apricot. 'Mmm... These *are* much better than usual.' She hastily wiped her chin as some of the juice escaped. 'I wonder if they have their own greenhouse. I suppose it's possible...' A distant wail only she could hear reminded her it was time to leave. Aurora, waiting in a small anteroom off the medcentre foyer, was evidently fed up with waiting!

'Alright, must go, even though I'd rather stay,' she said, standing up. 'Let me know when you're home again and I'll drop by to see you both.' Karla kissed Marie on the cheek and left, but turned around to grin and wave when Marie called out, 'Thanks again for the beautiful chocolates. I'll enjoy them!'

Aurora met Karla at the anteroom door, purring loudly and smooching as if it were days since they last saw each other. 'Oh, you're such a sweetie, aren't you, Aurora,' crooned Karla, as she gave the cat one last hug. 'Want to walk for a bit, or shall we take a railcar straight away?'

Never having taken a trip to this particular area before, Aurora made it clear she preferred to walk and bounded joyfully towards the front entrance, still relishing the freedom of not having a leash. Karla followed her out into the warm sunshine, where a slight breeze cooled their faces and brought them the delicious scent of the trafficway's living surface of bright blue flowers. Since there was only the occasional pedestrian and landjet, they both thoroughly enjoyed their peaceful surroundings while they walked.

The people they were to meet were the reluctant 'volunteers' who, after Marie's miscarriage, refused to continue taking part in the taste testing of the rye bread. Everyone had agreed to gather at the home of the least vocal of the 'dissidents', in Harkaway, about twenty minutes distant if they caught a railcar. To make sure of arriving on time, Karla stopped at the next callstation and entered their destination into its terminal, then sat down to wait. Several minutes later, they were on their way, Aurora standing next to Karla, gazing out the window and making small cat sounds when she saw something of interest, at the same time giving her companion a running 'commentary'. Used to her by now when they were in public, Karla had no problem answering Aurora without speaking aloud, although this art had taken some time to perfect. However, the hardest part was not to burst out laughing when Aurora 'said' something particularly amusing, being rather prone to commenting on people's appearance or behaviour. Earlier in their relationship, there were embarrassing moments when either fellow travellers or pedestrians stared pointedly at Karla, wondering why she was conducting an apparently one-sided conversation with her cat! Not everyone realised how often they tended to 'talk' to their companions.

When they arrived at their stop and were about to alight, Aurora happened to notice the animated conversation taking place amongst the people waiting for them inside the nearby house. She was particularly drawn to the vivid image in the mind of their host as he gazed in awe at one of the women and struggled to control his expression. Aurora showed

Karla what the woman looked like, then asked whether she was trying to imitate a parrot?

'*Please* don't do that once we're inside,' said Karla, holding a hand to her mouth to smother a giggle. 'I suppose she doesn't realise dark purple hair clashes with bright green cosmetic contact lenses, or that red shoes don't really go, either. She might just like lots of colour, puddums. Some people do – me for example – and it can often look surprisingly good. Not in this case? Oh well...'

Briefly giving in to the laughter as they walked towards the greenhouse entrance, Karla managed to control her expression and pressed a hand to its identification panel. Fortunately, when the door opened, the woman with the purple hair was not the one who greeted them. Instead, Antonio, the owner of the house, welcomed them, and with a touch of formality, said, 'Please, do come in, Researcher.'

Karla immediately noticed his gentle manner, slow, careful way of speaking, and unusually deep, mellow voice, which added distinction to his otherwise unremarkable appearance. 'The others are already here...downstairs,' he added, rather unnecessarily since it was obvious they weren't gathered in the small greenhouse. 'Perhaps you would follow me?'

The others, three women, were sitting around a small table and turned towards them as they approached. One of them stood and held out her hand. 'Hello, I don't think we've met. My name's Cynthia and this is Abhaya.' She indicated a tall dark-haired woman, who also stood up to greet Karla, then turned to the third woman, the one with the purple hair, and said, 'This is Afina.'

Without getting up, Afina smirked and held out a hand. Karla tried hard not to flinch at the ice-cold, flaccid handshake, and quickly released her grip. 'Hello,' she replied, smiling. 'This is Aurora.' Afina glanced at the cat but took no further notice, whereas Cynthia held out her hand to be sniffed. Aurora gave it a quick lick, then studied all the new faces, probing their surface thoughts. Deciding her companion had no need of any assistance in dealing with them, she twitched her tail and settled down in a corner of the room to listen, head resting on her front paws.

When they all sat down, Cynthia, Abhaya and Antonio turned expectantly to Karla, who began by saying, 'I asked you to meet me here because, instead of speaking with each of you individually, it's easier to explain the situation in person to everyone at the same time. You might have questions others have too, and your being here together may bring something to mind that you feel needs to be discussed properly as a group.'

Before Karla could continue, she was interrupted by Afina. 'You should never have given the bread to a pregnant woman to try.' She tossed her head, then said, in her high-pitched voice, 'I know the

Ferntree Gully medcentre has announced it had nothing to do with her miscarriage, but as far as I'm concerned, they're just covering up for your blunder!'

With these last words, her voice rose even higher, and when Aurora covered her face with one paw, Karla noticed, but managed not to smile. Taking a conciliatory tone, she said, 'Do you honestly believe the Federation would stoop to deceive the public like that? What would be the point?'

Afina's face reddened as she leaned back in her chair, sneering. 'To make sure their shiny reputation isn't tarnished, of course! To make everybody think that what is virtually a dictatorship, is in everyone's interests, and to keep us all quiet. This isn't a real democracy, and anyone who believes it is, is a fool!'

Astounded by her words, Karla almost gaped at the woman, but managed to remain calm, replying as if she took her views seriously. 'I know the Federation Assembly may at times seem remote to most of us, and there are sometimes too many layers of bureaucracy to deal with when we want to approach them, but I assure you, we take our research very seriously and would never do anything to compromise its integrity. All our studies are available on the lattice, too, once the results have been finalised and gone through peer review. You're welcome to read anything you like about the work we've done up to date, and if you wanted to, you'd be welcome to tour either Willsmere or the Narre Warren facility.' Karla smiled pleasantly and waited, but Afina merely narrowed her eyes, then pursed her mouth and looked away, studying her bright red fingernails.

The others stared at Afina, startled by her outburst, but after a few moments, Cynthia said, '*I'd* like to tour your facilities. I'm sure it'd be fascinating. Who do we see to arrange it?'

'You can contact the gatekeeper at either place and they'll make sure you see whatever you wish, other than secure areas which need to be kept under sterile conditions, for example, or which house sensitive information not yet ready to be released. Our rooms housing the security systems are off-limits to the public as well, as you'd expect.'

Afina gave a small snort of disgust. 'You can show the public anything you want them to see, and hide the rest. No one would ever be the wiser.'

Deciding there was no point in trying to reason with her, Karla replied, 'Yes, we could, that's true, though it seems a great deal of trouble to go to for no good purpose. Now, I'd like to give you all an update on what we've done to deal with the suspected case of poisoning, then answer any questions you may have.' She looked pointedly at Afina, and this time was allowed to proceed without interruption, outlining the steps the medcentre had taken and the inspections organised to ensure neither Phil's bakery nor the grain delivered to him were responsible for Marie's miscarriage. 'I'm relieved to say,' Karla concluded, 'that when I saw Marie this morning she was recovering well and looking forward to applying for the right to try for another baby. She fully accepts it was an unfortunate problem with the placenta that caused her to lose this one, and that the bread was not to blame.'

'Do you intend to continue your crop trials in Narre Warren?' asked Cynthia, smiling, pleased with what she had heard.

'Yes, we do,' answered Karla. 'As you probably all know, there was a fire on Wednesday night that burnt all our fields, but we've decided to use them as they are to give us some extra information, then continue on next year with the approach we were to take this April, but which we now can't.'

Abhaya still seemed uncertain: 'You won't be asking locals to test your products, will you? I'm still not sure I'd want to.'

'I understand, Abhaya, and no, we won't ask anyone in this region to taste either our bread or any other products again. We're considering approaching one of the universities. They're used to dealing with experimental situations and might even find a way of doing some joint research to fit in with their own aims. It seems our best option.'

Abhaya nodded, but Aurora told Karla that as one of the people who cancelled their orders with Phil, she was still not entirely convinced. 'Would *you* like to see the facility at Narre Warren, or even Willsmere?' offered Karla.

'Thank you. I'll consider it and let you know, but I expect I'm only nervous because I intend to try for a baby myself and it was such a shock to hear about Marie. I know her well, you see.'

'Oh... Yes, and I can understand how being a friend of Marie's would make a difference! In future, just to be on the safe side, I may screen out pregnant women, or women trying to become pregnant. To explain what I mean, even though I can guarantee our products are completely safe and not contaminated in any way, on the other hand, being new crops, theoretically, they *could* contain natural ingredients which in very rare instances might trigger either an allergic reaction or a sensitivity reaction in those with some form of food intolerance. Normally, this wouldn't be a critical problem for an otherwise healthy person because treatment would usually be available, but for someone who's pregnant, there'd always be the small chance the baby or the pregnancy could be affected.' Karla paused, considering the possibility more closely than she had previously.

'What you say sounds sensible,' said Antonio. 'Could men contemplating fatherhood somehow be affected by these new crops?'

'I doubt it, but as you've asked the question, I'll make sure my team takes this into account. We've done the usual background research, but there's no harm looking at the issue again, and perhaps screening them out as well.'

'Thank you,' he answered. 'That was my main concern.'

Karla smiled and said, 'Are there any other questions?'

They all shook their heads, except Afina, who shrugged her shoulders and looked away.

'Would you like something to drink before you go?' offered Antonio. 'Tea? Coffee? Some fresh lemonade? No?' As Karla made ready to leave, he stood up, held out his hand, and added, 'I may take you up on your offer to see Willsmere one day. It sounds like a very interesting place.'

'It is, and yes, you'd be most welcome, any time.' Karla shook hands with him, and then, relieved to have dealt with the situation reasonably well, she and Aurora left for their midsun appointment with Jonathon.

Karla and Jonathon had arranged to meet at a small café-restaurant in Ferntree Gully and arrived at almost the same time. Aurora watched contentedly as Jonathon quickly found a table and then waited until Karla was seated before he himself sat down. 'Remarkably polite,' thought Karla, suppressing a chuckle.

Arching her back and tail, Aurora stretched luxuriously before settling down by Karla's feet to wonder what would be offered as *her* midsun meal. She didn't have long to wait, since Jonathon had, as promised, done some reading beforehand about cats and about their food preferences in particular. He had even pre-ordered a bowl of water and a serving of pumpkin lasagne for both Aurora and himself, asking for his own meal to be served at the same time as Karla's, once she had made her selection.

'Thanks, Jonathon, you're very thoughtful,' said Karla, with a bright smile, when Aurora's food and water arrived and he told her what he had done. Quickly scanning the menu, she chose a Chinese-style sweetcorn soup, plus a small serve of fried rice and two steamed red bean dumplings. 'What do you want to drink?' she asked Jonathon, looking up from the menupad.

'I wouldn't mind a light ale. What about you?' he replied, leaning his elbows on the table, hands together, and admiring how well Karla looked in her loose-fitting, dark red, sleeveless blouse and calf-length black skirt, printed with matching swirls of colour. A pair of elegant black sandals and a beautifully engraved silver bracelet completed the outfit. If he was any judge, thought Jonathon, she had chosen it with care, and was glad he too had paid attention to his appearance.

'Yes,' agreed Karla, 'a light ale sounds good.' She placed the order, and shortly afterwards, as they were eating their meal, she said, 'Aurora seems to have taken an instant liking to you, Jonathon, which means I'll be allowed to finish this in peace.'

'Well, that's a relief!' he replied, gazing at Aurora, who raised her head from her bowl to look into his eyes. For an instant, he felt dizzy and nearly dropped his knife and fork, but then the sensation disappeared. He took a deep breath before saying, 'By the Sun, that was strange! Would Aurora read my mind, Karla, to find out more about me? I felt almost faint for a moment when she looked at me just now.'

Karla carefully studied Aurora, who ignored her and kept eating. 'I'm not sure,' she said slowly. 'It's certainly possible. She occasionally does do things like that, but doesn't tend to go beyond surface thoughts. Cats are trained to respect people's privacy, on the whole, although they don't always obey the rules. Are you all right now?'

'Yes, but I can see there's a lot more to them than I realised, even from the reading I did, though I admit I didn't have time to do a great deal. Anyway, you said you'd tell me more about them, and about the Willsmere case, too.' He drank some of his ale and continued eating.

Swallowing a mouthful of soup, Karla said, 'I'll finish this while it's hot, and afterwards, I'll tell you part of the story. It'd take all afternoon to tell you the whole thing!' She grinned, then began on the next course, which had just been served.

Jonathon finished his lasagne, then ordered another light ale for them both and sat back in his chair, relaxed and at ease. Aurora watched them, also at ease and occasionally observing the other diners, lightly touching their minds to see who they were and where they had recently come from. Unlike Jonathon, none of them noticed her touch.

After drinking a few mouthfuls of ale, Karla set the glass down and said, 'Most of what I can tell you is on public record, but some of it isn't. I've been working at Willsmere since I finished studying, which is now a long time ago, and for most of that time I've worked together with my good friends Mik Theophanous and Tamara Solanum. I'm sure you'd like them, if you ever meet. They're bondmates, and they've recently applied for fertility rights...which isn't something I'd be interested in, that's for sure, even if I had a bondmate, which I don't.'

Jonathon raised an eyebrow and nodded, but when he didn't comment, Karla began her story: 'About six and a half years ago, I was on my way to work one morning when I received a frantic telepathic message from one of Mik's three cats, telling me something was terribly wrong. When I got there, I found Mik unconscious and bleeding, and the cat, Fliedermus, locked in my lab, next to his, totally beside herself. I called an ambulance, and when Tamara arrived not long afterwards, she called the peacekeepers. Fortunately, Mik wasn't badly hurt, which of course was a huge relief for us all. However, it turned out that staff in other Federation labs had been attacked as well, here in Australia and in

Brazil, so FSIU agents were called in to assist with the investigation. Various valuable forestry research results and related items were stolen during the attacks, and my set of rare reference plants, which I'd spent ten years collecting, was destroyed. Luckily, I'd sent samples to the Federation Herbarium in Oslo, so at least I didn't have to try finding them again, which was just as well, but even so, it was terrible when I first saw what had happened!'

Karla grimaced as she remembered the dreadful day when their peaceful world had been turned upside down. Jonathon reached out to briefly touch her hand. 'Thank you,' she said slowly. 'The investigation went on for over a year, and during that time, other government labs were sabotaged, in Papua and Myanmar, and Tamara was attacked. Luckily, one of Mik's cats, Possum, saved her...by killing the attacker. She even drank some of his blood, but vomited afterwards, thank the Sun!'

Jonathon stared at her, then stared at Aurora. 'What?!' Aurora blinked sleepily, but laid her head on her paws again and dozed off. All this was old news to her.

'Yes, and that last piece of information isn't something the public knows about, so you need to keep it to yourself... Anyway, Possum was taken to the Melbourne Detention Centre, and Mik, who turned up at the scene not long after the attack, went with Tamara to the nearest medcentre. He called Søren Thorup to go to the Detention Centre to be with Possum, who was totally traumatised, and Søren then called me when he'd almost given up trying to calm her down. He asked me to bring Fliedermus and Mik's other cat, Red Matilda, to the Detention Centre. It was the middle of the night, so I had to get out of bed, go to Mik's place, fetch the cats, and persuade them to come with me in the patrol car that Søren had somehow managed to convince the peacekeepers to send for us. Mind you, once the cats woke up properly, they weren't in the least worried, and when we got to the Detention Centre, they soon worked out what was going on. They even influenced the peacekeepers to agree with Søren's suggestion to release Possum on bail...which isn't in the records either, so I'm trusting you not to tell anyone.' Karla looked steadily into Jonathon's grey eyes, which were wide with astonishment. He promised to keep it all to himself, so Karla told him what happened next.

'At the time, no one realised cats could choose to affect how we behave, but it soon became clear to us that they could, although not generally without a good reason, and I've never known one to harm anyone unless it was somehow to defend their companion...' She paused to drink more of her ale, while Jonathon remained silent, glancing at Aurora as Karla began speaking again: 'In the end, we managed to arrange for Possum to be tried, just like a human, and the Breeding Centre staff helped Søren do a great deal of research into cat behaviour, which was used as evidence in her defence. Fortunately, she was acquitted. Since then, cats have had status under the law and have gradually been given more rights, such as not having to wear a leash in public, and being able to have a seat on airjets, instead of being put in the cargo hold. Mik managed to pioneer that one.' Karla grinned, remembering his humorous account of the occasion when he needed to convince a reluctant bookings clerk that his cats should travel with him, and if they didn't and were put in the cargo hold instead, then all the other passengers would soon suffer the effects of the cats' annoyance.

'Cats have even given evidence at trials since then, via an official Witness, and are sometimes used as guardians when someone's in need of special protection.' Karla nudged Aurora with her foot. 'You're all rather wonderful, aren't you... Yes, you are, my sweetie.' At these last words, lost for a moment in Aurora's soothing mind, she didn't notice Jonathon's wistful expression. Looking up, she said, 'I suppose it's almost time for you to go back to work? Pity... Still, we can always continue this another time, if you want?'

'Yes, to both questions,' replied Jonathon. 'I'm astounded by what you've told me, though, and it seems I'd better watch out while I'm around your cat!'

'You'll be fine, I promise. If she didn't think we should be friends, it'd be obvious by now.' Karla stood up and held out her hand. 'So, when would you like to catch up again? You could come to Willsmere to take a look around, perhaps some time next week, if you want? I could show you some of the forestry-related work we're doing.'

'That'd be great! What about Tuesday? I know we'll have plenty of staff on then, so it should be safe enough for me to take a few hours off. I could meet you there at around 14:00.'

'Good. I need to know for certain because it's a secure building, which means I have to arrange for temporary access rights. If you change your mind, or something comes up, you'd need to give me at least twenty-four hours notice before another visit.'

'Oh, I see, but that wouldn't be a problem at all.' Jonathon hesitated, then bent down to hold out his hand for Aurora to sniff. 'Goodbye,' he said, smiling when she briefly licked his fingers. 'She *does* seem to have taken a fancy to me, doesn't she.' He straightened up, and on impulse, kissed Karla on the cheek. 'I'll see you next Tuesday,' he said, gently touching her on the shoulder.

'I'll look forward to it,' said Karla. 'Call me, if you like, in the meantime. If I'm too busy to talk, I'll just say so.'

'Alright, I will.' Jonathon grinned, then left to return to his workplace, on the way trying to make up his mind whether to bring Karla a small gift when he next saw her...or would Tuesday be too soon? Probably, he eventually decided.

## CHAPTER SIXTEEN

Not being a day he was required to work unless he wanted to, Yngwie chose to sleep in until 09:00, luxuriating in the feeling of not having anything in particular demanding his attention. After dressing, followed by a tasty breakfast in the communal dining room, he called his friend Torleif, at midnight, local Norwegian time. Like Yngwie, Torleif was now working for the Federation on Kaj's team, and had finished his day a few hours earlier, but as he tended to enjoy staying up late, was glad enough to talk.

'By the Sun, you look different!' exclaimed Yngwie, when he saw him. 'What inspired the haircut?'

Laughing, Torleif explained that he simply wanted a change. 'What do you think of the tat?' he asked, his brown eyes crinkling at the corners as he grinned. He had just come out of the shower and was drying himself when Yngwie's call came through. His formerly shoulder-length jet-black hair was now very short indeed, and his bare torso displayed an intricately designed hexagram proudly tattooed on one shoulder.

'It's okay,' replied Yngwie, who wasn't overly fond of them.

'I can always have it removed.' Torleif was unperturbed by Yngwie's lack of enthusiasm.

'True, or even have it replaced with something else, if you wanted.'

'How's Kaj treating you?' Torleif finished drying himself then put on a warm dressing gown.

'Fine, though he was a bit hard to get along with at first. What about you?'

'I'm glad he's not here in person. Can't say I'm crazy about him, and he doesn't seem to have *any* sense of humour! Wasn't at all happy when I sent him his very own portrait.'

'A caricature?'

'What else? He's perfect!' Torleif chuckled.

'Maybe we shouldn't annoy him too much. After all, we got off fairly lightly, other than the notation on our Federation records.'

'We certainly did. I mean, twenty-five hours a week. How easy is that compared to all the time we've put in these last few years!'

'Oh yes, it's easy work, and in the meantime, I can do what I like in my free time... I didn't tell you about the cat I was taking care of, did I?'

Laughing at Torleif's surprised expression, Yngwie elaborated. 'Her name's Dandelion, and she's a ferocious beastie when she wants to be, but otherwise, simply gorgeous! She's companion to a Greenlander staying here, by the name of Søren Thorup. He's a research zoologist doing some work on the spiders I told you about. The problem is, the cat's scared of going into the forest with him, and even had a real dust-up with a friend's cat when they went in there together. Apparently it was quite something!' Yngwie shook his head as he remembered the aftermath. 'When she was brought back here, she got away, and we had to chase her down the street, where she almost got into a fight with *another* cat, though luckily we'd caught up with her by then. Unfortunately, the cat's companion called the peacekeepers, but we managed to sort it all out and were allowed to take her home. So now, when Søren wants to go into the forest, I look after Dandelion, although not today, otherwise I'd get her to say hello! I've even taken her into work with me, and at first Kaj was furious. However, it turns out that the woman who's the FSIU Coordinator is a friend of Søren's, and when she saw Dandelion, recognised her immediately, so really, what could Kaj do?'

Torleif burst out laughing and Yngwie joined him. It was such a release, it was some time before they could speak again without laughing at each other. When they finally sobered up, Yngwie gazed at Torleif, suddenly serious. 'You know, it's just dawned on me for the first time how big an event we created and how massive the ramifications are. Did they tell you there's a possibility the flaw we found has been used to create false identities and even to remove all traces of people who don't want a Federation record?'

'No! How extraordinary!' Torleif ran a hand through his still damp hair and said, 'Do you mean to say they've come to the conclusion we've done them a favour?'

'In a way, though they still see what we did as serious enough to leave the notation on our records. I suppose the main problem is, we've been a bit too smart and so they feel we can't be trusted, which may be fair enough, when it comes down to it.'

'Yeah, I guess so. Of course, we can be, can't we? Trusted, I mean.'

'Oh, yes, I'm sure we can...for now.' Yngwie grinned, unable to remain serious for long. 'The other thing they said was that if their suspicions are right and we'd gone to the wrong people with this information, we might have been 'removed'. Not good, eh?'

Torleif stared at Yngwie for a full five seconds before replying. 'What!'

'I don't think they were just trying to scare me, and I suggest we keep this strictly to ourselves. For example, I won't be telling my parents any of this, so you shouldn't either. They're upset enough already.'

'They are, yes, they certainly are,' agreed Torleif, his face now grim. 'If I'd been any younger they would've stopped me from going out with my friends for months!'

'Hmm... That wouldn't have done you any harm, my friend. Too much partying isn't good for anyone.'

'I guess not. Speaking of which, it's time I got some sleep...and I'll try not to dream about being assassinated!' He yawned, then said goodbye and closed the connection, leaving Yngwie to ponder what he felt like doing with the rest of his day off. Despite his English being near perfect, he enjoyed the lingering sensation of having had the chance to speak in his native Norwegian for a while.

As he was about to walk out the door, Shahid called. 'Hello!' said Yngwie, pleased. 'Have you forgiven me? How are your parents? Are they prepared to talk to me yet?'

'They want to speak with you over a midsun meal. Today, if you have time?' answered Shahid, without smiling. 'I suspect my father wants to tell you off and then be friends again. He hasn't forgotten you saved my life.'

'Ah, I see. Well, in that case, I'll be there. What time?'

'13:00, if that suits, and afterwards, I have a small favour to ask. Laurita has written the words to a song, but asked me to come up with a tune. I said I'd do it by today, so I'd like you to sing it for me while I play my lute. She's due to come over for afternoon tea and I want to be sure it sounds right before then. It'd be a good chance to record your singing too, if you wouldn't mind?'

Yngwie grinned. This sounded promising. He would have been sorry if Shahid and his parents hadn't decided to forgive him. As for Laurita, well, they could at least be friends, if nothing more. 'Yes, it's all fine with me, Shahid. Will you be going into the forest this morning, or have you already been in?'

'No, not today. I'll spend all day in there tomorrow and take Tuesday off. The weather report predicts an extremely hot, windy day in the afternoon, and I'm due to go to the Breeding Centre anyway, for Yedda's training session. Laurita will be coming with us and we'll be spending the morning on the bay, taking the trip I promised in one of the sailing ships.'

'Sounds good,' said Yngwie, raising an eyebrow. 'Well, I'll see you later, Shahid, and thanks for the invitation. I appreciate it.'

'I'm glad you could come over at such short notice. My parents will be pleased.' He smiled this time, before ending the call.

Yngwie spent the remainder of the morning relaxing and reading a novel, then arrived at Shahid's house promptly at 13:00. Wania met him at the door, her expression neutral, but with a welcoming handshake. 'Come in,' she said. 'We'll eat straight away, and talk afterwards.'

Yngwie followed her to the dining room, where Shahid and his father were waiting. Unsure whether to shake hands with Shafiqur, Yngwie greeted him courteously, but was a little put out when he merely waved a hand, indicating they should all be seated.

For some time no one spoke, other than to ask for something to be passed to them. Yngwie did his best to focus on eating and enjoying the food, but found it difficult. At home, his own family chatted about the day's events whenever they saw each other, with the conversation usually continuing on throughout their evening meal and often for long afterwards, even if nothing of any particular importance had happened during the day.

Eventually Yngwie made up his mind to risk being seen as ill-mannered and broke the silence: 'I'm not sorry for what Torleif and I did, and the Federation Special Investigation Unit Coordinator has even told me it was probably just as well we managed events to make sure we spoke with their most senior members. Otherwise, there might have been a risk that someone within the organisation would exploit the security flaw we found and could even have decided we were expendable.' Feeling his face begin to colour, he gazed at each of them in turn, then studied his plate of food for a few moments and began eating again.

The others stopped eating and put down their knives and forks to stare at him. 'Really?' said Shafiqur at last.

'Yes, it's true. I was interviewed by the FSIU Coordinator, Morag MacIain, and this is exactly what she told me. It seems they've been investigating a number of incidents over the years where Federation identity records have either gone missing or have been falsified. They now suspect it's the security flaw that made this possible. The question is still whether it was discovered accidentally and then used for criminal purposes, or whether it was created deliberately. One of our tasks is to help answer this question...if we can. We might not succeed.'

Shafiqur nodded, his elbows on the table, resting his chin on his clasped hands, eyes half-closed, considering what to say. 'I want to ask you something,' he said slowly, 'and I want a completely honest answer. When you first decided to see if you could hack into the Federation's secure sections of the lattice, did you do it for fun, or did you do it to see if you could find a flaw and report it?'

Yngwie's colour deepened as he replied, 'We did it for fun. Only later, when we understood how serious the flaw was, did we begin working out how to let the Federation know about it without risking too much.'

'Which is precisely as I suspected,' said Shafiqur, in a neutral tone and looking directly at Yngwie. 'My next question is, did you enjoy yourselves creating the image you sent out, and did you enjoy the powerful experience of sending it to virtually every comlink on the planet?'

'Not *every* comlink, but yes, we enjoyed the whole thing, and as I said earlier, I don't regret what we did, although we now realise the image we sent out wasn't the right one. I'm horrified by the copycat events that have happened since, and wish we'd chosen something less 'inspiring', shall we say. The only thing Torleif and I can do now is to complete the work we've been set by Coordinator MacIain to the best of our ability and hope nothing more serious happens because of what we've done.' Yngwie frowned and looked down at his hands, which were clenched as they rested on the edge of the table.

'Do you enjoy flouting authority?' asked Wania earnestly, her voice steady and her tone friendly enough.

'Yes, and no,' answered Yngwie, his expression serious. 'I respect the person, not the position, although I also assume people are competent until they show me otherwise.' He leaned forward and said, 'If we bow to people because they have a certain title and don't hold them to account if they are corrupt or incompetent, that cannot be good for society as a whole, can it?'

'No,' replied Wania, smiling for the first time. 'You are quite right, and I think this has gone on long enough. Your questions have been answered, Shafiqur. It's time we enjoyed our meal properly. After all, Yngwie and Torleif eventually did what they considered best, and if they had a wonderful time doing it, well, perhaps they can be forgiven. What do *you* think, Shahid?' She looked at her son, expecting a well considered answer.

Shahid settled back in his chair, picked up his hand reader and said, 'With all due respect to you, Yngwie, we should keep in mind that you *are* very young, and were even younger when you began all this. It isn't always easy to know what's best, and at least you accept the consequences of your actions and are working to set things right. I'd prefer to forget about the whole thing now, and instead remember that you did, after all, save my life, and seem to be a thoroughly decent person.'

He looked pointedly at his father, who hesitated before saying, 'Yes, enough has been said. We'll enjoy this good food, and afterwards, I gather you will sing for us, Yngwie?'

Yngwie smiled. 'Yes, I have that honour. I believe Laurita has written the words to a new song, which Shahid has set to music. I hope it's good!'

'I think so,' replied Shahid, 'but we'll see what *you* have to say.'

The remainder of the meal was eaten with far more pleasure than when they first sat down, and once the table was cleared and the kitchen tidied, everyone assembled in the lounge room, where Shahid's lute and the music to the song were placed ready for him to begin. He turned to Yngwie, giving him a copy of the words and the music. 'Read it first, and afterwards, I'll play the tune. It's pretty straightforward, so I'm sure you'll easily pick it up.'

Yngwie read through the song, looking up when Shahid began to play, first the introduction, followed by the main melody, repeated twice. After the last soft note sounded, Yngwie waited for a few moments, then said, 'Yes, I have it.' Shahid smiled and began again. This time, Yngwie joined in, his voice true and steady. Wania and Shafiqur listened, entranced.

'What a beautiful song!' exclaimed Wania when the music finished. 'Yet so sad. Laurita seems to have put a great deal of herself into this, although she mostly shows us the happier side of her nature. I wonder if she has written anything else?'

'I don't know,' replied Shahid. 'I didn't ask. Maybe I should.'

'Yes, and if there are others as good, you could put *them* to music for her as well. You could even put together a collection and publish it. Would you be willing to sing them, Yngwie, if she doesn't want to, or can't?' Wania smiled happily and Shafiqur put his arm around her shoulders, kissing her. 'Always my beautiful romantic,' he whispered. She took his hand in hers, returning the kiss, and they held each other close, thinking only of the moment.

'Such love,' thought Yngwie, noticing. 'True bondmates. How lucky they are.' Aloud he said, 'Yes, why not, it might be fun.'

Shahid, used to his parents and their relationship, noticed too, and smiled. He strummed a few notes on the lute and said, 'Yngwie, I managed to record the song, and as you sang it so well, I don't think we need to do it again, unless you want to?'

'Perhaps we had better check the recording?' replied Yngwie, sitting down next to him.

'You're right... Let's see what we have.' Shahid replayed the song and even Yngwie was impressed with how well it sounded. He began to take Wania's suggestion seriously, which he hadn't at first. Turning to her, he said, 'You may have come up with a good idea, Wania. Laurita will be here soon, won't she? We could ask her.'

Wania smiled, and Shahid, pleased at how relaxed Yngwie sounded when he spoke Laurita's name, quickly agreed, then added, 'Before she arrives, Yngwie, if you like, we could record a few of your own songs. If they're well known, I could most likely accompany you.'

Yngwie grinned and put a hand on Shahid's shoulder. 'Yes, I'd be very pleased if you would play. Do you have any favourites?'

They discussed songs for a while, with a few suggestions from Shafiqur and Wania as well, and before long were able to agree on three traditional ballads that would suit both the lute and Yngwie's voice. Then, just as they had almost finished recording the third one, the household security system silently displayed Laurita's image on the room's screen, alerting them to her presence on their doorstep. Wania tiptoed out to let her in, and then together, they listened quietly while Shahid played the last few notes.

Surprised to see Yngwie here and to learn they were recording his singing, she was even more surprised when Yngwie said, 'Laurita! Great to see you. I love your song! Shahid was as good as his word and has put it to music. I've even had the privilege of being the first to sing it.' Laughing good-naturedly at her astonishment, he added, 'Here, listen.' He turned eagerly to Shahid, who picked up his hand reader, selected the song and set it playing.

Laurita sat down beside Shafiqur to listen. He patted her hand, smiled, and said, 'It *is* good. In fact, it's lovely, and we were wondering if you've written any more.'

'Why, yes, I have. Not many, perhaps a dozen or so. Why?'

'We thought of putting them to music and having either you or Yngwie sing them while I play,' said Shahid, 'just as we have with this one. You could try singing as well, if you wanted?'

Laurita shook her head. 'Oh no, not me! I'm not good enough. It would ruin the songs. No, no, I'd be delighted if you and Yngwie performed them.'

'We also thought a collection could be published,' said Wania, now seated and leaning forward, eager to hear what Laurita would say.

Laurita half opened her mouth in disbelief, then shut it again. Recovering, she said, 'Truly? You believe my song is good enough to be listened to by others?'

'Oh yes, my dear, more than good enough. Truly lovely. Few could fail to be moved by your words, and even though Shahid is my son, I think I'm allowed to say he captured the meaning perfectly with the music he chose. Yngwie's voice is just right, too.' Wania stood up. 'Would you like coffee, Laurita? I was about to prepare some.'

Delighted by the easy, relaxed atmosphere in the room and the enthusiasm with which her song had been received, Laurita smiled and nodded. This was all far more than she had anticipated. When Yedda stood up from where she was lying by Shahid's feet and padded over to her, placing one paw upon her knee and gazing into her eyes, Laurita received no images or feelings from the cat, yet nevertheless had the distinct impression Yedda totally approved of her! She scratched her beneath the chin, and when the cat turned her head for more, purring softly, continued scratching her around the head and neck.

Yngwie, entranced by the beautiful picture they made sitting there together, took out his comlink, captured the image, and sent it to Laurita's comlink. When it chimed and she saw what he had sent, she gave him a quick smile, before sending the file to Shahid.

Shahid, who had been speaking quietly with his father, excused himself when he heard the chime of the incoming message. Seeing the image on his hand reader, he began to say something, but changed his mind and smiled at Laurita instead, then showed the picture to Shafiqur.

'Oh how lovely!' he exclaimed, immediately understanding what had happened. 'We could almost use this for the music collection.'

Standing up, he showed the picture to Wania when she came in with a tray of coffee and an assortment of homemade sweet cakes. The fragrant aroma of the coffee soon filled the room as she set the tray down on a small table in the centre of the room and examined the image properly. 'It really is wonderful. Did you take it, Yngwie?' She had realised from the angle of the composition that it was most likely his work.

'Yes. The opportunity was too good to miss,' he answered, with a grin, 'and the lighting was perfect. The music collection didn't occur to me, but I agree with Shafiqur. It might even make a good publicity image.'

'I agree,' said Wania, after considering the idea. 'I think it has just the right romantic touch, without being over-sweet. With a cat in the composition, it also leaves the viewer wondering about the music, since this doesn't say directly what the style might be. What do you think, Laurita?'

'I feel almost as if I am being swept up in something quite outside my experience, but yes, if you all think this would work, then how can I say no? We could always take more and add them to the collection, couldn't we? A series of images might be interesting.'

'What an excellent idea!' exclaimed Yngwie, beginning to see all sorts of possibilities. 'We could have some of Shahid playing, and perhaps of me singing, even a group scene, with Yedda too... Out in the forest, for example, which would be good visually and also relevant to the work you both do.'

Shahid nodded slowly, then said, 'Laurita, would you like to send me your other songs? We could look at them and develop an overall theme, both for the music and the publicity images. Is there any particular one you'd like us to begin with?'

Laurita quickly located the songs on her hand reader and sent them to everyone's comlink, which seemed the easiest thing to do. 'There's one that would fit well with a romantic theme,' she said. 'It's called *Love's Season*.' She moved over to where Shahid was sitting and stood by his shoulder while he read the words.

'Yes, it's good,' he said, then turned to her and added, 'We should have at least one piece with you reading. You read so well, even if you say your voice isn't good enough to sing in public. Yngwie could sing it afterwards, if that would work.'

'Perhaps you could read it to us now?' suggested Wania, reaching for another cake and taking a sip of her coffee. 'We could even record video as well as sound, if you want?'

Initially rather nervous at the idea, Laurita suddenly grinned and said, 'Why not! If I make a mess of it, we can always try again. The acoustics seem to be good in here, and the setting is lovely, so let's see if I have beginner's luck!'

Yedda leapt up from where she was sitting to dance around Laurita's feet, but soon realised it was a distraction and sat down again. Meanwhile, Wania fetched their recorder, made sure Laurita stood in just the right light and with a good background, then positioned the equipment and set it to standby. The room was silent as Laurita began, her voice mellow and confident, with a certain lilting quality well suited to the words:

Come to me before the Autumn time,
Come to me before the leaves do fall,
Come to me before the Winter time
and you can lay your head
upon my shoulder fair,
untie your golden hair.

Bring to me no chill of Winter time,
Bring to me no tale of sad farewells,
Bring to me the fruit of Summertime
and you will find your love
in our soft embrace,
kisses rained upon your face.

Speak to me of time when love was strong,
Speak to me of Springtime's morning light,
Speak to me of evenings sweet and long
and you can dwell within this place
where you once were free,
and gave your thoughts to me.

Come to me before the Autumn time,
Come to me before the Winter storms,
Come to me before the Spring sunlight,
and warmth of Summertime
will ease your aching heart,
and we will never part.

Come to me before the Autumn time,
Bring to me no tale of sad farewells,
Speak to me of evenings sweet and long
and you can lay your head
upon my shoulder fair,
untie your golden hair.

'She certainly didn't write this for Yngwie,' thought Shahid, surprised by his own sharp sense of relief. 'When did you write this?' he asked, after Laurita had taken a seat again and composed herself. From her expression, she seemed somewhat overcome by her own emotions and how they related to the memories the song evoked... At least, this was what Yedda told him, although she didn't share any of Laurita's actual memories, which was probably for the best. 'She's learning,' he realised, smiling at her. Yedda 'smiled' back and for a brief while their intense feeling of companionship almost made them forget the others in the room.

Yngwie brought them back to the present by saying, 'Do you want to play it back for us, Shahid?'

'Oh, yes, of course,' he replied, with a slight start, and set the equipment to relay to the screen on the room's wall, turning up the volume.

'Yes, this should definitely be part of our collection,' said Shafiqur, once they finished listening. 'I'm not even sure it's necessary for Yngwie to sing it as well. To me, this piece sounds more like a woman's song, so perhaps it should be followed by Shahid playing the melody. What do you think, Laurita?' He turned to her, approval of this young woman clear in his expression.

Laurita lowered her head for a moment. It was a long time since anyone had accepted her so readily into their family, as it were, and she felt tears come to her eyes. But this was not the time to weep or to show her emotions too clearly. No, this was a time to simply be and to enjoy the remarkable generosity of these good people, Yngwie included. 'Yes,' she managed to say, although with a catch in her voice. 'Yes, what you say is true, and I am sure Shahid could compose something that will work well.'

'Good!' replied Shafiqur, standing up. 'It's time for our afternoon prayers, Shahid, and afterwards, I regret to say I must go to work. I will look forward to hearing and seeing whatever you come up with next. This is such an exciting project!' He smiled broadly and bent down to kiss Wania on the cheek, then, with a wave, left them to plan how next to proceed.

# CHAPTER SEVENTEEN

When Wania invited both Yngwie and Laurita to stay for the evening meal, they gladly accepted. Afterwards, they continued discussing their plans for the production of the music and poetry collection – having realised by now that poetry could also be included. Laurita soon sorted through her writing to select the poems that seemed to fit in well with the songs and gave a copy to everyone so they could decide on which to include.

Needing to get up early for work the next day, Yngwie eventually announced it was time for him to leave, expecting Laurita would leave as well, but was surprised when she remained behind, even though by now it was almost 23:00. Pushing the thought away, he walked to the nearest callstation. While he waited for his transport to arrive, he located his ancestry records and sent them to Karla, not expecting to receive a reply until at least some time the next day. It seemed, however, that Karla was also up relatively late because she immediately called to thank him.

'Hello!' she said, with a grin. 'Thanks for this. I'll run a comparison with mine tomorrow. I was about to go to bed when it came through. Søren and our mutual friend, Morag MacIain, were at Willsmere today for afternoon tea, which you may already know, but Søren and Dandelion have only just left. I had to leave Aurora at home, of course, but she didn't mind, although Dandelion still sulked all day and even hissed at me. Perhaps it was Aurora's scent on my clothes, I'm not sure, but it could be she just doesn't like me.' Unsure whether he was aware of all the details of the situation, Karla chose not to tell Yngwie about Dandelion's jealousy of her relationship with Søren. 'Still, enough of that... We won't repeat the experiment. What have you been up to?'

Yngwie told her about their plans to publish a collection of Laurita's songs and poetry, then had a sudden inspiration: 'Karla, would you like to be part of this? I don't see why you and I couldn't sing a few duets. Some of the pieces might lend themselves to it. What do you think?' His transport arrived at this point, so there was a pause in the conversation while he boarded.

'I'm flattered,' replied Karla, which was true, 'but is my voice really good enough?'

'Yes, it is, or I wouldn't make the suggestion. I'd have to ask the others first, but I can't see why they shouldn't agree. We'll be doing a set of images to go with the collection, and if you don't mind me saying so, you'd make a wonderful addition, particularly if we posed together. Also, if we took some in the forest, they'd fit in with both the overall theme and the work you all do.'

Karla smiled, and considered the idea for a few seconds. 'I can see you're intent on doing this, so what can I say, but yes! Let me know when you want me to be somewhere, and I'll fit it in somehow. We're rather busy at Willsmere at the moment, but you wouldn't need me for long, would you?'

'It depends upon how well the recordings go, and whether we manage to get good footage of the actual performances. We'd have to rehearse too, I imagine.'

'Okay, I like the idea,' replied Karla, 'but we'll have to wait for the right time. I can't say I fancy being in the forest when it's this hot. Still, next week might be good to at least begin. The weather report says it should be cooler by then. I'm assuming you'd prefer to rehearse outside?'

'Yes, otherwise the acoustics won't be the same. Anyway, there's no rush. The better we do this, the bigger the audience we'll attract.'

'Were you intending to ask people to pay for the collection?'

'We haven't discussed it, to be honest. Do you think we should?'

'I'm not sure, but my initial response is, probably not. I don't need any extra income, do you?'

'Not at the moment, but who knows, it might come in handy if the Federation notation on my record prevents me from earning anything extra once I finish university!' Yngwie grimaced, but it was obvious to Karla he wasn't overly concerned about the issue. After all, the Federation made sure all its citizens' basic necessities were well taken care of, which meant additional income was only required for what were regarded as luxury items.

'Hopefully by that time you'll have earned their trust and respect and the notation can be amended, or even removed. Anyway, I'm easy, so I don't really mind if you or the others want to charge a fee for the publication. We can talk about it later.' Karla yawned, then said, 'Sorry... I should go to bed, so goodnight, and I'll let you know if we're related.' She gave him one last smile and closed the connection.

By this time, Yngwie had arrived at the communal house in Ferntree Gully, and after a quick shower, went to bed and slept soundly until his alarm woke him at 07:30.

*

'Please be seated,' said the Judge, in its mellow, neutral, disembodied tone.

Everyone in the room sat down, including Matthew, with a guard next to him to ensure he didn't try to abscond, remote as this possibility might be. Others present included a Witness to ensure the proceedings were conducted fairly and in accordance with the law, the Prosecutor, the Defence Psychologist, who interviewed Matthew soon after his arrest, and Jonathon, who was the primary informant for the Prosecution. Since this was not an open hearing, no other interested parties were present. The charges, together with the defence and prosecution cases, had already been entered into the Judge's database, so this was now a formality to provide Matthew with an opportunity to challenge any of the evidence provided and to ask questions if he wished – as well as for the Judge to deliver its verdict.

'Matthew Robertson,' continued the Judge, 'you are charged with deliberately setting fire to fields located in Narre Warren and which are owned and used by the Federation for research purposes. You have admitted to using an accelerant to start the fire at approximately 01:45 on the fifteenth of March this year. The flames immediately spread, causing extensive damage to the fields.

'Prior to your admission, which the Court notes in your favour, Jonathon, the forest guardian who was first alerted to the fire and who subsequently conducted the investigation, instituted a search at the Pakenham Recycling Plant for a discarded container of this particular type of accelerant. A container was subsequently found with your fingerprints on it. As a result, he and his colleague, Aaron Jacobs, went to your home to search for any gloves that might have been used while setting the fire. When they met you on your way home, you surrendered a pair of gloves, which were later shown to have traces of the same accelerant upon them. It is my verdict, therefore, that your admission to being guilty of arson is upheld by the evidence.

'Your Defence Psychologist has entered extensive information into my database relating to your state of mind at the time you committed this act of arson. The Court accepts that you acted in a manner far outside your normal behaviour and also accepts that you are unlikely to repeat offend, or to commit any other criminal acts. Nevertheless, the crime was a serious one, and the Federation research effort being conducted by the Willsmere group has been compromised – although, due to their willingness to adapt their work to the circumstances, not as severely as might otherwise have been the case.

'Before I pass sentence upon you, Matthew Robertson, do you wish to ask any question, request any further explanation or clarification of this Court's procedures, or provide any new evidence on your own behalf?'

Matthew gazed around the room, met Jonathon's eyes and blushed, then looked down at his folded hands. Finally, he stood and said, in a clear, strong voice, 'No, Your Honour, I do not, but wish to take this opportunity to offer my sincere apologies and regrets to the staff at Willsmere and to those at the Narre Warren research facility. I deeply regret my actions, and can, to the best of my ability, undertake never to behave in such a foolish and irresponsible manner again.' He heaved a sigh, took a kerchief from his pocket and blew his nose, then abruptly sat down to hear what his fate would be.

'The Court accepts your apology, which will be noted and given to the people mentioned. Nevertheless, on this date, the nineteenth of March 2457, the Court sentences you to six months community service as an attendant to the patients at the Ferntree Gully medcentre, where you will work for a minimum of fifteen hours per week. During this time you will have the opportunity to reflect upon the harm you might have caused to anyone in the vicinity of the fire had it spread out of control, and the damage it could have done to the nearby forests and farmlands had it not been promptly contained. The region has a long history of catastrophic fire events, many of which were the result of arson or carelessness. It is your good fortune that in comparison, the harm your actions caused was relatively minor.'

The Judge paused, then in conclusion said, 'The Court is now adjourned and thanks are given to those who provided evidence in a timely and efficient manner. Matthew Robertson, you will be notified of your commencement date and time once arrangements have been made with the manager of the Ferntree Gully medcentre. In the meantime, you are not to leave this city and should you fail to perform your duties for the required period of time or to the standard agreed upon with the said manager, you will be required to attend this Court for an adjustment to your sentence. You are now free to go.'

His lips compressed in a determined line, Matthew left the room, accompanied by the guard. Jonathon and the others followed a few steps behind. Once outside, Jonathon waited until he was sure Matthew had left the vicinity, then called Karla. When she answered, he told her what had happened.

'Well, that seems fair,' she replied. 'Six months as an attendant won't do Matthew any harm, and the Judge is right in saying it might give him a new perspective on life. There's nothing like dealing with the seriously ill to do that!'

'How's Marie?' asked Jonathon.

'She's doing well, now she's home again. I'm sure she'll be relieved Matthew wasn't sentenced to home detention, which would have made running the farm rather difficult. Even so, fifteen hours out of Matthew's working week will still have an impact.'

'Yes, that's true, though I suspect the Judge took their circumstances into account. I'm sure the Defence Psychologist will have entered everything relevant into its database.'

'I suppose so. All that's needed now is for them to apply for the right to try for another baby, and then they can leave all this behind and get on with their lives.'

'Which reminds me, Karla... Is everything organised for me to see you tomorrow at Willsmere?'

'Oh yes, no problems with the security clearance.' Karla grinned. 'The gatekeeper will be there if there are any issues, but the gates should open for you once you've used the retina scanner. Afterwards, you just place your hand on the identification panel at the main door. I'll meet you in the hallway soon afterwards.'

'Excellent! I'll make sure I'm on time. Will Aurora be there too? I'd like to see her again.'

'Yes, she usually comes to work with me. We like going for a run along the riverbank when the weather's fine, but I think we'll give it a miss tomorrow. It sounds as if it'll be too hot.'

'It shouldn't be too bad in the morning, but the afternoon does sound as if it'll be a bit warm, and the prediction is for strong winds, too...' Jonathon paused. 'I probably shouldn't leave work, but if I stay every time the weather sounds dangerous, I'd almost have to live in my office!'

Karla smiled. 'Well you can't do that. You need some time off now and again, and there are plenty of other staff on hand, aren't there?'

'There are, yes, and my friend Aaron will be working, so I should stop worrying and instead look forward to seeing Willsmere in your good company, and Aurora's. It'll all be fine.'

'I'm sure it will. Anyway, I'd better get back to work, so see you tomorrow.'

'Yes, see you tomorrow.'

Jonathon smiled as he put his comlink into his pocket, then walked back to his office.


Standing at the windows of the twentieth floor of the Rialto building, in the city centre, and gazing out at the vast panorama of Melbourne before him, Søren waited for Morag to return from saying goodbye to her bondmate, Peacekeeper Chiu Liow Jones. She would be taking the evening flight back to Switzerland and Søren had used the opportunity to see her again, even though, just yesterday, they had thoroughly enjoyed their afternoon with Karla at Willsmere. Søren suspected he and Morag might not have the chance to catch up with each other in person for quite some time, so it was worth the trip from Ferntree Gully to spend a short while together and say goodbye properly. He would accompany her to Tullamarine airport, then return, with Dandelion for company. The cat now stood next to him, her paws resting on the low window ledge, also enjoying the scenery. When Morag entered the room, Dandelion turned around and bounded towards her, dancing around her ankles, tail in the air, begging to be cuddled. As Morag knelt down to oblige, Søren said, 'Are you ready to go?'

'Yes, but it's always hard to leave Chiu... He was sorry he couldn't talk longer with you when you first arrived. Still, at least you managed to see each other, even if only for a few minutes.' Morag gave Dandelion another hug, then stood up and brushed a few white cat hairs from her dark grey, tailored suit. Søren smiled, noticing how the tone brought out the highlights in her auburn hair. He was glad to see her looking so well after a recent viral infection. Modern medicine could deal with most things, but viruses still found new ways of defeating it, and perhaps always would.

Once outside, they took a seat in the Melbourne Peacekeeping Force patrol car waiting for them, and were soon skimming across the surface of the Collins Street waterway towards the Parkville transport exchange, where the patrol car could safely fly at greater height until it reached the airport, twenty minutes later. Meanwhile, Dandelion curled up between Morag and Søren for a short nap, leaving them to pay attention to each other, rather than to her.

'Morag,' said Søren, 'Karla seems to have taken a fancy to someone...by the name of Jonathon, a forest guardian. They met while he was investigating the fire we told you about at Narre Warren.' He looked away for a moment, unable to continue, despite having intended to tell her how much he hoped Karla had finally met someone she could be happy with. 'Sorry,' he managed to say. 'I'm sure you know how I feel about her, and although she feels a great deal for me too, I have long since resigned myself to the fact that we will never be bondmates. At least, I thought I had, but clearly, I haven't – I suddenly mind very much. Morag, it hurts dreadfully to think she may form a relationship with this fellow!'

Dandelion woke, and with her blue eyes half closed, studied him, then stood up and licked his face. 'Oh Dandelion, I always have you, don't I,' murmured Søren, burying his face in her soft, thick fur and holding her close.

Morag moved towards him and put her arm around his shoulders. 'I know, Søren, I know, and I'm so sorry. Perhaps it's time you tried to move on. If you don't, you may never be able to meet someone you can love enough to be with for the rest of your life. You're such a beautiful person, and one of the most handsome men I have ever seen. There must be many women who could easily fall in love with you. Surely you know that?'

'Not really,' replied Søren, his voice tinged with a note of bitterness. 'I realise it may sound strange, Morag, but women still seem to prefer men who are *at least* as tall as them, or hadn't you noticed? When I worked at Willsmere, six years ago, Tamara used to call me 'Alf', the Danish for pixie. Even Karla began calling me that for a time. I am *short*, Morag, tiny compared to most women. I have met only a dozen or so who were my height or less. Nearly *everyone* is taller than me!'

Morag hugged him a little tighter, but could hardly refute what he said. Unfortunately, it was all true, but she suspected that although Karla was some fifteen centimetres taller than Søren, this was not the reason she had never become his bondmate. She had an independence of spirit and an unwillingness to be constrained that did not sit well with Søren's tendency to want everything in life to be orderly, measurable, and to a certain extent, predictable. It was not that he was inflexible, or unimaginative, or even the least bit conventional in his actions or ideas, but whereas he and Karla worked well together and had a great deal in common, their domestic habits did not seem at all compatible. 'You *know* you and Karla would be at each other's throats within a week if you tried living together,' she said. 'Love isn't enough, you see. It's often the small, day-to-day things that make or break a relationship.'

Søren sighed. 'Yes, *I* would drive her mad, and *she* would drive me insane. Drat and damn and blast our personalities! We're far too old to change now.'

'You're no older than Chiu and I were when we fell in love, so don't give up on finding someone...but you may need to stop dreaming about Karla, my dear.' Morag kissed him lightly on the cheek and smiled.

'Yes, you are right, and I will try. Perhaps the best thing would be to see her with this Jonathon person. It would then become a reality and I could sincerely wish her well and move on, as you so wisely suggest. Naturally, I would try to make his life hell if he didn't live up to *my* expectations *and* hers!'

Morag chuckled, sure Søren meant every word.

At this point, the patrol officer turned to them, saying, 'Coordinator MacIain, we've arrived. Is there anything else I can do for you?'

'Oh yes, so we have, and thank you, but I travel light. I can easily manage my luggage and it isn't far.'

Morag and Søren said goodbye to their driver, then walked to the main airport building, Dandelion leading the way, sniffing the breeze to pick up all the new scents.

'Good luck, both with your spider project and with letting go of Karla,' said Morag, when they reached the flight lounge. She gave Søren one last hug, hugged Dandelion as well, and was rewarded with a lick on the nose.

Laughing, and rubbing her face, she stood up, then turned and walked away, but waved before boarding her flight. Søren and Dandelion watched through the plastiglass barriers until the international airjet lifted off and eventually disappeared from view.

On their way back to Ferntree Gully, Søren had the sudden impulse to see Jonathon for himself. After all, he had an excuse to contact him, even if it *was* rather late in the day, since it was perfectly reasonable to provide an update on the work he was doing mapping the distribution of the funnel-web population and the likelihood that a public safety warning would be required. A forest guardian was as good a person as any to give this preliminary report to, although a more senior person in his department would need to be notified of the final results.

When Jonathon answered the call from his office computer, he looked just as Søren had expected: handsome features, and by the breadth of his shoulders, strong and probably tall. He even had thick, dark brown, wavy hair, which he could just imagine Karla would enjoy running her fingers through... 'Bah!' he said to himself, then forced a smile: 'Hello, I don't believe we've met, but your friend Karla may have mentioned me. My name was in one of the recent requests for regular access to the Dandenong Ranges forests in order to perform a study of the spider population, in particular, the recent influx of funnel-webs from New South Wales... Søren Thorup.'

'Oh, yes, hello! Karla *has* mentioned you. I gather the survey is progressing well?' Jonathon was struck by the extraordinary beauty of the man, yet there was something in his expression that was not quite what he would expect, despite the charming smile. Hostility? Surely not...

'Yes, it's going as well as one could hope for, although the hot weather tends to make them hide more than usual. I wanted to let you know that I should manage to provide a final report in about one week's time, but it seems there are more than enough of the Southern Tree-dwelling Funnel-web Spiders in your forest to justify your department issuing a public safety warning, together with the appropriate action to take if some other unfortunate person is bitten. I can send through the data I've gathered so far, if you like?'

'Yes, please, that would help us prepare an appropriate warning message, which can be done once your final report is delivered...or shouldn't we wait?'

'I think you can wait before sending out the message. It's quite rare for anyone to be bitten, and you have a medcentre close by, so the risk in delaying a week or so is minimal.' As they spoke, Søren sent his results through.

'Thanks,' said Jonathon, when he received them. After quickly scanning through the data, he added, 'This all seems to be extremely thorough and easy to understand. I'll send it to the person responsible for dealing with these issues. They can contact you so you know who to send your final report to. It will save you wading around through our departmental structures trying to work out who the right person is...or do you already know?'

'Karla has told me, but thank you for your thoughtfulness. I appreciate it.' Søren was beginning to like this helpful, friendly man, despite feeling almost unbearably jealous of him.

'Oh, that's good, then. To change the subject slightly, I gather you've known Karla a long time?' Jonathon leaned back in his chair, relaxing when he noticed Søren seemed to be thawing towards him.

'Yes, for a long time. We have worked together, on and off, for more than ten years. She is a dear friend as well.' Søren hesitated as he said this, which Jonathon noticed.

'She's a remarkable person, that's for sure,' he answered, but didn't pursue the subject. There was more than friendship between these two, he was certain of it. 'How long are you staying in Melbourne?' he asked instead.

'It depends upon the weather in Greenland, where I come from,' replied Søren. 'I and my cat, Dandelion, were snowed in, and food deliveries were so unreliable we had almost run out when Karla called to ask me to come to Melbourne to do some detective work. If the situation hasn't improved by the time I finish my survey, I may well take a holiday until it has. No doubt the weather in France will be quite good at this time of year.' Søren chuckled, imagining the fine food he could enjoy there.

'Yes, it probably is.' Jonathon grinned. 'Particularly in the south, I gather, though I've never been there. Have you?'

'Many times, and you are right. The south of France is wonderful. You must go there some day.'

'Perhaps I will, now you've put the thought into my head. However, I'm at work, so I'd better get back to it. Thanks for calling, and for all this useful information. Good luck with the rest of your survey, and we may even meet up before you go. I'd like that.'

'I would too, Jonathon,' said Søren, his expression hard to read. 'I would like that very much. Well, goodbye.'

'Damn!' he swore softly, after closing the connection, then put his arm around Dandelion and hugged her. 'Thank goodness I have you, my darling,' he murmured, kissing the top of her head. She purred and snuggled closer, fully aware how unhappy he was, and why.

# CHAPTER EIGHTEEN

The vast white sails of the ship billowed above them as Shahid and Laurita stood on the deck gazing at the blue-green waters of Port Phillip Bay. A brisk breeze blew their hair away from their faces, and when a small flock of gulls screamed and danced nearby, they watched them with pleasure. Other than the birds and the occasional soft voices of their fellow passengers, the creaking of the ship's timbers and ropes were the only sounds. Nothing to disturb their peace for two blissful hours.

When they boarded, at 10:00, the temperature on land had already risen to thirty-two degrees, so it was a relief to be out on the bay, where it felt a great deal cooler. Yedda sat by them, intrigued by this totally new experience, sniffing the salty sea air and watching the gulls, never having seen them before. When one landed on the deck, she crept forward, crouching down, tail twitching ever so slightly, but she sat up again when the gull flew off, never in any danger from the cat; she was just curious.

One of the other passengers noticed Yedda and whispered to her female companion, pointing, though with a smile, not disapproval. Yedda padded over to them and sat at their feet, placing one paw on the woman's knee. She bent down to stroke her soft grey fur, then looked over towards Shahid and Laurita, giving them a small wave. They smiled and walked over to join them.

Laurita held out her hand and introduced herself, then introduced Shahid as well. 'This is Yedda,' she added, looking down at the cat, who gazed up at them, basking in all the attention and purring loudly.

'We haven't met many cats,' said the woman. 'This one's particularly beautiful.' Yedda stood up and rubbed herself against her legs, tail in the air, its tip curling back and forth. 'And so friendly too!'

'Yes, she is, and it's not long since she came home with me from the Breeding Centre,' said Shahid, using his hand reader.

The woman and her companion both stared at him, gaping. 'Oh, sorry!' they said in unison. 'Aren't you able to speak...um...in the usual way?'

'No,' replied Shahid, with a grin, used to this reaction from strangers. 'I've never been able to, and it seems there's nothing to be done about it. My father's a doctor, so I'm sure it's true.'

'Oh! Well, you seem to manage.' They were still staring at Shahid, but then glanced at each other, a little embarrassed.

'Please don't be embarrassed,' he said. 'Yedda is being trained to help me communicate even better. We're due at the Breeding Centre in Werribee this afternoon for our second session. It's all an experiment. Cats have never helped people with a problem like this before. At least, not to the knowledge of the Centre's staff.'

All this took longer to say than if Shahid had been speaking with his own, natural voice, and Laurita was intrigued by the expressions on the women's faces. They were clearly amazed by his dextrous use of the hand reader, as well as its entirely natural tone and inflexions, which created a voice that suited Shahid extremely well. Yet they were still somewhat taken aback by the experience of dealing with someone with such a rare disability.

'I see!' said the second woman, this time staring at Yedda, who stared back, without blinking. 'Will she understand everything you want to say?'

'Not yet, but with time, I gather she will,' replied Shahid, smiling.

'They're highly sophisticated,' added Laurita, taking Shahid's hand and clasping it gently. He returned the light pressure, grateful for the reassurance. After all, to many people, having Yedda communicate for him might seem even more remarkable than using the hand reader.

'Ah... Well, I'd be willing to try her out, if you like,' said the woman, giving Shahid a bright smile.

As her friend laughed, delighted by the novelty, Yedda swivelled her head to face Shahid, long whiskers fluffed out, eager to test her skills. Shahid grinned and asked her to tell the woman that he and Laurita were enjoying their trip around the bay. 'That should be simple enough,' he thought, but when the woman's eyes widened in surprise, he hesitated before asking, 'What did Yedda tell you?'

'Um, she said you and Laurita were simple enough to enjoy being out on the bay!'

'No, no, that's not what I told her to say!' exclaimed Shahid, blushing, although his dark skin hid this from them. Laurita immediately burst out laughing and patted Yedda, who trilled a high-pitched 'Mrroww' before asking Shahid what she had done wrong.

'Not much,' he answered aloud, forgetting for a moment that his onlookers wouldn't know what he meant. Realising, he turned to them and, with a shrug of his shoulders, explained: 'She asked me what her mistake was. Do you want to try again?'

The two women laughed and nodded, so Shahid tried to focus purely on what he wanted Yedda to tell them. It was difficult, though, to prevent the background murmur that nearly everyone has in their mind from interfering with his message. He then recalled that after giving Yedda exact wording to convey to someone, he was supposed to use the word

'Stop'. For some reason, he had forgotten, most likely because he was becoming used to their almost constant undercurrent of communication. This time, however, they succeeded, and the two women smiled as Yedda managed to tell them that Shahid was enjoying their company...and would they like to have morning tea together?

'Yes,' said the taller of the two women, 'that would be lovely.' When Laurita looked at her questioningly, she explained, and Laurita bent down to stroke Yedda, saying, 'Well done, pussycat!'

Purring, Yedda trotted off, tail in the air, towards the dining room, where the morning repast was set out in grand style. Turning to check they were all following, she found a table towards the back of the room, which had the best view of the city skyline. How the cat knew they would enjoy this was a mystery, but enjoy it they did. The sunlight glittered off the Rialto building, as well as all the other glorious structures soaring high and proud into the blue sky, where not a single cloud marred the scene.

While Shahid helped himself to sparkling apple juice, the others enjoyed a fine pinot noir from the Mornington Peninsula. Yedda, meanwhile, contentedly ate a serving of scrambled egg, much to the amusement of the crew member who, at Laurita's request, served it to her. 'I thought cats ate meat,' he said, looking down at Yedda's eager face.

'Oh no, not for a long time,' replied Laurita. 'There may still be a few wild ones around who do, though hopefully, not many.'

'No, I guess not,' he agreed, before leaving to serve the other passengers. When he had gone, Yedda turned to Laurita and 'said', 'Wild ones?'

'Yedda has asked about the wild cats,' Laurita told the two women, then answered the question: 'Yes. Cats weren't always like you, and weren't always properly looked after, so the wild ones needed to kill other small creatures to live.'

'Eww!' replied Yedda, so 'loudly' the two women heard her as well and gasped in surprise.

Laurita added, 'She has just told me she never wants to meet one.'

'It *would* be strange,' said Shahid thoughtfully. 'They were a lot smaller than Yedda, weren't they?'

'Mostly, although some of the ferals, as they were called, did grow quite big...to a little over half her size.'

'What happened to them all?' asked one of women.

'We don't know the whole story.' Laurita put down her glass of wine and thought about the question for few moments. 'Cats are highly adaptable and can live almost anywhere,' she explained, 'but here in Melbourne, there wasn't anywhere left for them when the inner city drowned. Then, as the suburbs were gradually placed underground, there weren't many structures aboveground where they could hide – only in unmanaged gardens. There were trapping programs as well to eradicate them from the few natural forests on the mainland that survived all the fires, the logging, and changes in climate. I've heard too there was a virus released, designed to make the females sterile. They were almost completely wiped out. If they hadn't been, we wouldn't have as many small animals and birds as we do now. It wasn't the cats' fault, of course; it was ours. They were doing what they evolved to do, but we were the ones who let them loose here in Australia in the first place, just as we did with so many other foreign creatures, which then caused such terrible damage to the environment. An interesting point, though, is that apparently on some islands, the cats kept the population of introduced rats down, which seemed to help some native species survive.'

'Not a pleasant subject for such a lovely day,' said Shahid. He understood Laurita's passion and shared it, but could see the two women were becoming uneasy, both at her tone of voice and at the idea of the cats being trapped and killed. Yedda was becoming agitated as well. He sent her a soothing thought and she settled down to finish the last of her scrambled egg.

'No, it isn't,' agreed Laurita, and changed the subject.

They spent the next half hour enjoying their food and each other's conversation, Laurita making an effort to return to her former light-hearted mood. After all, they were here to enjoy themselves, not to dwell on the past and all its horrific problems. When the ship finally docked at Williamstown, everyone disembarked in the best of spirits, and Laurita and Shahid thanked the two women for making their morning even more pleasant than it already was. It was then only a relatively short trip to Werribee, where they enjoyed a leisurely midsun meal in a small café, afterwards making their way to the Breeding Centre in time for their appointment with the same gentech Shahid saw the previous week for their training session.

As they began to walk the few hundred metres from the callstation nearest to the Centre, the breeze, which had grown stronger since the morning, blew Laurita's long hair about to such an extent that she fished around in her pockets for something with which to tie it back. While she did, Shahid noticed once again how beautiful she really was. Her bare arms, so lithe and strong, were accentuated as she held them up to tie her hair, and he saw how well formed she was in all respects. Unable to resist the impulse, he offered to help and felt a tightening in his stomach as he gathered her hair in his hands, lifting it from her long, smooth neck. His breath quickened and it was all he could do to prevent his hands from trembling while he tied the small, dark green scarf into place. She turned around and they stood there in silence, looking at each other, dark eyes serious, questioning – and then the moment was lost as Yedda pounced on Shahid's feet, curling herself around his ankles and kicking him with her hind feet, pretending to attack.

'Oh you little monster!' exclaimed Laurita, laughing and bending down to swat her on the backside. Unable to join in the laughter in a literal sense, Shahid smiled, and when they eventually entered the Centre's foyer, he linked arms with Laurita, kissing her softly on the cheek.

The gentech was already there and held out a hand to greet them. 'The Guardians are looking forward to meeting you,' he said, with a broad smile. 'They're as excited as we are by Yedda's potential, so let's go and meet them!'

As they neared the habitation enclosure where the Guardians lived, Yedda leapt forward, eagerly pacing to and fro outside its door, impatient to enter. 'Not yet, Yedda,' said the gentech. 'Wait a bit. They first need to understand more about you and your companions. Just let them become accustomed to your presence before we go inside.'

While Yedda grew increasingly excited, repeatedly leaping on and off a nearby chair, Shahid and Laurita felt the lightest of touches in their minds as dozens of cats probed and explored their surface thoughts and feelings. Eventually Yedda stretched up to place her paws upon the heavy plastiglass barrier, then immediately rushed inside when the gentech opened the door. The others followed more slowly. However, Shahid and Laurita stopped in astonishment when they felt their skin begin to tingle and the hair on their forearms stand on end. Shaking his head, Shahid gazed at the gentech, who chuckled as he watched Laurita rubbing the back of her neck.

'When they're all together in one place, they usually affect our guests this way,' explained the gentech. 'We're so used to it, we hardly notice, but it's quite an experience for first-time visitors. Come on, let's sit down and wait for them to come closer.'

He led them to a garden seat, overhung by an elegant ornamental maple, and they all watched as Yedda touched noses, first with one huge black cat, then with a smaller, longhaired brown tabby. One by one, the other cats approached and either touched noses or sat down close by. After a time, when Yedda was virtually encircled by them, it seemed almost as though they were conducting a meeting. Laurita giggled, holding a hand over her mouth, and Shahid, glancing at her, grinned. The gentech noticed, but simply smiled and waited. At last, Yedda walked towards them, followed by the brown tabby, an elegant creature with long legs, small paws and a bushy, plumelike tail. Her green eyes stared straight into theirs as she came closer, studying these new wights. Apparently they met with her approval, because she sat down and began to purr, then licked Yedda's face. Yedda lay down by her side, also purring.

'What now?' asked Shahid.

'Ask Yedda to tell Laurita something very specific, without letting the other cats know as well,' replied the gentech, leaning forward and scratching the tabby beneath the chin. She raised her chin and purred even louder as the gentech obliged by scratching a little longer. He finished by asking her not to 'listen in' to anything Shahid or Laurita were thinking. The tabby stood up and stroked herself against his legs, tail in the air, perfectly happy to cooperate.

Shahid thought for a while, then asked Yedda to tell Laurita that his mother's Namingday was on the tenth of April, remembering this time to say 'Stop' at the end of the message. Yedda sat up straight, fixed her gaze upon Laurita and passed it on. When the gentech silently asked the tabby what, if anything, Yedda had told Laurita, she 'replied', 'The wight's mother has a Namingday on the tenth of April.' The tabby then stretched out her front legs, sharpened her claws on the thick carpeting, and sat down to watch Yedda, who flopped onto her side and began playing with the tabby's tail. Swishing it out of her reach, she touched Yedda on the face with her paw and waited to hear what the wights would say next.

'What happened?' asked Shahid.

'The Guardian heard Yedda's message. Not to worry – this *is* quite difficult.'

'Oh! Well, I'll try again,' and Shahid asked her to pass on a request to Laurita: Would she write a song just for him?

'Yes, of course I will!' exclaimed Laurita, before she could help herself.

The tabby swivelled her head to look first at Shahid, then at the gentech, and finally, at Laurita, who was by now blushing. 'This young wight wants Laurita to write a song for him,' she told the gentech, purring as he suppressed a chuckle. 'No, luck, I'm afraid,' he said. 'It appears Yedda's directional shielding will take a bit of practice.'

Just then, the gentech's comlink chimed. Excusing himself, he read the message displayed on the small screen. 'It seems the weather has turned harsh,' he announced. 'There's a gale warning for the entire Melbourne region and the temperature outside has reached forty-two degrees. It may be too unsafe now for you to travel far. What do you want to do?'

In order not to interrupt their session, Laurita and Shahid had set their comlinks to silently take messages, so when they looked at their listings, they saw the weather warning sent out by the government.

'Is there a communal house here in Werribee where we could spend the night if we needed to?' asked Laurita, unperturbed.

'Yes, there is, about half a kilometre from here, so you could walk safely enough if you went now, before the gale sets in.' He paused while they located it on their comlinks. 'We can make a time for you to come back for another training session later in the week, if you like?'

When Shahid nodded, the gentech suggested 14:00 on the Friday. They agreed to this, then waited for Yedda to finish smooching with the tabby. A loud chorus of cat burblings and trills followed them as they finally left the habitation enclosure.

'What is it about these cats that makes them so special?' asked Shahid, as they walked with the gentech towards the main entrance.

'They're particularly reliable, better able to be specific in their communications with us *and* with other cats, and better at judging when to influence our emotions and behaviour in their role as Guardians. They're part of the Melbourne Peacekeeping Force now, and can be sent interstate if necessary. For example, if someone was in danger from some criminal element, which, although rare, can still happen, one of these cats might agree to become their protector, either for a set period of time, or even permanently. It depends upon whether the cats consider the person in question to be worthy enough.' At Shahid's raised eyebrows, the gentech added, 'They can't be forced to protect someone. There has to be a mutual understanding, just as there was when you met your Yedda.'

'Which seems to indicate the cats couldn't be trained to behave in an anti-social manner,' remarked Laurita, intrigued.

'Oh no, not at all. Quite impossible, as far as we're aware. The risk would be far too great otherwise. They can influence our emotions to a fair extent if they choose to, and can even make themselves invisible to our eyes by making us forget we've seen them. Yes, yes... They're very powerful, but thankfully, also highly cooperative and reasonably placid...until the person they're protecting is threatened. Then, Sun help the one who's doing the threatening!'

'Ah, I see!' said Laurita, with a grin, looking at Yedda and wondering what she might potentially be capable of. Yedda turned around, her eyes gleaming. She had already learnt a great deal from her meeting with the Guardians.

Once outside, they were all struck, literally, by the force of the wind and the oven-like heat. 'You'd better hurry,' the gentech told them, taking a step back into the shelter of the entrance. 'Go on. I'll see you on Friday.' As he waved goodbye, Laurita, Shahid and Yedda leaned into the burning wind and walked as fast as they could towards the communal house.


Earlier, while Shahid, Laurita and Yedda were spending their morning sailing on Port Philip Bay, Karla was giving half her attention to her work and the other half to making preparations for a sumptuous afternoon tea to share with Jonathon. He was due to arrive at 14:00, so after showing him their facilities and her own work area, she intended to take the rest of the afternoon off to enjoy his company.

She and Aurora had managed, after all, to have their morning run along the banks of the nearby Yarra River while it was still reasonably cool, and although they had intended to take a walk in the Willsmere gardens at midsun and eat their meal outside, when she checked the temperature, Karla saw it was already far too hot. Instead, she decided to take a swim in their indoor pool, located in the staff entertainment complex at the rear of the building.

To her delight, it had turned out that Aurora was one of those relatively rare cats who actually liked water, and she had no objection whatsoever to learning how to swim. Therefore, while Karla stripped off her clothes and hung them neatly on the rack provided for the purpose, Aurora jumped in, making a huge splash, then slowly paddled towards the end of the pool, twenty-five metres away.

There was no requirement for swimming costumes, unless people wanted to wear them, which Karla didn't, being quite satisfied with her appearance, so she soon made a highly competent racing dive into the water and quickly caught up with her cat, who by this time was halfway along the length of the pool. When Karla dived beneath the water and rose to the surface at Aurora's side, grabbing her around the middle, Aurora wriggled free and tried to push her under. Not succeeding, she pretended to bite Karla on the neck. They laughed and wrestled for several minutes, until Aurora had had enough and swam off. Karla followed at a leisurely pace and after several lengths of the pool, climbed out to dry off. There were stairs for Aurora to use and Karla chuckled as she watched her leave the water; the sight of the wet cat never failed to amuse her, and Aurora never took offence. Instead, she kept perfectly still while enjoying being dried off with one of the towels the centre provided. Purring loudly as her fur was combed into place, she rubbed her head against Karla's hand, making every attempt to slow down the whole process.

'Alright, that's enough, puddums. I'm hungry, so it's time to go to the kitchen and have something to eat. What do you want, sweetie?'

Aurora sent her an image of unsweetened egg custard, made with rice milk, followed by a small piece of tasty cheese. Karla gave her a pat on the head and soon obliged. While they were eating, Karla's comlink chimed, and when she answered, it was Jonathon, his expression grim.

'Karla,' he said, 'I'm so sorry, but I've had to come in to work. We've all been called in, and everyone will shortly receive a weather warning. The wind has picked up and will soon be blowing at around eighty kilometres per hour, possibly even more. You probably already know the temperature's heading towards the low forties. It's the perfect situation for bushfires, so we have to be on full alert. I'm so sorry, I really am. I was looking forward to seeing you, and Willsmere, today, but we'll have to make it another time.' He turned away for a moment as one of his colleagues spoke to him. 'I have to go, Karla. I hope we'll see each other soon, and in the meantime, take care, and I mean it. Stay indoors, preferably somewhere away from bushland or grassland. It isn't safe.'

Disappointed and alarmed, Karla managed to say, 'I will, I promise. I'll go home after I finish off a few things here. You be careful too. I don't want to hear you've had an accident, or worse.'

'You won't. I'll be fine. We know how to look after ourselves and don't take unnecessary risks... Karla, sorry, I definitely have to go.'

Karla nodded, then sat there, thinking. They hadn't suffered any major bushfire disasters for decades. The forest guardians knew what they were doing. Everything *would* be fine, but nevertheless, if he'd told her to go home, she would do as promised and leave.

In Clayton, Yngwie was enjoying the air-conditioned comfort of their office as he and Kaj worked through the latest set of data collected from the satellites used by the messaging system. Today, Dandelion had stayed in Ferntree Gully with Søren, since he only needed to visit the forest shortly after dawn to inspect the spider traps, then check the female burrows to ensure they were still inhabited. This meant he could leave Dandelion in their room until he returned, after which they intended to go for a walk. Oddly enough, Kaj felt vaguely sorry the cat was absent, having become used to her by now and interested in the way she related to him – so like a human in many respects, yet still very much her own being.

When they were ready for a break, he and Yngwie went to the nearest servery for coffee and sweet biscuits. As they sat down, their comlinks chimed and they were astonished to read the gale warning being issued by the government. Inside their secure building, the world was comfortably excluded and the day sometimes passed so quickly it was almost a surprise to find that outside, when they went home, the weather had completely changed since morning, or it was nighttime and dark.

'What should we do?' asked Yngwie. 'Should we stay here or leave?'

'I'm not sure... We could ask the Gatekeeper. She will know.' Kaj fished his comlink from his tunic pocket and made the call. 'Oh, I see,' Yngwie heard him say. 'We should be safe here, but if the gale continues, it might be better if we went home now? Very well, and thank you.' Kaj put his comlink away and looked at Yngwie. 'You heard everything? It seems it is our choice whether to stay or to leave, but if we stay, it might well be overnight. I think I will stay, but you may go if you want to.'

Yngwie thought of Laurita and wondered if she and Shahid would return from Werribee. Probably not, he concluded. It was a long way to travel if the gale hit *en route*. What about Søren and Dandelion? Were they safely inside by now? Surely they would be sensible enough not to be wandering around outside? Still, there was something making him uneasy. He felt the strongest urge to return to Ferntree Gully.

'In that case,' he told Kaj, 'I'll go home,' and stood up to leave. As he did, he nearly fainted from the impact of the scream inside his head. He staggered and was only saved from falling by Kaj's hand gripping his arm.

'What on Earth!' exclaimed Kaj. 'What *is* the matter?'

Yngwie could only groan and mutter, 'There's something wrong. There's something wrong with Søren and Dandelion. I have to go!' He tried to straighten up and almost fell over, but with Kaj's hand to steady him, managed instead to sit down. He took a deep breath, and as suddenly as he felt ill, felt fine again. Giving his head a shake, he said, 'I don't know how she's done it, Kaj, but Dandelion is in trouble and is calling for help. She's in the forest and Søren is in there too.'

While Kaj gaped at him, astounded, Yngwie turned and left, running as fast as he could towards the entrance of the building, leaving several startled bystanders wondering whether they too should be leaving.

During the morning, at around 08:30 the same day, when the breeze was pleasantly cool and the sky a bright wonderful blue, with only a few fluffy clouds near the horizon, six-year-old Preeti said to her mother, 'May I play with Lawrence today? We could take some food and have our midsun meal down by the creek then come straight home again. Please?'

Preeti's mother looked down at her daughter and smiled. She was always a good girl and never got into trouble. Her glossy black hair was plaited into a long, thick braid and, with her mother's help, she had just finished tying a scarlet ribbon around its tip. 'There,' said Preeti. 'Don't I look beautiful?' She twirled around to let her mother see the full effect of her outfit: a red and blue silk tunic; a pair of matching blue, loose trousers; and dark green, comfortable yet robust, slippers.

Her mother kneeled down to hold her close, saying, 'Yes, my beautiful daughter, you look just as you should, and yes, I will make something special for you and Lawrence to eat together. But please, remember not to wander off too far.'

'I promise we won't, and anyway, you always know where I am.' Preeti held up the small ID tag hanging from its silver chain around her slim throat.

'Well, this is as it ought to be, my dear. You are too precious to lose.' She released her daughter, stood up and went into the kitchen. Meanwhile, Preeti called Lawrence and said, 'Yes, we're allowed to play together and have our picnic by the creek. Mummy is making the food now. You could bring something too, if you wanted?'

Lawrence, also six years old, replied, 'Oh good! I love what your mother makes! I can bring our drinks...some lemonade or apple juice. What do you like best?'

'Oh,' replied Preeti, trying to sound grown up, 'I prefer apple juice.'

'Right,' said Lawrence, 'I'll bring the apple juice, and some chocolate in a cooler bag so it won't melt. We can have it for dessert. When do you want to come over?'

Preeti looked at the clock on her ID tag. 'Mummy says she'll be finished cooking in about an hour, so I can meet you at your house at about 10:00.'

'Alright... And I have something special to show you!' Lawrence grinned, showing the small gap between his two front teeth, which gave him a somewhat cheeky appearance, enhanced by his curly blonde hair and a sprinkling of freckles across his nose.

'What is it?' replied Preeti.

'I'll show you when we get to the creek. It's a surprise. I found it in the toolshed.'

'Oh.' Preeti couldn't imagine what might be in a toolshed that would interest her...unless, perhaps, it was something with which to paint pictures? She loved digital painting, even more so if the colours were bright, and often used her hand reader for this purpose.

'No, you'll like it. I know you will!' insisted Lawrence. 'Anyway, my Mum's calling me, so I'd better go. See you soon.'

Preeti wandered into the kitchen, thinking about what the surprise might be. However, she soon forgot about it when her mother invited her to help make the savoury pastries she loved so much. At last, everything was packed neatly into a small backpack and off she went, first skipping along, then walking, and finally running as fast as she could down the grassy hillside to where Lawrence lived. She pressed her small hand to the greenhouse identification panel and waited until he appeared at the door. 'Are you ready?' she asked.

Lawrence grinned cheekily, then pointed to the cooler bag he was carrying and cried, 'Come on! Let's run!'

By the time the two children reached the creek, about half a kilometre from Lawrence's house, they were laughing so much they were out of breath. The creek was shallow and had a smooth bed with only a few rocks, so they left their bags in the shade of an old gum tree, took off their shoes, rolled up their trouser legs, and were soon paddling around in the water, splashing each other and searching for anything of interest along the banks. A bright blue dragonfly hovered nearby, but when Lawrence tried to catch it, the insect flew off, its body gleaming in the sunlight, its wings a small rainbow of colour. They even came across a lizard, though it quickly skittered away and hid itself in amongst some fallen branches. A kookaburra, perched in the gum tree, was following its movements with great interest, but when no other lizards presented themselves to its keen eye, it flew off, yet was soon replaced by a small flock of crimson rosellas, who closely studied the children. Deciding they weren't a threat, the birds flew down into an area of long grass to search for seeds. The two children kept perfectly still, watching them, until Lawrence became bored and let loose a loud cry, which sent the birds screeching off into the distance.

'What did you do that for!' protested Preeti. 'They're so beautiful! I wanted them to stay a bit longer.'

'They'll come back, or some other birds will.' Lawrence gave her shoulder a little shove, whereupon Preeti gave his a harder one, and before long they were in the water, clothes and all, shrieking and splashing each other and generally having a wonderful time. After a while, they became hungry, so clambered up the bank and raced each other to where their food was waiting for them beneath the tree. As they ate and dried off, they could see the heat haze and feel the breeze pick up, but being children, were unworried and not at all uncomfortable, except when the flies wanted to share their food. Fortunately, they had repellent with them, so even this small nuisance was quickly dealt with.

Their meal finished, they lay contentedly on their backs, watching the gum leaves shimmer in the sunlight. 'What's the surprise you brought with you?' asked Preeti, still gazing up into the branches of the old tree.

'Oh yes! Here, I'll show you.' Lawrence rolled onto his side and pulled an old magnifying glass from his pocket, handing it to Preeti. 'What do you think this is?' he said, with a grin.

Preeti turned it over in her hand, fascinated by what seemed to be real glass, something she had rarely seen. The handle was made from wood, too, also a rarity. She stroked its smooth surface and then the glass, which seemed to her to have an almost silky feel. 'What does it do?'

'It makes things look bigger.' Lawrence put out his hand and Preeti reluctantly gave it to him. He found a small stone, held the magnifying glass over it, looked through it, and told Preeti to do the same, moving away slightly. She rolled onto her stomach and shuffled herself closer, letting out an amazed 'Oh!' when she saw what the device could do. 'Oh!' she exclaimed a second time, then grabbed the magnifying glass and ran off with it towards the patch of long grass, dropping down and hiding from sight. Lawrence leapt to his feet and ran after her. When he reached Preeti, she was holding the glass over a small line of tiny ants scurrying towards their nest not far away. 'They're so big!' she exclaimed, laughing. 'Look at them! I never knew they had such funny little legs. They're so cute!'

Lawrence crouched down beside her and she gave him the magnifying glass to see for himself. As he did, a beam of sunlight went through at precisely the right angle to burn the ants. It was his turn to exclaim 'Oh!'

and then 'Ah!' when it happened again. 'You hurt them!' cried Preeti. 'How did you do that?'

'I don't know,' said Lawrence, moving the glass away from the ants and onto a seed head of grass. 'Let's try again and work it out.' He squinted up at the sun, then held the magnifying glass so it would focus the light onto the seed head. With a tiny puff of smoke, it burst into flame, which almost immediately went out. Lawrence ran his finger over the surface of the glass and noticed it was rounded on both sides. 'It's called a 'lens',' he announced proudly, remembering something his mother, who was a preceptor, once told him when they were looking at the stars together one night using a telescope. 'It brings the light into one spot and because it's so strong, the light gets hotter.'

'Let me try,' said Preeti eagerly, taking the glass from Lawrence. She held it over some of the grass tips and watched, spellbound, as they also burst into flame, but this time, the small fire spread into the twigs lying at the base of the clump of grass. They leapt to their feet, looking for something to put it out with, but they hadn't brought a picnic blanket to sit on, which they could have used to smother the flames, and their feet were still bare, so they couldn't stamp them out. The only thing they had was the cooler bag, so Preeti grabbed it and ran to the creek, quickly filling it before sprinting back to the burning grass. The flames hissed, but the fire only smouldered where the water fell, while the rest continued to spread, fanned by the strengthening breeze.

'Run, Lawrence!' she screamed. 'Run!'

## CHAPTER NINETEEN

'There's a hotspot near Montrose, moving fast, towards the forest, and a second one developing near the old Olinda township site,' said Aaron, frowning. 'I'm picking up five comlink signals in the second area, although three of them seem to be heading away from the hotspot and are about two kilometres south-west of it. The other two are in the immediate danger zone.'

Jonathon swiftly alerted the firefighters, but it was a race against time, which, with wind speeds of ninety-two kilometres per hour, they were set to lose. By the time the airjets reached the second hotspot, the flames were already climbing the loose bark of the eucalypts and heading towards the canopy. Before long, dark columns of smoke were visible from as far away as Clayton, where Yngwie saw them while he waited at a callstation near the Computer Site. 'Transport in six minutes,' droned the terminal in answer to his request, its tones annoyingly neutral.

'Shit!' Yngwie swore a second time as he stood there, watching the smoke. Six long minutes ticked by and when the railcar arrived, he leapt onto it, fervently wishing that despite its speed, it would go even faster. At least it was cool inside, which was something to be thankful for. As he wasn't the only person to have noticed the columns of smoke, or to have received the gale warning, the railcar stopped many times to pick up passengers before it arrived at Ferntree Gully, full to overflowing with anxious people talking about the situation and what they intended to do next. There were children still at school to worry about, farm animals outside to gather and lead to safety, family and friends to contact to find out if any of them needed help...and for those who cared about such things, the likelihood there would be terrified and injured wildlife to assist as they tried to escape the flames.

However, none of these matters were on Yngwie's mind as he made his way through the crowd towards the communal house, where he intended to change his clothes, pick up supplies, set his comlink to take silent messages, then get to the forest as quickly as he could. When he eventually left, he was carrying a backpack containing water, emergency rations, first-aid equipment, a lightweight power saw, a torch, rope, a facemask, and a fire blanket, all of which a dumbstruck manager had given him when he told her what he was about to do. Dandelion's presence was in his mind the entire way, but whatever was happening, she couldn't put together a coherent message...or at least, for some unknown reason, he was unable to 'see' what was happening to either her or Søren. He paused to check where the worst of the smoke was coming from and which way the wind was blowing. As far as Yngwie could make out, the direction Dandelion's pleas for help were coming from was not in the direct path of the fire, but if the wind changed by even a few degrees, they almost certainly would be.

Today, being the third Tuesday of the month, was, as usual, set aside for the senior students of the Mitcham regional school to take time off for private study. The previous day, Vera, Lenni and Yeasmin, all seventeen years of age, had persuaded their parents to allow them to spend their free day hiking in the Dandenong Ranges, rather than studying. Practiced bushwalkers, with a thorough knowledge of the area and the western slopes of the forest, they promised to be back well before their evening meal.

'Well, start early, at around 08:00,' said Vera's father. 'Take plenty of water and a fire blanket each, and whatever you do, don't turn off your comlinks. Keep close to the access ways so you don't have far to a clearing if anything happens, and if a weather warning is issued, make sure you return straight away.'

'Yes, Dad, we'll be sensible. There hasn't been a fire in the area for ages, so we'll be fine, and I promise to be back by 17:00 at the latest. Don't worry!' She kissed her father's cheek then went to her room to tell her friend, Yeasmin, that she had permission to go on their hike the next day, as planned.

'Good,' said Yeasmin. 'My parents were a bit worried, but they're so trusting, I had no trouble convincing them this was just an ordinary bush walk and nothing at all would happen to worry them.' She laughed, and Vera grinned, saying, 'Oh no, nothing out of the ordinary at all! Won't they be surprised! Them, and everybody else... Has Lenni called?'

'Yeah, a few minutes before you did. Same story, though her Mum was a bit suspicious when Lenni told her she was going with us. She knows I've had a few rows with the preceptors at school, and that you're my best friend. Anyway, not to worry. The main thing is, Lenni will be coming with us. It'll be even more fun with someone else along...and Lenni can take the blame if something goes wrong. With *her* interests, it wouldn't be hard for everyone to believe it was her fault.'

'No,' agreed Vera, laughing. 'Okay, so we'll still meet at the callstation at the base of Mount Dandenong at about 08:30, and walk on from there, yes?'

'Yes, so here's to our success!' Grinning, Yeasmin pretended to raise a glass to toast the occasion, then said goodbye to her friend.

The next morning saw the three girls decked out in hiking boots, fireproof clothing, and hats to protect their heads from the sun. They had food and water in their backpacks, heavy gloves, a fire blanket each, and facemasks, in case of emergency. Most importantly, Yeasmin carried a fire lighter and a small, yet highly efficient, fire extinguisher of the latest design, borrowed from her parents without their knowledge and carefully tested beforehand.

As they set off towards the base of the mountain, they concentrated on walking – in single file and making sure they didn't veer off from their path, which led towards where the township of Olinda once thrived. It was heavy going, through rugged terrain, but they were fit and strong, and even as the temperature began to rise, it hardly worried them. Besides, it was significantly cooler within the forest and they made good headway. By 12:30, they had reached their destination and took off their backpacks.

'We deserve a break, don't you think?' said Lenni, with a grin.

'Definitely!' agreed Yeasmin, and Vera began by taking out her fire blanket and spreading it on the ground near a fallen tree so they could sit in comfort with their backs against it. The air smelled of clean earth and the ever-present eucalypts, as well as, very faintly, of smoke. 'Smoke?' said Lenni. 'That's weird. It must be a campfire. They shouldn't be lighting one in the forest at all, and particularly not on a day like this. It couldn't be a bushfire, could it?' She glanced at Yeasmin for guidance.

Yeasmin looked up from rummaging through her backpack and sniffed the air, then listened. 'No, there are heaps of birds singing. If it was a bushfire, they'd have left by now. It's probably some idiot lighting a campfire. Still, maybe we'd better investigate before we have something to eat. Lenni, you stay here while Vera and I see what's happening. We won't be long.'

A few hundred metres further in, towards Olinda, the girls spotted two men, one relatively young and the other somewhat older looking. They were indeed sitting by a small campfire, lit within a depression made in the earth and surrounded by large stones. The clearing where they sat seemed to be remarkably regular in shape, with no overhanging trees or even small shrubs growing inside it. 'Must be part of the old town,' whispered Vera. 'Something must have been built there once and whatever it is, is stopping the forest from growing back. Their fire seems safe enough. Should we tell them to put it out anyway?'

'No,' answered Yeasmin. 'It looks as if they're boiling water in an old-fashioned billy. They could be just soaking up the atmosphere of the old town. The fire looks safe, too. I think we can leave them to it, particularly since it wouldn't be good if they knew we were here. It would ruin our plan.'

'True. Okay, let's go back.'

Not long afterwards, they were all sitting down to their small meal, their legs stretched out comfortably, backs against the fallen log. 'This is amazing,' said Vera, her mouth full.

'Isn't it though,' agreed Lenni, taking another sip of ice-cold water. 'Listen to those birds! What do you think they are? Lorikeets?'

'Yes, I think so. There are currawongs here too. Did you hear that? There's a whole flock of them.'

Yeasmin had little interest in the birds so didn't bother to comment. She enjoyed bushwalking mainly for the exercise, the sense of isolation, and the challenge. 'Are you almost finished?' she asked the others. 'We should do what we came here for, then get back before it gets any hotter. The wind's picking up too, so we'd better get a move on.'

Vera stood up and stretched, packed away her things, then took out her comlink. Yeasmin handed the fire lighter to Lenni and took the fire extinguisher from her backpack, then positioned herself ready to use it. Lenni collected a small bundle of twigs and dry leaves, piled them into a tidy heap, broke a small branch into three pieces, and added the pieces to the heap. She then took a sheet of old wrapping paper from her backpack, tore it into four pieces, scrunched them up, and carefully poked them in beneath the twigs. 'There,' she said, 'that should do nicely. I'll just add one more piece of wood and we should be right. Are you ready, Vera? This has to look good!' When Vera nodded, Lenni applied her fire lighter to the paper. The twigs and leaves instantly crackled into life. The small branches were soon alight as well, and when the larger piece of wood began to burn strongly, Vera recorded the fire, with sound, making sure to catch the best close-up effect. 'Okay, Yeasmin,' she said, 'you can put it out.'

Yeasmin started the fire extinguisher and fire retardant immediately spurted forth – for only two seconds, before it failed! 'Oh crap!' she exclaimed and leapt forward to stamp out the fire. While Lenni stared in horror, before running to her backpack for the water container, Vera rushed off to grab a fire blanket. Meanwhile, the larger piece of wood exploded, sending embers into a nearby shrub as well as in three other directions. The shrub and undergrowth burst into flame, and before the girls could beat it out, the fire had spread into the leaf litter and into the thick layers of loose dry bark and small twigs lying on the ground. The heat was incredible as the flames began to make their way towards a nearby gum tree, which was shedding its bark, providing the fire with all the fuel it could ever want. A brushtail possum, which had been sleeping in a hollow further up the trunk, came rushing down, head first, and then, bewildered by the sunlight, the smoke, and the presence of people, ran in a circle, before disappearing down the hillside at full speed. Several smaller ringtail possums soon appeared as well and followed the brushtail, fleeing for their lives. Above them, a lone raven cried out, while a small flock of pink and white galahs flew overhead, shrieking in fear.

The three girls could feel the intense heat through the thick soles of their boots as they continued to stamp and beat at the flames, but it was no use. The wind blew the debris into the air and hurled it ahead of the main fire, starting new ones, and it soon became obvious that if they were to save themselves, they had to leave. Lenni threw the fire lighter into the nearest pile of burning bark and they fled, not thinking to activate their emergency signals until long after, when they were safe, running along the nearest access way, two kilometres upwind from the fire they were responsible for igniting.

'What's that?' said Andre, standing up. 'I can smell smoke, other than what's coming from our campfire.'

His friend, Maarten, stood up as well and looked around, listening. Apart from the distant screeching of a flock of cockatoos, the forest had become silent. 'We'd better put our fire out and leave,' he said. 'I think a bushfire may have started.' He stared hard at the treetops to judge which way the wind was blowing. 'We should head upwind, further up the mountain, then move along the ridge towards where we left our landjet. It's only about one and half kilometres, so we should be safe enough.'

He used the spade they had brought with them to break up their small fire, then shovelled soil onto it, moved the hot rocks well away from each other, making sure there were no twigs or leaves nearby, and finally, stamped the soil down and poured water onto it. Satisfied, the two men packed their few belongings and began walking at a steady pace up the mountain, away from the smoke that was now becoming visible.

'We should notify the guardians,' said Maarten, once they were about five hundred metres from their campsite and feeling safer.

'You're right.' Andre stopped, sat down on a rock and made the call. 'Yes, we're in the Dandenong Ranges forest, about three hundred metres north of the old town of Olinda, and there seems to be a bushfire here.' He waited for a response, then said, 'We don't seem to be in any immediate danger, and there's only about one kilometre to go before we reach our landjet, which is parked on a broad access way. It should be safe enough, unless the wind changes direction. Do you want us to wait for someone to get here, or should we leave now?'

He put away his comlink, saying, 'They want us to leave. Another fire has broken out as well and they predict the wind will become even stronger. It doesn't sound too good, my friend.' Andre briefly put his hand on Maarten's shoulder and they continued on, increasing their pace a little. As they walked, the light took on a different quality, a strange, dusky tinge. A wallaby hopped past, and then another. Normally shy creatures, they too were fleeing for their lives and paid no attention to the two men. A snake crossed their path, also looking for safety, and they hastily moved out of its way. When they finally arrived at the access way, two uniformed peacekeepers were there waiting for them.

'Oh dear,' murmured Andre. 'I think perhaps we shouldn't have lit our little fire. Someone has most likely seen it and reported us for having started all this.'

'Perhaps,' replied Maarten, 'but they may have tracked our comlink signals and are just checking we're safe.'

'I hope so,' replied Andre. 'Hello!' he called out as they came closer. One of the peacekeepers took a step forward and held out his identification. Putting it away, he said, 'Hello. Andre and Maarten? Yes? We want you to accompany us to the Montrose Detention Centre. One of you will come with me in our airjet and my colleague will drive your landjet. We have information that you may be responsible for starting this forest fire, so we can discuss the details once we're there. Do you have any questions?'

Both men shook their heads and did as they were asked, feeling guilty, even though they knew the bushfire was not their doing. Still, they had broken the law, and as a result, would in all likelihood face charges.

Half an hour later, as they sat in the wonderfully cool detention centre, Andre admitted to having lit a small campfire, even though they understood it was illegal, but they'd made sure it was safe, and afterwards, that it was properly put out before leaving their campsite. 'We came to Olinda to trace where our ancestors lived, about three hundred years ago, before the town was abandoned. We even stumbled upon a few old artefacts, including this billy, and we wanted to test it – get back the atmosphere of the place for a while.' He delved into his backpack and withdrew the battered, rusty utensil, which although old, appeared to be from more recent times.

'I can understand your wanting to connect with the past, Andre, but lighting the fire was unbelievably irresponsible, so I hope your tea was worth it,' said the peacekeeper, 'and I hope we can corroborate your story when we inspect the campsite. That's assuming it doesn't end up being nothing but ash over the next few days. At the moment, it's far too dangerous to go back to check. You're lucky to have got out in time. Now, did either of you see anyone else in the area?'

Andre shook his head, while Maarten said, 'No, we saw no one at all during the three days we were there. It was wonderfully peaceful...until now, that is.' He looked down at his hands. 'You *must* believe us. Our fire wasn't the problem. We're experienced campers, and yes, we shouldn't have lit it, but truly, this bushfire started some distance further down the mountain. We could smell the smoke, which is why we left when we did, and why we reported it as soon as we safely could. It was our intention to stay a few days longer. You can check with the forest guardians because we lodged a request to be allowed to camp there.'

'Well, that would certainly help confirm your intentions in being there were honest, but it doesn't rule out the possibility you accidentally started the forest fire. Until we can check your story, you'll have to stay here. Anyway, it's too risky to be wandering about outside.' The peacekeeper stood up, indicating Andre and Maarten should come with him, then led them to a modest but comfortable room containing all the basic necessities, including a servery, small bathroom, and two beds. 'You'll be fine here until tomorrow morning,' he said, not unkindly, 'and you're welcome to use your comlinks to call anyone you want, or to access the lattice for anything else you need.'

He left them to ponder what would happen next and to hope that, somehow, their story could be corroborated.


When Søren returned from his early morning spider-hunting trip in the forest, he found Dandelion fast asleep in their room, tightly curled up on the bed. He looked at her for a few moments, then tiptoed into the bathroom to tidy up before crawling into bed, careful not to disturb her. They slept for nearly three hours, until almost 10:00, when Dandelion awoke, patted Søren's face with one paw and loudly demanded breakfast. He rolled over, stroked her head, and tried to go back to sleep, but this, it seemed, was out of the question.

Sitting up, Søren yawned, climbed out of bed, put on his dark red, ankle-length silk dressing gown and looked at the weather forecast for an update. 'It will be a hot, awful day, Dandelion,' he said. 'Are you sure you want to go outside?'

When Dandelion made it clear that she did, he sighed, but dressed and fetched her leash. At first she wriggled in protest as he fastened it to her collar, then gave in and followed him meekly to the dining room. Half an hour later, they were ready for their walk, even though Søren had serious misgivings when he felt how hot it already was outside. Still, if they were back in time for a late midsun meal, they might avoid the worst of the heat.

He paused, then decided it would be best to head uphill rather than down to the flatter areas, where the temperature would most likely be a few degrees higher. Skirting the edge of the forest, they walked steadily onwards, with Dandelion slowing them down by seeming to investigate almost every leaf and twig she came across. When the breeze caught one of the leaves and sent it into the air, she leapt after it, but was stopped short by the leash. Annoyed, she pulled against it, but after a sharp reprimand, settled back into a more sedate walk – for all of ten minutes, after which she was intent on seeing what lay beneath a rotting branch about two metres into the forest. While Dandelion scrabbled about, digging a small hole, Søren waited as she then crouched down to see whether she had unearthed anything of interest. Finding only a few ants and a small millipede, she stood up and went a little further into the forest, sniffing the air. Reluctant to allow her to continue, Søren called her back, gently tugging the leash. As he did, a black form appeared where the trees began to grow more densely. Dandelion froze, her tail down, ears pricked.

'What on Earth is that!' exclaimed Søren under his breath, peering into the shadows.

When the black form came closer, Dandelion crept forward until she could just make out that it seemed to be a creature with four legs and a tail, like her, but almost twice as large. Growling softly, she crouched down and waited, and as she did, the creature bounded forward and leapt for Søren's throat. With a yell, he thrust it aside, shocked by the weight of the animal, but slipped as he stepped backwards. He fell to his knees, dropping Dandelion's leash, then saw it was some type of dog, enormous and snarling, savage teeth bared, its small eyes fixed on him, preparing to pounce.

Having never seen one in real life, only in old video footage, for a few precious moments, utterly confused, Søren lost the advantage he may have gained by recovering more quickly and standing to confront it. Instead, the dog saw him as an easy victim and attacked, only to meet Dandelion in its path, screaming in rage, tail fluffed out to its full extent, hackles raised and ears flattened, bracing herself to strike. Søren scrambled to his feet, grabbed a small rock lying nearby and threw it at the dog, hitting it on the shoulder. With a low growl, the dog hesitated, then turned to lope away, but Dandelion hurled herself forward to leap onto its back, sinking her teeth into its neck, claws tearing at its face. Howling in pain and anger, the dog reared up on its hind legs, furiously shaking itself, flinging her off. She hit the ground, hard, but swiftly rolled over, set to rip the dog's chest with her powerful hind feet as it loomed over her, attempting to grasp her in its jaws. Dandelion lashed out, her front claws striking its nose. With blood streaming from its wounds, the dog gave up and fled, with the cat in pursuit. She had lost all control, racing into the forest, intent on catching and killing her foe!

Søren, who had watched, horrified, unable to do anything for fear of being attacked, yelled at the top of his lungs for her to come back, but nothing penetrated her mind. All was an intense, blood-red blur, inhabited only by the desire to defeat this predator who had dared to attack her companion. They ran on, deeper into the forest, with Søren following as fast as he could, stumbling on rocks and tripping over fallen branches, but not giving up. Panting, he stopped for a moment to catch his breath, fumbled in his pocket for the electronic device used to unlock a cat's collar, activated it, then continued on, still following the sound of them crashing through the undergrowth. He caught sight of Dandelion's white coat, and glimpsed the black dog as well. They were running at almost the same speed, but the dog's legs were longer and Dandelion was beginning to lose ground. 'Stop!' he shouted. 'Dandelion, stop! We can't be in here. It's too dangerous. Please, stop!' She ignored him, lost to everything except her quarry.

After almost half an hour, Søren's legs gave out and he sank to the ground, exhausted. On level ground, it would have been another story, but running uphill at such speed, in this heat, was too much for him. Trying one last time, he called Dandelion, but she had disappeared. With a sob of utter frustration and near panic, Søren stood and began walking in what he hoped was the direction they had taken. The trees soared above him, majestic, mysterious, age-old: his friends, or so he considered them. Taking a deep breath, he sat down with his back against a mountain ash and did his best to calm down. She would come back eventually and it was unlikely the dog would return to attack. Dandelion had successfully frightened it off, and may even have saved his life; he knew what dogs were capable of, which is one of the reasons they were now a rarity. But a wild one! How could that be?

'Damn it!' He swore, loudly, then tried to think rationally. Could Dandelion become lost, unable to make her way home? No, that seemed equally unlikely, not unless she became confused by something else in the forest, something which frightened rather than angered her. A snake? Possible, he thought, quite possible in this weather and at this time of day. What about the leash? Could it have caught on something? If it did, with her collar unlocked, both it and the leash should fall free. Surely she wasn't trapped somewhere?

He couldn't simply return to the communal house and assume she would as well. All he could do was continue on, call out regularly and focus his mind on hers as best he could. She would eventually respond, he was sure of it. 'Focus,' he reminded himself, and pictured her as she was this morning: curled up on their bed, calm and contented, then afterwards, enjoying her breakfast. 'Keep this clearly in mind,' Søren told himself as he stood up and began to walk. He looked at his comlink: 12:42. 'No midsun meal for you, my friend,' he thought, wishing he had at least brought some water. Well, too bad! He'd be fine, although missing meals was not something he was used to...until recently, that is, in Greenland.

Some time afterwards, his comlink chimed and he saw the government-issued gale warning. 'Oh, how wonderful!' he muttered. 'We can only hope none of these trees decide to fall on my head...or on Dandelion's! Blast it!' He grimaced when he realised what he'd said and sat down to rest for a while. The wind had picked up and the sound of it in the treetops reminded him of surf striking a beach. Damnation! This was becoming dangerous. 'Come back you stupid cat!' he yelled at the top of his voice. 'Forget the damned dog! Come back, Dandelion!'

Nothing... He heard nothing, either in his mind or in the forest, to tell him she was listening, or had even heard him, but then a distant wail sounded in his mind. 'You're not stupid, my darling,' he cried, leaping to his feet. 'Stay where you are, I'm coming. Don't go any further, just wait!'

The first thing Shahid did when he and Laurita reached the communal house in Werribee was to call his mother. 'We can't return home yet,' he told her, using the keypad on his hand reader, 'and may have to stay overnight here in Werribee. Where are you?'

'I am at home, dear, and your father is at work. We're quite safe, and I intend to rest this afternoon in case I'm needed tonight or early tomorrow. Everyone seems to be handling the gale warning extremely well and we haven't received any reports coming in of anything serious, only the usual small mishaps we'd expect. The medcentre is on alert, of course, and the staff will be on call. I am too, naturally.' Wania smiled to reassure her son. 'How is Laurita, and is Yedda all right? It must be dreadful for her, having lived in the safety of the Breeding Centre until so recently.'

Laurita peered over Shahid's shoulder to say hello, and when Yedda clambered onto his knee to add her face to the 'conversation', Wania laughed as the cat pushed her nose and whiskers closer, taking up almost the entire screen. She blew Yedda a kiss, then said, 'Well, I'm glad to see you're all fine! Let me know if anything happens, and I promise to do the same. Otherwise, I'll assume you will all come home when this storm blows over.'

'Yes we will, and promise me too that you won't go outside unless it's absolutely necessary?' Shahid knew his mother might be needed if anyone was injured or required counselling, and he also knew she sometimes tended to ignore her own welfare when she felt others' was at stake.

'I promise. Now go and enjoy yourselves. You may as well.'

'True. We *could* see what the communal house has to offer in the way of entertainment.' Shahid grinned, and while he and Laurita said goodbye, Yedda placed her paw on the small screen, making Wania laugh. 'Goodbye, Yedda,' she said, pressing a finger to the screen and then closing the connection.

# CHAPTER TWENTY

As the smoke thickened and walking became more difficult because of the decreased visibility and his need to wear a mask, Yngwie concentrated on the task of putting one foot in front of the other and keeping Dandelion's presence focused. Until he found her, and hopefully Søren too, there was little point engaging the emergency signal on his comlink, but meanwhile, he had set it to broadcast the emergency reports. He trudged on, stopping now and then for a sip of water and ignoring the fact that he seemed to be heading straight towards the fire front. Yngwie was able to sense which direction to walk by following Dandelion's 'voice', which was becoming increasingly desperate in its pleas for help. Unfortunately, he was finding this so stressful it was wearing him out far more than the physical exertion, which under normal circumstances would have been relatively trivial.

Startled by a large body crashing through the undergrowth at speed, grunting loudly as it went, Yngwie hesitated, then saw that the sound came from a terrified wombat, presumably seeking shelter. Clearly it had either lost its way or was heading for its burrow. He hoped it was the latter and the creature would be safe, yet knew that many would be injured or killed. He pushed the thought away, unable to deal with it. Yet what of Shahid's trees? The mountain ash? Would *they* survive this fire if it spread? Too awful if they should die, and just when the seed gatherers were anticipating a good crop.

How long had he been walking? Too long... Why were they so far into the forest? What were they thinking! Still, there had to be a good reason...surely... He paused again, listening, trying to filter out the roar of the wind in the treetops, to hear if there were any voices other than Dandelion's inside his head. No, nothing. 'Walk on, keep walking,' Yngwie told himself. 'Just keep walking and you'll find them.'

Søren stumbled on, his legs almost giving out as he breathed in the smoke of the oncoming bushfire. 'Please, please let me find her,' he whispered, his throat raw and his eyes stinging. He stopped to listen. She was close, he could hear her, but the darkness that had fallen over the forest made it difficult to see anything other than the outlines of the trees. He nearly tripped over a rock, but managed not to fall. Odd, Dandelion's voice seemed to be coming from below, even though he was walking uphill, so how could that be?

Moving slowly now, Søren trod carefully. If her voice was coming from somewhere lower down, there could only be one explanation: she had fallen into a hole of some kind – and he didn't particularly want to follow in after her! He could see a mound ahead of him, which seemed to be where her wailing was coming from, although this hardly made sense. At last, as he carefully put one foot forward to feel his way along the edge of the mound, he realised he was standing on something regular and firm. Kneeling down, he cleared away the leaves and debris and saw a stone surface; he was standing on the remains of a building and realised what must have happened – this place was buried long ago, perhaps by a landslide, and Dandelion had followed the dog as it bounded across what was left of either its roof or floor, but she had fallen through into a space below.

Crawling now on hands and knees, Søren cleared away more of the debris as he went and eventually found the place where Dandelion had indeed fallen through. He lay on his stomach, edging forward until he found a jagged gap. There she was, gazing up at him, some four metres below, her eyes glinting in the light of the small torch he habitually carried when out walking. He could see there was something wrong with her hind leg and her white fur showed where blood had seeped through. Her plaintive cries were almost more than he could bear. What to do? If she was unable to find a way out, then how could he find a way down? No choice...he had to!

The wind was becoming stronger and the reports coming through on his comlink told him that the fire was nowhere near under control. If he engaged the emergency signal, how long would it take for someone to reach them? Possibly too long, but either way, it should be done before he did anything else. In the meantime, it might be safer to be inside this old stone building.

Søren felt along the surface of what appeared to be a main wall. It seemed to be sound enough and the drop seemed clear – nothing to snag himself on, as Dandelion had most likely done when she fell. If he let himself down, then dropped the remaining two metres or so, he would probably land without being hurt. He knew how to roll on impact. On the other hand, there might be something sharp down there – it was impossible to tell. However, leaving Dandelion was out of the question and trying to find his way back was pointless; he would simply become lost. There was nothing for it but to make the attempt. At least he could examine Dandelion's wound, bind it with his kerchief if necessary, and comfort her.

As he hung by his fingers before letting himself drop, a sudden gust of wind toppled one of the mountain grey gums growing nearby. It crashed down over the old building, a branch struck him on both the shoulder and the side of his head, and he fell. Dandelion screamed in terror, then dragged herself to Søren's side, licking the wound on his head and meowing piteously.

'Mummy, Mummy!' screamed Preeti. 'We didn't mean to! We were playing. It was an accident!' She ran into her mother's arms as she waited outside, scanning the hillside, her long dark hair blowing in the wind.

Hugging her daughter and forcing herself to remain calm, Preeti's mother quickly said, 'Come inside, both of you.' She opened the door and ushered the two children into the greenhouse. 'Now, tell me, what did you and Lawrence do?'

Preeti looked up into her mother's face, glanced at Lawrence, who was staring down at his bare feet, then blurted out, 'We started a fire! Mummy, we didn't mean to! Lawrence had a magnifying glass and we were looking at the grass, and it caught fire!' Tears began running down her little face, while Lawrence tried hard not to cry as well, though didn't succeed. Rubbing his eyes, he pulled the lens from his pocket and thrust it at Preeti's mother. 'Here,' he said. 'You take it. I borrowed it from our shed.'

Having never seen such a thing before, she took it from the boy, turning it over in her hand. However, this was not the time to worry about the strange object... There was a fire outside, moving across the hill – away from their homes, thank the Sun – and she needed to notify the authorities in case they hadn't already spotted it. 'Come downstairs and we'll call the forest guardians. They'll know what to do, and we can show this to them if they come here asking to speak with us. So, sit down in the kitchen, and afterwards we can have something good to eat and drink. Lawrence, I'll let your mother know you are here and she can come to fetch you. Yes?'

Lawrence nodded, and followed them into the kitchen, listening while the two calls were made: 'Yes, the children accidentally began the fire here in Montrose. They were playing in the grass, looking at it with something called a magnifying glass, which seems to have set it alight. I don't fully understand, but I have it here if the guardians want to see it. My daughter and her friend will explain a little more. I should call the boy's mother, though, or she'll worry.'

When the call ended, Preeti's mother turned to the two children, seated at the kitchen table, watching her with big eyes, and said, 'Don't worry, Lawrence, I'm sure the fire will soon be put out and the guardians will know you are both telling the truth. Now, I'll call your mother.'

Ten minutes later, the two women were sitting in the kitchen, waiting for the guardians to arrive. They sipped their tea and stared at their children, who were doing their best to deal with the situation by behaving as quietly and as properly as they could, despite the remarkably difficult circumstances.

Søren woke to find Dandelion by his side, but when he tried to turn over to put his hand on her head, he groaned in pain, unable to move his left arm. Dandelion whimpered and put out a paw to touch him. 'I'm sorry, my dear, but I seem to have a problem,' he said, trying to reassure her, while making another attempt to sit up. Succeeding this time, he rubbed his eyes to clear away the dust, then tentatively explored his head, which hurt abominably. Grateful to feel only a large lump and a graze, but no blood, Søren decided he would probably live and that attending to Dandelion was the priority. He fumbled in his pocket, pulled out his torch and turned it on.

The cat blinked in the sudden bright light and Søren could clearly see that her hind leg was badly gashed, most likely as she crashed through the rotting wood and rusting metal of the building's roof and ceiling; or perhaps on the way down, she hit some of the jagged pieces of wood sticking out from the walls, or even one of the large metal nails loosely holding the timber in place. Fortunately, the bleeding had stopped, but it appeared the leg was either broken or sprained, perhaps even dislocated, although judging by its appearance, he thought not. If only he wasn't so thirsty! She must be as well. Best not to dwell on it...

He looked up towards where the top of the building had once been and could see only a faint glimmer of light. The rest of the opening was obscured by a massive tree. Realising now what must have happened, Søren tried to think of something constructive to do. What *could* he do though? Impossible to climb out in his condition and equally impossible to somehow haul Dandelion out at the same time. There was little choice but to stay where they were. With luck, someone would find them before the fire did.

'There's an emergency signal coming through from the forest, five kilometres northwest of Ferntree Gully,' announced Aaron, double checking that the exact coordinates were being passed to their rescue team. Meanwhile, he checked for other comlinks in the immediate vicinity and, to his astonishment, found one, moving slowly towards the coordinates of the emergency signal.

Simultaneously, both comlink numbers, and their associated details, appeared on Jonathon's screen. 'The fire front's heading towards that location,' he said grimly, 'so assuming the wind maintains its speed, and assuming our firefighters can slow the front down, it will arrive in sixty-eight minutes.'

Using their satellite software, he zoomed in on the coordinates, but all that was visible were the treetops. There were no clearings within easy walking distance. 'Damn! It'll have to be a ground crew. They'll need to walk up from Ferntree Gully. There's no other way of getting there in time and even *that's* cutting it fine.' He swore again, then mobilised the team, before he and Aaron called the comlinks' owners. Of course, Jonathon already knew who they were: of all people, Søren Thorup, Karla's friend, and the Norwegian, Yngwie.

Yngwie knew he was heading in the right direction when he heard – physically heard – Dandelion's scream, almost immediately after he heard a large tree crashing down. *Please don't let that be the reason for the scream,* he prayed, to no one in particular – or perhaps to the ancient spirits of the forest; or even just to reassure himself. The problem was, he could barely see where he was going; the torch was almost useless, its beam bouncing off the swirling fog of smoke. Yngwie had one advantage though, and this was an excellent sense of direction; he had found his way home in snowstorms many times.

Moving cautiously forward, he searched for the white shape of the cat. Presumably it would stand out, even in this gloom? No, nothing... He took off his mask to call out to them, instantly regretting it and shoving it back on his face as quickly as he could. Alright, he would borrow an idea from Shahid and use his comlink to 'call' them. Crouching down, he keyed in a few instructions, then the message, and set it to full volume. It sounded bizarre, but it worked. An answering wail came from Dandelion, although nothing from Søren.

The cat's voice seemed to have an echoing quality to it, which made little sense. It also seemed to be coming from somewhere to his left, so Yngwie moved forward again, but still could see neither Dandelion nor Søren. What he did see, however, was the trunk and canopy of the massive stricken mountain grey gum, and in amongst the canopy was one of the most peculiar sights he had ever encountered. A group of luminescent green lights were floating around within the branches, uttering a high, keening sound. When Yngwie came closer, they drifted towards him, then back again to the fallen tree, moving upwards, then down again. He stopped in his tracks, unable to believe what he was seeing and totally convinced he was hallucinating, the effect of overexertion and the whole bizarre situation. As he stood there watching, he heard the faint sound of a comlink chime, which seemed to be coming from almost below where he was standing. 'Odd,' he thought, then understood: they had fallen into some sort of pit, now covered by the tree canopy.

Slipping in and out of consciousness, Søren felt ill – so ill he could hardly move. Concussion, he guessed. Perhaps also lack of food, having had nothing since breakfast, which now seemed a long time ago for someone like him, who was used to eating frequently throughout the day. Also, his mouth and throat were so dry he felt as though he would choke.

'Dandelion,' he whispered hoarsely, 'we *will* be fine. Someone will rescue us soon. I'm sure of it.' He coughed and held her close as best he could. She licked his hand and meowed softly.

When Søren looked up to see whether the daylight was fading, he noticed the light had changed colour. It was now green, rather than a dull, smoky grey. How could that be? Not only had it changed colour, the light was shifting around, becoming more intense, then fainter. As some of the green light drifted down towards them, he thought he must be dreaming, but it hovered around his head, and when he reached out to touch it, the icy coldness hurt his fingers, bringing him to his senses. This was definitely not a dream! He gasped, and when Dandelion hissed, whatever it was shot upwards and disappeared, although the light above them remained green. Staring at it, he heard someone call out in a loud voice, strangely artificial, yet almost familiar. While Søren did his best to answer, although at first he could only whisper, Dandelion wailed as loudly as she could, and shortly afterwards, his comlink chimed.

'He's alive,' said Jonathon, turning aside to glance at Aaron as he spoke. Looking back at his screen, he could see Søren and Dandelion lying amongst an incredible assortment of rubble, leaves and broken glass. 'Where are you?' he asked, unable to clearly make out the surroundings and equally unable to explain why there seemed to be an unusual greenness to the dim light. 'Could you hold your comlink up a little more so I can see what's above you, please?' he added. When Søren did as he asked, Jonathon could make out the shapes of tree branches and a large mass of leaves, then, as Søren faced the comlink towards the inner walls of the place where they were lying, Jonathon understood what had happened. 'You're inside an old building of some sort, aren't you?' he said.

Søren nodded wearily. 'Yes, we are. My cat, Dandelion, chased a wild dog into the forest after it tried to attack me, and I followed. That was this morning, and when I eventually found her, she was injured, so I tried to climb down to help, but that dratted tree came down, almost on our heads.' Søren discovered he was able to speak far better than he expected, which was odd, but he accepted the fact gratefully and said, 'Tell me, does the light look green to you?'

'Yes, it does, which is a bit peculiar... However, Søren, we need to get you out of there, though I can't get anyone in by air. There's nowhere to land nearby and the tree canopy is too thick for us to rappel down. We have to send in a ground crew, but it'll be a while before they get to you. Can you hold on?'

'Well, we aren't intending to leave, Jonathon, so yes, we'll do our best to stay alive until your crew get here. Mind you, I thought your people had already arrived. A moment or so before you answered my signal, I heard someone call out... Oh! Dandelion tells me it's a friend of ours, a Norwegian by the name of Yngwie, but surely that cannot be true! She must be confused.'

'No, she's quite right. When we checked the area after receiving your emergency signal, we found his comlink nearby, but he isn't answering our call. Well, perhaps he's out there searching for you... If that's the case, my advice is to let him help, and if Yngwie can get you both out, head down the hill towards Ferntree Gully. You'd be moving away from the fire front and it would save time if we could meet you on the way down. Now that we have your comlink signals, we can track you.' Jonathon decided not to tell Søren how close the fire was. No reason to upset him even more than he already was.

'Good, thank you,' said Søren, managing a weary smile. Noticing a rustling sound above his head, he looked up, and heard Yngwie's unmistakable voice calling to him as he briefly removed his mask. 'It *is* my young friend!' exclaimed Søren. 'I had better speak with him, so with luck, I will see you soon, or at least, your crew.'

'Excellent! I'll stay online in case you need me,' answered Jonathon, then returned to examine his screen for the latest fire update. By now, there were others in need of assistance as well.


In Werribee, Shahid and Laurita's plans for a relaxing afternoon were cut short by the news that fire had broken out in the Dandenong Ranges and was spreading at an extraordinary rate. Shahid immediately called his mother again, who was still at home and quite safe. The household security system had closed the fire door leading to the greenhouse, so even if it imploded due to the impact of flying debris, the house itself would not burn, and being energy and water self-sufficient, provided a good medium term refuge for as long as there was food available. In the meantime, her concern was for Laurita, Yedda, and her son. 'You won't be able to return,' she said. 'By the time you reached this region, the transport system would only be taking emergency arrivals and departures, and bringing in supplies.'

'We can't stay here doing nothing,' replied Shahid, pacing back and forth in agitation. 'The trees, Mother! What if we lose all the trees! I can't bear it!'

Laurita placed a hand on his shoulder and he briefly covered it with his own. Feeling helpless at first, she suddenly had an idea. 'What if we contacted the operations centre in Ferntree Gully? Surely they could use more firefighters? I'm fully qualified and you would be as well, wouldn't you, Shahid?'

When he turned to her in surprise, he exclaimed, 'Why, yes, I am! Maybe they're calling in other units now and one of them could swing by and pick us up. Yes! Mother, we'd better go. Did you hear all that? Good... If this works out, we'll have to leave Yedda at the Breeding Centre. You won't mind that too much, will you?' he added, turning to her. When Yedda promptly reassured him, he quickly said goodbye to his mother, promising they would take care and call again with news of their situation.

The operations centre was being flooded with calls, so an automated system took their offer of assistance, calling back twenty minutes later to let them know it had been accepted and that the forest guardians from the Geelong region were preparing a task force, which would pick them up in around forty minutes. 'We have just enough time to deliver Yedda to the Breeding Centre, then come back here and pick up supplies,' said Shahid, staring at them both as he focused on their task.

'Right, let's go!' he said, after calling the Breeding Centre, where the gentech on duty had instantly agreed with their plan.

Outside, the wind roared and the air was full of dust and leaves flying in all directions. No one else was making the attempt to walk along the trafficway. They struggled on, at last managing to reach their destination.

Utterly miserable by now, Yedda crouched down, gazing up at them, her pupils huge and black. Shahid knelt down, hugging her, and in his mind saying, 'I'll come back, I promise. I don't know when, but it won't be long. We'll be safe and so will you. See, here's someone you already know coming to look after you. Goodbye my dearest Yedda.'

When she pressed herself against him, he kissed her forehead, then stood up and approached the gentech, who shook hands with Laurita and patted Shahid's shoulder. 'We'll take care of her,' he said. 'See you soon.' He bent down to stroke Yedda, before leading her away.

The tree branches blocked the opening to the old building where Søren and Dandelion lay, but Yngwie could just manage to shine his torch down to see how they were faring. He also needed to see what the best approach would be to clearing away enough of the branches so he could safely lower himself down and then bring them back up. Søren shielded his eyes from the glare of the torch. 'How did you find us?' he called out.

'Dandelion sent out a message to bring me here. I don't know how, but she succeeded. I can't speak much though. The smoke is too heavy. I'm about to clear away some of the tree, so move towards the back of the room, if you can.' Yngwie coughed, sipped some water, and put his mask back on.

Søren tried to stand, found he could, and walked slowly towards the other side of the rubble-filled space, while Dandelion pulled herself after him, whimpering when the pain in her leg and hindquarters became too much. It tore at Søren's heart to hear her, but he was completely incapable of giving any help, other than encouragement. When they had gone far enough, they both sank down in a huddled heap, then watched as Yngwie began to cut through the biggest of the branches blocking his way. The sound of the small power saw was almost a relief in comparison to being alone and hearing only the wind in the trees above.

Ten minutes later, Yngwie threw down two lengths of rope, each securely fastened to one of the tree branches, then lowered himself down and crouched next to Søren and Dandelion. 'Here,' he said, 'drink some of this, and I have something for you to eat as well, but once we're out of here, I won't be able to carry you both, so Søren, you'll have to walk.'

Dandelion sniffed eagerly at the water, but Søren said, 'Dandelion is hurt and may need an operation, so we cannot give her much. I am so sorry, my darling,' he added, when she meowed in protest. 'Only a little... Here, have this.' He poured a few mouthfuls of water into his cupped hand and held it out to her. All too soon, it was gone.

'We don't have much time, Søren. We *must* go.'

Søren nodded, drank a cupful of water, coughed, then ate a bar of the emergency ration Yngwie handed him. Yngwie broke off a small piece from his own and gave it to Dandelion, followed by a few more mouthfuls of water. After eating the rest of the ration himself, he said, 'Are you ready? We'll take you first, Dandelion, then come back for Søren. You must keep still. Can you do that for me?'

He took the fire blanket from his backpack, lifted Dandelion onto it, tied each end together, then looped one length of rope through the ends, making it taut. After using the other length of rope to climb to the edge of the opening, Yngwie braced himself and slowly hauled Dandelion to the top. She cried out in pain as the sling swung and her leg hit the side of the opening, though he had no choice but to ignore this and keep hauling. Once Dandelion was safely up, he undid the rope, threw it into the opening and went down again for Søren, taking the first aid kit with him. 'Put this on,' he said, handing him a spare facemask.

Without something to wrap Søren in, the rope would chafe when he tied it beneath his arms, so Yngwie took off his fireproof jacket and hood and wrapped it around Søren's upper body, using the arms to tie it into place. Next, he used a roll of bandaging from the first aid kit to firmly secure Søren's injured arm, and another piece to bind his free hand so he could hold the rope and use his legs to brace himself against the wall of the building.

'This will probably hurt,' said Yngwie as he finished. Søren mentally prepared himself, then moved to where he needed to stand for Yngwie to pull him up. He coiled the rope around his hand, gripping it firmly, and waited while Yngwie put his facemask back on and climbed to where Dandelion lay, listening to everything happening below. She sneezed and coughed as the smoke irritated her nose and throat, so hid her head beneath her front leg, which helped a little.

Bringing Søren up was a great deal more difficult than bringing up Dandelion, but fortunately, the bandaging of his injured arm kept it from hurting too much. With a sigh of relief, he finally crouched at Yngwie's feet, taking a few moments to rest before gathering his strength to stand.

Once the ropes were untied and put away, they were ready to leave, with Yngwie carrying Dandelion, still inside the fire blanket, and Søren now wearing the fireproof jacket and hood, while Yngwie did his best to support him. Nevertheless, it was slow going over the treacherous terrain and with the smoke of the fires obscuring their vision. Behind them, the fire front blazed – the roar of the flames lent its voice to that of the wind, terrifying in its fury. The trees screamed and groaned, as if in the knowledge they were about to burn, while Dandelion, her fear finally overwhelming her, went into a state of complete withdrawal – which immediately affected Søren: despite her distress, without her presence in his mind, the struggle to reach safety seemed almost impossible. However, for Yngwie, her silence came as a small relief.

# CHAPTER TWENTY-ONE

All the long afternoon and throughout the night, the airjets plied back and forth over the burning forest in an attempt to extinguish the fires that were consuming everything in their path. At first light, the firefighters would begin their arduous work of last resort – bulldozing firebreaks. The access ways were well maintained and strategically located, so although the work was difficult, it was not beyond them. The problem was that pieces of burning debris were being hurled forward, often over long distances, creating spot fires along the ridges and well down towards the populated areas along the forest fringe.

Fine ash filled the air and heavy smoke choked those who ventured outdoors and were foolish enough not to be wearing a facemask. Meanwhile, frantic forest creatures were beginning to turn up everywhere, some injured, some dehydrated and exhausted, others dying from their wounds. The birds able to leave had already gone, and flocks were gathering in the nearby farmlands, seeking food and water.

Every able-bodied person who could be spared was outside fighting the perimeter fires wherever they safely could. They were all trained and well equipped, even though the last major fire in the region had been long ago. The history of the area was well known and complacency was not in the nature of these people. After all, their homes were built underground for a reason, and their small greenhouses were made from reinforced, fire-resistant plastiglass. Even the entertainment centre in Ferntree Gully was built to withstand the extreme temperatures of a forest fire, although it was highly unlikely to be faced by any real threat due to its distance from the forest and any substantial vegetation. It did, however, serve as a refuge, should it be needed.

Inside the forest, Shahid and Laurita fought the flames, side by side, steadily and with the sense of calm that comes from the dedication required for both their usual work and this immediate crisis. They worked their way along the fringe of an access way, putting out spot fires. The men and women working with them did the same, holding back the fire front, preventing it from reaching further down the mountain range and from spreading to the east. Meanwhile, Shafiqur and the other medical staff were treating a host of relatively minor conditions, ranging from burns, smoke inhalation, cuts, exhaustion, dehydration, and even a few crush injuries from tree branches falling on the ground crews. So far, though, no one was critically ill or severely injured. However, unless the fire was contained soon, it might only be a matter of time before someone was badly hurt.

Earlier, in amongst this furore of activity, the two-person team making their way up the hillside to find Yngwie, Søren and Dandelion began to wonder if they would reach them in time. Not only did they have to reach them before the fires did, they had to return, possibly carrying someone. In spite of this, they were still optimistic. The steady stream of information coming in from their operations centre told them that the wind had lessened slightly, so for the time being, the fire front was slowing down – and the comlink signals they were tracking were now moving towards them. They estimated that, all going well, the two parties should meet in approximately ten minutes. However, unless luck was with them, the final kilometre or two would be travelled in amongst burning trees.

In Kew, Karla watched the news broadcasts with horror. All their work in the forest could be lost. At this stage, no one seemed to know for certain whether the fire was the result of accident or arson, but there were no reports of lightning strikes, so it seemed unlikely to be natural. Wondering how her friends in the region were, she called Søren, but received no answer, only a message to say he was unavailable for an unknown period of time. Karla asked him to call her when he could, then tried to contact Laurita. Oddly enough, she didn't answer either and hadn't left a message to indicate when she would be available. Beginning to worry, Karla tried Shahid next, and when the same thing happened, her stomach tightened in a knot and she stared at her comlink as if it was somehow playing tricks on her. Yngwie, she would call Yngwie... Oh no, not again! This was ridiculous! There must be someone who knew what was happening and could be reached. Finally, Karla called Wania, and this time received an answer.

'Thank the Sun you're there, Wania!' exclaimed Karla, her voice trembling.

'Why? What's wrong?' Wania felt she knew Karla well enough now to expect that she wouldn't normally panic, which meant something must have seriously upset her – other than the obvious fact of the fires.

'I can't contact Søren, Shahid, Yngwie or Laurita. Do you know where they are?'

'I know where Shahid and Laurita are, approximately. They've volunteered to fight the fires. They were in Werribee for Yedda's training session, but left when the gale warning was issued and went to the nearest communal house. When the fires began, they took Yedda back to the Breeding Centre, then returned here with a crew from Geelong. Unfortunately, though, I have no idea why Søren or Yngwie wouldn't be answering their comlinks. That *is* strange...'

'Well, if by some chance you hear anything, could you call me?' Karla gripped her comlink tightly, as if she could somehow force the situation to resolve itself.

'Of course I will. In the meantime, are you alright?'

'Yes, I'm quite safe at home, and I gather you are too?'

'I'm fine, but I might be called out if someone needs me. At the moment, the medcentre in Ferntree Gully has everything under control, and although there have been numerous injuries, nothing serious so far. Shafiqur called not long before you did and he's confident everyone will manage. He even met Matthew this afternoon. He's working a voluntary shift, which, under the circumstances, is very good of him. Marie is at home and has promised to stay inside, with the fire door shut. Matthew made sure everything was safe at the farm before he left for the medcentre, so I'm sure they'll come through this if the fire spreads that far, although I'm hopeful it won't. At worst, it will be a grass fire, but even so, that can be damaging enough. Mind you, the debris flying around out there is travelling long distances, so spot fires could even start here fairly soon... We'll simply have to deal with it if it happens... Karla, I know it's rather peculiar of me to say this, but at least *your* fields have already burned, so nothing worse can happen to them!'

'No, I suppose not,' replied Karla, smiling, despite the situation. Trust Wania to see something positive in all this.

Wania returned the smile, even though, inside, concern for her son, and for Laurita and all the other firefighters, blotted out nearly everything else. At least Yedda was safe...

The two forest guardians who had arrived to speak with Preeti and Lawrence shuffled their feet and at first spoke a little awkwardly, never having dealt with children this young before in circumstances as serious as these.

'Are you able to...ah...show us, this...um, magnifying glass...you used to start the fire with?' said the older of the two, a sturdy woman in her mid-forties.

Preeti's mother reached into her pocket and said, 'Yes, here it is.'

The woman took it from her and turned it over, curious, never having seen one before, although she knew they existed. Holding it in a beam of sunlight coming into the room, she focused it on the table's surface and saw how the lens condensed the light, then put her hand beneath it to feel the faint warmth. The light, and therefore the heat, would be far stronger outside.

'They didn't realise this could happen. They're only children,' said Lawrence's mother, frowning. 'The lens came from our toolshed. I recognise it.'

The other forest guardian, a man in his fifties, looked at Lawrence, his expression serious. 'Will you promise me never to do anything like this again?'

Lawrence hung his head, then raised it and returned the guardian's gaze. 'I promise,' he said, his voice steady. 'I didn't know the magnifying glass could do this, but I'm so sorry...and Preeti is too, aren't you,' he added, turning to her.

Preeti stole a glance at him, then looked up at the two guardians. 'Yes, I'm very, very sorry and I'll never do anything like this again, though *I* didn't know it could happen either.' With a small, grubby fist, she rubbed her eyes, then her face. 'Did you put out the fire?' she asked, in a low voice, almost a whisper.

'Yes, we managed to put out the fire before it spread too far into the forest. We were lucky, and you were very brave trying to put it out before you ran home.' He nodded to emphasise his words, then turned to the two women and said, 'We'll file an account of the incident and won't be taking the matter any further. It's clear what happened, but if you don't mind, we'll keep the lens as evidence.'

Suppressing a sigh of relief, Lawrence's mother quickly agreed, while Preeti's mother stroked her daughter's head and managed a tentative smile.


In the distance, Yngwie could make out two figures labouring up the hillside, fully kitted out in fireproof clothing and carrying backpacks. He gestured to Søren to look, and then paused to let him gather his strength for one last effort. 'Two hundred metres,' thought Yngwie. 'They're only two hundred metres away. We'll make it.'

They trudged on, and the figures below moved steadily towards them. They had caught sight of Yngwie and Søren and were relieved to see both of them walking. Embers and flying pieces of burning bark were beginning to land all around, some of them setting fire to the leaf litter and undergrowth. Despite the hot weather, here in the denser areas of the forest the ground still held some moisture, so at first most of these fires remained small, often only smouldering, and in some cases, even going out. One, however, managed to set alight a particularly flammable shrub and tongues of flame soon travelled into the loose bark at the base of a nearby eucalypt, sending out a shower of sparks.

When the two groups met, there was no time to waste, so one of the rescuers took Dandelion from Yngwie, who flexed his arms and neck, which were beginning to cramp. Because of Søren's injured shoulder, it was considered best if one of the rescuers supported rather than carried him during their arduous journey back down the hill. Unfortunately, the terrain contained far too many obstacles for them to have been able to bring a hoverbed, yet although their progress was slow, it was better than before, when Yngwie was hampered by both carrying Dandelion and supporting Søren.

Tendrils of flame followed the small group and the smoke became even heavier, while the dull orange-grey light gave them all an eerie sense of walking through an alien world, filled with the howling, roaring fury of the wind and the fire behind them, as well as the crashing of branches as they weakened and fell. Intent on not losing a moment in their attempt to reach safety, none of them noticed several luminescent green lights hovering nearby, following closely behind. If anyone had noticed them, they would have thought they were either an illusion or the result of gaseous vapours being released by the heat of the flames.

After almost three kilometres without mishap, their path was blocked when a tree fell to the ground, its canopy on fire. Searching for a way around that wouldn't require a retreat, one of the rescuers saw a narrow opening in the forest that seemed safe to enter. He gestured for the others to follow. However, his movements were made more difficult by having to carry Dandelion and he stumbled, but recovered his footing and went on, followed by Yngwie, then Søren with the second team member. They clambered down a small, steep incline, into a gully filled with tall tree ferns, where the ground was slippery with rotting branches and moss. A small stream trickled along its centre. When Søren slipped and almost fell, he was saved by the strong arm around his waist. Steadying himself, he focused on putting one foot in front of the other. Close to exhaustion and increasingly unable to think clearly, it seemed to him that the light ahead was changing colour, becoming green, just as it did when he was inside the derelict building. This time, though, the others saw it too and stood still, unable to decide whether it was safe to go on. On either side, the fire was closing in and the only clear area seemed to be where the green light lingered, fluctuating in intensity. There appeared to be no choice but to move towards it. After all, they were wearing masks, so if it was some type of gas, then presumably they wouldn't be affected too much, although Dandelion might.

As the group approached, the green glow moved on ahead of them, and at one point, when a sapling directly in their path burst into flame, the light scattered and one section sped towards the burning tree. Watching in astonishment, they saw the flames die down and go out. Nevertheless, this wasn't the time to wonder at the strangeness of it, for they still had almost a kilometre to go and Søren was fast losing the strength to continue. His head had begun to hurt again and his legs felt like lead. Yngwie, walking behind, noticed Søren's difficulty and signalled for them to stop. There was only one thing left to do, and that was for one of them to carry him, despite his injuries. They would make far better time, and Yngwie, as he volunteered for the task, thanked their good fortune that his new friend was light. As he lifted him onto his shoulders, Søren was grateful to some extent that his own shoulder had by this time lost nearly all feeling.

The group walked on in this fashion until they reached the edge of the forest, where the ambulance was waiting. As they approached, the green light disappeared, yet not before they heard, despite all the noise surrounding them, the sound of what could only be described as whispering, which they all assumed was an artefact of the fire.

Twenty minutes later, while Søren was being tended to by the medcentre staff, Yngwie and Dandelion were on their way to the nearest animal healer. When they arrived, the premises were full to overflowing with injured forest creatures, bewildered and terrified, often with burnt feet and paws, as well as stinging eyes and damaged lungs from inhaling smoke. An attendant and several animal healers, who had come in from other parts of Melbourne, were dealing with them as best they could, but it was clear no one had time to deal with an injured cat.

Wondering what to do, Yngwie stood by the entrance for a moment, then gently laid Dandelion down on a nearby bench, took out his comlink and asked it to locate any other nearby animal healer still on duty. It told him there was someone available in Endeavour Hills, ten kilometres away. 'Too far!' he thought, then instantly remembered Wania. With luck, she'd be home. They owned a landjet, and she might need it if she was required to come to the assistance of someone traumatised by the fires or the storm, so it might be there with her rather than at the medcentre with Shafiqur. Would she help? He had to try.

When Wania answered, she was at first speechless. Yngwie suddenly realised what he must look like, covered in soot and, for all he knew, burn marks from the embers that had landed on his partially unprotected head and neck as they walked through the forest.

'Yngwie!' she exclaimed. 'What's happened? Where are you?'

'I need your help, Wania, please. Søren and Dandelion were in the forest and were caught in the fire zone, so I went in to rescue them after I heard Dandelion calling for help... Don't ask me how, but she did, even though I was at work in Clayton. Søren was injured and is in the medcentre, and Dandelion is hurt too, but the healer here in Ferntree Gully is overwhelmed by all the injured animals, so I need to take her to Endeavour Hills. There's someone available there, but I have no means of getting to them. Are you able to take us? Do you have your landjet with you?' Yngwie tried to keep his voice steady, but failed. The thought of Dandelion not receiving treatment was more than he could endure.

'Yes, I can help. I'll be there in about ten minutes. Don't worry, Yngwie. Just call ahead and let them know we're on the way and what the problem is with Dandelion. They'll know what to do, I'm sure.'

The afternoon's effort finally took its toll on Yngwie. Collapsing into the nearest chair, all he could say was, 'Thank you, Wania, thank you,' then followed her advice and called the Endeavour Hills clinic.

'A cat, you say?' said the animal healer. 'We don't get many of them, but don't worry, we'll take care of her. If necessary, she can be transferred to the Breeding Centre. They'll know how to treat her if she doesn't come out of this...shock, shall we say, for want of a better word. What about yourself, young man? You don't look too good, if you don't mind me saying so?'

'I'll be fine once Dandelion is taken care of,' answered Yngwie, bending the truth. His head was beginning to spin, possibly from having breathed in too much smoke when he removed his mask to speak with Søren earlier on. On the other hand, he might also be dehydrated. 'We should be there in about twenty minutes or so,' he finished by saying.

'Very good. We'll be waiting for you. In the meantime, take it easy.'

Yngwie knew this was probably good advice, so after checking Dandelion one more time, found a dispenser and drank three full cups of the most delicious chilled water he had ever tasted. Taking a deep breath, he carried a fourth cup back to where the cat was lying, sat down again and this time sipped more slowly, savouring every mouthful.

Just as he finished drinking the water, Wania arrived, looked at his face, then at Dandelion, and put her hand on Yngwie's arm, saying, 'Can you carry her? I can help if you want.'

Yngwie stood up. 'I think I can manage, but thank you. I'll follow you out.'

Without another word, Wania led the way, then helped manoeuvre Dandelion into the landjet, ensuring she was well fastened into place. Once Yngwie had taken his seat, Wania set course for Endeavour Hills. When they arrived, the animal healer, a tall, rotund man, was waiting for them, together with an attendant, who carried Dandelion into their operating room. She was still in a state of complete withdrawal, totally unaware of what was happening. Meanwhile, Wania remained with Yngwie in the waiting room, ready to assist with whatever else might be required.

Thirty-five minutes later, the animal healer returned, wiping his hands on a cloth. 'Physically, she'll be fine. There was a large gash in her left thigh and a mild dislocation of the hip. The worst of it, though, was a piece of old-fashioned glass which seems to have entered in beneath the skin, between the top of her inner thigh and her belly. We found just a small fragment left and luckily it hadn't done any major damage, but it must have been dreadfully painful.' He shook his head and pursed his lips. 'The problem is, we won't know how she is mentally until the anaesthetic wears off, although that shouldn't take too long. We gave her a nice twilight one, which should make her feel quite happy when she wakes up, but we'll keep her under close observation for at least twenty-four hours. Then, if there are any psychological problems, we'll let you know. Any questions?'

Yngwie shook his head, then realised he hadn't told the healer Dandelion was Søren's cat, not his. 'If there are any issues,' he said, 'it might be better if you contacted her companion, Søren Thorup. I'm just their friend, but if for some reason they need my help, let me know, won't you? Søren's in the Ferntree Gully medcentre because he was injured too.'

'Ah!' said the healer. 'I see. Well, I'm sure we can work it all out. Now, it'd be best if you took yourself off home and got cleaned up. You might want to have those burns checked too, don't you think?'

'I don't know... Do I?' said Yngwie, touching his head.

'Yes, I think so. Look, I know I shouldn't give you advice, but if this kind woman could take you to the medcentre here in Endeavour Hills, that might be best. They can wash off the grime and see if anything more than a good salve is needed. They most likely won't be as busy there as they are at Ferntree Gully.'

'Thank you so much for your kindness,' said Wania. 'I'll take him there now, and here's my comlink number. It doesn't do any harm to have backup in these situations.' She put her hand on Yngwie's arm and said, 'Are you ready?'

Yngwie held out his hand to the healer, who shook it, saying, 'Take care of yourself. I'd better get back to my patient. Perhaps I'll see you later.' He smiled and then left them to see themselves out.

When they arrived at the medcentre the animal healer had recommended, there was a twenty-minute wait before a practitioner could see Yngwie, and when he did, he was somewhat taken aback by his appearance. 'You look as if you've been involved in the fires. If you sit down here, I'll clean those burns and see how serious they are.'

Yngwie did as he was asked, while Wania took a seat nearby and watched. The practitioner worked quickly and efficiently and soon found that of the five burns only the one on Yngwie's forehead seemed to require more than an ointment. 'I'll apply artificial skin to this one,' he said. 'That'll keep it moist and comfortable until your own skin grows back underneath. You should come back tomorrow afternoon and have it checked again, but I'm sure you'll be fine in about two weeks. Not even a scar to brag to the girls about!' The practitioner grinned as he put a final touch to his work, then stood back and added, 'Pity about your hair though. Still, it'll grow back soon enough.'

Realising what a sight he must be, Yngwie glanced at Wania, who gave him a sympathetic smile and said, 'I can take him home and bring him back tomorrow. What time?'

'Oh, let's see. We can make it at 16:40. Will that be convenient?'

They both agreed and then left. 'Do you want to go back to the communal house, Yngwie, or would you prefer to come home and stay with us?' Concerned, Wania wondered whether Yngwie would suffer an emotional reaction if he was left alone overnight.

'If you don't mind, I'd prefer to return to the communal house, have a bath and then something to eat. Afterwards, I just want to sleep, though I should tell Kaj, my supervisor at work, what's happened. He'll want to know.'

'You could leave that until tomorrow,' suggested Wania. 'The news broadcasts will be full of what's going on, so he'll understand.'

'Yes, I suppose so. You're right. I'll call him tomorrow. I wonder how Søren is...'

'You can call him tomorrow as well. I imagine he'll be asleep by now. At least, I hope so.'

'I hope so too. He *has* been through a lot.'

'So have you,' thought Wania, but said nothing until they reached the communal house a few minutes later. 'If you need anything at all,' she said, 'call me. I may be out somewhere, but if necessary, I can arrange for someone else to help either you, Søren or Dandelion. Promise?'

'I give you my word,' replied Yngwie, climbing out of the landjet and looking back at her.

Wania smiled. 'Good. I'll see you tomorrow at 16:20.'

'Yes, and thank you. Good night.'

Yngwie walked wearily to the entrance and went inside. The manager was nowhere in sight, which was just as well, he thought, not wishing to speak with anyone else for the time being. He went to his room, fetched what he needed, and continued on to the bathing area. There was no one in there either, for which he was thankful, so was able to relax for as long as he wanted. Eventually, feeling a great deal better, he managed to find enough courage to look in a mirror. Wincing at what he saw, Yngwie turned away and put on the clean clothes he had brought with him, then headed off to the dining room to help himself from the servery. Finally, after finishing his meal and returning to his room, exhausted, he dropped onto his bed, fully clothed, and fell asleep.

## CHAPTER TWENTY-TWO

The next day, as the fires continued to burn in the distance, a group of school students stood talking while they were having their midsun break.

'Have you had enough to eat yet, Tubby?' taunted Vera.

Tomas – Tubby Tomas, as the others called him – turned bright red, as he always did when any of the other students teased him about his weight. Few children were overweight, so Tomas was keenly aware that as far as they were concerned, it was entirely his own fault, and he was not only lazy, but didn't have the willpower to simply resist eating too much. Reluctant to tell them the truth, that he was ill and so far the practitioners were unable to cure his condition, Tomas kept silent and tried to eat his meals away from the others. Today, though, Vera and her two friends, Yeasmin and Lenni, had followed him. After wiping his fingers on a kerchief, Tomas carefully put away the remainder of his meal and stood up.

'What do you want?' he asked them.

'We have something for you, Tubby,' said Yeasmin, moving closer. She held out the comlink she was holding. 'We have some music for you. It's a new piece by your favourite singer. We could load it onto your comlink, if you want.'

Suspicious, Tomas shrugged his shoulders. 'Why would you want to do that for me?'

Yeasmin turned to Vera, saying, 'You shouldn't have teased him, you know. It isn't fair at all. He can't help being fat. It's just the way he is.' Turning back to Tomas, she added, 'It's an apology for how we've treated you, although sometimes Vera just can't resist.' She gave Vera a shove on the shoulder. 'Why don't you apologise properly, eh? You should.'

Vera pulled a face. 'I'm sorry, Tomas. I know I'm mean sometimes, but I promise I won't tease you again. Friends?' She held out her hand, which Tomas reluctantly shook, then quickly let go, still not sure what they wanted from him.

'So,' said Yeasmin, 'do you want the music?' She showed him the comlink screen, where an icon of the singer was displayed, together with the label of her latest piece, which Tomas recognised as being released only two weeks ago.

'Really?' he said. 'You'd give this to me?'

'Yes, really. After all, we bought four copies so we could give you one.'

Tomas' eyes widened. Surely this couldn't be true. It seemed far too generous, but on the other hand, given the way they mocked and humiliated him, it was certainly a fair apology.

'Alright,' he said. 'Thanks,' and after setting the appropriate permissions, handed Yeasmin his comlink. She gave both comlinks to Lenni, who copied the file over, then handed his back, saying, 'Do you want to listen to some of it now?'

Tomas smiled, and then activated the icon. To his horror, the icon opened not with a song, but with the message "New World ~ Pass the Flame" and an image of fire consuming the Federation Assembly flag. His mouth open, he stared at Yeasmin and her two friends, then frantically tried to delete the file, but couldn't! Instead, within moments, it transmitted itself to nearly everyone in his contact list, and when they in turn activated the icon, to even more people, until it passed around the world and made the news headlines. 'Another Cascade!' screamed the broadcasts. 'Why hasn't the Federation brought the person who started this to justice? We were told the case was over, solved, and the perpetrator found!'

Meanwhile, the girls made sure to delete all evidence from their own devices, which included the imagery they used when creating the file: the footage of the fire they lit the day before.


Still feeling remarkably tired, even after a quiet day inside, Yngwie decided to go to bed early. After having slept for only an hour or so, he woke to the sound of someone knocking loudly on the door. Confused, he rubbed his eyes and staggered out of bed, then hastily pulled on some clothes before opening it. There stood two peacekeepers, frowning. One had been about to knock again. Withdrawing his hand, he said, 'Yngwie? We need you to answer some questions. May we come in?'

Yngwie studied the peacekeepers for several seconds before standing aside for them to enter. 'Do you mind if I fetch myself a coffee?' he said, smothering a yawn. 'Do you want any?'

'No, thank you,' they both answered. 'But we can wait while you get yourself some,' said the taller of the two men. Noticing the marks on Yngwie's head and on his forehead, he added, 'How did you get the burns?'

'I was out in the forest yesterday afternoon, searching for some friends, and once I found them, the fire front caught up with us. We were lucky to get back without anything worse happening, mainly because a rescue team met up with us not long afterwards and helped us down the mountain. One of my other friends very kindly took me to the Endeavour

Hills medcentre to have this treated.' Yngwie touched his forehead. 'They were a bit busy in Ferntree Gully... I didn't return here until quite late and haven't been outside all day, or done anything other than read a novel.' He paused to sip his coffee, then sat down, looking up at the peacekeepers, who were still standing. 'Do you want to take a seat?' he asked them.

They sat down opposite. 'So you haven't heard about the latest comlink event?'

Yngwie stared at them. 'No. What do you mean?'

'There's another image being sent around the world of a fire burning, but this time with a message. It isn't being sent using the technique you used; it's more like an old-fashioned trojan, and activates itself when someone opens an icon of a popular singer. The entire thing then transmits itself to at least some of the people in the comlink's contacts list. The peculiar thing is, though, the lattice security systems aren't preventing it from spreading, which in theory, they should...or at least, so we thought. We wondered if you might have some insight to share with us as to why this might be. Also, this is the second time you've rescued someone from a bushfire, and not long afterwards, images of fire have spread throughout the communications network. Odd, don't you think?'

'Um...yes, I suppose so. Do you have a copy?' Yngwie took the hand reader one of the peacekeepers gave him. When he saw the icon, he could understand why anyone would open it. Why not, after all? 'So in your opinion, I did this because I want to be seen as a hero, while at the same time laughing at everyone because I've cleverly succeeded in sending out this message, yes?'

The peacekeepers looked steadily at him, saying nothing.

'And of course, since I'm now working for the Federation on their messaging system, I'm in the perfect position to bypass their security? Well, I didn't do it, and for that matter, I couldn't! They haven't given me the access I'd need. It takes time to put this type of thing together, or otherwise it's beginner's luck, exploiting a security loophole that already exists – some type of anomaly.' Yngwie glared at them, not realising how fierce he looked, particularly with the missing patches of hair.

'Beginner's luck?' replied the taller peacekeeper, raising an eyebrow.

'Yes, and actually, I can already see how it might have been done.' Yngwie leaned forward, picked up his coffee and drank a mouthful, then put it down again, his irritation at the accusation forgotten. 'It's simple, really,' he said eagerly. 'If this icon was flagged as secure by the section of the lattice it came from, and the person who sent it out managed to discover how to retain the setting and permanently tag it as 'send to all close friends', for example, then any of their contacts who were listed as being 'close friends' would automatically receive it. When these friends then opened the icon, it would automatically be passed to *their* 'close friends', and so on – *if* the friends had set their comlinks to do this, of course, and *if*, in turn, their close friends had them listed as being 'trusted contacts'. Some people like sharing nearly everything, so it's astonishing how many people the message would automatically be passed to in a relatively brief space of time.'

'The clever part of the scheme,' continued Yngwie, 'is linking the image and message to the icon without changing its security tag. However, come to think of it, that's not so difficult either. Anyone with an interest in IT and the patience to work it out could probably do it. Hmm.... I must tell my team leader, Kaj Jonsson, about this. We need to do something about it... Close off the loophole...'

Lost in thought, Yngwie drank another mouthful of coffee. When he noticed the mug was now empty and stood up to get a refill, he realised the peacekeepers were staring at him in amazement. He grinned, his confidence returning. 'See, it wasn't me. Too easy, and why would I bother? We achieved what we wanted with the first one. Speak with Federation Special Investigation Unit Coordinator Morag MacIain if you need to...and if you haven't already.'

'Cheeky, aren't you,' said one of the peacekeepers, with a wry smile. 'You'll be glad to know we *have* spoken with her. She suggested we discuss it with you to find out for sure if you did have anything to do with this, and if not, how you thought it might have been done. Also, she didn't think this was your doing, but wanted to be absolutely sure.' He stood up. 'We've been asked to request that you go in to work tomorrow to help sort this out and to see if your team can track the message to its source. Coordinator MacIain said it shouldn't be too difficult and that you and this Kaj Jonsson might as well take on the task to save her the trouble of finding someone else to do it.'

'Oh, I see!' replied Yngwie, with another grin. 'Well, that makes sense, so perhaps I might be allowed to go back to bed?'

The peacekeepers smiled, more broadly this time. When they left, they were satisfied in their own minds that the real culprit would soon be in custody.

The sound of Dandelion calling him woke Søren from a deep sleep, but when he sat up to see what she wanted, remembered, with a start, that he was still in the Ferntree Gully medcentre, so how on Earth could she be calling him? He listened again, and although he couldn't actually hear anything, her voice was clear in his mind: distressed, begging him to come to her, to tell her he was all right. However, there was something in the tone of her voice that wasn't quite the same as usual – a strangeness, as if there was a faint echo; an echo that reminded him of Aurora, even

Yedda, or possibly another cat... 'Was that it?' he thought. Was she managing to transmit to another cat, perhaps even more than one? Was this how she contacted Yngwie? During his seven years of researching cat behaviour, he had never heard of such a thing.

After visiting Dandelion at the animal healer's premises, Yngwie had reassured him that, physically, she was stable, although, as she hadn't returned to full consciousness, he was still unable to connect with her mentally. Now, desperate to return her contact, Søren tried to focus as hard as he could, but eventually gave up. Whatever method Dandelion was using to contact him, he couldn't answer. Agitated, utterly incapable of ignoring her pleas, and despite the late hour, he called the animal healer's premises, which his comlink told him should still have staff in attendance.

An alert, brightly smiling young woman answered, but her tone and expression changed to one of concern, as well as amazement, when Søren told her the reason for his call. 'Your cat, Dandelion, reached you? And you say you're in the Ferntree Gully medcentre? Are you sure you weren't dreaming? No? Okay, I'll look in on her now.' She turned away for a moment. 'She doesn't seem to be awake, but her heart rate is up and her blood pressure is far too high. Bear with me... I'll take a proper look.'

Søren waited. When the animal healer spoke to him again it was from the room where Dandelion was lying, her eyes closed, a drip inserted into her forearm. It was almost too much for him to see her like this. If it were possible, he would have leapt out of bed and taken the nearest transport over there... Instead, he asked, as calmly as he could manage, 'Could you put your comlink close to her ear and set it so *you* can hear as well? I'll talk to her, and I believe she will recognise my voice and pick up the meaning from your mind. Please?'

The animal healer did as he asked. Almost immediately, the crying inside Søren's mind changed to a low purring and Dandelion opened her eyes. Tears ran down his face as he did his best to control his voice, saying, 'I'm fine, my darling, I'm fine, and so are you. Our friend Yngwie saved us both and we will soon go home, I promise.'

Dandelion tried to raise her head, but was still unable to do more than meow softly.

'Perhaps you should talk to her about ordinary things for a while,' suggested the animal healer, intrigued. 'I don't mind staying, though if someone else calls, we'll have to finish up.'

'Thank you,' said Søren, smiling in relief. With the comlink in place again, he told Dandelion that he needed to remain in the medcentre for another day to be sure no further treatment was required. 'Afterwards,' he said, 'I will visit you, and once I finish my work here, if you want, we will go home, even if I have to bring a supply of food to last us both a month!'

When Dandelion purred, quite loudly this time, Søren knew she understood, so finished by saying, 'But if you ever chase another dog, my dearest, don't expect me to come after you!'

Dandelion's ear twitched and she raised her head ever so slightly. She was used to his teasing and this was the best way Søren could think of to let her know he really was fine and not just pretending.

'All her vital signs seem normal now,' said the animal healer, smiling, 'so if you visit as soon as you can, I'm sure Dandelion will make a full recovery. It's been quite an experience tonight... Something to learn from... Sorry, but I have another call coming through, so I must go.'

'Thank you so much for all your help,' replied Søren, taking a deep breath. 'Perhaps we will see one another when I come in.'

'I hope so, and it's the least I could do. Goodnight – and try to get some sleep. I'll keep an eye on Dandelion, and if anything happens, I'll be sure to let you know.'

'Thank you again. Goodnight.'

Søren put his comlink away and settled down beneath the bed covers, vastly relieved and certain everything would work out. Still, he was not at all sure how relevant his work on the spider population would be; the fires may well have destroyed a significant number. He would submit his final report after doing one more survey – if that was even feasible within a reasonable period of time. Afterwards, the authorities would need to employ someone else to monitor the situation, no matter what the outcome. Pleased with this decision, he finally fell asleep.

The Guardians knew the Dandenong Ranges were burning. They knew the city's resources were being stretched to their limit fighting the fires, dealing with the terrible damage. Since Yedda knew as well, they used their combined powers to help her search for Shahid and Laurita. Unable to sense them, she began wailing, until, with the full force of their psychic powers, the Guardians shattered the plastiglass wall of the enclosure. As it crashed down in an explosion of sound, Yedda leapt out, racing towards the main entrance, intent on escape.

The gentech on duty gaped in astonishment when he saw her. He had jumped up from his workstation when he heard the wailing, and as she rushed forward, had the presence of mind to disable the automatic door from opening. Yedda threw herself against it, howling in desperation. Just as she was about to be caught, the door too shattered and she was out, while the other cats followed with their minds, giving her the strength and direction she needed.

Before long, Yedda knew where Shahid and Laurita were – and that they needed her help. The distance was enormous, but she ran on throughout the night, following the trafficways, and eventually, the glow of the fires in the distance. Occasionally she was able to travel on a railcar when one happened to stop at a callstation as she was passing and the driver's mind told her it was heading in the right direction. Sometimes there were other passengers, who stared at her in surprise, but they were easily dealt with by diverting their attention to other matters; they soon forgot she was even present.

When Yedda arrived in Ferntree Gully she paused, searching, confused by all the noise and activity, frightened by the nearness of the fire, coughing from the smoke in her lungs. Even so, with a small sigh of relief, she managed to locate Shahid and crept silently into the forest, seeking the best way through the undergrowth. Startled, she hissed as a wallaby hopped by, then found what she was after: a clear path through, where a number of wights were assembling heavy equipment to take with them further up the mountain. Now, running at full speed, Yedda knew her companion was only a few kilometres away.

As he rolled onto his side, Shahid gazed up at the trees, completely unable to remember what had happened – until a sharp pain in his left ankle reminded him. Laurita, where was Laurita?! He struggled to his feet, wincing as the pain travelled up his leg. Looking down, he saw that his trouser leg was torn and a long splinter of wood had embedded itself in his calf muscle. His backpack was lying nearby, so he limped over to it, took out a bandage from his first aid kit, pulled out the splinter and immediately bound it tightly to stop the bleeding. His ankle seemed to be sprained, so the safest thing to do was leave his boot on and keep his weight off it, difficult as that might be on the uneven, rocky ground. It was hard to see, too, with all the smoke and lack of light. He had no idea, either, how much time had passed since the explosion.

Searching for something to lean on, he picked up a slender piece of dead wood and tested it for strength, then found his torch and hoisted his backpack into place. A minute or so later, he saw Laurita, lying face downwards in a shallow depression. Pressing his fingers to her neck, Shahid detected a pulse, weak and thready, but definitely there. *Thank God!* After taking off her backpack, he rolled her gently onto her side, then made sure her airway was clear and that her pulse hadn't weakened in the process. Finally, he took the fire blanket from her pack and covered her with it.

A little further into the small clearing, he discovered the third member of their crew, Aziz, lying in a pool of blood, which had drained from the severed artery in his neck. There was no chance at all he was still alive. Shahid mentally said a prayer for his soul as he searched for the fourth and final member of their team, Mei-Ling. Although severely injured by flying shards of metal, she was alive, but unconscious. Deciding it was safest not to move her, he made sure none of the wounds were still bleeding, then covered her with a fire blanket.

Reaching into his jacket pocket for his comlink, he found it was gone! For an instant, he almost panicked. Without it, there was no way to notify their air support that they needed assistance. He had left his hand reader behind so as not to have more than the most essential equipment and supplies in his backpack. He couldn't even use anyone else's comlink to activate an emergency signal since every comlink was set to be accessed only by its owner. His one hope was that either Laurita or Mei-Ling would wake up and be able to use theirs, or that he searched one of them and attempted to press a finger to the comlink's signal activation button. Shahid flinched at the idea, but decided to explore those of Mei-Ling's pockets that he could easily reach without moving her – but luck wasn't with him.

He didn't dare leave them in case their condition worsened, and he certainly couldn't carry the two women to safety. Should he disturb Laurita and search her as best he could, or wait a while, and in the meantime, use his torch as a visual signal in case anyone was searching for them? He had water and emergency rations in his backpack and his own fire blanket to keep him warm. Despite the heat of the day, which had continued into the late evening, he felt cold, and increasingly weak and confused.

'Shock,' he thought vaguely, as he leaned against a tree trunk. Nevertheless, he began to recall more clearly what had happened, recalled the shower of earth as an underground explosion tore the forest floor apart and sent them all reeling to the ground, while amidst the deafening noise, pieces of metal, glass, timber and plastic were thrust into the air. An old gas cylinder, he concluded. Most likely in a disused fire bunker, or cellar. The ceiling must have collapsed after they unknowingly walked across it, and then an ember had set fire to the whole thing. The forest in this region, near the old towns, was full of such places. They should have been cleaned up. But then, so many things should be done, yet never were...

Nearby, he heard a groan, and straightened up, nearly falling because he forgot to use his makeshift walking stick to support himself. Laurita was waking up! More carefully this time, Shahid limped over to where she was lying. *Oh God, if only I could speak!* Instead, he knelt and stroked her cheek, taking her hand in his and pressing it tenderly. She opened her eyes, tried to move, tried to say something, then closed them again and lost consciousness. Frantic, Shahid felt for a pulse. It was still there. Relief washed over him, and although he longed to stay with her, he stood and once more made his way to where Mei-Ling lay. After making sure she was still alive, he went back to Laurita, took his fire blanket from his pack, covered himself with it, and lay down by her side, with his torch set to full beam, facing skywards to alert the airjets if any were close by.

When Yedda found them, Shahid, overcome by exhaustion, had fallen into a light sleep, one hand lying over Laurita's. The cat licked his face and he immediately awoke, eyes wide, staring at her as if she were an apparition.

# CHAPTER TWENTY-THREE

After six hours sleep, a shower and a hasty breakfast, Aaron and Jonathon were back at work, scanning their screens for the latest fire updates. Yawning, Aaron noticed one of their firefighting teams hadn't reported back on schedule. 'This is a bit strange,' he said. 'Do you remember the two volunteers who came over with the Geelong crew? We teamed them up with two locals and should've received a status update from them by now. Their air support should've notified us if anything was wrong, too. This doesn't look good.'

Jonathon brought up the records of both the ground and air crew and saw that the airjet had been out of action for some time, after being caught in a fierce updraught. Why hadn't anyone followed up? The simple answer was that as the fires spread throughout the hills, their resources were being stretched to breaking point. Although the wind had dropped to more manageable levels, the natural build-up of fuel within the forest was turning the bushfire into an inferno, far beyond the ability of anyone to control, no matter how well resourced or organised. Their best hope now was to contain it, to prevent it from spreading into the grasslands below, where there were farms and small outlying areas of Melbourne. Other states had sent in as many firefighters and support crew as they could spare at this time of year, when they still had their own concerns to deal with. There were even volunteers coming in from other countries, particularly New Zealand, yet still the battle raged and the toll, in injuries and damage, was mounting to enormous proportions. To add to this, some fool had sent out another comlink image of a fire!

Jonathon ground his teeth, then made a conscious effort to relax. He would never last the distance if he allowed the incident to bother him more than it already did. Yet what an insult! Such a stupid, callous thing to do! Forcing himself to focus on the latest updates from the area where the missing firefighters were last seen, he gasped, then exclaimed, 'There's a cat out there! What?!'

Aaron stared at him before checking his own screen. 'Oh my! Not only is there a cat out there, she's trying to get the attention of the people erecting the force field. I'd better call them to make sure they listen to her. This is too weird!' Aaron made the call, and when the team leader replied, said, 'Yes, that's right, you need to let her speak with you. I know it's out of the ordinary, but cats don't normally wander around in the forest. If she belongs with someone, they may be injured or lost, and she's looking for help.' Aaron had a cat of his own, so knew how intelligent and resourceful they were. He waited while the woman he was talking to knelt down and gently stroked her.

After a few moments, she said, 'Well, this is incredible! Her name's Yedda. She's found one of our firefighting teams and wants us to go back with her. One of them is dead, two are badly injured, including a woman named Laurita, and the fourth is her companion, a fellow by the name of Shahid, who has only a minor gash and a sprain. *We* can't leave our work though. You'll have to send someone else. I'm sorry, but we have to get this field up. It's our only chance of making sure the fire doesn't reach the old stands of mountain ash. In the meantime, though, I'll keep the cat with me. I don't want her running off.'

Aaron swore under his breath, but agreed and said, 'Thanks. I know you're stretched. We all are, and yes, don't let the cat out of your sight. Just reassure her that help's on the way.'

He wasted no time before contacting the Ferntree Gully medcentre to arrange for a pair of ambutechs and a practitioner to travel out to the injured firefighters. When the call came through, Shafiqur was on duty, and on hearing Shahid's name mentioned, immediately volunteered to be the one to attend, but was told it was out of the question. 'He's your son,' said the administrator in charge. 'You can't be objective. No, someone else will have to go instead.' She touched him on the shoulder. 'We'll make sure he's okay, I promise, and you can see him when they arrive, which hopefully won't be long.'

'Is there a woman named Laurita with him?' asked Shafiqur, doing his best to remain calm.

'Yes, I believe so, though at this stage I don't know what her injuries are. All I know is, she's alive.'

Shafiqur breathed a deep sigh of relief, then turned away to attend to his patients. Many were now coming in with burns, smoke inhalation, and assorted cuts, breaks and crush injuries. The firefighter was the first who had died though, thank God, and he fervently prayed there wouldn't be others.

Sitting in the front of the ambulance, Yedda did her best to give clear images of how to get to where Shahid, Laurita and the two other firefighters were, but she was beginning to tire. They were now tracking Laurita's comlink signal and had located those of the two other team members – although not Shahid's – yet they were sometimes forced to turn back due to the obstacles in their path. Satellite imagery and echolocation were of some help, but the dense smoke covering the area limited how useful they could be, and trees, weakened by both the gale and the fire, were falling in increasing numbers. Eventually, however, they found them. Yedda used her last reserve of strength to clamber out of the ambulance and run to where Shahid sat, staring at the ambulance headlights.

Laurita, conscious by this time, was still unable to move anything other than her free arm and, thank the Sun, one of her feet. At least she seemed not to have suffered any serious spinal damage. Mei-Ling had regained consciousness as well, but was too weak to do anything other than endure the pain of her injuries and the thirst – dreadful, dreadful thirst, which Shahid hadn't dared alleviate, as it seemed highly likely she had internal damage and would need an immediate operation.

With the aid of his walking stick, Shahid stood up, pointing to Mei-Ling, but was unable to tell them anything about her condition. He looked meaningfully at Yedda, and she passed on to the practitioner and the two ambutechs what he wanted to say. They stared at her in surprise, then looked at Shahid, who nodded, so while one of the ambutechs examined Laurita and the other verified that the fourth firefighter was indeed dead, the practitioner gave her full attention to Mei-Ling.

Since they were in a clearing, it was possible to lift her onto a hoverbed and then into the ambulance, after which the practitioner gave both the women a fast-acting painkiller. Laurita smiled weakly at Shahid, who briefly clasped her hand as she also was lifted onto a hoverbed and placed into the ambulance. Finally, Shahid followed her inside and Yedda climbed in after him, collapsing onto the floor by his feet.

Realising she would be hungry and thirsty, Shahid fumbled in his backpack for water and a ration bar, poured some of the water into a cup, and gave it to her. Yedda drank eagerly, then looked up, ready for the food. He broke it into small pieces and offered them to her one at a time, slowing down her eating to reduce the chance of her vomiting. Gradually, instead of anxiety, the tone of her mind changed to one of contentment; she purred softly after he gave her a little more water.

'Thank you,' said Shahid silently, while he stroked her head and back. 'You most likely saved our lives, but how did you get away from the Breeding Centre and how did you know we were in danger?' There had been no time to ask when she first arrived, only to tell her what he needed her to do.

Yedda showed him what had happened. Astonished, and in awe of this creature who had managed to travel all the way from Werribee, alone and without hesitation, Shahid's eyes filled with tears and his heart with gratitude. When they arrived at the medcentre, he used sign language to ask one of the ambutechs to lift Yedda onto Laurita's hoverbed. 'You've travelled far enough on foot for one night,' Shahid told her, when the ambutech did as he was asked, assuming there must be a good reason. While Yedda curled up and fell asleep, covering her face with the tip of her tail, the ambutech returned Shahid's smile of thanks. Laurita smiled too, although she still seemed too weak to say anything, other than to murmur, 'Thank you.'

Shafiqur met them in the foyer, where, in his agitation, he had waited since hearing the ambulance was on its way and would soon arrive. He rushed forward to embrace his son, kissing his forehead and cheek. 'Thanks be to God, you are alive!' he exclaimed. Shahid warmly returned the embrace, then pointed to Laurita and Mei-Ling. 'Yes, yes, I understand,' said his father, and turned his attention to them instead, leaving Shahid to be seen to by the practitioner who accompanied the rescue team.

'Unless Dandelion is happy for us to have a holiday somewhere, I intend to go home once she has recovered,' said Søren, as he lay in his medcentre bed, speaking to Karla on his comlink. 'In the meantime, if the area where I did the survey is safe to go into, I will do one more round, then finalise the report. If not, at least someone else can use my results to work with, which would no doubt have been the case anyway.'

'I'll be sorry to see you go,' replied Karla, 'but I do understand. Both you and poor Dandelion have been through more than enough – though I'm still amazed about the dog! I didn't know there were any left in area. Unfortunately, we may have to hunt it down...if it's survived the fires. A wild dog population is all we need! Still, I must admit, I wouldn't have minded seeing Dandelion chase after it – I'd never have thought she'd dare!' Karla grinned, hoping to cheer him up, as well as herself, although under the circumstances, he wasn't doing too badly. With rest and physiotherapy, his arm was expected to be back to normal in about two weeks, and the head injury was, apparently, relatively minor.

Søren saw the humour and laughed. 'Yes, when I look back, it *is* amusing, but it certainly wasn't at the time! And after being buried beneath snow in Greenland, we are buried here in Melbourne! Well, we have survived both burials, and should think ourselves lucky. So tell me, how is Yngwie? Have you heard from him? He called in yesterday, looking rather different from his usual handsome self, I must say, but otherwise, seemed to have survived our ordeal extremely well. I'll invite him to visit once we are home again. After all, it isn't so far from Norway to Greenland. I probably owe him my life, and so does Dandelion...' Søren paused, then said, 'Which reminds me, Karla. There were some very odd things in the forest which I simply cannot explain. Have you ever seen, or heard of, a phenomenon involving green, luminescent lights floating amongst the trees? I saw them while I was still inside the old building, and when I touched one, it was icy cold. Later on, we all saw them as we walked back down the hillside; they almost seemed to be leading us to safety. I know how this must sound, but it's what I felt.'

Karla stared at him, then thought a little more about it and decided not to dismiss what he described as a hallucination. 'No,' she said slowly, 'I've never come across anything like that, but I'll do some research to see if I can find any references to it. Was there a lot?'

'Not a "lot", but enough. It looked like a series of smallish balls of light and when we reached the ambulance, they seemed to be making an odd sound...almost like whispering. Ask Yngwie – I'm sure he could give you more information, or at least confirm what I saw.'

'I will,' replied Karla, intrigued. 'I haven't the faintest idea what it might have been. If it occurred in only one spot – for example, inside the old building – I'd have said it was some type of gas, but if it followed you, or led you, then that doesn't sound likely. Hmm...' Karla frowned, thinking hard, but came up with nothing. She would have to ask Jonathon as well, and perhaps even Shahid. Since they spent so much time in the forest, it was possible they might have heard of something similar.

'How far has the fire spread?' asked Søren, knowing how deeply the devastation would affect her, as well as the rest of the team at Willsmere. He had sporadically watched the news broadcasts, but only someone like Karla would know the true story.

'Too far, Søren, too far... They've managed to get a force field up to save our best stand of mountain ash, and are working to extend it, but it's just as well no one lives in these forests any longer. I'm sure anyone who stayed wouldn't have survived. The toll on the wildlife is dreadful, though.' Karla paused, unable to continue. The images of burnt and injured creatures being broadcast over the lattice were horrifying, and almost more than she could cope with. 'Mik and Tamara have called,' she said at last. 'They're thinking of coming back from Queensland, but I told them not to. There's nothing to do here until the fires are brought under control and we know the worst. Thank the Sun for our seed banks, Søren! Without them, some of our rarer species might not be saved... Still, I'm being pessimistic. Some plants will have left a store of seed in the soil, and some even benefit from fire; the mountain ash generally only regrow from seed when the area's been burnt. Poor Shahid though... The trees are so important to him.'

'Has he called, or Laurita?'

'No, I haven't heard from them – only that he and Laurita volunteered to join the firefighters. In the meantime, Yedda was left with the Breeding Centre.'

'Oh! It must be hard for them to be separated after being together for such a short time...and just as they were getting to know each other.'

'I agree, but Shahid's mother promised to let me know if there was anything wrong, and she hasn't called, so I'm assuming they're all fine.'

'I hope so...but Karla, I must go. The practitioner is here to see how I'm faring. I'll call you this evening.'

'Good, I'll look forward to hearing from you. In the meantime, I'll see what I can find out about those green lights...and to answer your earlier question, no, I haven't heard from Yngwie either.'

'I see... Well, goodbye, Karla,' and Søren turned away to speak to the practitioner.

As Karla closed the connection, her computer chimed an incoming call. When she answered, it was Jonathon. 'Hi... I only have a few minutes,' he said, speaking more quickly than usual. 'Everything's crazy here, but I wanted to see your face and hear your voice. Are you alright?'

'Yes, why wouldn't I be?'

'I had this awful feeling you weren't. I suspect it's the fires...this whole disaster...affecting me. Still, I can see nothing's wrong with you, so that's a relief. Have you heard about your friend Søren?'

'Yes, I have. I was talking to him just before you called. He's fine, and should be allowed to go home either this evening or tomorrow morning. Dandelion should be okay too, but it'll take a bit longer before she's fully recovered. She was quite badly hurt and is being treated by the animal healer in Endeavour Hills. The Ferntree Gully practice was overwhelmed, so Yngwie took her there.'

'Good, I'm glad to hear she was looked after. That's one incredible cat! And speaking of extraordinary cats, have you heard about Shahid and Laurita...and Shahid's cat, Yedda?'

'No! What's happened?' Karla could feel her heart pounding as she waited for him to answer.

'They're alive, but Laurita received some fairly serious injuries from an explosion in the forest, possibly caused by an old gas cylinder, according to Shahid, and he's probably right, though we haven't had the chance to examine the area yet. He only received a sprained ankle and a small gash in his leg, but one of the other firefighters died, and the fourth member of the team, Mei-Ling, may not live. We won't know for a while yet.' Jonathon paused to get control of his voice. 'Sorry... It's hard. She's a friend.'

'I'm sorry too, Jonathon, really sorry. I hope she makes it. What happened to Laurita?' Karla had to work hard to prevent herself from weeping. *Please, please be all right...*

'She has concussion, a fractured pelvis, three broken ribs, damage to her lungs and shrapnel in one kidney. The shrapnel's been removed by now, and the bones will mend, but the lung damage may take longer to heal, so she's having trouble speaking.'

With a catch in her voice, Karla managed to say, 'So there's no point calling her?'

'No, you'd be better off sending a message. Shahid lost his comlink during the explosion, so couldn't call for help. He didn't have his hand reader with him either and the only reason we located them when we did was because Yedda turned up...all the way from the Breeding Centre in Werribee, it seems. I haven't yet heard how the miracle happened, but once she found them, she went for help, then showed the rescue team where they were, as well as the quickest way back through all the debris and smoke.'

'What!' exclaimed Karla. 'How under the Sun could she have done that?'

'I have no idea, but perhaps Shahid can tell you, if you call him. I imagine he either has his hand reader by now, or a replacement comlink.' Jonathon shook his head, raising his eyebrows in remembered astonishment at Yedda's journey and what she managed to do.

'Yes, I will. Does Yngwie know what's happened?'

'I haven't had time to catch up with him and don't even know where he is. You might want to call him, too.'

''Yes, I'll do that... There's something else I wanted to ask you about, if you have a moment?' Jonathon nodded, so Karla said, 'Søren told me he saw some mysterious green lights while he was inside the buried building, and again when they were making their way down the hillside. The others saw it as well and he thought it was almost as if the lights were showing them the safest path through the forest. We've never heard of anything like that before. Have you?'

'Well, yes, I have actually. How peculiar... One time I was doing an inspection tour of the same area, just as the sun was about to set, and I saw a green light, which I assumed was something a little out of the ordinary associated with the sunset, so stopped to take a better look. As I did, a huge tree fell, right in front of me. If I hadn't stopped, I would have been crushed, most likely even killed. So, I'll ask around and see if anyone else has ever heard of or seen anything like this. What do you think it could be?'

Karla hesitated, then said, 'I don't know, but I promised Søren I'd do some research. If I find anything, I'll send you the information, or call.'

'Thanks. Look, I'd better go, but I'll talk to you again when I get the chance.' Jonathon gave her the best smile he could muster, while Karla did the same.

'Just one more question? Do you know yet how the fire started?'

'It definitely wasn't lightning, so we're investigating the possibility it was either accidental or arson. So far, two campers are in custody because they've admitted to lighting a fire to boil water, but say they saw smoke in the forest nearby, close to where the old town of Olinda used to be. Apparently they put out their own fire and shortly afterwards reported the smoke. We intend to inspect their campsite this afternoon, as it doesn't seem to be burnt out. We can't hold them for much longer without charging them.'

'Oh, I see... I wonder if the people who sent out the second comlink cascade had anything to do with it?'

Jonathon understood what she meant, and said, 'It's a distinct possibility and we're looking into it. There were three comlink signals moving away from the Olinda area not long after the fires began, and one of these people also reported seeing smoke, though quite some time after the campers informed us. That's all I can tell you for the time being. Anyway, I really must go, but wish I could see you in person.'

'This may have to do for a while, Jonathon, but I'll be thinking about you,' replied Karla, wistfully.

Jonathon smiled briefly, then closed the connection.

All that morning, Tomas struggled to make up his mind whether to show his comlink to someone – one of the preceptors for example, or even his parents – but would they believe him? How could he prove Yeasmin had given him the file? The simple answer was, he couldn't. He was sure Lenni and Vera wouldn't rat on her, and he was also sure that by now she'd have erased all trace of the file and anything they'd used to make it.

Utterly miserable, he sat alone, as always, and ate his midsun meal, trying to enjoy it, but failing. All it did was make him fatter! And the fatter he became, the more people like Vera teased him. It wasn't fair!

Thinking of Vera made up his mind for him, so he swallowed his last piece of food, carefully wiped his mouth, and went to the room the preceptors shared for their meal and other breaks. Knocking on the door, Tomas resisted the temptation to run. He *must* do this! The door opened and the preceptor who stood there asked what he wanted.

'I...I have something to show you,' he said, trembling slightly. 'May I come inside?'

'Of course. What is it?' The preceptor stood aside to let him in, then told him to follow her into a private office nearby. 'Sit down, if you like,' she said.

Tomas sat on the edge of a small sofa, fumbling in his trouser pocket for his comlink. 'It's something on my comlink,' he said, 'and *I* didn't put it there...Yeasmin did. It's what started the fire message that's been going everywhere.'

Staring at him, the preceptor sat down by his side and Tomas showed her the icon he was given, saying, 'Don't touch it, or it'll send itself to my friends all over again.'

'Can you delete it?' she asked, taking the comlink from him to examine the icon.

'No, I can't, and I don't think anyone it's sent to will be able to either... At least, that's what I've been told by the friends who got it from me.'

'Tell me exactly what happened, Tomas, and I'll try to help,' answered the preceptor, handing back the comlink.

Tomas related the whole incident, and as he did, realised he was angry. Not just upset or embarrassed, or afraid of what would happen, but really angry. At a time when the entire mountain range was at risk of burning, Yeasmin and her stupid friends had sent this out, using him as their dupe!

The preceptor noticed his expression and how red in the face he'd become. 'If what you've told me is true,' she said, 'you have every right to be angry.' Privately, she could easily picture the whole scene.

'It's true!' protested Tomas.

The preceptor patted his shoulder. 'I believe you, but we have no proof, have we?'

'No, but maybe the peacekeepers could talk to them, and maybe they'd give themselves away.'

'Perhaps, though perhaps not.' The preceptor knew the girls well and thought they would all be quite adept at maintaining their innocence. 'Do you want me to call the peacekeepers? You understand I'd have to speak with your parents first?'

'Oh, would you? I suppose you would... Alright, yes please.' Tomas began to feel that if the preceptor believed him, then so might his parents and the peacekeepers.

Thirty-five minutes later, Tomas' mother sat across from him, her face red, arms crossed, hands clenched, glaring at her son. His father sat next to her, frowning, clearly worried. The preceptor could see Tomas might have inherited his condition from his mother, since she was a large woman, overweight and with the same facial features... Although, if that was the case, how did they succeed in their application for fertility rights? Presumably some other factor was at work here... Poor lad... On the other hand, Tomas appeared to have followed after his father in having a mild temper and an overall eagerness to please, whereas his mother seemed just the opposite. 'What have you done, Tomas?' she demanded, leaning towards him.

'I didn't do anything wrong!' he protested, wringing his hands. 'It wasn't me who started it. Like I told Preceptor Gregory, it was one of the girls who gave it to me... Yeasmin... She pretended it was some music she bought for me, the latest songs, and then copied it onto my comlink. When I opened the icon, that's when the message began to spread!'

He tried hard to hold back the tears, glancing at his father, who sent him a sympathetic look, but said nothing. Instead, his mother retorted, 'You fool! Did you honestly think she'd buy music for *you*? You're not even their friend!' It was all she could do not to slap him, but of course, not in front of the preceptor.

Tomas hung his head and this time the tears trickled down his chubby cheeks. He hastily pulled out a grubby kerchief from his pocket to wipe them away, then blew his nose, as quietly as he could. The preceptor, shocked at his mother's tone, said, in a steady voice, 'I'm not sure your behaviour is particularly constructive, Veronica. I'm impressed by Tomas coming forward and am inclined to accept what he says. He needs support, not criticism.'

Veronica threw her a vicious look of contempt, saying, 'Support! If he wasn't such an idiot, this whole thing would never have started. Have you listened to what the news broadcasts are saying? It's a criminal act, and they're calling for the culprit to be charged and brought before the Judge. My son, a criminal! How *could* you, Tomas!'

At this, his father mumbled a few incomprehensible words, then cleared his throat several times and at last managed to say, 'Dear, our son isn't a criminal. The girl who made this thing and gave it to him, pretending it was something else, is the criminal and the one who should be charged. Think about it. Would Tomas do something like this on purpose, just when the fires have broken out? He's not that kind of boy at all. Only someone really callous would do this, and he isn't callous in the least.' He sighed and shook his head, then leaned over and patted Tomas' hand. Tomas gave him a look of gratitude and put his kerchief away. 'Thank you, Father,' he said quietly.

'Hrrmph!' said his mother. 'Still, you may be right, Eric. Let's hope so, because I don't want to see our names in the broadcasts, and when it comes down to it, I don't want the peacekeepers dragging Tomas off to some detention centre, either.' Softening a little, she added, 'Tomas, promise me it wasn't your fault, eh?'

'I promise, Mother. Truly, it wasn't me!'

Veronica abruptly stood, and while Eric gazed at her in astonishment, she said, 'Well, what are we waiting for? Let's call the peacekeepers and have that rotten little Yeasmin witch arrested!'

# CHAPTER TWENTY-FOUR

While Tomas confessed his role in the second cascade to his preceptor, Kaj Jonsson was organising a full trace of all the comlink messages back to their source. Vastly relieved that Yngwie appeared not to have had a hand in the event, he even gave him sufficient lattice authorisation to access the records directly once they had been retrieved by the infotechs at the Central Computer Site.

'Here you are,' he said, sitting down next to Yngwie and placing a scanner in front of him. 'Put your right hand, palm down, on this, and then your left. You will only have limited rights, but more than you had before. I am trusting you, Yngwie, and I expect not to be let down. If I am, I warn you, it will be something you will regret for a very long time.'

His dark brows came together in a fierce glare, and Yngwie, startled, stared back at him, at first, lost for words. 'Um...I don't know whether to thank you or tell you where to get off for being such a pompous ass,' he eventually replied.

Kaj laughed and punched him lightly on the shoulder. 'A joke, my friend,' he said, 'a joke. If I didn't trust you by now, I wouldn't give you this authority.' He laughed again, completed the authorisation process, then showed Yngwie where the comlink records were located. 'It should be easy enough to track this down. Let me know when you have worked it out.' He grinned, then stood up and, whistling a tune from the collection that should have been on Tomas' comlink, went off to make himself another cup of coffee, leaving Yngwie smiling to himself while he began putting together a routine to sort and analyse the records.

An hour later, after having double and then triple checked the results, Yngwie walked over to where Kaj was sitting, enjoying yet another cup of coffee while he worked on their original project. 'The message was sent out by a young boy named Tomas Perry, who lives in Montrose, here in Melbourne,' announced Yngwie. 'He was at school at the time and is now in the Montrose Reconciliation Centre with his parents and one of the preceptors from his school. It seems he may have confessed, or has already been caught.' Yngwie grimaced. 'Oh well, we needed the proof.'

Kaj looked up, eyes wide, completely taken aback by the news. 'I suppose we did, yes, I suppose so. Still, I must say, that was quick,' he added, meaning the confession. 'The boy may have realised he'd soon be caught and thought the Judge would be more lenient this way. Hmm...'

'Perhaps,' answered Yngwie. 'Do you want me to send this information to the peacekeepers?'

'Oh yes. I am sure they will be grateful to have confirmation the boy is involved... Clever little bastard...'

Yngwie raised his eyebrows at the epithet, but said nothing. After all, if Coordinator MacIain hadn't believed him and given him this position, he might still be under suspicion for having created this second cascade, which would have been extremely inconvenient! He returned to his workstation, contacted the Montrose Reconciliation Centre, and told them what they had discovered.

'Thank you, Yngwie,' said the peacekeeper who took his call. 'Yes, this will be extremely helpful, both for us and for the Judge to consider. When we checked for updates to the case in our central records database, we were told you would most likely call, either today or soon afterwards, so thank you again for giving us this information so quickly.'

The peacekeeper was obviously busy, so Yngwie accepted the thanks gracefully and said goodbye. Sitting down next to Kaj, he asked, 'What next?'

'After you work out how to prevent a trojan like this from spreading in the future, you can go back to our main project. We still need to determine whether the flaw you found in our satellites was accidental or not.'

'True. So may I have direct access to the messaging system yet...or not?'

'Not... Sorry. It would be too much too soon, Yngwie, even if I *do* trust you. If anything were to go wrong, you might be blamed, and that wouldn't do at all, would it?'

'No, you're right, as always.' Yngwie grinned, and soon put the fate of poor Tomas out of his mind, although he couldn't help briefly wondering what would become of the boy and having a certain amount of sympathy for him.


A replacement comlink had quickly been organised for Shahid, and while he transferred the language programming from his hand reader, he made Laurita laugh by telling her a few jokes. However, without warning, she closed her eyes and fell silent. The concussion, more severe than the treating practitioner originally thought, was causing her to intermittently lose consciousness.

The medtech, who came immediately when Shahid called for help, reassured him that their scans showed no brain damage. 'Once the swelling inside her head goes down, which we don't expect to take much longer, this will stop happening,' she said. 'Just stay with her. Keeping her company and keeping her calm will help.' She smiled to reassure him, then left the room.

*Dear God, please help her get well*, prayed Shahid, as he sat by Laurita's bedside, holding her limp hand and wishing he could infuse it with the warmth of his own. Understanding his distress, Yedda meowed softly from her place at the foot of the bed. She had refused to leave and the medcentre had little choice but to allow her to stay, since every time they tried to persuade Yedda to leave with Shahid's father, Laurita's heart rate and blood pressure increased, even when she was unconscious. They could only conclude that, somehow, the cat was having a beneficial effect.

Shahid gazed fondly at her, conscious now of a bond between them that nothing could break. 'You are the bravest, truest cat anyone could wish for,' he silently told her. Yedda purred and rolled onto her back, luxuriating in his emotions, despite his fears for Laurita.

However, unknown to Yedda, Shahid had earlier received a call from Genevieve at the Breeding Centre and he was doing his best to shield her from the knowledge. For once, the gentechs were angry with their charges, though needless to say, vastly relieved when told that Yedda was with Shahid and not lost. After being informed of Yedda's disappearance, as well as the damage to the enclosure, Genevieve, as the person who helped Shahid choose a cat, was almost beside herself with a combination of anger and worry.

'Outrageous behaviour nevertheless!' she insisted, once Shahid explained that Yedda had almost certainly saved Laurita's life, and possibly even his own. 'The Guardians are to blame, of course. Without them, I'm sure Yedda could never have done this.'

'I guess not,' said Shahid, utterly bemused by the whole situation and wondering why Yedda hadn't simply told the gentech on duty that she needed his help. Then again, it was unlikely they would have released her.

As if in answer to his unspoken question, Genevieve said, 'She could have told us you were in danger. We'd have called the forest guardians, and if necessary, sent someone out there with her. She needs to understand she can ask us for help.'

'Oh, I see. Maybe we can cover it in our next training session?' Shahid wondered when that would be. As things were, it might need to be put off until such time Laurita had recovered sufficiently for Yedda to agree to leave her.

'I think that would be an exceedingly good idea, Shahid!' retorted Genevieve. Calming down a little, she added, 'Still, she's a brave one, and to manage to use the transport system to help her travel so far, so fast, is astonishing. I suspect the Guardians have taught her a great deal. The problem is, their knowledge without their discipline is a potentially dangerous combination. I may need to have a long talk with them about this.'

'The situation was extreme, surely,' answered Shahid, in their defence.

'True, very true...and presumably they had their reasons. Well, I should leave you in peace and simply ask you to arrange for the next training session when it's convenient. In the meantime, we'll repair our enclosure!'

'Thank you, Genevieve,' said Shahid, smiling.

'What for?'

'For helping me choose Yedda.'

Genevieve returned his smile. 'Yes, it seems you two have already developed a marvellous relationship. I must admit, it makes me feel a great deal better about the situation, and after all, she *is* very young and can't be expected to know everything.'

'Do you want to see her?' Shahid turned the hand reader around so she could see Yedda, exhausted and sound asleep.

'Oh how sweet!' exclaimed Genevieve, forgetting her anger. 'She looks so at home there. Fancy the medcentre letting her stay!'

'They don't seem to have much choice. She refuses to leave, and Laurita seems better when she's nearby.'

'Ah ha! That makes sense, actually. They do sometimes help people recover from illness and injury. But on that note, I'd better leave you to it, so goodbye, and no doubt we'll see you soon.'

'Yes, goodbye,' replied Shahid, with another smile, then closed the connection.

Now all he wanted was to see Laurita open her eyes again and for Mei-Ling to come out of her coma. Deliberately pushing away the thought of the fires and what they were doing to his beloved forest, he smoothed a few strands of dark hair away from Laurita's brow and kissed her. As he did, she opened her eyes, gasping in surprise at seeing him so close, then took his hand in hers and pressed it gently, lifting her other hand to stroke his face. 'How do you feel?' he asked, via Yedda, who was fast becoming an adept at transferring his words.

'Woozy,' whispered Laurita, 'and hungry. I wonder if they might let me have something to eat now? My mouth is so dry, too. Could you give me a sip of water?'

Shahid poured a little iced water into a cup and helped her drink it. Lying back, Laurita sighed and said, 'That's better. Thank you.' Raising her head, she saw Yedda watching her. 'Hello, puss,' she said. 'I'm so glad they let you stay. Do you want to come up here?'

Yedda walked carefully up to the head of the bed and nuzzled Laurita's cheek, tickling her with her whiskers until she laughed – but then grimaced at the resulting pain in her ribs. Fondling Yedda's ears and head, Laurita looked at Shahid and said, 'We owe her so much, but how did she know where we were, and how did she get there? It doesn't seem possible.'

Before answering, Shahid called the medtech to tell her Laurita was awake again and hungry. However, the medtech said that until more tests were done, it was safest if she waited a while longer before eating. Laurita made a face, but reluctantly accepted the situation, so Shahid told her everything that had happened, only leaving out certain parts of the conversation with Genevieve. 'It seems we have the first known case of collaboration between cats to defy human-imposed restrictions,' he concluded, but chose not to mention that the Breeding Centre seemed concerned about it setting a precedent, which is how he interpreted Genevieve's words.

'In a good cause,' remarked Laurita. She attempted to sit up, but with a groan, sank down again onto her pillows. 'No, it hurts too much. I'll simply have to lie here until I'm better.' She spoke slowly from the effort to form the words, then tried to smile, but failed.

'Relax, Laurita,' said Shahid. 'You've had an operation and you have a number of broken ribs, as well as a fractured pelvis, so don't try to be brave. Just give in and let yourself be taken care of. Please?'

'I'll try.' Laurita sighed, having never been seriously ill before.

'Good! In which case, maybe it's time I called Yngwie. I'm sure he'd want to know how we are, and would also want to visit, if you like?'

'Yes, please...' Laurita managed to say, her voice beginning to weaken. 'I'd like to see him.'

'I'll call him now,' said Shahid. 'Hello, Yngwie? How are you? My mother's told me all about your rescuing Søren and Dandelion. You seem to be making a habit of this...and it looks as if you've hurt yourself this time.'

'I'm fine,' replied Yngwie, which was true. 'How are you and Laurita? Wania said you'd volunteered as firefighters.'

'Yes, and unfortunately our team was caught in an explosion. I'm only slightly hurt, but one of us died, another may die, and Laurita has some serious injuries.' When Yngwie, in dismay, began to interrupt, Shahid reassured him: 'She'll recover, don't worry. You could visit, if you like. I won't be going home for a while.'

Yngwie stared at him for a few moments, turned away to speak with Kaj, then said, 'I'll be there in about forty-five minutes.'

'Thank you. Do you want to say hello to Laurita first?'

'Yes, please.'

Shahid held the comlink for Laurita while she spoke: 'Hello, Yngwie,' she said.

'Hej! You look awful. What happened?'

'Well, *you* don't look too great either, my friend,' replied Laurita, with a lopsided attempt at a grin.

'No, and people keep staring at me, but never mind. What about you?'

'I'll let Shahid tell you everything when you get here because I can't speak for long. Some damage to my lungs, you see.'

'Alright, I'll see you soon.' Yngwie blinked away the sudden tears, said goodbye to Kaj, and left.


Glad to be out of the control centre for a while, even though it was to inspect the burnt-out forest and nearby areas, Aaron and Jonathon arrived at the approximate place where their satellite images suggested the main fire began. The stench filled their nostrils to gagging point, but they concentrated on the task at hand and did their best not to be overwhelmed by the sight of the blackened trees, ash-covered earth and the occasional bloated body of an animal not fortunate enough to escape the flames. The dreadful eerie silence gave them the impression of being in an alien place, so unlike the life-filled, verdant forest they were used to. Smoke issued from the ground where the roots of trees still burned and would likely do so for some time yet. 'If it existed,' thought Aaron, 'this is what hell would be like.'

An hour later, after thoroughly combing the area, there was nothing to show how the bushfire might have started, so they walked further up the hillside to where Andre and Maarten said they lit their campfire to boil water. The rocks they used and then moved away were exactly where they described, and sure enough, the actual fire pit seemed to be safe and the fire itself properly put out. Scratching around in the soil, after taking appropriate images for their records, Jonathon found the cold cinders and took an image of them as well.

'I think we have enough,' he said. Aaron agreed, so they walked back to their airjet and returned to Ferntree Gully, where the evidence was entered for the Judge to consider as it held the two men accountable for their lesser transgression.

Ninety minutes later, at the Montrose Detention Centre, Andre and Maarten looked up from their hand readers when a burly peacekeeper arrived and told them to come with him. They glanced at each other, then did as they were asked. The peacekeeper escorted them to a medium-sized, sparsely furnished room and told them to sit down. As they did, a woman entered the room and took a seat a short distance away. A voice then said, 'As this is a formal hearing, a Witness will be present while I, the Judge, give you, Andre and Maarten, the Court's determination in relation to the crime to which you have both pleaded guilty.'

The seated woman inclined her head in acknowledgement and the Judge continued:

'Andre and Maarten, this Court accepts your statement that on the twentieth of March 2457 you deliberately lit a campfire in the forest near the site of the former town of Olinda, but soon afterwards extinguished it in such a way as to ensure it could not spread. Earlier today, being the twenty-second of March, two forest guardians, Aaron Jacobs and Jonathon, inspected the area and found evidence to corroborate your statement.

'During the intervening two days, you have been held in the Montrose Detention Centre and have been of good behaviour. While your reason for lighting the fire is to some extent understandable, and the conscientious way in which you subsequently put it out, commendable, you have both nevertheless committed a serious offence. To your credit, however, you reported the forest fire that began nearby as soon as you safely could, which the Court will take into account. Before I pass sentence, do either of you wish to make any further statement or call anyone to speak on your behalf?'

The Judge waited until Andre and Maarten shook their heads, saying they had nothing further to add to what they previously told the peacekeepers. 'Very well,' continued the Judge. 'You are each to pay a fine of two thousand credits and are required to leave Australia immediately. In addition, you are banned from re-entering this country for a period of eighteen months. You may return to your home country if you so desire. Once the fine has been paid, a guard will escort you to your place of lodging and then to the airport. This Court is now adjourned.'

The peacekeeper motioned for Andre and Maarten to follow him back to their room, where they collected their few belongings before leaving with their escort. Once outside, they looked back towards the mountain range, deeply thankful their small fire hadn't started this massive conflagration, which continued to rage, fanned by the wind and its own momentum.

Sitting in the Montrose Reconciliation Centre, with her parents present, Yeasmin scowled at Welcome, who, after being contacted by Morag MacIain with a request to lead the investigation, was conducting the interview. When he asked Yeasmin to give him her comlink, she reluctantly handed it to him. During a visit to her home, the peacekeepers had already confiscated her computer and hand reader. These pieces of equipment were currently being examined and the results were expected shortly.

'Here's a temporary replacement comlink,' said Welcome, placing it on the low table between them. 'You'll have yours back once we've finished with it.'

Yeasmin shoved the comlink into her shoulder bag and folded her arms, saying nothing. Unsure whether to comment, her parents chose to wait until the situation became clearer.

'We have received information that yesterday you gave a file to Tomas Perry, one of the students at your school, and that this file contained malicious code which spread a message and an image to his contact list, after which it continued to spread, worldwide. You will no doubt have heard about this on the news broadcasts.' Welcome waited for Yeasmin to react, but she only shrugged her shoulders, while her parents stared at her, too stunned to say anything.

'Do you deny doing this?' said Welcome, leaning forward.

'Yes, of course I didn't do it!' retorted Yeasmin. 'Why would I?'

''There are many reasons why someone would do this,' replied Welcome, holding her gaze. 'One of them is to prove how clever they are and then sit back and laugh at other people's reactions. Is that why you did it?'

'I *didn't* do it!' Yeasmin insisted, unfolding her arms and resting her clenched fists on her knees.

'Tomas Perry tells us that your two friends, Vera and Lenni, were there at the time, and as a result, they are both being detained. We've also seized their computing equipment and comlinks. What do you think they'll say when we interview them and what do you expect we'll find on their equipment?'

Yeasmin shrugged, saying, 'If either of them did this, it has nothing to do with me.'

'Do you think one of them might have created the malicious code and given it to Tomas?'

'No, I think Tomas did it himself and is blaming us.'

'We've examined his computer and hand reader, as well as his back-up drive and section of the lattice, and have found nothing to indicate he was involved. We believe him when he says he didn't do this, which inclines us to also believe him when he says you were the one who gave him the code, disguised as music.'

'Well, he would've deleted everything he used to make the code, the message, and the image, wouldn't he?' Yeasmin was confident Tomas would still take the blame.

'Perhaps, but then why confess?'

'Because he's too stupid to carry the whole thing through to its conclusion. He might be smart enough to create the code, but he got scared when it hit the headlines, so is blaming me instead.' Yeasmin fiddled in her shoulder bag for a kerchief, blew her nose, and then smiled.

'He's such an idiot, you know, but smart too, in that totally behind the scenes way, if you know what I mean.'

'Oh yes, I know exactly what you mean,' replied Welcome, also smiling.

'It's so awful, too,' continued Yeasmin, relaxed now and beginning to enjoy herself. 'What with all these fires, it's such an incredibly horrible message to send out! I know it gave *me* a shock when I heard about it. Luckily, it didn't get sent to me, but I've seen it, of course. Others at school showed me. I have to admit, though, that if it wasn't so dreadful, it's rather well done...as an artwork, I mean, and as a social statement.'

'Do you really think so?' Welcome sat back in his chair and folded his hands over his somewhat ample stomach.

'Oh yes. It looks great, and a bit more rebellion might do some good, wouldn't you say? No, perhaps not...' Yeasmin grinned, and then laughed as Welcome shook his head. Meanwhile, her parents were coming to the realisation that there were things about their daughter they knew nothing about. They had never heard her speak like this before.

'I want to ask you about something else,' said Welcome, 'and that's to do with where you, Vera and Lenni were on Tuesday afternoon, at the time the fires broke out. When you activated your emergency signals you were two kilometres from where we think it started. What were you doing in the area?'

'We were given the day off school, like they always do on the third Tuesday of every month, and were out bushwalking. We began early in the morning, stopped to have something to eat, and when we were about to go home, saw smoke in the distance, which I reported. I don't know if that's where the fires started. It might have been, but anyway, we headed back down the mountain, where we met up with the peacekeeper who answered our emergency signal.'

'Yes, we have all that on record, thank you, Yeasmin. Now, also for the record, did you or either of your two friends light a fire while you were out walking?'

'No! Certainly not! We're not stupid,' she replied, scowling again. 'We go on bushwalks all the time and we know the rules.'

'I'm sure you do,' said Welcome, standing up. 'That will be enough for now. You may all return to the waiting room, where, if you like, you can help yourselves to refreshments.' He looked sternly at Yeasmin's parents, saying, 'Once we allow you to return home, I want you both to make sure your daughter stays put until further notice. Do you understand?'

They nodded, then left with their daughter, without having said a single word other than to introduce themselves when they first entered the room. Shortly afterwards, Welcome consulted the Montrose Reconciliation Centre's specialist information technologist, who had finished examining Yeasmin's computing equipment, as well as the section of the lattice reserved for her use.

'Anything?' asked Welcome.

'No, not a trace,' replied the infotech, with a frown.

'Oh what a nuisance! I didn't expect that. Here's her comlink.'

The infotech took it, then sat down and after deactivating its security settings, began examining the contents. Welcome waited, using the opportunity to fetch a much-needed mug of hot, strong, sweet tea. Just as he was finishing it, plus the second of two rich chocolate biscuits, the infotech handed him the comlink, saying, 'Nothing on this either.'

'Not even a trace of anything suspicious?' said Welcome, raising his eyebrows.

'Nope, nothing at all. Whoever did this, it wasn't her... Or at least, there's no evidence to show it was her. She may have helped someone else do it, of course.'

'Hmm... Yes, quite likely. It'll be interesting to see if there's anything on the other equipment. I'll be back after the next interview.'

Welcome returned to the interview room, where Vera was waiting, also accompanied by her parents. Unlike Yeasmin's, however, they were more than ready to voice their opinion of the situation.

Her father stood up, glared at the peacekeeper, and said, in a loud voice, 'This is outrageous, and I demand we have a Witness present!'

'Certainly,' agreed Welcome. 'I'll arrange for one now.'

Several minutes later, the Witness entered the room, took a seat and studied everyone with an air of quiet assurance. Vera's father abruptly sat down, and her mother, mouth compressed into a thin line, joined him in making her displeasure known by staring at the Witness then looking meaningfully at Welcome. Meanwhile, Vera did her best to appear unconcerned, but had to force herself not to fiddle with the ends of her long, blonde braids. Instead, she nibbled on a fingernail, until her mother reached out a hand to prevent her doing it. With a small sigh, Vera put her hands in her lap and tried to focus on what Welcome was saying.

'Oh,' she said. 'Yes, here you are.' She handed him her comlink and accepted the one she was given in exchange, holding it as if it would bite, but then put it into her pocket and took a deep breath, waiting.

Welcome let her wait for a few moments. Eventually he said, 'Do you think we'll find anything on your comlink that we shouldn't?'

Vera shook her head. 'No. What are you looking for?'

'Tomas Perry has told us you were present when your friend Yeasmin gave him a file, which she pretended was music, bought for him, yet which turned out to be the trojan which has since spread around the world. Do you know anything at all about this? Is he telling the truth?'

Colouring, Vera said, 'He's telling the truth about us being there when Yeasmin gave him some music, but she didn't give him a trojan! If that's what he's saying, then he's trying to get us into trouble.'

'Why would he do that, Vera? Why would Tomas Perry try to get Yeasmin into trouble, and you as well?'

This time Vera blushed. 'I tease him, and I teased him yesterday, but I did apologise. We even shook hands, so I can't see why he'd want to do this.'

'He may have only pretended to accept the apology. What do you tease him about, Vera?'

'He's fat, and eats too much, which he shouldn't, though I suppose I shouldn't tease him.' Vera managed to look contrite.

'I agree, you shouldn't, and I suspect you don't actually care that he might become upset, and possibly even want revenge. Does Yeasmin ever tease him as well?'

'No, and she was the one who said I should apologise.'

'I see. What about your other friend, Lenni? How does Tomas feel about her?'

Vera shrugged and made a face. 'I don't know,' she said, nibbling another fingernail.

Welcome waited for several seconds before saying, 'I understand you and your two friends went on a bushwalk on Tuesday and told the authorities about a fire you saw, near where the township of Olinda used to be. Now I want you to think very carefully before you answer my next question.' He paused, looking directly at Vera. 'I put it to you that you and your friends started the fire now spreading across the Dandenong Ranges, and that you did this as a stunt so you could create the image used for the trojan and benefit from the added drama. What do you have to say?'

As Vera's mouth opened and her eyes widened, her mother jumped up from her seat, exclaiming, 'How dare you suggest such a thing! We're leaving! Come on, Vera, we're going!'

Welcome stood up and said, 'No, none of you will leave until Vera answers my question. Now sit down.'

Vera's mother turned red in the face and tried to push past him to the door, while Vera's father stood close to Welcome, saying, 'You'll regret this. We'll make a complaint the minute we're out of here.'

'You may make as many complaints as you like,' replied Welcome, with a smile, 'but I strongly suggest you sit down and keep quiet while Vera answers my question.' He turned to Vera, ignoring her mother.

Still seated, Vera shook her head. 'No! *We* didn't start the fires! It wasn't us, and I didn't have anything to do with making the trojan. I wouldn't know how to, anyway.'

'Then who did?'

# Chapter Twenty-Four

'Tomas Perry,' insisted Vera.

'How did he get the imagery of the fire?'

'I don't know!'

'Very well, you may all return to the second waiting room,' said Welcome, standing up again and giving them the same warning he gave Yeasmin and her parents, in relation to her staying at home once they were allowed to leave.

After they were gone, he took Vera's comlink to the infotech, who told him there was nothing incriminating on Vera's computing equipment or in her section of the lattice. 'Let's see if she's telling the truth about her comlink,' said the infotech, connecting it to his equipment and commencing a deep scan. This time, Welcome watched.

'We have something,' said the infotech, turning around and grinning. 'She tried to erase it, but didn't manage to remove all traces. I should be able to reconstruct a fair bit of this. Just give me a few minutes.'

Before long, they watched as a small fire burned brightly for about twenty seconds, crackling and spitting. 'Now I wonder what will turn up when we compare this to the image used for the trojan,' said Welcome, smiling in satisfaction.

'Yes, I'll do it now,' replied the infotech, also smiling. 'Won't take long.' He soon showed Welcome the results, saying, 'It matches, and the timestamp on the resurrected file fits with the time the fires began spreading.'

'I think we can safely say those three were in this together, but we still don't have the actual trojan, so Vera can't be charged with anything...yet,' said Welcome. 'Let's see what the third one has to say for herself, eh? What about *her* equipment and section of the lattice? Did you find anything?'

'I haven't finished examining it all yet,' answered the infotech, 'but it shouldn't take much longer. There was something interesting during my first scan, but not much, so I'm doing another one, using a different algorithm.'

'Good. I'll be back after I've spoken with her.'

Lenni and her mother were waiting for him, and this time Welcome had already arranged for the Witness to be present. Their hunch about the girls seemed to have paid off, which meant this interview could be critical to their line of evidence.

The late afternoon sun brightened the small room, enhancing the delicate beauty of both the girl and the woman, who were strikingly similar in appearance. Welcome wondered why the father wasn't present, but since this was irrelevant to the immediate situation, didn't ask. Instead, he began by saying, 'Thank you for waiting so long. Did you use the servery? If not, do you want anything to eat or drink before we begin? No? Very well. Lenni, we have evidence that your friend Vera has comlink footage of a fire that was taken at about the time when the outbreak currently burning in the Dandenong Ranges began and which has already cost the life of one firefighter and put another in a critical condition.' He paused to watch Lenni as her eyes opened wide and she glanced at her mother, who took her hand and held it tightly.

'I need your comlink, please,' he continued, 'and have one you can use while we examine it.' Welcome handed her the replacement, which Lenni looked at with interest, before carefully putting it away. It was a newer model than her own, sleek and beautiful to hold. She handed Welcome her existing one.

'Thank you,' he said, with a slight smile, having noticed how she handled the new comlink. 'Tomas Perry has accused Yeasmin of giving him the trojan that's been spreading around the world and which contains the words "New World ~ Pass the flame", together with imagery of fire consuming the Federation flag. The flames match those found in a file on Vera's comlink. Do you know how she came to have these images, and why Tomas Perry has accused Yeasmin of giving him the trojan, rather than Vera?'

Lenni met Welcome's gaze. 'He's afraid of Vera. She teases him a lot, which she shouldn't. Yeasmin may have given him some music – she did say something about wanting to – but I don't know why he'd claim it wasn't what it was supposed to be. Sorry...'

'And the images,' Welcome reminded her.

'Oh, yes... After the fires broke out, and while we were out bushwalking, Yeasmin reported seeing two campers lighting a fire. She and Vera went to see what they were up to before we left the area, but didn't think their fire looked dangerous...although of course they shouldn't have lit it. Maybe Vera took the footage then in case it was needed as evidence.'

'Glib,' thought Welcome, 'very glib.' Aloud he said, 'Yet she didn't mention this to you? A little odd, don't you think?'

Lenni shrugged and said nothing, and neither did her mother.

'Are you good at your schoolwork, Lenni?' asked Welcome, his tone friendly.

'Yes, I am. Why?'

'Are there any particular subjects you're better at than others?'

'I do well with them all,' said Lenni, hesitating.

'What about information technology? Do you like studying that field?'

'Yes...about as much as anything else.'

'Would you be capable of creating the trojan if you wanted to?'

'Probably...but I couldn't be bothered. I have better things to do.'

'Such as?'

'Well, bushwalking and swimming. I like dancing and music, too.'

'I see. And what about friends? Do you have many friends?'

'Enough, but I mostly hang out with Vera. That is, until recently. I don't have as much time for her as I used to.' Lenni glanced at her mother, who gave her a reassuring smile. Welcome suspected there was more to this particular aspect of the story than either of them were prepared to tell.

'I understand. Now, Lenni, I want you to stay here with your mother while we see what your comlink has to tell us, if anything. I won't be long.' Welcome stood up and left the room.

'Did you find anything?' he asked the infotech, giving him Lenni's comlink.

The infotech nodded. 'Yes, I certainly did. There's nothing in her section of the lattice or on her hand reader, but there was something on her computer. I managed to resurrect the icon used for the trojan, as well as part of the code, although there's no trace of the imagery or the message wording. She kept them separate, it seems.'

'I'm not sure if that'll give us enough to charge her,' replied Welcome, frowning. 'Well, I wonder what we'll find on her comlink.'

What the infotech found was precisely nothing – only the default settings and Lenni's identification details remained on the device. It had been completely and expertly wiped clean.

'Damn!' Welcome was increasingly sure the three had worked together to produce the trojan, but not at all sure they started the fires, unless by accident, and Lenni's story about the campfire was quite plausible. He stroked his chin, thinking. What to do? He went back to the interview room and sat down, studying both Lenni and her mother for several seconds before saying, 'Lenni, why is your comlink wiped clean?'

'I do it every now and again when everything gets too cluttered,' she replied, smiling. 'I hate mess and it's easier than trying to tidy it all up. If there's anything important I definitely want to keep, I back it up to my computer.'

Another plausible explanation. Welcome sighed inwardly. 'Your computer contains the icon used for the trojan, together with part of the code. I want you to explain how this came to be.' He leaned towards her, his expression grim.

Lenni was completely unfazed. 'I liked the artwork in the icon, so downloaded it, and the code is common property on the lattice. If you look at it closely, it's just a routine used for creating complex comlink messages that combine imagery, text and sound from a variety of sources, but without having to first collect all the components in the one place. It also has switches that can be set to send the message to selected people on a contact list. It comes in handy sometimes, and I used it for a school project. You can ask my preceptors, if you want.'

Welcome could barely prevent himself from gaping in surprise. Instead, he pursed his lips and waited a few seconds to recover, then said, 'I will, Lenni, I will. Which one in particular do you suggest?'

Lenni gave him a name, after which Welcome allowed them to return to the waiting room, intending to have a detailed discussion with both the infotech and Morag MacIain about how best to proceed.

'All my new friends, other than Karla and Yedda, are injured,' thought Yngwie, as he stood looking at Dandelion while she slept. At least it was healthy sleep, according to the animal healer on duty, and he decided not to interrupt it. Turning aside, he retraced his steps and was on his way back to the communal house when his comlink chimed. It was Welcome, who he remembered as being present during his first interview in relation to the cascade he and Torleif created.

Yngwie's first reaction was annoyance; all he wanted to do was have a quiet evening reading something light to take his mind off Laurita and Dandelion and the injuries they had suffered. Lying there, in bed, Laurita seemed so vulnerable, so unlike the vibrant, confident woman he first met... When? Nearly three weeks ago, yet it felt so much longer. Forcing himself to be civil, he answered Welcome's greeting: 'Hello, and yes, I have time to talk.'

'Good,' replied Welcome. 'Yngwie, I've a favour to ask. You're now someone Morag and Kaj seem to trust, and you were the one who traced the person whose comlink this latest cascade was initially sent from, so we'd like you to do something else for us, if you're willing?'

'Possibly. It depends upon how much time it takes. I still have a few loose ends to deal with, as well as our original project, and to be honest, I'd like to spend more time with my friends here. Some of them have been injured in the fires, and we've all been through a lot these last two days.' The impact was beginning to tell on him and the thought of even more involvement suddenly seemed more than he could manage.

'I'm very sorry to hear it, Yngwie. Which friends?'

When Yngwie told him, Welcome raised his eyebrows in surprise. 'Søren Thorup? I know him! He's a friend of Morag's.'

'Yes, he is, and I'm just on my way back from visiting his cat, Dandelion, who was injured as well. They were caught in the fires not long after they first began. I saw Søren earlier on, as well as my other friends, who are still in the Ferntree Gully medcentre.'

'You seem to be hurt yourself,' said Welcome.

'It's nothing,' replied Yngwie, not wanting to elaborate.

'I see. Would you at least listen to what I propose before making up your mind?'

'Okay, I'll listen,' said Yngwie, stifling a yawn. He realised that what he needed above all else, was sleep.

'I've spent the best part of the afternoon questioning three young women, who are from Montrose, and who Tomas Perry claims gave him the trojan you tracked to his comlink, disguised as music he was fond of.' When Yngwie was about to interrupt, Welcome said, 'Let me tell you the rest before you ask any questions.'

Yngwie nodded, so he continued: 'Their names are Yeasmin, Vera and Lenni, and we believe Tomas when he says he didn't create the trojan, as do his parents and preceptors. I have yet to interview him, but will if necessary. In the meantime, our infotech here has examined the comlinks we took from the young women, along with their computing equipment and lattice segments. Yeasmin's contained nothing to incriminate her. However, Tomas said it was her who gave him the file.

'We discovered that Vera had erased a file from her comlink, which we managed to resurrect: it contained footage of flames matching those used for the trojan. Lenni thought it might have been taken of a campfire they saw in the forest near Olinda while out bushwalking on Tuesday, and which they later reported. However, Vera herself didn't volunteer this information, and when I confronted her with Lenni's account, she was a little too quick to agree, but couldn't really explain why she deleted the footage instead of giving it to the peacekeepers, and why the footage contained a close-up of the campfire. I'd have thought a scene showing the people who lit the fire and what they were doing would have been far more useful, but she said the campers were in the rest of the file, and what a pity we couldn't have resurrected that part as well.'

Welcome paused, but when Yngwie didn't comment, continued his summary: 'Lenni's computer contained an erased copy of the icon used for the trojan, as well as some partial code similar to that contained in the trojan, but which she proved was readily available on the lattice and quite innocuous. However, her comlink was completely clear of anything other than its default settings and her identification information. She explained this away by saying it was something she routinely did when her comlink became too cluttered.'

'So you have nothing to charge them with,' concluded Yngwie.

'No, and we couldn't keep them any longer, so sent them home with a warning to stay put until further notice.'

'And you're convinced they're responsible?'

'Yes, I am. There are far too many coincidences here, and my biggest question is, why were they bushwalking on a day like Tuesday? Why didn't their parents stop them? I gather they're highly experienced, but still, on a day like that!'

By this time, Yngwie's transport had arrived at Ferntree Gully. As he walked to the communal house, the starlit night sky and the faint sounds of nocturnal creatures going about their business gave him the illusion of safety. The fires had moved eastwards by now, so apart from the smell of smoke, he could almost imagine things were back to normal, but of course, they weren't. 'I agree,' he said, 'but people do, often. It's cooler in the forest too... And I can't see how I can help if you already have your own expert checking their equipment.'

'Well, this is obviously a copycat crime,' said Welcome, 'mimicking the cascade you and your friend Torleif sent out, and based on other evidence we have, the worst of it is, I suspect these three are responsible for the fires in the Dandenongs.'

'What!' Yngwie stopped walking and sat down on the nearest available object, which happened to be beneath the lighting outside the entrance to the communal house, which meant Welcome was able to see his expression.

'I'm sorry to upset you like this,' he said, 'but I'm afraid the repercussions of what you did are far greater than you may have anticipated, which is why I want your help...and I'm fairly sure you *can* help.' Welcome waited, wondering whether Yngwie would cooperate, because if he didn't, neither Yeasmin, Vera nor Lenni were likely to answer for their crimes.

'What do you want me to do?' asked Yngwie, carefully controlling his voice.

'We want you to speak with Lenni. She seems the most vulnerable of the three and also the one most likely to have undertaken the work to put the trojan together. If you tell her what you did and why, there's a chance she might confess, to impress you. If you don't mind my saying so, you're a handsome young chap, and if you manage to exercise enough charm, being a copycat crime, she may succumb to a certain degree of hero worship. Though I must admit, you're not looking your best right now.'

Yngwie grimaced and said, 'Wait a week or so and I'll look a great deal better!'

'Good! I take it you agree?'

'Yes, I agree. I could hardly refuse, could I?'

'Possibly not. Now, an idea springs to mind. Did you say you were visiting Søren's cat when I called?'

'That's right. Why?'

'Cats can be very useful in situations like this, if they can be persuaded to help. Is there any chance Dandelion will recover enough to leave the animal healer's premises in about a week's time?'

'I'm not sure, but I think so.'

'If she does, could you borrow her for a few hours?'

'Yes, easily. I've been taking care of her while Søren goes into the forest. She doesn't like it in there. He's doing some research...but it's a long story, and I'd prefer not go into it all just now.'

'I quite understand... What I want to ask is this: if Dandelion is well enough, and agrees, I'd like you to bring her with you when we speak with Lenni. Cats are able to read our minds if they want to, which you no doubt realise by now?' When Yngwie nodded, Welcome said, 'If *she* can find out exactly what happened, even if it's only to corroborate what Lenni tells you, then Dandelion's evidence can be entered into the Judge, via a Witness.'

'So I've heard,' answered Yngwie, raising an eyebrow.

'Good, I'm glad you understand. They're usually extremely reliable.'

'Dandelion may not be. She has sometimes behaved rather badly while they've been here.'

'Which sounds like another long story,' said Welcome.

'Yes, and perhaps if you ask Søren's permission first, then at the same time you can ask him what she's done and whether he thinks she would be reliable enough to do this.'

'You're quite correct. I'll do as you suggest, but if Dandelion can't help, I still think, even alone, there's every chance you could achieve what we're after. Either way, I'll let you know once I've spoken with Søren. If he agrees, I'll see what Dandelion herself has to say.'

'Okay. Now if you don't mind, I'd like to go inside and have something to eat.'

'Of course. I'll contact you again soon, and thank you, Yngwie.'

## CHAPTER TWENTY-FIVE

While lying in bed that night, unable to sleep, Karla wondered if there was any valid reason for her to be allowed into the bushfire zone to visit her friends. Probably not, she concluded, and reached out to stroke Aurora, her main source of comfort these past three days. She had called Yngwie earlier in the evening, but his comlink told her he was unavailable, and when she called Shahid, his said the same. Presumably they were both either sleeping or attending to something important. This time, Karla decided against contacting Wania, who almost certainly had enough to keep her busy, and no doubt so did Shafiqur. Instead, she sent a video message to Laurita, telling her she knew what had happened and if there was anything at all she could do to help, to please let her know...and that she was looking forward to hearing from her when she was well enough.

Aurora moved up the bed to softly lick Karla's cheek. The comforting warmth of the cat's furry body and her gentle affection, together with the soothing, ever-present background link of their minds, finally allowed Karla to fall asleep – only to wake two hours later thinking about the green lights Søren and Jonathon had seen. Having failed during the afternoon to find any reputable reference to the exact phenomenon, and wishing she could have talked to Yngwie and Shahid about them, she sat down at her computer and did one more search.

Karla knew there were many species of bioluminescent fungi, some of which also grew in Australia, such as *Omphalotus nidiformis*, or 'ghost fungus' – but they were all, of course, flightless, and certainly not known to have voices! Sometimes referred to as 'foxfire', their luminescence, often green, was occasionally seen on rotting bark, dead and dying trees, and in amongst leaf litter. A number of species, such as *Mycena lamprospora* and *Mycena pruinoso-viscida var. rabaulensis*, had luminescent spores, which could explain why the light was seen to be floating, but not why Søren felt cold when he touched it. Of course, this may simply have been an illusion associated with his state of mind, or even the effect of having breathed in the spores, which might contain an hallucinogen. However, for Karla, the interesting question was whether there was an undiscovered species in the forests of the Dandenong ranges which did in fact have spores of this type, and which perhaps were only released under certain conditions.

As well as fungi, there were also bioluminescent bacteria; insect larvae and caterpillars; adult insects, such as fireflies and various beetles; earthworms, and creatures such as millipedes. So, while clouds of small flying insects sounded like a possibility, there were also phosphorescent gases and other materials such as inks, paints and dyes to consider.

After reading for a while, Karla concluded that without a systematic investigation by someone far more qualified in this particular field than herself, it was unlikely an explanation for the phenomenon would be found. Meanwhile, she could at least give this information to Jonathon, in case he knew of someone interested enough to take it further.

Yawning, Karla noticed Aurora sitting by her feet, gazing up at her, eyes wide, pupils glinting greenly and ears twitching as she 'listened' curiously to her thoughts.

'That's it!' Karla exclaimed, giggling and reaching down to pat her. 'A pride of giant meat-eating cats wandering around the forest, their eyes glowing in the dark, waiting for poor sods like Søren to fall into a trap so they can pounce on him! Grrrrrr...' She ruffled the long fur around Aurora's neck and scratched her beneath the chin. 'What do think, eh? Should we be hunting for giant puddytats, hmm? Maybe that's why the dog left the forest. He was being chased by them and had the bad luck to be chased back in again by Dandelion! Oh dear me, I'm being silly, aren't I? Still, better than worrying about everyone... Okay, definitely time to get some sleep. Come on,' and she wandered back to her room, followed by Aurora, who purred softly as she leapt into bed after Karla and buried herself beneath the covers.

Two days later, when Søren arrived in Endeavour Hills to fetch Dandelion, the animal healer on duty was not the young woman who had been so helpful when he called, but the one who was there the night Yngwie and Wania brought her in for treatment.

'Thank you so much for everything,' said Søren, shaking his hand.

'Not at all, not at all. She's a wonderful cat, and we don't see many here. Quite a novelty.' The animal healer smiled and added, 'She's recovering well. Come this way and I'll show you.' He led the way to where Dandelion was waiting, eager to see Søren, who was shocked, however, by the shaved area on her rear quarters, which of course he should have expected. As he knelt down to stroke her, she purred loudly, pressing herself against him, tail in the air.

'Keep her as quiet as you can until the wounds have completely healed and encourage her not to jump around,' said the animal healer, looking meaningfully at Dandelion, assuming she would understand and pleased when she sent him a quick acknowledgement.

'I will,' agreed Søren. 'A friend of ours should be here in about fifteen minutes to take us back to Ferntree Gully.'

'Good. You can come out front to our waiting room, if you like. I don't have any appointments for an hour, so you shouldn't be disturbed in there.'

Having called the day before to see how Søren and Dandelion were faring, Wania had made the offer to bring them home. When she arrived, right on time, Søren was quietly pleased to see she was no taller than him, and even though this was the first time they had met in person, they formed an instant liking for each other.

Before he left the room, the animal healer noticed that besides being of a similar age, they were both uncommonly attractive, Wania's darker-skinned and raven-haired elegance of feature and form perfectly complementing Søren's blonde beauty. Wondering whether they were more than just friends, he observed them for a few moments longer, then left them to their privacy.

'It's wonderful to see you up and well, Dandelion,' said Wania. 'I helped Yngwie bring you here when you were hurt,' she added. Dandelion gazed back at her, ears twitching, the pupils of her eyes huge and black, puzzled as to why she couldn't remember meeting this wight before. Wania could sense her confusion. 'You weren't yourself that night,' she explained, 'so there may be many things you don't recall, but the important thing is, you're fine now.'

'She was semi-unconscious for a long time,' said Søren, 'which, under the circumstances, is probably for the best.'

'I agree,' replied Wania, stroking Dandelion's head. 'Shall we go?'

'Yes, thank you. Can you walk a bit further?' he asked Dandelion.

Since she still couldn't put much weight on her hind leg, Dandelion took a few three-legged steps, then looked up at her companions, meowed softly, and hopped onwards towards the entrance, with Søren and Wania following close behind, watching in case she stumbled. Fortunately, they reached the landjet without mishap, but Dandelion needed help to clamber inside. Once en route, she chattered almost constantly, commenting on everything she saw, her relief at having left the animal healer's premises overcoming any reserve she might normally have felt with a relative stranger such as Wania. Her cheerfulness, so like her usual self when they were home in Greenland, affected her companions, who found themselves talking about common interests, their backgrounds and their work, hardly noticing the dark, almost lifeless vista of the burnt forest in the distance. However, once they arrived at the communal house, it became all too apparent.

As they stood outside for while, saying nothing, only looking at the devastation, Wania said, 'Would you like to share our evening meal with us tonight? I could pick you both up at 18:30. It would cheer up my bondmate, I'm sure. You may already know that he's a medical practitioner and works at the medcentre here in Ferntree Gully? Yes? Meeting you both would do him good, particularly as Shahid and Yedda have chosen not to come home yet. They're staying with Laurita. She isn't recovering as well as expected, and we're all very worried. My son seems to have developed a great affection for her, and I believe she returns it.'

'Yes, I noticed when I visited them yesterday,' replied Søren, 'but I thought Laurita was looking remarkably well. Has something happened since?'

'A small clot formed in her lungs, which dislodged and caused a stroke. It has yet to fully resolve itself.' Wania paused to gain control of her voice. 'Laurita can't speak. Ironic, is it not?'

Søren gaped at her, and his hand trembled slightly as he brought it to his mouth. Then, shaking his head, he said, 'It is, and I hardly know what to say, other than yes, I'll be very glad to share a meal with you this evening.'

'Thank you. We'll see you soon,' replied Wania, watching while he helped Dandelion climb out of the landjet. She returned Søren's small wave as they reached the entrance to the communal house, then went home to prepare their evening meal, and to pray for Laurita.

While his father waited in their landjet, Tomas Perry walked slowly up to the entrance of the house where Lenni and her mother lived. He placed his hand on its identification panel, almost wishing Lenni wasn't home, even though his comlink confirmed that she was. When she came to the door, he swallowed a few times and coughed, but managed to say, 'Lenni, I want to talk to you about the trojan. May I come in?'

'Sure, why not,' answered Lenni, standing aside for him to enter. He waited for her to say something else, but when she didn't, mumbled something about comlinks, then cleared his voice and said, quite loudly, 'I know it was you who wrote it, not Yeasmin. I've remembered. She gave the comlink to you and then you copied the file to mine. Why would she do that if it wasn't your comlink in the first place? And anyway, you couldn't have copied the file from hers to mine. It isn't possible.'

Lenni gazed at him for several seconds. 'Do you want to sit down?' she asked, her tone polite yet neutral.

Tomas nodded, and sat down on a nearby chair big enough to take his bulk. Lenni took a seat opposite, studied her fingernails for a while, then looked up and said, 'You're not actually stupid at all, are you Tomas.

You're really quite clever. The problem is, you're not clever enough. It doesn't matter what you think you saw, or what you think you remember. It's over. Forget it.'

'I can't, and I don't think you're at all clever in doing what *you* did. It's stupid to upset everybody. Why would you want to do something like this?' Red in the face, Tomas forced himself to continue: 'You should be sorry for wasting the peacekeepers' time, and everyone else's, especially when all these fires are burning and they have enough to do already. Why aren't you sorry?'

'Who says I'm not?' replied Lenni. 'I mean, sorry about the fires,' she quickly added, looking him in the eye.

'You shouldn't be friends with Vera and Yeasmin,' replied Tomas. 'You wouldn't have done this on your own. They talked you into it, didn't they.' He took his kerchief from his pocket and blew his nose, wishing he didn't feel so nervous. Unfortunately, he always felt nervous when he was anywhere near Lenni.

'No, they didn't! And anyway, we're not friends anymore.' Lenni turned away for a moment to hide her expression. Damn Yeasmin and Vera! Why did she listen to them? Damn this stupid boy, too!

'I want you to go, Tomas,' she said, standing up, her voice tense. 'My mother will be home soon and I don't want you here when she arrives.'

Tomas stood as well, then made one last attempt: 'Lenni, you should tell the peacekeepers what you've done. If they find out it was you, and you didn't tell them first, they won't like it.'

'Just go away, Tomas!' shouted Lenni, slamming her hand against the household security system's panel. The door opened and she grabbed Tomas by the elbow, thrusting him towards it. 'Keep away from me at school too, Tubby!'

Tomas nearly tripped as he was forced to leave, but managed to recover his balance. 'It's your choice, Lenni,' he said, taking a deep breath as he turned back to face her. 'Your choice, not mine.'


'Welcome! How wonderful to see you!' exclaimed Søren, when he answered the comlink call. 'I am in Melbourne at the moment, doing some work for the Federation, or did you already know?'

'I knew, Søren. I've called on business, but it's good to see you anyway. How are you? I've heard you and Dandelion were hurt during these dreadful fires.'

'We are almost better now, but how did you hear about us?'

'Karla told Morag, and Morag told me.' Welcome smiled. 'You know how it is with Karla. She often tends to be the conduit for information.'

'Yes, that's very true.' Søren returned the smile. 'And what about yourself? Is the world treating you well?'

'It is, Søren, it is. I still live alone, but I'm happy to enjoy my wines, my friends, and a regular swim in the City Baths. However, the main reason I've called is to ask to borrow Dandelion, if you think she'll be up and around in about a week's time?'

'You want to borrow Dandelion? What for?' Søren raised an eyebrow and stared at him, completely taken aback.

'We need a sleuth, and she seems the best candidate. She's friends with a mutual acquaintance – young Yngwie, the Norwegian. I gather you know him fairly well, particularly since he rescued you both.'

'I do, yes. Well, I don't know why you want a sleuth, though I can guess.'

'You were always good at putting the story together, my friend,' said Welcome, with a grin, 'and even more so when it comes to cats... I've pressed Yngwie into service to help work out who set this latest cascade loose, and we'd like Dandelion to be present when he and I interview our likeliest suspect. Without their assistance, I doubt if we'll have enough to lay charges.'

'I won't ask who your suspect is, but I must ask if there'll be any danger to Dandelion. She has been through a great deal lately.' Søren proceeded to tell Welcome the whole story, beginning with the attack on Aurora, the escape and confrontation with the black cat in the streets of Ferntree Gully, and finally, the chase after the dog that led to their being trapped in the forest not long after the bushfire began. 'She needs peace and quiet,' he concluded, 'not more excitement.'

'What you've told me does seem to make it far too risky, on all counts,' agreed Welcome. 'Perhaps another cat could be there instead.'

'I would suggest Aurora,' replied Søren. 'She has considerable experience dealing with difficult situations and knows how to keep secrets, too.'

'You're absolutely right! I'll ask Karla straight away.'

'She happens to know Yngwie, and I believe Aurora has met him as well.'

'Good, that may help. Karla seems a little distracted, have you noticed?'

'Oh yes, which is understandable. Just as well she isn't able to see the fires from where she lives or works. That would be far too distressing. I can't say I like it either.'

'Could anyone, except perhaps the people who started it?'

'No, presumably not... Do you know if the investigation is any closer to finding out whether it was done on purpose, rather than being an accident?'

'We may be close, but we're not sure.'

'Are you helping with that investigation too?'

'Yes, I am. We think that whoever sent out the trojan may also have started the fires.'

'In which case, it's even more out of the question to use Dandelion for your interview. If your suspect did in fact start the bushfire, she could easily attack them.'

'Because of what you've been through... Well, that makes Aurora the better choice by far. I don't expect she'd ever attack anyone.'

'No, she's a remarkably even tempered cat.'

'I agree... Well, I'll contact Karla now, so look after yourselves and try not to have any more misadventures! You've had more than enough for anyone.'

Søren laughed. 'We have a dinner invitation for this evening from an extraordinarily delightful woman, but sadly for me, she has a bondmate, or otherwise I'd consider exercising all my considerable charm on her.'

'Oh?' said Welcome. 'Who?'

'A friend's mother. She helped bring Dandelion to the animal healer when Yngwie needed transport, then fetched us back here this afternoon once Dandelion was well enough to be released. You may know her... Wania.'

'What a coincidence... Yes, I do know her. She's a valued colleague, who's being kept busy by the repercussions of the fires, and beforehand, some of the copycat crimes that began here after Yngwie's stunt. It's dreadful how situations like this bring out the worst in people.'

'And don't forget, Welcome, also the best.'

'True. Thanks for reminding me, and do enjoy yourselves this evening. I'm sure you'll like her bondmate, Shafiqur. Their son's name is Shahid, isn't it?'

'Yes, it is, and he was injured in the fires as well, together with one of his dear friends, Laurita, who is also a friend of Karla's. Hasn't she mentioned them to you?'

'No, which is odd. I assumed she was upset because of the fires, but there must be more to it. I'll ask her about it all when I call.'

'She may not know how ill Laurita is. I was told only this afternoon. She has suffered a stroke and is unable to speak.'

'Oh, poor woman! Should I tell Karla?'

'Yes, but I suspect *her* main problem is that this is still a restricted area, which means she can't visit any of us. Worse, Laurita has damaged lungs, so Karla couldn't even speak with her – and now, with the stroke, it will be worse still.'

'Dear oh dear... This isn't at all good. I think I should visit Karla, rather than just call.'

'I agree.'

# Chapter Twenty-Five

'Goodbye then, Søren, and let me know if there's anything I can do to help.'

'I will, and thank you.'

After the call, Søren spent the remainder of the afternoon resting, listening to music and enjoying Dandelion's company, glad to have her with him again. When Wania came to pick them up, they were both in a mood to appreciate their evening and to be pampered with good food and even better company, while, for a few brief hours, they all made an effort to push away the outside world.

Tears filled Shahid's eyes as he and Yedda watched Laurita struggle to take a few, laboured steps, helped by a support rail and a medtech, who held her fast by one arm. With her pelvis now pinned and stabilised and her ribs beginning to heal, these steps were vital if she was ever to recover from both the stroke and the damage to her lungs.

'Just a little further,' encouraged the medtech.

Laurita tried to smile, but the frozen left side of her face made it a mockery. When Yedda sent her a calming thought, Laurita briefly turned to look at her, raised the fingers of her right hand a little in acknowledgement, then focused on the next, arduous movement.

Shahid's own injuries were healing well, yet he felt unable to leave the medcentre; it seemed too much like desertion. He took Yedda for a walk twice a day; to begin with only as far as the nearest stretch of garden, but this morning, before Laurita's exercise session, he managed to reach the trafficway and half a kilometre towards the forest. However, the sight of the blackened trees in the distance was heartbreaking, so they turned back, Shahid leaning more heavily on his new walking stick. Now, all he could think about was Laurita and her work – their work – and pray that she recovered sufficiently to return to it.

Silently entering the room, Shafiqur approached his son and laid a hand on his shoulder. 'Her condition will almost certainly resolve itself,' he said softly.

*Almost certainly...* Shahid looked up at his father, his lips pressed together in a thin line, his brow furrowed. He placed his hand over Shafiqur's and turned back to watch Laurita – as she almost stumbled, saved only by the medtech's hold. Her long hair, tied back in a ponytail, seemed to have lost some of its lustre, which was hardly surprising, and rather than its normal healthy tan, her skin had taken on a slightly sallow tone, yet to Shahid, this accentuated her beauty rather than detracting from it. Even as she was, ill and unhappy, her depth of character, her courage, shone through everything else and he found it impossible to believe she would fail to win this battle. *He* might be condemned to remain silent, but surely, she would not... She *would* read her poems and songs aloud for the world to hear. She *would*, one day, return to the forest with him, where they'd once again climb to the heights of the great mountain ash and have the chance to watch clouds of butterflies dancing in the treetops.

Tears ran down his cheeks and he hastily wiped them away. It wouldn't do for her to see him weep. When Yedda placed a paw on his knee and licked his hand, he stroked her head, then stood up and walked over to the other side of the room, leaving his father wondering what he intended to do.

While Laurita was still several metres away from her goal, Shahid waited, facing her, his eyes fixed upon hers and with a warm smile of encouragement. When she and the medtech were close enough, he held out his hand, and as she reached out to him, grasped hers. 'Well done,' he said, sending the words to Yedda to pass on. Laurita steadied herself, and with his and the medtech's help, sat down on a nearby chair. She noticed Shafiqur still watching and beckoned him to join them, then patted the chair next to her for him to sit down, which he did.

'You're doing well, Laurita,' he said. 'I've spoken with your treating practitioner this morning and we expect that you *will* return to normal, though it will take time. However, I have some very bad news. Mei-Ling died twenty minutes ago, and I thought it best to let you both know now rather than have you hear it from someone else. I am so sorry.'

Laurita hid her face in her hands as it contorted in grief, and she wept uncontrollably, yet without a sound. Shahid sat down, also silently weeping. While the medtech stood by, unable to do anything, other than wait, Shafiqur put an arm around Laurita's shoulders. Meanwhile, Yedda crept to Shahid's feet, crouching down, her shoulders hunched, tail curling to and fro. So much sadness, yet nothing she could do to take away their pain, for if she did, it would only resurface at another time.

At last Laurita dried her eyes and turned to face Shahid, then took his hand in hers and raised it to her cheek. Shafiqur stood up, patted her shoulder and gestured to the medtech to come away. As they left, Shahid turned to Laurita and gently put his arms around her. Together, they silently mourned the loss of their new friend – and the forests they fought to save.

## CHAPTER TWENTY-SIX

For a distance of nearly twenty-five kilometres, almost the entire southern face of the Dandenong Ranges was now a blackened, ghostly land of silent trees, ashen earth and empty skies. As the wind dropped and the temperature fell, the last of the fires were quenched – before they reached the small communities nestled within the eastern foothills. The people of Gembrook and Beaconsfield had watched as the flames approached in the distance – had watched the airjets, ceaseless in their efforts to save the remaining forests, the farms, and surrounding grasslands; they watched as the firefighters did their utmost to prevent the flames from escaping over the northern ridge should the wind spring up again and change direction, as was predicted.

The forest creatures who had managed to escape were gradually returning to search for food and water, but the ash-laden creeks and streams gave little relief. Occasionally wombats, hidden deep beneath the ground in their burrows, emerged to lumber through this alien landscape, so entirely different from their former home. Confused and frightened, they returned to their burrows to wait for nightfall, hoping the darkness would bring safety. Some of the birds and other predators found more than enough to eat as they scratched around in the earth for the bodies of those who had not escaped. Sometimes, when they uncovered still hot cinders, burning their feet, they hopped away or flew up with an indignant squawk, but soon returned to their feast.

Yet even amongst the devastation, small pockets of verdant greenery remained, miraculously untouched, and here and there a few small springs were already beginning to run clear. Jonathon, in his ash-stained boots and soot-covered gloves, stretched his back and for a few moments surveyed the team of volunteers who were searching for injured wildlife to take to the animal healers in the surrounding district. These small oases were often the best place to find the injured, especially the ones with the greatest chance of survival. Those found elsewhere were sometimes beyond help and so were euthanized and buried. The work, heartbreaking at times, inspiring at others when, against all odds, a struggling creature was saved, had become one of their priorities – other than to ensure the still ember-hot areas where the fires had burned most recently did not rekindle a fresh outbreak.

When Jonathon's comlink chimed and he answered, it was to see Karla's face, drawn from lack of sleep and wary of what he might say. 'How bad is it?' she asked.

'It's not good,' he said, taking a deep breath to steady his voice. 'I suspect we may have lost some of our more fragile populations of plants and animals, where they were too localised. We won't know until a full survey has been done. Could you help?'

'Yes, of course,' replied Karla, without hesitation. 'When can I start?'

'When do you want to start? We're working with aerial data first, but we need people on the ground as well.'

'I can begin today if you tell me where to go. Willsmere can do without me for the time being and I can leave Aurora with a friend who called around yesterday, asking for her help. You may know him. His name is Welcome.'

'Oh, yes, I do know him. Unusual fellow, but charming, and a good choice to assist with our investigation. What does he need Aurora for?'

'He wants her there when he interviews a suspect, and he's asked Yngwie to help as well because he agrees that whoever's responsible for the latest comlink cascade may be the same person who started the fires. Yngwie's inside information into how these things are done could be invaluable.'

'Ah, I see. I've been a bit busy, so I didn't know Welcome was planning this. It could work.'

'He also thinks Yngwie may be able to trade on his good looks and track record to charm the suspect into confessing. Apparently it's a young schoolgirl.'

Jonathon grimaced and said, 'Yes, that's right. There were three of them...three young girls from Montrose. It was their comlink signals I told you about earlier.'

'It's almost too incredible to believe that they did this on purpose. Surely it must have been an accident?'

'It's a possibility... Sorry, I need to get back to my group here, so I'd better find one for you to join.'

'Yes, but before you do, Welcome brought me some other news. Laurita has had a stroke and hasn't recovered yet. She can't speak.'

'No! How awful!'

'And I'm not allowed into the area yet, other than to help with your survey. It's a bad situation. Anyway, I know you have to go, so where do you want me to begin?'

'Just a moment... I'll check our latest maps. Yes, there's a group being put together to follow the Monbulk Creek, to see if there's anything left alive. You could join them. I'll send you the coordinates.'

'Thanks... I can borrow one of the Willsmere airjets for this work. I suppose these coordinates are where there's a clearing for good access?'

'Yes, that's right. There's no other way in at the moment. You might want to bring supplies for a few days. They intend to camp out and do as much as they can in one go.'

'Right, I can do that. I'll call you when I get there.'

'Good. Everyone needs to report in regularly anyway.'

'Okay. I'll talk to you soon, Jonathon.'

'Take care.'

'I will, and you too.'

Karla put her comlink away and explained the situation to Aurora, then, after a quick call to Welcome to arrange for him to fetch her, began assembling everything she needed. A highly experienced field scientist, she was used to taking part in expeditions lasting far longer than this one and in far more rugged terrain, so it took very little time before she was ready to leave and not much longer to reach the designated meeting point. Seven others were already there, inspecting the remaining mountain ash and the reasonably large patches of intact vegetation surrounding the headwaters of the creek. After introducing herself, Karla made the promised call to Jonathon.

'Everything seems extremely well organised,' she told him. 'There are quite a few stands of mountain ash still very much alive, thank the Sun, and the creek seems reasonably unspoiled here... Sorry for the short call, though. I should talk to the team now and find out how I can best fit in. Call me if you can. I wish you could be here.'

'I wish I could too, but we'll see each other soon, one way or another. In the meantime, let's hope you manage to spot a platypus, though I suspect it'd be a miracle. Still, we can always hope.'

'Yes, and an echidna or two would be something, that's for sure.' Karla turned away as one of the team members tapped her on the shoulder, indicating they were ready to discuss their plans. She nodded, said goodbye to Jonathon, and set to work.

When Yngwie arrived at work on the Monday morning, after spending most of the previous afternoon with Shahid, Yedda and Laurita, he found Kaj staring at his computer screen, so lost in thought he hardly noticed him. 'Hej,' said Yngwie, and Kaj turned around, eyes wide.

'Your friend, Torleif, seems to have beaten us to it,' he said slowly. 'He has identified who engineered the fault in our messaging system and is convinced it was done on purpose. Look!'

Startled, Yngwie peered over Kaj's shoulder, and there were the names of two information technologists, each associated with the changes made to one specific satellite, eleven years ago, and buried within multiple layers of complex maintenance routines, each one verifying the validity of the preceding one. Consequently, none of the changes would normally have created any cause for concern, particularly as the standard authorisation system had been used: the ID of the first infotech was associated with the individual changes within the sequence, while that of the second, the authorisation for them to proceed.

The only reason these routines were picked up by Torleif as suspect was because they were all put into place within far too short a period of time to be credible: three days. However, this was as far as he could go because he didn't have the authority to access the records of the two people concerned. All he could do was give the information to Kaj, who could then take the issue further. In typical Torleif fashion, though, instead of signing the message with his name, he had used his current avatar: a troll bearing a remarkable resemblance to Kaj and eating a bowlful of struggling people, each with carefully detailed features.

Ignoring the attempt at humour, Kaj added the checks Torleif had outlined to the collection of routines they intended to use to verify that nothing similar had been done to any of the other satellites. He then handed this task to Yngwie, who shrugged in resignation and sat down to begin coding the required procedures. Meanwhile, Kaj informed Morag MacIain of their progress and began hunting for the two information technologists. He soon located them. The first was dead, and had been dead at the time his name was attached to the maintenance routines, while the other was still alive and currently working for a company called Wyvern Meridian, of which Kaj knew very little; only that it was large, had facilities worldwide, and dealt in a wide variety of products and services.

As dead people don't usually undertake work of this or any other description, Kaj immediately realised that something must presumably be wrong with the death, or at least the records of the death. His problem was, though, he was unused to thinking in a devious, and perhaps even criminal, manner, so stood up and asked the person he thought most capable of quickly answering his question: 'Yngwie,' he said, 'if you wanted to use a dead person's identity to make unauthorised changes to a piece of software, what would be the best method of going about it?'

Yngwie stared at him. 'One of the information technologists Torleif found was dead at the time?'

'Yes.'

'Which one?'

'The one who made the changes.'

'When did he die?'

'Five days before all the changes were made.'

'So how did he die and where did he die?'

'Ah, I see. Yes, that could be it. If he died under, shall we say, unusual circumstances, and his death wasn't made known immediately, plus if the person who authorised the amendments knew he was dead, but also knew the death was being investigated, for example, he could take the opportunity to make these changes himself, *if* he knew how to forge the identity. Hmm... It may be best if I consult Coordinator MacIain. It should be far easier for her than it would be for me to discover how and where he died... Thank you,' he added absentmindedly, then wandered over to the servery, made himself a hot chocolate, and sat down, sipping his drink carefully so as not to burn himself.

'What about the other one?' asked Yngwie, sitting down next to him.

'Oh, he's alive and working for a large corporation. Once I tell her, I expect Coordinator MacIain will want him interviewed.'

'I think you're right,' answered Yngwie, with a grin. 'Perhaps you should thank Torleif first?'

'I should, yes.' Kaj took the remainder of his hot chocolate over to his workstation and typed for a while. Before long, he received a reply in the form of Torleif's new avatar: the same troll, but this time drinking a toast from what appeared to be a bowl made from a human skull. Kaj shook his head, but Yngwie could see he was smiling. 'Progress!' he thought, and after sending his own message to Torleif, returned to work. The troll he received some fifteen minutes later had his friend's own features and was raising its hands to its ears, twiddling its fingers and poking its tongue out at him.

Thirty-two firefighters, eleven forest guardians, fourteen peacekeepers, dozens of friends and family members, along with almost half the population of Ferntree Gully, all gathered together to say goodbye to Mei-Ling and the fourth member of their team, Aziz. Jonathon, as one of the pallbearers, led the procession, which began in the outdoor pavilion near the entertainment centre then wound its way towards the old cemetery, where the two would be cremated and their urns placed in a memorial garden. A silver birch stood ready to be planted on the site. During the ceremony, which various news teams were recording, there were few dry eyes while Mei-Ling's bondmate gave his farewell speech, followed by Aziz's father, Akram, who had flown in from Pakistan for the occasion. His pleasantly accented English lent poignancy to the funeral as everyone was reminded of the future his son had lost and of his family's grief at the death of their only child and grandchild.

'He came to this country six years ago,' said Akram, 'and learned to love it as his own. Now, he has given his life to protect it, and I am honoured by those of you who have come here today to pay your respects. I thank you for this gift and pray that my son will know everlasting peace and joy.' He raised his fine features to the sky and pressed his hands together, before bowing his head in silence.

Hardly a murmur was to be heard amongst the listeners. The only sounds were the background calls of the birds and the rustling of the trees as the breeze, which had picked up during the morning, brought relief from the heat of the day before. Everyone watched as the two coffins were lowered into the cremation chamber and many wept when they at last disappeared from view. Akram stepped down from the podium, shook Jonathon's hand, then Aaron's, and finally, greeted each of Mei-Ling's parents and her bondmate with a kiss on the cheek. 'My deepest sympathy,' he said, at which her parents burst into tears, while her bondmate looked down for a long moment, utterly miserable.

Akram turned to Jonathon and Aaron and quietly suggested they move away to give them privacy. Joining the others gathering inside the entertainment centre for the traditional funeral meal, they met with Shahid, Yedda and Laurita, who sat in a wheelchair. Jonathon introduced himself to Laurita and Yedda, then introduced them all to Aaron and Akram, who said, 'You were with my son when he died. Please, tell me what you know.'

He was slightly taken aback when neither Laurita nor Shahid replied straight away, but Jonathon explained that Laurita's lungs were damaged in the explosion that killed Aziz and Mei-Ling, and that Shahid was permanently unable to speak using his own natural voice. He glanced at Shahid as he said this, then let Shahid 'speak' for himself: 'My friend Laurita and I were volunteers and assigned to the crew your son and Mei-Ling were members of, so we only knew them for a short time, although under circumstances such as these, friendships form quickly. We were impressed by their courage, their commitment and their willingness to work with us as a team. We are both deeply sorry for your family's loss, and ours.' Shahid held out his hand, which Akram clasped in both his own before embracing him and then turning to Laurita, holding out his hand. Unable as yet to smile properly, she inclined her head and shook hands.

'And the cat?' asked Akram, curious. He had rarely met any before today.

'She's my companion,' answered Shahid, 'and came to our rescue when we weren't able to communicate with anyone about our situation.' He saw no reason to elaborate further unless Akram wanted him to. He was therefore surprised when Akram said, 'How did she do this?'

'Yedda was far away, on the other side of Melbourne, yet sensed we were in trouble and managed to find us and go for help. It's an extraordinary feat.'

'Indeed it is,' said Akram, kneeling down to hold out a finger for Yedda to sniff. She rubbed her head into his hand and he began lightly stroking her. As she purred with pleasure, Akram hid his face and wept. Yedda pressed herself against him until the worst was over, then sat down as he put an arm around her and kissed the top of her head. Standing up, he said, 'Thank you, for everything. I hope you recover soon, Laurita. Now if you don't mind, I would like to leave this gathering and return to my hotel. I need to be alone for a while. I'm sure you understand.'

'Of course,' said Jonathon, 'and if there's anything we can do for you, please let us know.'

'Thank you, I will,' replied Akram, then slowly walked towards the main entrance, looked back once, and was gone.

'Poor man,' said Aaron.

'Yes, and all this because someone was too stupid to consider how easy it is for a bushfire to start and get out of control!' The anger Jonathon felt showed for an instant, but he controlled himself and turned to Shahid, saying, 'I have something for Yedda, if you think she'll accept it. Here, let me show you.' He took a small case from his pocket, opened it, and inside they saw a finely engraved silver disk with Yedda's name and the date of the rescue on one side. On the other were the words: "For heroism beyond the call of duty".

'I don't see why only humans should be recognised for their acts of courage, do you?' he said, kneeling and showing the disk to Yedda. She sat down, trilled her approval, then stayed still while the disk was attached to her collar, where it hung neatly at the front, gleaming in the soft lighting of the room.

'It's lovely,' said Shahid, smiling, 'and she definitely deserves it. Thank you, Jonathon. It was so thoughtful of you.'

A journalist had noticed them and approached, saying, 'Do you mind if I take an image?'

'No, not at all,' answered Shahid.

Startled by his 'voice', the journalist hesitated, then said, 'May I take one of you as well?'

Shahid also hesitated, but agreed, standing next to Yedda as several photographs were taken. The journalist thanked them, confirmed a few details, having already heard the story of the cat who rescued the firefighters, then sent it all to her newsroom.

Later that day, after their evening meal, Vera and her parents watched the coverage of the funeral, and when they saw the shots of Shahid and Yedda, Vera's mother exclaimed, 'Isn't she beautiful!' Her father murmured his agreement, then turned to Vera and said, 'Are you absolutely certain you had nothing to do with starting the fires?'

Giving him a look of disgust, Vera stood up and stalked off to her room. 'Damn Yeasmin and her idiotic schemes,' she thought. 'It's one thing to tease Tubby Tomas and have him take the blame for the trojan, but it's another to set the whole damned mountain range on fire and kill people! Shit, shit, shit! Damn that fire extinguisher for not working! Well, at least they can't prove anything, even if they do suspect us...unless someone rats, of course. Lenni... She's the one who might. I know Yeasmin won't, and I know *I'm* not admitting to anything either, even if Lenni *does* confess!'

She sat down at her computer and tried to focus on her homework, but failed miserably. Instead, she kept seeing the image of the cat in her mind, as well as her companion, the seed gatherer turned firefighter. There was something about his face which haunted her, as if she should know him...then suddenly remembered. She had seen him in the forest one day, when she and Yeasmin were out walking. He had waved to them before continuing his climb up the trunk of one of the gigantic trees, just as his workmate finished getting his own climbing gear ready so he could join him. Glad neither of them were the ones who died, Vera comforted herself with this knowledge and tried hard to put it all out of her mind.

After fetching Aurora, then enjoying a highly satisfactory dinner at a local restaurant with some friends from work, Welcome returned home to his apartment in Brunswick to find the cat curled up on the couch in the living room, her head resting on one of its cushions. She stretched out her legs, yawned, and turned to look at him, clearly expecting to be fed.

'Come on,' he said. 'I have a treat for you.'

Aurora leapt off the couch and padded after him, plumed tail in the air and a satisfied expression on her face. They were old friends and he knew exactly what she liked best: creamed potato and pumpkin pie with melted cheese sauce. He had brought back a piece of pie from the restaurant especially for her and carefully cut it into bite-sized pieces before placing it in her bowl by the kitchen window. While she ate, he took off his jacket and put on his comfortable old slippers, as well as a somewhat tatty grey cardigan, then made himself a whisky and soda, and carried it into the living room. With a sigh of contentment, he sat down on the couch, put his feet up on a footstool and told the household computer to resume playing an early twenty-fifth-century drama, made in Germany and with a strong romantic theme.

After a while, Aurora joined him and put her head on his lap, purring softly. Stroking her, Welcome allowed himself to relax, immersing himself in the drama and shedding a few tears as the lovers found themselves in difficulties. The spell was broken, however, when the real world, in the form of a comlink call from Morag MacIain, decided to intrude on this peaceful domestic scene. Sighing, Welcome paused the drama and answered, transferring the call to the screen on the wall. 'Hello, Morag. Is it morning where you are?'

'Yes, it is, and I have some news for you. Am I interrupting? Oh, yes, I see I am, and you've got Aurora with you, too. Is Karla away somewhere?'

'She's on a field trip surveying one of the creeks in the Dandenong Ranges, checking to see what's survived and what hasn't. Not a place for Aurora, needless to say. So, tell me your news.'

'Kaj Jonsson has contacted me with the names of two people associated with the changes to the satellite software. It seems the flaw was discovered by Yngwie's friend Torleif, which I'm sure miffed him no end. The odd thing is that one of these people was apparently dead at the time and the other now works for Wyvern Meridian.' At Welcome's startled expression, she raised an eyebrow and said, 'Yes, I suspect we finally have the solution to one of the puzzles that's been bothering us for so many years. I think we now know how all those people disappeared or were given false identities.'

'How was the flaw picked up?'

'Torleif searched for maintenance anomalies and discovered a series of routines that were put into place within a suspiciously short period of time. When Kaj passed the information on to me, I discovered that the dead person, whose name was associated with the actual changes, was admitted to a medcentre in Italy after a landjet accident. He was still alive at that point, but his injuries were severe because he collided with a bridge pylon at high speed. The accident was subsequently treated as suspicious because there was a fault in the landjet's engine, despite having recently been serviced. The Coroner's inquest lasted several days, and it was during this period that the changes to the satellite software took place, before the infotech's access was permanently revoked. It's an issue which I'll take further since it should have been revoked immediately after he was pronounced dead and not delayed until the Coroner's verdict. Now, obviously all this indicates either prior knowledge on the part of the person who made the changes using the forged identity, or else timely knowledge obtained from inside sources. Personally, I'd say both.'

'I tend to agree,' said Welcome, absentmindedly playing with Aurora's ears, until she moved her head away.

'The individual who authorised the changes to the system was employed by the Federation at the time and did have sufficient security clearance to do so. However, the records tell me he was on leave, which makes it difficult to establish whether he was in fact involved, or whether his identity was also forged. It's likely he *wasn't* actually on leave, but after all these years, it may be extremely difficult to verify. We can try, of course.'

'Could he have made the changes even if he was on leave?'

'Yes, though it would have taken some doing because normally his access would be temporarily suspended.'

'There must be some way of establishing all this,' said Welcome. 'How long has he worked for Wyvern Meridian and what does he do?'

'Ten years. He's their marketing director for wood products, such as fine furniture, and has been for eight and a half years.'

'No! Truly? It fits in rather too well with the situation we were investigating seven years ago.'

'Yes, doesn't it,' replied Morag, with a wry smile.

'I gather he was one of the board members who escaped prosecution for the company's illegal activities?'

'He was, which is remarkable, isn't it. Still, hopefully our forests are now safe from him and his kind.'

'Will you put him under surveillance?'

'Yes, but it's doubtful we'll find anything.'

'What about an interview, perhaps with our feline friend present?' Welcome looked down for a moment and stroked Aurora's head.

'Not a bad idea at all. She'll remember the situation well enough.' For many years, Aurora's former companion, Morag's predecessor, Rohan Maerz, had attempted to gather evidence to bring Wyvern Meridian's international director, Kenjiro Kakura, to justice for his criminal attacks upon the Federation and their efforts to control the trade in forest products; one aspect of the global strategy designed to rehabilitate and recover vast areas of badly degraded lands, a legacy from the past.

'And she'll have had some practice by then too,' said Welcome. He proceeded to tell Morag about his plan to have Aurora and Yngwie present during the interview of the young woman who was suspected of having played a part in starting the fires in the Dandenong Ranges, on the outskirts of Melbourne.

'If it goes well, let me know,' said Morag, impressed, 'and then if Aurora agrees, we may take up your suggestion.'

'Good,' replied Welcome. They then talked for some time about ordinary, everyday things, until Morag allowed him to get back to his German drama. However, he was now somewhat preoccupied, remembering the past and how they very nearly failed to prevent Wyvern Meridian and Kenjiro Kakura from destroying the Federation's work, which had taken so much time and effort to achieve. 'Not unlike our arsonists,' he concluded, 'even if *their* efforts *are* on a much smaller scale.'

## CHAPTER TWENTY-SEVEN

When Laurita awoke, she sat up, pressed her fingers lightly to her face, tried to smile – and succeeded! Taking a sip of water, she looked around to see if anyone was nearby, and finding no one, slowly formed the one word which had become so important to her: 'Shahid'. At first it was only a whisper, so she picked up a mirror to see what would happen when she said his name a little more loudly.

Profound relief washed over her when she saw there was no longer any trace of the dreadful grimace that distorted her features when she made the attempt last night before going to sleep, all the while remembering the soft touch of his lips on hers. Climbing out of bed, she put on slippers and a robe and walked slowly to the adjoining bathroom, taking care to use the handrail running along the wall. Without it, she still had difficulty standing for long, and even the simplest of tasks, such as brushing her hair and cleaning her teeth, seemed to take forever. Yet at least she was able to do them for herself and there was simple joy in this achievement.

Deciding to surprise Shahid, sleeping in a room two doors down from hers, Laurita made her way down the corridor and tapped on his door. Opening it slightly, she peeked inside and saw he was still asleep. Wondering how to cross the room without a handrail, she saw his walking stick leaning against the wall, just within reach if she stretched out her hand. Balancing carefully, and taking small steps, she managed to reach the bed, where she sat down on a nearby chair and leaned over to kiss his dark cheek, a little below where his long eyelashes lay. Shahid moved his head, then opened his eyes. Startled, he raised himself on one elbow. 'Hello,' she said, smiling.

Shahid held out his hand to stroke her left cheek, amazement and joy in his answering smile. 'Yes,' said Laurita, 'I walked here all by myself. I wanted to have breakfast with you and Yedda, and I wanted to see you asleep. I was lucky, wasn't I.' She took his hand in hers, kissing its palm and wrist.

Yedda, who had been curled up asleep on the other side of the bed, woke, stretched luxuriously, yawned, then jumped down and padded over to where Laurita sat, laying her head on her knees and purring loudly. With a final caress, Laurita released Shahid's hand and ruffled

Yedda's fur instead. 'Hello, gorgeous,' she said, laughing when Yedda repeated the words back to her. Shahid sat up, drew the sheet halfway up his smooth, bare chest and reached for his hand reader, but Laurita stopped him. 'You don't always need to speak. Sometimes words aren't important, are they?'

Shaking his head, Shahid noticed how her skin was regaining its former healthy lustre and how the morning sunlight streaming in through the window made her dark hair shine. With her good humour restored, she was even more beautiful than before, although by now, even if she could never speak again, or walk, nothing on Earth would have convinced him she wasn't perfect in every way...flaws and all! Laurita returned his gaze, her eyes holding his, a wordless promise in them.

Even a worried medtech searching for Laurita failed to break their mood. Smiling, she turned to look at him, while Yedda bounded over to the doorway, demanding breakfast. Shahid grinned, modestly wound the sheet around himself, and got out of bed to fetch his hand reader. 'She can speak,' he told the medtech, who raised his eyebrows and grinned, then calmly said, 'Good! That's very good. It won't be long before she'll be dancing again! Now, what would you like to eat?'

For a few brief moments, Karla imagined herself in a clearing where the canopy consisted of its usual mixture of grey-green eucalypt leaves, interspersed with the bright green of tree fern fronds, and in late winter and spring, the powdery yellow of wattle flowers. The illusion lasted only as long as she kept her eyes closed and could keep the smell of burnt forest at bay by holding a kerchief to her nose. Ash covered nearly everything she owned, or so it seemed. Inside her tent, she at least felt at home, its familiar surroundings a much-needed comfort. She slid out of her sleeping bag, unzipped the tent opening and crawled outside, where thankfully, it was now cool, with no wind to make things worse than they already were. Taking a few moments to stretch her arms and back, she steeled herself to be cheerful, then walked over to the small group making their breakfast.

'Good morning!' she greeted them. They returned her greeting and one of them offered her a mug of coffee. 'Thanks,' said Karla, taking a sip. 'Is there any bread left?'

'Plenty,' said the youngest of the team, a woman of twenty-six, and a talented zoologist.

'Excellent!' Karla gave her a quick smile and made herself a toasted cheese sandwich, which tasted particularly good outdoors, even in this setting. A lone kookaburra sat perched on a nearby branch, watching the ground. 'At least someone benefits,' she thought. Until the plant cover grew back, prey would be far easier to see.

After breakfast, Karla took the opportunity to call Yngwie and Shahid to ask if they had ever seen any of the strange green lights in the forest. Yngwie told her about his sightings during Søren and Dandelion's rescue, which made Karla incline towards the theory of it being some form of gas, either released or ignited by the heat of the fires. When she spoke with Shahid, he hesitated, then said he had never seen, or heard of, anything like it.

'Alright,' replied Karla. 'Thanks. How's Laurita?'

'She's recovering well,' said Shahid, with a brilliant smile. 'Her face is back to normal and this morning she managed to speak again.'

'Oh, how wonderful! I'm so glad,' exclaimed Karla, returning the smile. 'I'll call her later today, if you think it'd be okay?'

'Of course it would, Karla. She's talking non-stop now, and misses you.'

Tears gathered in Karla's eyes as she said, 'I miss her too, and you... Did you know that some of our mountain ash survived? I'm taking part in a survey along Monbulk Creek, and yesterday evening, just before sunset, we even saw a pair of black cockatoos. We haven't come across any platypuses in the creek, though. I have the horrible feeling they're all gone, but we're not giving up; we still have the lower reaches to look at. There's a fair bit of bird life returning, and amongst other things, we've seen three wombats, two wallabies, several lizards, and even a few possums of various types, so we're hopeful at least this part of the forest will eventually recover.'

'Do you think we'll still be able to gather seeds?'

'I don't know. We'll need someone to climb up and see. How's the ankle? Will you be able to take on the job again fairly soon?'

'Yes, maybe in another week or so... Karla, I have to go. Sorry... My mother is trying to call me. I'll talk to you again before too long.'

'Okay. Give Laurita my love and pretend I've given each of you a hug.'

Shahid smiled. 'I will, and thanks.'

The team spent the rest of the morning continuing their survey, without finding more than the occasional patch of unburnt forest. Dispirited and hungry, they stopped for a midsun meal, then stood completely still for a few moments to watch a small flock of white, yellow-crested cockatoos as they flew into the blackened branches of a nearby tree, shrieking and calling to each other, the young birds begging for food.

'Even here, there's beauty,' thought Karla, undoing the straps of her backpack to find her eating utensils, at the same time noticing a tiny green shoot poking its way out of the earth. Kneeling down to look more closely, she saw it was a tiny wattle and moved away to avoid standing on it. The seed had escaped the ever-hungry ants, which were busily scurrying around searching for food and rebuilding the entrances to their nests. The yabbies too had been busy, their ventilation towers of mud dwarfing those of the ants. Safe in the their subterranean reservoirs, these remarkable and unique creatures, who, like so many Australian animals, only emerged at night, provided a major source of food for the kookaburras, who often spent hours digging for them with their huge beaks.

Comforted by these homely beginnings of normal life, Karla and the rest of the team were soon discussing their morning's work while they ate, quickly arriving at an agreement about where to camp once their afternoon drew to a close. During this discussion, Karla's comlink chimed. It was Jonathon.

'Hi Karla,' he said, with a grin. 'Thought I'd catch up to see how things were going. We've almost finished here, so I decided I deserved the evening off and wondered if you felt like some extra company?'

'Um, sure,' answered Karla, her mouth full. 'Hang on a minute.' She finished chewing then hastily used her fingers to wipe her mouth. 'I'll send you the coordinates of where we'll stay for the night. If you get there at dusk, we should either be there already, or not be too far off. I suppose you have your own tent with you?'

'I do, but I was wondering if yours was big enough for two?' Jonathon hesitated before adding, 'You can tell me I'm an idiot if that's presuming too much.'

'No, no, the last thing I'd ever call you is an idiot,' replied Karla, with a half-smile, half-teasing grimace.

'What would you call me instead?' Jonathon held his breath, wondering what the answer would be.

'I'll tell you tonight.'

'That's not fair!' he exclaimed, laughing.

'Probably not, but it'll give you something to look forward to.'

'Ah, that sounds promising.'

'Oh, before I forget, on a more pragmatic note, I've asked Yngwie and Shahid about those green lights you saw, and Yngwie said he not only saw them in the forest last week, after the fires started, he heard them: a high, keening sound, apparently, and it was almost as though they were trying to help him find Søren and Dandelion. Possibly just his imagination, but if you want to take this any further, it's something to consider. Mind you, Shahid, who spends most of his life in the forest, says he's never seen or heard anything like it. Overall, though, I'd suggest there is something to look into, but what it is, I don't know, other than the possibilities I've already sent you.'

'Yes, I read the notes you gave me, and I'll speak with Yngwie, but as you say, it's a bit difficult to know what to make of it all, particularly if

Shahid hasn't seen anything. Hmm... I'll have to mull it over a bit more. In the meantime, I'd prefer to think about you, if you don't mind?'

'I'd be honoured,' answered Karla, with a chuckle. Standing up, she added, 'The others are getting ready to leave, so I'd better join them. I'll see you tonight... Oh, and it'd be wonderful if you happen to have anything to get rid of the smell of soot.'

'Soot? What's a bit of soot between friends?'

'Nothing, I suppose. I'm just a bit fed up with it.'

'I can see that. You have smudges all over your face.'

'Do I really?'

'Yes, mostly on your nose. It's rather cute.'

Karla pulled out her kerchief and gave her nose a quick rub. 'Any better?'

'No. Forget I said anything.'

She grinned and closed the connection.

'We're having a visitor tonight,' Karla told the others, some of whom knew Jonathon. 'He'll meet us at the campsite and stay for dinner, then possibly overnight, with me.' Blushing slightly, she was relieved when no one made any comment. 'Good,' she thought. 'I'll see how this works out and *then* decide what I want to call him, other than "Jonathon"!'


With Laurita so much improved, Shahid decided it was time to pay the Breeding Centre the promised visit for Yedda's training session, although he was almost certain she no longer needed it. The gentech he saw the last time happened to be available that afternoon, and knowing what happened to Shahid, as well as what Yedda had done, he was more than eager to see them. When they arrived he was waiting at the entrance.

'Come in, come in!' he greeted them. 'What a relief to see you both so well and in good spirits. It could all have turned out rather differently, don't you think? Yes, of course you do. Come this way and we'll see how Yedda manages with a few simple exercises. Afterwards, we'll discuss what happened here last week. I'm sure we can all learn from the experience.' He looked meaningfully at Yedda, who met his gaze, and if a cat could wink as humans do, she would have. Instead, she sat down and began cleaning herself, until Shahid gave her a gentle nudge. Standing up, with tail waving, she led the way to the room the gentech had chosen for the session.

'Cheeky cat,' thought the gentech, chuckling to himself. When they were all seated, he asked how she came to have her silver medallion. Shahid told him about the funeral for the two firefighters killed during the explosion in the forest and how Jonathon, a forest guardian, had decided she should receive the decoration in honour of her courageous rescue.

'Does he know the full story?' asked the gentech, a far more serious expression on his round, good-humoured face.

'Not as far as I'm aware,' replied Shahid, wondering why he asked. 'I don't think anyone other than Laurita and my parents know how she escaped.'

'I seriously suggest we leave it that way, and it might be best if you ask them not to mention this to anyone. If word gets out, there may be a reaction amongst the general population. There are people who would see the cats as a threat if they realised how powerful they are – and that they're also willing to defy us.'

'It was a situation no one could have predicted,' protested Shahid.

'Yes, but at this stage we don't know how far the cats will choose to go. In fact, we have an ethical dilemma.'

'What do you mean?' Shahid could easily guess, but didn't want to make an assumption, in case it was wrong.

The gentech looked at Yedda, who stared at him, unblinking, not sharing her thoughts. 'We choose to breed them, train them, keep them in enclosures, and restrict their movements even when they leave here. Without us, they have no means of either reproduction or of fending for themselves. Is this, when it comes down to it, right?'

Shahid also looked at Yedda, considering the question. 'I'm not sure,' he said slowly. 'As far as I understand, this breeding program originally began in response to the issue of feral and stray cats, didn't it?'

'Yes,' answered the gentech. 'There were millions of them, either becoming sick and neglected, starving to death, or creating havoc with the native wildlife, all because people didn't care enough to look after them properly or even to prevent unwanted kittens being born. Dreadful!'

'I agree,' answered Shahid, 'and if people wanted cats yet weren't prepared to be responsible, this program may have seemed the only rational response. Cats' mental abilities arose by accident, didn't they?'

'They did, and have gradually progressed without any intervention from us. The question is, what do we do now?'

'You can't discontinue the program!' exclaimed Shahid, shocked.

'No, after much discussion, we agree it must go on, particularly as the small remnant population of natural domestic cats would almost certainly be exploited again and we'd be right back to where we started, centuries ago. No, that wouldn't do at all, but we have to consider our cats' rights. They now have legal status, but do they have sufficient legal protection? For example, if Yedda had accidentally harmed someone when she escaped, what would have happened if she was then caught?'

'I gather there was a cat named Possum who was put on trial for killing someone, six years ago,' said Shahid. 'Wouldn't any other cat have the same legal right if they accidentally hurt someone, or had no other choice but to defend themselves, or their companion?'

'In theory, yes, but if a peacekeeper, for example, wasn't fully aware of the cat's rights, they might even choose to shoot them, assuming she was 'just' an animal out of control.'

Shahid's eyes widened at the thought and he shook his head. 'Surely not! How could they do something like that?'

'It's unlikely, I agree, yet some people still don't recognise that all creatures have fundamental rights, and those we breed and have live with us as domestic or farm animals have special rights because they are utterly dependent upon us. We have a sacred duty to protect and care for them, if you like.'

'Yes, I think so too,' replied Shahid, 'but if people become frightened of cats, knowing what they might be capable of, they may resort to doing what they've always done, which is simply to get rid of them.'

'Precisely,' replied the gentech, while Yedda wailed, terrified now of the prospect, something which had never before entered her world.

'I'm so sorry, Yedda, but you have to know the truth,' said the gentech, kneeling down to put his arms around her. 'You must never, *never* do something like this again, unless there is definitely no other choice. You must *always* ask for help first, and you *must* understand that not all humans are good people.'

Yedda wailed even more loudly and it took both Shahid and the gentech a long half hour of comforting and explaining to her before she eventually calmed down, crouching at their feet and uttering one final plaintive meow.

'We should take her to the nursing mothers now,' said the gentech. 'Yedda's nurse is still with us, of course, and her company may help. We've already discussed everything with the Guardians, and being far more worldly, they were able to deal with it quite well, which makes me optimistic that Yedda will too, after a while.'

Shahid and Yedda followed him down a long corridor until they reached an enclosure containing several dozen large, mature cats in a wide variety of shapes and colours, as well as numerous younger ones and small kittens. As they entered, they heard a chorus of burblings and chitterings, trills and purring, soft meows and tiny mewing sounds. Altogether, it seemed almost as if the cats' voices were combined into a unique and charming orchestra. Yedda immediately bounded over to one of them, tail in the air, all her concerns forgotten in the joy of greeting her. Bearing no resemblance to Yedda whatsoever, her nurse had long, dark brown fur, a plumed tail, large feet and bright golden eyes. She licked Yedda on the forehead, then proceeded to give her a thorough clean. Yedda purred contentedly and rolled onto her back, paws drawn up to her chest. Meanwhile, several kittens wandered over to meet her and were soon climbing over each other to play and be played with. The multicoloured bundle of furry little bodies squeaked and leapt around to such an extent that Yedda stood up, licked her nurse on the forehead, and joined in, while the big brown cat watched, purring and kneading the floor with her paws. The cats' intense pleasure transferred itself to Shahid, and this time, even to the gentech, who was so used to their emotions they rarely had any effect on him. With a broad smile, he took Shahid by the arm, and together they walked over to a nearby bench to sit and watch the cats playing. At last, Yedda gave the kittens a parting lick and capered over to them, tail in the air and with every appearance of having completely recovered from the earlier distress. Her nurse followed more sedately, jumped onto the bench, and as the gentech stroked her head, settled down next to him.

'Yedda will be fine now,' he said.

'Are you sure?' asked Shahid.

'Almost, but if you ever think she needs to come back for while, just let us know.'

Shahid nodded. 'Should we do those few simple training exercises now? It might make her feel things are back to normal.'

'Yes indeed, good idea. All you need to do is tell her something you don't want any of the other cats to know and her nurse will soon tell me if you've both succeeded. Keep it simple and everyday.'

Shahid thought for a few moments then told Yedda that he and Laurita enjoyed their breakfast that morning of milk coffee, croissants with orange marmalade, and fresh peaches. They waited while Yedda narrowed her eyes and looked at them intently, before replying that she had enjoyed her own breakfast of scrambled eggs and soymilk yoghurt. Her nurse continued to purr, seemingly oblivious to the interchange – which turned out to be the case when the gentech asked her specifically if she had overheard the 'conversation'.

'Excellent,' he said, smiling. 'I didn't overhear anything either. Next, let's try something a little more complex that only I should hear.'

Shahid leaned down, lifted Yedda by her front paws until she could rest them on his knees, and looking into her eyes, 'said', 'Tell our friend here that Laurita and I love you dearly, Yedda, and nothing you do will ever change that. You probably saved her life, and even though you should have asked for help from one of the staff instead of allowing the Guardians to help you escape, I know you did it out of love and I will be forever grateful.'

Yedda leapt onto the bench beside him, licked his forehead, then lay down with her head on his lap, purring loudly. They stayed like that for some time, in this wonderfully peaceful place, until the gentech patted

Shahid on the shoulder and said, 'I think Yedda has graduated from our little school. You've both done wonderfully well.'

Instead of the usual chorus of a multitude of different birds, a lone magpie warbled as the sun rose above the small campsite where Jonathon and Karla lay together in their tent, sleeping. Two hours after sunrise, Karla woke and kissed Jonathon's cheek, then laid her head back on his shoulder, luxuriating in the warmth of his presence. Stirring, he turned to her and murmured, 'What do you want to call me this morning, dearest Karla?'

'"Dearest" is good,' she whispered, kissing his ear, 'or sweetheart, darling, blossom, possum, or even my love.' She giggled, adding, 'I think 'Jonathon' is okay too.'

'Just okay?'

'No, more than okay. Much more than okay – wonderful, lovely, beautiful, exciting, romantic, gorgeous, and do you very much mind if we stay here just a bit longer?'

'I don't mind at all, and from the sound of it, I don't think anyone else is up and about yet.'

'Mmm... I'm glad,' murmured Karla, snuggling closer and stroking his chest and shoulder, then placing one long, lithe leg on his.

'One more time?' Jonathon kissed her lips, which parted beneath his as she drew him to her.

'One more time,' she agreed, looking into his grey eyes and running her hand slowly through his hair. 'Life has a way of never giving up, doesn't it.'

'Yes, it does,' and as she arched her back in response, he kissed her throat.

Forty minutes later, a voice outside the tent interrupted their delicious contentment by saying, 'Are you interested in breakfast yet?' A faint chuckle made them both laugh and then sit up, only to spend the next few minutes simply looking at each other in the daylight, not having had the chance to really do so the night before, since it was completely dark when they went to bed.

'You're incredible, Karla,' said Jonathon softly.

'So are you, Jonathon,' she replied, kissing his forehead, then tracing the long scar on his left, upper arm. 'How did you get this and why didn't you have it removed?'

'Years ago, I slipped down an embankment and gashed my arm on a piece of sharp wood, at the same time knocking myself unconscious and breaking an ankle. Fortunately, I woke up and managed to engage the emergency signal on my comlink, so was rescued soon after. However, I decided I liked the scar... Reminds me to be more careful, and that in spite of the odds in my line of work, I'm still alive. Don't *you* like it?'

'I do, strangely enough, and I understand what you mean.'

'I'm glad. So, should we get dressed and have something to eat?'

'Yes, but we could always have a bush shower together afterwards. Just a quick one, of course.' Karla grinned.

'You're on!' Jonathon returned the grin, then pulled on some clothes while Karla did the same.

Outside, the day was becoming overcast and the air full of the promise of rain, which although good for the slowly recovering earth on the lower slopes of the mountain, would make their job more difficult, and if too heavy, would cause erosion on the steeper areas. Despite this knowledge, everyone was in good spirits and once breakfast was over, showers finished and their equipment packed away, the team began another day's work following the course of the creek. Jonathon worked with them for the remainder of the morning until he needed to return to his office in Ferntree Gully.

'I'll call you tonight,' he said, kissing Karla on the cheek.

She put a hand on his shoulder and returned the kiss, properly. 'I'll be back tomorrow. We could have dinner, if you like?'

'Somewhere special, maybe,' he replied, holding her hand.

'Yes, that'd be great. Okay, you'd better go or we'll never get this survey finished!' Karla gave him one last hug, then rejoined her team as they continued their work.

Once Jonathon was back in Ferntree Gully, he called Yngwie, and when he answered was astonished to see the close resemblance to Karla.

'Hello,' said Jonathon. 'It's good to finally speak with you in person. We have a friend in common, Karla, and she told me you saw something rather peculiar when you rescued Søren and Dandelion, as did Søren and the other members of the rescue team... Something to do with green lights?'

'Yes, we did see something unusual, though I'm still not quite sure what I saw and heard.' Yngwie described how he almost thought the lights were trying to lead him to Søren and Dandelion, and afterwards, were helping them find their way back to safety. 'It's most likely a natural phenomenon,' he concluded, yet there was a certain reluctance in his voice that told Jonathon this was his logic speaking and not necessarily what he truly felt.

'I once saw an unusual green light at sunset,' he replied, 'and when I stopped to look, a tree crashed down in front of me. If I hadn't stopped, I'd have been crushed. Odd, don't you think?'

For several seconds, speechless, Yngwie gazed at him, then recovered and said, 'Yes, very odd! Is it possible they were alive and trying to save us?'

'I don't know, Yngwie. Karla has done some research and come up with a number of reasonable explanations, all natural, but I'm still not sure what to make of it all. I can't say I believe in the supernatural, so, if they're a species we haven't come across before and they have enough intelligence to want to save us from harm, then why not accept they exist and really were trying to save us?'

Taking a deep breath, Yngwie said, 'I agree. I'm glad to hear you say this, but may I make a suggestion? Don't tell anyone else about them. They could come to harm if people go hunting through the forest searching for them. My feeling is that if we haven't come across them until now, then it's likely they're extremely shy and possibly quite rare.'

Jonathon stared at him for a moment, considering. 'Good point,' he agreed. 'You're right, and I must pass on what you've said to Karla. By the way, are you two related by any chance? It's extraordinary how alike you are. If she was slightly older, she could easily pass for your mother.'

Yngwie laughed. 'Yes, we've noticed, and I've sent her my ancestry records, but she hasn't done a comparison with hers yet, or if she has, hasn't told me what the results were. Things have been a bit hectic lately, so I do understand.' He made a face and Jonathon nodded.

'Well, let me know if she does find out. It'd be interesting.'

'I will, and I'm glad to have spoken with you. Perhaps we'll meet one day.'

'Oh, I'd be surprised if we didn't, Yngwie,' said Jonathon, smiling before he closed the connection and turned to Aaron to discuss their day's work schedule.

## CHAPTER TWENTY-EIGHT

At Welcome's request, Yngwie took more than usual care with his appearance and made sure to arrive on time for the interview with Lenni and her mother. He and Aurora now sat directly opposite them, while Welcome fussed around at the room's servery, making sure the tray he was setting up was exactly right. Lenni took no notice as he filled an old-fashioned, dark blue ceramic teapot with boiling water and placed a selection of small iced cakes onto a matching serving plate. Instead, she stared at her fingernails. Meanwhile, her mother fidgeted, alternating between patting her hair and hunting through her shoulder bag for a variety of small things that would normally be entirely inconsequential but which suddenly seemed essential, such as lip salve. It was all Lenni could do not to smack her, even though such a thought had never before entered her mind.

Welcome let them wait a while longer before presenting the beautifully prepared tray to Lenni, who, without meeting Welcome's eyes, took the offered cup and saucer, as well as a plate and cake. Her mother almost dropped her own cup and saucer as she accepted them from him, but fortunately, caught them just in time. When Yngwie, by reflex, stood up to help, she gave him a look of thanks, then managed to take a cake and put it onto a plate without further mishap. Smiling, Welcome poured the tea for them, before turning to Yngwie, pot in hand.

'Thank you,' said Yngwie, and as Welcome filled the cup he held out to him, he cast a glance at Lenni, who met his eyes and smiled, unable to resist. Yngwie, with his closely cropped blonde hair and regular features, was the most handsome young man she had ever met. Even the slight mark on his forehead lent interest to his face, while his grey eyes held a depth which seemed to say that he found her attractive, which indeed she was. Lenni wore her wavy black hair cut short, and she was tall, though not quite as tall as Yngwie. Slender, and wearing a severely tailored grey suit and ruby ear studs, with matching lipstick, nail varnish and shoes, she was someone who immediately attracted attention. They had shaken hands when Yngwie first entered the room and he had been impressed by her firm grip and the direct gaze of her beautiful hazel eyes. However, she soon began to lose her confidence as the silence lengthened and Welcome spent far longer than necessary fetching their morning tea.

284

As they sipped their tea, Aurora stood up to stretch, then yawned, showing her long sharp teeth. She walked over to each of the two women and studied them closely, probing their minds. Neither of them dared stretch out a hand to touch her. The Witness brought in for the occasion remained silent and inconspicuous in the background, but noticed Aurora's behaviour and accurately guessed what the cat was doing.

'Do help yourselves to more when you're ready,' said Welcome, sitting down and drinking his tea. After eating a cake, then dabbing his mouth with a serviette, he put his cup, saucer and plate onto the small table in front of them, saying, 'Lenni, I want to give you one last opportunity to clear your conscience. You have now met Yngwie, who is someone I've had dealings with recently.' He paused to wave a hand in Yngwie's direction. 'Like you, he has a strong interest in information technology and can easily understand why someone would take on the challenge of creating the trojan. Perhaps I should let him tell you about his own experience with something similar?'

Startled, Lenni stared at Yngwie, her finely outlined eyebrows raised, her eyes wide.

Yngwie leaned forward slightly and in a low, sympathetic tone said, 'Yes, I fully understand the attraction of meeting this challenge, although I don't condone the method used to spread the trojan. Using Tomas Perry as your scapegoat was cruel and mean, and I would have expected more from someone as intelligent and well brought up as you.' He nodded to Lenni's mother, who smiled and simpered as if hypnotised.

Intrigued, as well as charmed by his lilting accent, Lenni was tempted to defend herself. Instead, however, she looked down for a moment, then defiantly met his gaze, saying nothing.

'You see, I know how the trojan was constructed,' continued Yngwie. 'Can you guess why?' When Lenni shook her head, he said, 'I created the earlier cascade... I and my friend Torleif.' He sat back in his chair, watching as Lenni gaped at him, all pretence of composure forgotten. She tried to say something, but failed.

'Yes,' said Yngwie, 'it was me, and it took several years to find the flaw that allowed the cascade to be produced. Years of hard work, years of subterfuge and lies, as well as many, many hours of believing we were so much cleverer than everyone else. Is that what you are, Lenni? A liar? A cheat?'

When Lenni still said nothing, he stood up, walked over to where she was sitting, bent down, and whispered, 'I was caught, Lenni. Torleif and I were caught, and our crime will be on our Federation records for the rest of our lives. Is that what you want? Do you want to be branded as a criminal? I imagine you would rather be free to spend your life as you wish?'

Impressed by Yngwie's somewhat bent version of the truth and by his playacting, Welcome raised his hand to hide a grin, then used a kerchief to quietly blow his nose. Neither Lenni nor her mother noticed. Their eyes were fixed on Yngwie as he sat down next to Lenni, saying, '*You'll* be caught too, Lenni, no matter how hard you try to hide the truth. With all the resources of the Federation behind him, Welcome will soon know everything you've done, and then the Judge will require you to stand trial and be held accountable. You'll be alone as well, because neither Vera nor Yeasmin will help you, and we have no reason to believe either of them were involved. We think you tricked Yeasmin, as well as Tomas. She thought she was giving him a genuine piece of music, but you decided to play games behind her back, didn't you?'

Lenni gasped and before she could prevent herself, exclaimed, 'No! It didn't happen like that at all! It was all her idea!' Eyes wide, she put a hand to her mouth as she realised what she had said, then shook her head, unwilling to say more.

'I see,' said Yngwie. 'Yes, I can see how it might have been her idea after all. Yeasmin can be quite the bully when she wants to, can't she?'

Gaining courage, Lenni's mother spoke for the first time: 'You're right, she *is* a bully, and I didn't want Lenni to be friends with her, right from the start. I'm only glad she's finally seen through her. Vera's no better, and when the two of them get together, I pity anyone who stands in their way. Well, not any longer, if it's anything to do with me!' She turned to her daughter, put a hand on hers and said, 'Lenni, it's time to tell the truth, if there's anything to tell. If this young man is brave enough to be here today and confess to us what he's done, then you can too. Did you help them create the trojan?'

A quiet sniff greeted this gentle request, and Lenni turned away from her mother, as if angry at being doubted. Welcome decided it was his turn to say something.

'There's also the matter of the fires, Lenni,' he said, his voice firm and uncompromising. 'To obtain the imagery you wanted, at least one of you, possibly Vera, lit the fire, which then spread, killing two firefighters, injuring others, destroying large areas of our wonderful forest, and in the process, killing and injuring countless innocent creatures, who are still suffering because of what you did. This is something you will live with for the rest of your life and the only way you can compensate for what you did is to confess...now.' He stood up and pointed a finger at Lenni. 'Unless you take responsibility for your actions, this guilt will warp the rest of your life. Yngwie knows this all too well and has agreed to work with the Federation to make up for what he and his friend did. He has a future. Do you?'

Confused, Lenni looked up at him, a tendril of doubt creeping into her mind. She glanced at Yngwie, who still sat next to her, making every effort to appear as sympathetic as he could. With a sigh, Lenni gave in. 'We didn't mean to start the fires. All we intended to do was light a small one, get the imagery we needed, then put it out, but the fire extinguisher we brought with us failed, even though we tested it beforehand. I'm sorry, I really am...' Her mouth turned down at the sides as she resisted the urge to cry. Yngwie fished a pristine white kerchief from his pocket and handed it to her: the classic gesture, which Lenni gratefully accepted. She blew her nose, and told them the whole story. 'The problem is,' she finished by saying, 'there's no proof left that Vera and Yeasmin were involved with creating the trojan, or that it was Yeasmin's idea in the first place.'

It was then that she remembered what Tomas had said...that he knew Yeasmin was holding, not her own, but Lenni's comlink when she showed him the icon of his favourite singer, offering it to him. Why would she have done this if the music was legitimate?

Brightening immediately, Lenni exclaimed, 'I know who you can ask to confirm what I've told you...Tomas! He came to see me because he remembered that after showing him the icon, Yeasmin handed the comlink to me to copy the file over to his. I couldn't have done that unless the comlink was mine, and if Yeasmin had really wanted to give him music, wouldn't she have used her own comlink? Do you see what I mean?' Excited now, she smiled, her whole expression eager and alive.

Everyone did see what Lenni meant and returned her smile, including her mother, who took her hand and pressed it warmly. 'What will happen now?' she asked Welcome.

'Once our Witness here has watched the recording of this interview and confirmed it as being complete and accurate, Lenni's evidence will be entered into the Judge for its consideration. Afterwards, if there are any further questions, we'll be in touch. In the meantime, we'll speak with Tomas and will reinterview Vera and Yeasmin. They may choose to be as sensible as Lenni, but if not, we'll lay formal charges against them anyway and they *will* stand trial.' He looked directly at Lenni and said, 'The Judge may still call you to the same hearing and may choose to pass a sentence of some type. Naturally, I can't comment on what it will do. Now, before we finish, do either of you have any questions?'

After both Lenni and her mother shook their heads, Welcome escorted them from the room. When he returned, he knelt down next to Aurora, stroking her head and asking, 'Well, my dear, what did you see?'

Purring and rubbing herself against him, Aurora confirmed everything Lenni had told them, 'speaking' to the Witness as well to ensure he could enter this as evidence for the Judge to include in its deliberations. Watching them, Yngwie guessed what was happening and, intensely curious, asked Welcome whether his guess was correct.

'Yes, indeed it is, Yngwie,' replied Welcome, with a grin. 'We can ask Aurora to be present during the remainder of the interviews, then use her impressions as further evidence. I doubt very much whether either Vera or Yeasmin will escape us!'

'I'm glad to hear it,' said Yngwie. 'It would be a pity if Lenni shouldered all the blame, even though I'm still not sure she has as bad a conscience about all this as she should have.'

'No, I think you're right, and I sincerely hope the Judge will find a way to teach her to be more responsible in future. I feel sorry for her mother, though.'

'I do too. *My* parents are upset enough, even though our motives were good in the long run.' Yngwie fell silent for a while, thinking. 'Will you provide a counselling service for all the parents, Welcome?' he asked eventually.

'Yes, we should. Good idea... And thank you for your highly imaginative performance this morning. I was impressed.' Welcome held out his hand and Yngwie shook it. 'Glad to help,' he said. 'Well, I'd better go. Kaj is expecting me and I have a busy afternoon scheduled. Will you need me for anything else?'

'No, I suspect your charming presence would fail to have the least effect on either of the other two. Together with Lenni and Tomas' evidence, I'm fairly sure Aurora's 'word' will be enough for the Judge. After all, we also have confirmation that the three of them were there on the day, at the right time, and that Vera's comlink contained imagery of the flames, with the timestamp of the file matching the time the fires began. I'm sure all this will be enough to convict them.'

'Good,' said Yngwie, with a grim smile. Turning to Aurora, he added, 'Goodbye, and say hello to Karla for me. I look forward to seeing her soon.'

Aurora trilled her acknowledgement, and when Yngwie had gone, Welcome checked the time then sent a message to Morag to tell her about their success.


During the afternoon of the same day, Shahid, now almost completely recovered from his injuries, arrived at the Ferntree Gully medcentre with a huge bunch of red leucadendrons from his family's garden as a gift for Laurita. With a wave and a smile to the receptionist, who was now used to seeing him about the place, Shahid walked through to the second tower of the medcentre and, instead of taking the lift, climbed the stairs to the tenth floor. He needed the exercise since he was still not quite fit enough to take on the task of tree climbing. When he reached Laurita's room, he paused to adjust the flowers so they looked their best, then knocked on the door, and after she answered, went in.

Laurita was fully dressed and doing some light physiotherapy exercises under the supervision of a medtech, who stood with arms folded and an encouraging smile on his lips. 'Hello,' he said, turning to Shahid. 'Do you want a vase for the flowers?'

Smiling, Shahid handed them to him. After the medtech left the room, Shahid and Laurita used their few minutes alone to good effect, having missed each other, even though it was only two days since Shahid last visited. Two *very* long days, as far as they were concerned! When the medtech returned, Shahid still had his arms around Laurita as she returned his kiss, holding him close.

'Ah, hum...' said the medtech, grinning. 'Your flowers, Laurita.'

Laughing, she turned to him, and as he came closer, accepted the vase. 'Thank you, and thank you, Shahid. Are they from your garden? They're so beautiful!'

Pleased, Shahid nodded and grinned. Laurita gave the flowers back to the medtech, who placed them on her bedside table, then stood back to admire the arrangement. 'Perhaps I should leave you two to have some time together? We were almost finished the exercise routine anyway.'

'Thank you, Alex,' answered Laurita, returning his smile. 'I feel better every day, thanks mainly to your help.'

'It's a pleasure,' said Alex pleasantly.

Once he had gone, Shahid took his hand reader from its carry bag and 'said', 'When you're ready to leave the medcentre, my parents and I would like you to stay with us. Being a practitioner, my father thought it might be best, rather than returning to the communal house. That way, if anything happens, he can take care of you. Not that it will, but just as a precaution...and we'd like to have you stay with us in any case,' he added, with a somewhat bashful grin.

'How incredibly generous you all are!' exclaimed Laurita. 'I would love to stay with you until I'm well enough to work again.'

'Only until then?' asked Shahid. 'You could stay longer, if you wanted.' He put down the hand reader and held out his hands to her. Laurita gently clasped them in her own, softly saying, 'Ask me again, after I've been in your house for a while. You may change your mind.'

When Shahid shook his head, smiling, Laurita stroked his cheek, then ran her hand through his hair, reaching up to kiss his lips, lightly, and then with passion. The sunlight coming in through the window enveloped them in its warmth, while their joy in each other grew with every moment. Eventually, Laurita thought to ask, 'Where's Yedda today?' This was the first time Shahid had visited without her. Kissing her one last time, Shahid picked up his hand reader and said, 'My mother wanted to take her shopping, for the novelty...and the exercise. I haven't given her enough. She's an extremely energetic cat!'

Sitting down, Laurita looked up at him, her expression serious. 'Are you healing well? Tell me the truth.'

Shahid sat down next to her. 'Yes, I am. I promise... I'm just not as fit yet as I should be, but I climbed the stairs again today, so I'm getting there. The problem is, Yedda likes to run long distances and I can't keep up with her!'

Laurita laughed. 'I don't expect you ever would be able to, no matter how fit you were. You may need to teach her to slow down and not disappear into the distance.'

'Maybe. Still, it won't be a problem once I'm back to normal, which hopefully shouldn't be much longer.' He turned a little to face her, saying, 'Laurita, there's something we should talk about before you make up your mind about coming to stay with us.' Pausing, he waited for her to respond, and when she did, said, 'You know our family is religious, and I have the impression you aren't. How much of a problem do you think this will be?'

'You mean for your family, for me, or for us, if we're to have a future together?' Laurita spoke slowly, the sudden fluttering in her stomach telling her how nervous she now felt.

'All three,' said Shahid, his expression serious.

'I've never needed to consider this before, Shahid. I'm not sure how to answer... All I can say is, that if my not being religious isn't a problem for either you or your parents, then your being religious isn't a problem for me.'

'I have to admit that it'd be wonderful to share our beliefs with you,' said Shahid, with a wistful smile, 'but I'm sure both I and my parents will be able to respect your position. I'd like to know more about what it is, though, if you don't mind?'

Laurita moved closer, kissing him on the cheek. 'This is the real reason why Yedda isn't here today, isn't it? You wanted to be alone with me so we could talk about this without her presence in the background.'

'Yes, you're right. It's true what I told you, but it's also true that these days I sometimes have difficulty unravelling my thoughts and feelings from hers – and I suspect she's having the same effect on you.'

'Yes, she is, so in answer to your question, let me see if I can express what I feel. I hope I can.'

'Just try, Laurita, and I'll listen.' Shahid reached for her hand and held it in both his.

Laurita nodded, thought for a moment, then, in a steady voice, began to speak, gazing into the distance as she did: 'The vase of leucadendrons you brought for me represents so much of what is good in the world: beauty, generosity, nurturing and sharing, the joy a gift brings, and the ability to adapt and flourish. There is also the interaction between that which the universe has created and the things humanity has made. To me, the vase, the water and the flowers are a form of universal poetry, flowing and changing form over time, without, perhaps, an ultimate beginning or end, although some may say this isn't true. I realise many people believe there is a Creator, that all this could not exist without a guiding hand, but I do not feel the need for this type of belief. I don't know how all this has come about and regard it all with awe, with humility, and with acceptance. What I do *not* accept, though try my best to understand, is why humanity is at times evil and why they do not necessarily appreciate all they have freely been given. Instead, they have so often destroyed, are cruel, selfish, and have imposed their beliefs on others, each group claiming *their* God is the one true God, or in some cases, even that their many Gods represent the truth. Some still place their own creations above those of the natural world and put themselves above all other creatures, believing they have a God-given right to do so, all of which I utterly reject. What I do know is this: the universe is as it is, I am alive, you are alive, and there is so much to take joy from and care for, which is enough for me.'

Laurita turned to look into Shahid's eyes, studying him and waiting for a reply. He gently stroked her hand, then kissed her and held her close for long moment. 'I see no reason why I should try to change your mind,' he said at last. 'In all the important ways we are alike and can easily respect each other's views. That is all *I* care about and I'm sure my parents will feel the same. Thank you for sharing this, Laurita, and if you don't mind my saying so, bless you for your honesty, and for your acceptance of our way of life and our beliefs.'

'Acceptance is part of love, isn't it?' said Laurita, smiling.

Shahid nodded, put his hand reader away, and held her in his arms, barely able to comprehend how someone like her could love him as much as he now loved her.

'I'm sorry you and Dandelion must say goodbye to each other so soon, Yngwie,' said Søren, as they sat together in the dining room of the communal house, following their evening meal. 'I have booked our flight for Thursday morning and arranged for Karla to come with us to the airport. We have things we need to say to each other...personal things...otherwise I would ask you to be there too.'

Dandelion looked up from her place on the floor nearby and meowed, looking first at Søren, and then at Yngwie, her blue eyes wide, questioning them. Standing up, she padded over to Yngwie and put a paw on his knee.

'Yes,' he said softly, looking into her eyes. 'I promised to visit during my winter holidays, and I won't forget. I could never forget you...or Søren.' He stroked her head and held her paw until she purred, although with just a tiny note of anxiety still there.

'We'll have a whole two weeks together,' added Søren, smiling at Dandelion, then glancing at Yngwie, who nodded, returning the smile. 'In the meantime, we still have this evening and tomorrow!'

Yngwie grinned and said, 'We shouldn't stay up late tomorrow evening, since you need to be ready to leave, Søren, and I need to work on Thursday, but we can have a little party tonight, can't we? Where would you like to go?'

'Oh, what a good idea! Yes, we can have a glass of good Danish aquavit to toast each other with, then stay up late and watch the sunrise together. I have seen so many now, during my spider surveys, but it would be good to watch one together with you and Dandelion, though perhaps not in the forest. Instead, we could take a trip to the top of the Rialto tower. What do you think? I hear they have special sessions for people wanting to watch the sunset and the sunrise. Afterwards, we can all sleep-in as long as we like.'

'Excellent!' exclaimed Yngwie, taking hold of Dandelion's paws and standing up. When he bent down to kiss the top of her soft furry head, she quickly licked his nose, then pranced over to Søren, ready to leave.

It was all Karla could do not to weep as she hugged Søren, so tightly he had to protest: 'Karla! I adore you, but this is too much! My shoulder still hurts. Let go!' She kissed his cheek, then did as he demanded, but was unable to resist holding him close again for just a few seconds, although this time, more carefully.

He steeled himself to say, in as normal a voice as he could manage, 'I am so glad, my dear, that you have at last met someone you can share more with than just your work and your leisure. Jonathon is a good man and you have both made a sensible decision to continue living in a communal house, even if you *are* sharing rooms now. It gives you enough personal space to adapt to each other. Who knows, you may want something else one day, but there is no need to rush these things.'

'Thank you, Søren,' replied Karla, her voice husky with emotion. 'I hope the villa you've booked in Provence turns out to be as good as it sounds. I almost envy you!'

'No you don't. You have more than enough to keep you busy and happy. For the time being, *my* work here is finished. The funnel-web population is now less than it was before the fires, so I don't expect to be back for quite some time, although you are always welcome to visit.

Aurora might be happy enough to remain behind, now she has Jonathon to look after her.'

'You may be right, and I'll give it some serious thought. I'd love to see your home, and Greenland too, even in wintertime. We could even visit Morag! It's not far to Switzerland and I've never visited her either.'

Karla managed to smile as she considered the possibilities. Earlier, when Søren announced he was leaving, she had the sinking feeling she would never see him again in person, now that her relationship with Jonathon seemed about to become permanent.

'I'm sure Morag would be delighted to have us visit,' he said. 'Now, Karla, it's almost time for me to go.' He took her hand in his, pressing it tenderly, then let go. 'Send me copies of your music venture once it's completed. You all have great talent and the world will no doubt agree with me. It will be a success.'

'I hope so, but even if it isn't, I think it'll be fun. Oh, and I almost forgot to tell you: Yngwie and I are distantly related. Apparently we *do* have a Norwegian connection! One hundred and sixty years ago, our great, great, great grandparents were talented musicians from Trondheim. Isn't that a wonderful coincidence?'

Søren smiled, and then laughed. 'Yes, I like it very much. There is a lovely symmetry in these things, don't you think?'

'Yes, I do. We should probably mention it in the notes we put together with the collection. It'd be even better if we included an old photograph as well, come to think of it; I did find some.' Karla grinned, then added, 'By the way, are you sure you don't mind not telling anyone about the green lights you saw in the forest? I know we've discussed it at length, but I just wanted to say that I've thought about it since and still agree with Yngwie and Jonathan. We really do think it'd be for the best if we say nothing to anyone else, at least for the time being.'

'Yes, I'm quite sure. I realise I didn't agree at first, but I do now. Some things are best left alone. However, I must add that Jonathon would be wise to ask Shahid to share any future sightings with him, and vice versa, as otherwise, if they *are* a rare species, there's always the risk they may become extinct if steps aren't taken to protect them. What do they eat, for example? Where do they live? What if their specific habitat has been irreversibly damaged by these fires, or becomes damaged over time due to other issues?'

'You're right, I know, and I'll speak with Jonathon again. It may be possible to keep a watching brief without anyone else becoming involved. Anyway, I'll let you know.'

'Good. Thank you.' Søren held out his hand, which Karla grasped tightly, before kissing him on each cheek and giving him one last gentle hug.

'Take care,' she said. 'Call me when you've settled into your villa.'

'I will. Goodbye, Karla.'

Søren turned away and walked the short distance to a small, secure area, where Dandelion was perched on top of his luggage, waiting impatiently for him to return. Karla watched him go, and before long, she was on her way back to Willsmere, where Aurora was waiting for her – and where Jonathon would finally join her for the tour she had promised him.

# CHAPTER TWENTY-NINE

Rain poured down as a small crowd gathered outside the entrance to the nineteenth-century law courts in Lonsdale Street, central Melbourne. The soft, living carpet of flowering plants covering the surface of the arrivals and departures area added colour to the otherwise fairly gloomy, albeit highly decorative, sandstone buildings. Taking little notice of their surroundings, Vera's parents stood next to their daughter, who surveyed the crowd with an air of sullen defiance. Meanwhile, Yeasmin's mother fiddled nervously with her daughter's hair, wanting to make sure she looked as perfect as anyone could during her trial. When her bondmate reached out a hand to stop her, Yeasmin gave him a quick smile of gratitude. Doing her best to ignore both Yeasmin and Vera, Lenni waited several metres away, accompanied by her mother. With their arms linked in a gesture of mutual support, they avoided the others, wanting to put as much moral distance between them as possible. When Welcome arrived, hurriedly adjusting his formal, dark grey attire, it signalled the time for them all to enter the main building and to take their places within the courtroom.

Once inside, Vera, Yeasmin and Lenni had no choice but to sit together, although a little apart and flanked on either side by a guard. At the front of the courtroom, the Prosecutor, the three Defence Counsels, Witnesses, various official consultants, and a Court Official, were all assembling and taking their respective places, amid the usual sounds of foot shuffling and voice clearing that occurred during such gatherings. When everyone was finally settled and the Court silent, the Prosecutor identified herself to the Judge and the other officials followed suit. The Court Official then stood and asked the three Accused to do the same, which they did without hesitation and without looking at anyone else, not even each other.

'Now that all present have been properly identified,' began the Prosecutor, 'the trial of Vera, Lenni and Yeasmin can commence. They are each charged with intentionally lighting a fire on the afternoon of the twentieth of March 2457, within the forests of the Dandenong Ranges, approximately seven hundred metres south-west of the former site of the town of Olinda. They are also charged with having created a piece of malicious software, commonly referred to as a trojan, which, on the twenty-first of March 2457, they subsequently tricked a fellow school student, Tomas Perry, into accepting onto his comlink. He then, unwittingly, activated the trojan, which rapidly spread around the world. The Court notes that it contained imagery of flames and was released during the spread of the fire Vera, Lenni and Yeasmin are accused of lighting and which later caused widespread damage throughout the region.

'All evidence relating to these crimes has been entered into the Judge, together with the cases put forward by the Defence for each of the Accused. The Summary of this evidence, as well as any mitigating circumstances, will now be given to those gathered here today. Anyone wishing to provide or request additional evidence or explanation will then have an opportunity to do so, having previously registered their interest in being present or having been called by the Defence or the Prosecution. Silence will be maintained while the Summary is read.'

Lenni glanced at Yeasmin, but quickly looked away, while Vera, who sat on her other side, cast Lenni a look which promised retribution for her confession, should she ever have the chance. Lenni coloured and stared into the distance, without seeing anything in her future other than the prospect of having Vera and Yeasmin to deal with after the trial. Sitting two rows behind, Jonathon and Karla, Aurora, Yngwie, Laurita, Shahid, Yedda, Wania and Shafiqur, all focused on the neutral, impersonal tones of the Judge as it gave the Summary of evidence. At the same time, the text of its speech appeared on the comlink of everyone present:

'...On the day the fires began in the Dandenong Ranges, the Accused acknowledge having entered the forest, ostensibly for the purpose of bushwalking and with the permission of their parents. Lenni has confessed to lighting a small fire, at approximately 13:20 on the twentieth of March 2457, in order to provide the imagery required by the three Accused for the malicious software they were creating and which they planned to release the following day. She claims Vera stood ready to capture footage of the flames, while Yeasmin was prepared with an appropriate extinguisher to immediately put out the fire once they completed their recording. Apparently the fire extinguisher failed and the fuel used exploded, setting the undergrowth and a nearby shrub alight. Having insufficient equipment with which to adequately deal with the fire, and given the speed with which it spread, the Accused left the site and, once at a safe distance, activated their emergency signals.

'The Court notes that at the time, the Accused did not admit to lighting this fire. Instead, Yeasmin attempted to place the blame onto two tourists whom she and Vera saw in the vicinity, boiling water over a campfire. The tourists were subsequently detained and interviewed, and it was later established that their fire was not responsible for the outbreak that eventually devastated the region. Instead, they claim to have detected smoke from a fire that began a short distance further down the hillside, which they subsequently reported, without delay. The Court has accepted their account, while detailed investigations by the forest guardians indicate that the fire set by the Accused was in all probability the source of the abovementioned bushfires. It is noted, however, that the guardians found no physical evidence remaining at the site of the initial blaze.

'Despite the bushfires, the Accused proceeded with their plan to assemble a trojan using the imagery of the fire and to then release it the following day. Lenni has testified that she was asked to create this software by Yeasmin and Vera, which she subsequently did. During her second interview with Welcome, a Melbourne Peacekeeping Force psychologist, Lenni's testimony relating to what happened on the day of the fire and afterwards was also heard by a cat named Aurora, who has since confirmed, via a Witness, that Lenni's statements are true. The Court therefore accepts this evidence. Also, examination of Vera's comlink by an MPF specialist technician found imagery of the flames used for the software. Moreover, the timestamp of the file corresponds with the time the bushfires began. However, when Vera and Yeasmin were interviewed for a second time by Welcome, with Aurora present, neither were prepared to admit to any of their actions and it is mainly through the testimony of the cat that further evidence of their guilt was obtained.'

At the mention of Aurora, all three girls turned their heads to look around the courtroom, and upon seeing the cat, gaped and stared. Aurora stared back, purring, deeply satisfied her evidence was being used by the Judge in its determination. She eventually turned away, listening intently to Karla's impressions as the Judge continued its Summary:

'There is also the corroborating statement by Tomas Perry, whose comlink was used to initiate the spread of the trojan. When he realised the extent of the spread of the malicious software and the nature of its content, he had the presence of mind to take his comlink to a preceptor at his school, for which this Court commends him. Tomas states Yeasmin showed him what he believed was her comlink, offering him a gift of certain popular music, a copy of which she claimed the Accused had jointly purchased for him, as well as for themselves. Yeasmin then handed the comlink to Lenni, who ostensibly transferred the music to Tomas' comlink. When Tomas activated the music icon, it initiated the spread of the trojan to his contact list, and from there, throughout many parts of the world, creating outrage and concern.

'Lenni has since testified that it was in fact her comlink which Yeasmin used to show Tomas the music icon containing the malicious software. The Court accepts that if Yeasmin genuinely believed she was offering music to Tomas, rather than the malicious software, she would almost certainly have used her own comlink to do so, rather than Lenni's.'

Hearing this, Lenni turned to look for Tomas in the courtroom, and upon finding him, inclined her head in acknowledgement that he had kept his word; he hadn't told the peacekeepers about his realisation that the comlink was hers and not Yeasmin's. Instead, he allowed her to choose whether or not to confess. Tomas blushed, then briefly smiled, quickly turning his attention back to the Judge:

'The timing of this action by the Accused is particularly malevolent due to its being within the context of the bushfires raging in the outer east of Melbourne. The Court also notes that the consternation produced by this trojan was no doubt greater than it might have been were it not for a similar, although far more extensive, event that took place approximately two weeks prior, on the fourth and fifth of March, and which also contained imagery of flames. The Defence has argued that the Accused were influenced by this earlier event and offer this as a mitigating circumstance, particularly given their young age. The Court accepts this argument to the extent that the cascade may have provided them with the inspiration to behave as they did, yet asserts that the Accused were under no compulsion to do so and are therefore fully responsible for the crimes they chose to commit.

'While it is also accepted that the Accused did not intentionally cause a bushfire, and therefore are neither guilty of arson nor of deliberately causing the deaths of two firefighters and countless creatures living within the forest and nearby, they are guilty of extraordinary negligence. They are also guilty of having so little in the way of remorse that they went ahead and used the imagery of the fire to assemble their malicious software, which they then propagated at the earliest opportunity, in the process taking advantage of a fellow school student. It is therefore my initial determination that the Accused, Vera, Lenni and Yeasmin, are guilty on all three counts, as charged.

'Before giving a formal verdict, is there anyone who requires further explanation of this Summary, has additional evidence to enter in the presence of Witnesses, or wishes to challenge this initial determination? Once the final verdict has been delivered, the full transcript of this hearing will be made available to the public at such time when each of the Accused have reached the age of twenty-five years.'

Five long minutes passed while the Judge waited to hear if anyone had anything to say. A few whispered to each other, Tomas' mother turned to her son and, to his surprise, patted his hand, while Yeasmin's mother wept, holding a kerchief to her eyes. Meanwhile, Lenni's mother did her best to control her emotions, and Vera's father sat with arms folded, red in the face, fully determined to make sure his daughter never had the chance to disgrace the family ever again!

Eventually, since no one required further explanation or needed to provide additional evidence, the Judge delivered its final verdict. Vera, Yeasmin and Lenni were found to be equally guilty of lighting a fire in a prohibited area and on a day of extreme fire danger, of creating malicious software for unauthorised distribution via the lattice, and of deceiving Tomas Perry.

'It now remains to pass sentence,' concluded the Judge. 'The first condition this Court will impose upon the Accused is that they will have no further contact with each other in any form whatsoever for a period of at least five years, and this requirement will be monitored. To this end, and prior to this hearing, it has been agreed with Lenni and her mother that they move to Vermont, where Lenni will now attend school. Furthermore, it is ordered that Vera will continue her schooling in Mitcham, while Yeasmin will attend school in Wantirna, commencing Monday of next week. To expedite matters, preliminary negotiations with the relevant schools have commenced, particularly in relation to monitoring of their behaviour and their ongoing studies.

'In addition, the Accused will each perform ten hours of community service per week for a period of three years. Lenni is to work with the regional firefighting team and their emergency rescue service in whichever capacity her skills are deemed to be best suited, while Vera and Yeasmin are to work with their respective forest guardians on rehabilitation of the fire-damaged areas of the Dandenong Ranges, as well as any future areas requiring similar work. Should the Accused fail to fully meet the requirements of this sentence, this Court will reconvene and consider further options for the repayment of the debt they owe the community. To this end, they are each required to submit to their local peacekeeping force a weekly diary of their community service activities, verified by their relevant supervisors, the details of which will be given to them after the conclusion of this hearing.'

The Judge paused, then said, 'The Court encourages you all to make good use of this opportunity to finish your formal education and commence professional careers, while taking full advantage of the training you will receive in the performance of your extra duties. You are now free to leave. The relevant authorities will contact you shortly.'

The Defence Counsels stood and solemnly shook hands with first the Prosecutor, and then with Welcome. 'A good outcome,' said the Prosecutor, glancing at the three young women, who were slowly walking over to where their parents were waiting for them. 'I'll need to prepare a press release giving enough information to satisfy the public that justice has been done, but without more detail than necessary. We don't want their lives to be ruined, no matter how disgraceful their conduct has been. After all, they didn't intend to set the whole region alight! Still, I'd have felt happier if they showed more remorse, particularly since it'll take so long for the region to recover. We can only hope their community service teaches them some respect for others and for their environment.'

Welcome and the Defence Counsels wholeheartedly agreed, then went their separate ways. Welcome moved through the small crowd until he reached Karla, Jonathon and the rest of their group. 'What do you think?' he asked. 'Are you satisfied with the verdict and the sentence?'

Jonathon smiled, but his overall expression was one of severe disapproval. 'Oh yes. I look forward to getting to know Yeasmin and seeing how well she can manage to improve her attitude. Separating the three was an excellent plan and I suspect they'll all be the better for it. Tomas will be better off too, without having their little gang to deal with. I imagine Vera will keep well clear of him from now on. I'm glad the Judge commended him for his role.'

'So am I,' said Karla. 'Poor kid!' She looked over to where Tomas was waiting with his parents for the exit to clear before they left. He was standing close to his father, who had his hand on his shoulder.

Welcome touched Yngwie's arm, saying, 'And how are you?'

Yngwie shrugged, but didn't reply, instead looking decidedly glum.

'You're blaming yourself, aren't you,' said Welcome. 'You shouldn't, you know. This may have been a copycat crime, but they did it for a totally different reason, and you aren't responsible for their actions.'

Yngwie shook his head. 'We should have realised someone might do something as reckless as this. It was only a matter of time.'

'Not really,' offered Wania, moving a step closer. 'If the girls had had access to an open hearth or other domestic fire, for example, it might not have occurred to them to light one in a forest. You weren't to know that anyone would go so far as to do this. For example, where did you get *your* flames from?'

'We have highly efficient wood stoves in Norway and plenty of plantation timber,' he answered, brightening a little.

'There,' answered Wania. 'So stop being miserable. I understand you feel responsible, but there's no point. You did what you did, they chose to do what they chose to do, and we all need to move on. There's a massive task to deal with now, helping the forest regenerate, and this rain is making things even more difficult. It's too heavy and too soon.'

'The untouched areas will benefit,' said Shahid, 'and at least in some places it will clean out the creeks and streams.'

'And clog them up with silt and debris in others,' replied Karla, frowning. Jonathon put his arm around her waist and kissed the top of her head. She returned the kiss, but didn't smile.

Yedda and Aurora, who were sitting close together and giving each other the occasional lick, tried to send a comforting thought to Karla, but without much success – the subject was far outside their experience. Aurora stood up to rub herself against Karla's legs, trilling an inquiry. 'Yes, puss,' she said, bending down to stroke her, 'I know you want us all to feel better about this, and we will, eventually...perhaps when we see some green shoots on the burnt gum trees. I'm sure a lot have survived.'

'Quite a few of the tree ferns will recover, I'm sure,' added Shahid. 'It's amazing how they do it. It must be because they store so much water in their trunks.'

'And because in many places the fire moved through very quickly,' suggested Jonathon. 'It didn't have time to kill them.'

'I just wish so many birds and animals hadn't died,' said Laurita, in a low voice. '*They* can't simply regrow.'

Shahid briefly put a hand on her shoulder. 'No, they can't,' he replied, 'but we can care for the ones that survived.'

'Speaking of which,' said Shafiqur, 'I think we should go. Laurita is a little too pale for my liking.' This was her first real outing since leaving the medcentre and it seemed clear she was beginning to tire.

'Perhaps everyone would like to come back to my office?' suggested Welcome. 'It's not far and we could have something to eat and drink while we discuss all this.'

'Good idea,' agreed Shafiqur. 'It would be interesting to see your workplace.'

They walked slowly, for Laurita's sake. Once outside, Welcome took advantage of his position as a member of the Melbourne Peacekeeping Force to call a nearby patrol car to stop by and take them the short distance to the Rialto building. Its glass walls reflected the dull grey of the sky and loomed above them as they approached, the patrol car skimming over the surface of the waterways, which now replaced the old, nineteenth-century streets. As Yngwie stepped onto the plaza at the base of the building, he remembered the time when he first saw the Rialto, upon arriving in Melbourne, seven weeks ago. How differently he felt then!

When they reached Welcome's corner office, on the twentieth floor, everyone used the opportunity to admire the wonderful view of Port Phillip Bay on the one side and the panorama of Melbourne on the other. Small, choppy waves ran across the bay, chased by the breeze, the grey water also reflecting the leaden skies. Welcome rubbed his hands together in anticipation of a cosy afternoon, with cups of tea, chocolate or coffee, accompanied by whatever his guests wanted from the servery.

Just as they were sitting down with their orders, they heard a polite tap on the door and there was Welcome's close friend and colleague, Peacekeeper Chiu Liow Jones. Welcome waved him in, and as Chiu Liow entered the room, those who hadn't yet met him were fascinated by his appearance. Taller than average, slender, yet strongly built, with an unruly mop of straight black hair, his dark skin complemented highly unusual golden eyes. Dressed in the blue uniform of the Melbourne Peacekeeping Force, he immediately commanded attention, yet when he spoke, it was with a certain degree of deference, his voice soft and melodic. 'Having a tea party, Welcome? How delightful. May I join in?'

Smiling, he took Welcome's agreement for granted and sat down next to Karla, putting his arm around her shoulders and giving her a kiss on the cheek. 'Hello, we haven't seen each other in ages...and here's Aurora too! Come here, you beautiful pussycat.' Chiu Liow held out a hand for Aurora to smooch, which she did, with enthusiasm. 'And who is your friend, Aurora?' he asked, looking at Yedda, who sat nearby, intrigued by this new wight. 'Come on,' Chiu Liow encouraged her, 'I'd like to meet you properly.'

Yedda padded over to him, sat down by his feet to study his face, then sniffed his outstretched hand and, finally, purring loudly, stroked herself against his legs. 'Yedda,' announced Chiu Liow. 'Thank you, and your companion is Shahid. I see, and you think I should say hello to him too? Very well.'

Chiu Liow stood up, went over to Shahid and shook his hand, giving him a slight bow. 'And this is?' he asked, facing Laurita. Shahid introduced her, and Chiu Liow shook Laurita's hand too, then turned to Wania and Shafiqur. 'It's wonderful to see you again. It's been far too long since we dined together. Perhaps we should make up for it now?' He smiled and held out his hand to Jonathon. 'You are Karla's close friend, I suppose? Jonathon?'

Jonathon grinned and stood up to shake the offered hand. 'Yes,' he said, 'I'm Karla's close friend, and it's a pleasure to meet you at last.'

'Good to hear,' replied Chiu Liow. 'So, this must be Yngwie,' he added. 'I've been looking forward to meeting you. My bondmate, Morag MacIain, has told me all about your recent shenanigans, as well as the excellent work you've done to make amends.'

Startled, Yngwie shook his hand, almost wincing at the strength of his grip. 'Tell me,' said Chiu Liow, letting go at last, 'do you practice martial arts? From the look of you, I suspect you do.'

'Um...yes, I do,' answered Yngwie, staring into Chiu Liow's eyes as if transfixed by his gaze. 'Why?'

'It seems to me you would make a worthy opponent. We should have a practice bout one day.' Chiu Liow grinned and Yngwie smiled.

'Why not,' he said. 'I'm here for another month or so, and I could do with some practice.' Yngwie failed to notice Karla's expression when he said this, but Jonathon didn't and cast her a curious glance, as if to say, 'What's so funny?'

'Ah, well, I can certainly give you some practice,' said Chiu Liow. 'Shall we say 14:00 on Sunday? We could meet on the fourteenth floor of this building, where we have our gymnasium.'

'Are you sure you're being fair?' interrupted Welcome, with a chuckle.

'Of course I am,' answered Chiu Liow, laughing. 'I shall restrain myself and allow Yngwie every opportunity to exercise his skills. After all, he is young and fit and I am a great deal older than him.'

'You're a master, aren't you,' said Yngwie, suddenly realising what was happening.

'You're quite right, Yngwie, I am, but don't let that worry you. I won't take advantage, I promise. We'll simply enjoy a pleasant hour and a half, during which you may learn something new. There is nothing like our Wing Chun kung fu for learning discipline and respect for others. Am I right?'

For a few seconds, Yngwie considered what to say, and then in a calm voice replied, 'You are, and yes, if I have learnt anything these past two months, it's the need for self-discipline and a deeper consideration of the possible repercussions of our actions.'

Chiu Liow lightly put a hand on his shoulder, saying, 'I'm glad to hear it. The unintended consequences of what we do can be profound indeed.' He walked over to the servery and came back with a pot of green tea, as well as a bowl of mixed, dried fruit. 'What was the outcome of the trial?' he asked, as he poured his tea.

Welcome proceeded to tell him, while the others listened, sometimes adding a comment. Outside, the rain continued unabated, and as the afternoon turned to evening, the small group of friends, new and old, exchanged their views on the events of the past two months, until at last it was time to leave.

On a cool, peaceful, sunlit day in mid-May, Yngwie and his new friends gathered within an unburnt patch of forest alongside Monbulk Creek to record Laurita's songs and poetry. The first tiny green shoots had begun to sprout on the limbs of the blackened trees surrounding their small sanctuary, providing a starkly beautiful contrast to the greenery within. Bellbirds had taken advantage of the lack of competition and claimed the territory as their own. Their dramatic, echoing call added to the loud twittering of small flocks of tiny finches and wrens flitting in and out of the tree ferns, searching for insects. These and other birdcalls would provide a fitting accompaniment to Shahid's lute – although they hoped the cockatoos would be kind enough not to add their screeches to the orchestra!

While Wania critically evaluated the light, Shafiqur and Jonathon unloaded the group's equipment from their backpacks and set it up where she indicated would be best. Next, Yngwie, Shahid, Karla, Laurita and the two cats moved into their agreed positions. Laurita sat a little apart from the others, with Aurora and Yedda lying close together at her feet. Shahid sat to her left, while Yngwie and Karla stood behind him. Shafiqur and Jonathon provided the 'audience'. When everyone was ready to begin, Wania took some sound and lighting tests, then a number of still images for their collection's artwork.

'Beautiful!' she said. 'I think we can start.'

Laurita began with a reading from one of her poems, followed by an instrumental piece by Shahid. This melded in with Karla and Yngwie as they sang the first of Laurita's compositions, followed by a second and then a third. Prior rehearsals had perfected their performance, so they knew just how they wanted the full hour of music, singing and poetry readings to sound and appear. The pieces would be interspersed with short segments of imagery from the surrounding forest and close-up shots of the two cats, who were doing their best to look even more appealing than usual.

After a while, a pair of bright red and green king parrots flew down, sitting on a nearby branch to listen and to watch. With impeccable timing, these highly sociable birds added a few soft chattering calls to the overall sound effects. In the background, a small family of magpies strutted around, digging with their sharp beaks for anything edible. Jonathon watched them, wondering if they too would add their beautiful call to the concert, but this time the birds remained silent. Instead, Yedda chose that moment to sneeze!

Jonathon burst out laughing, Shafiqur chortled, Yngwie swore, loudly, while Laurita hid her face in her hands, giggling. Karla and Shahid looked at each other, shrugged, and turned to Wania, who had stopped the recording. 'We'll have to begin that piece again,' she said, with a broad smile. 'Perhaps Yedda still isn't sure she likes our music!'

Yedda apologised to them all and settled back down with Aurora – but sneezed again. 'She seems to be reacting to something,' said Shahid, concerned. He squatted down and held her face in his hands, examining her eyes, which were beginning to weep.

Shafiqur came over to them, knelt down to see, and said, 'Yes, you're right. What do you want to do?'

'If you like, I could take her back to the landjet while you finish,' offered Jonathon. 'She might be reacting to something growing here, or to dust. You were almost there. What do you think, Shahid?'

'I'm not sure. Maybe that would be best, but if she gets any worse, you'd better take her straight to an animal healer and come back for us later.' He took Yedda's paw in his hand, pressing it gently, and silently asking her what she wanted him to do. With a low meow, Yedda agreed they should finish their music, then turned to Jonathon, ready to leave. Aurora gave her a comforting lick on the forehead and sat down to watch them go. Once they were out of sight, she turned to the others, ready to continue.

Unfortunately, due to his concern for Yedda, Shahid fumbled the next piece, but with encouragement, managed to calm himself and they finished well, Karla's voice soaring high and clear on the final notes of the last song. As silence settled over the forest, with not even a birdcall to disturb it, Wania recorded a little more footage of the entire group, although she wished Yedda was still there and wondered how to make up for her absence. It would require some digital magic, she concluded, of which, luckily, she was perfectly capable.

'That's it,' she announced, and everyone laughed and hugged each other.

'Well done, Cousin,' said Yngwie, releasing Karla from a bear hug. 'You have a lovely voice. With a bit more practice, you could become a professional.'

'Thank you, Cousin,' replied Karla, kissing his cheek. 'You are most gracious!'

'How are you feeling, Laurita?' asked Wania. 'Are you well enough to walk back, or would you prefer to rest first? We could have some of the tea I brought, if you like? There should still be plenty left from earlier.'

'Yes, please, I'd like that,' replied Laurita, 'but I'm sure I'll be fine. This was such a wonderful experience and one I'll never forget. Thank you, everyone... Sorry, but I'm about to cry.' She took a kerchief from her pocket and wept, but they were tears of happiness – happiness in sharing her work, her feelings, and now, her sense of achievement.

Shahid put an arm around her shoulders, fully understanding. Meanwhile, Wania fetched the tea, an assortment of sweet biscuits, and the fresh fruit left over from their midsun meal here in the forest. As they shared this small celebration, Shahid's comlink chimed. When he answered, it was Jonathon, with the good news that Yedda was fine; it seemed she had merely reacted to something in the forest after all. 'She should probably be checked out by an animal healer anyway, to find out what she reacted to,' he suggested, 'but I'm sure there's no need to worry. It can most likely be treated, so take your time and I'll wait here.'

'Oh, that's a relief! I'll take her to one later this afternoon, when we get back,' answered Shahid, smiling.

'What about the rest of the concert. Did it go well?'

'Yes, the recording went extremely well, although it *is* a pity Yedda wasn't here at the end. Still, we'll make up for it somehow, I'm sure.' He glanced at Wania, knowing her capabilities, and she nodded.

'Good. We'll see you soon,' said Jonathon, with a grin, then closed the connection.

Shahid turned to the others to tell them what Jonathon had said, then carefully packed away his lute and sat down next to Laurita, holding her hand, content and at peace with the world.


Later that day, everyone helped prepare a sumptuous dinner, and afterwards, viewed the results of their afternoon's work. They were delighted with it, even though it still required editing and enhancing, particularly to fill in the sections where Yedda should have been present. Still, all in all, this was a minor factor; the most important thing was that it looked and sounded wonderful!

'We don't have a name for the collection,' remarked Yngwie, which was something no one else had even considered.

'You're right, we don't!' exclaimed Karla. 'Um...that's hard.'

Laurita giggled. 'After all this creativity, we're stuck for a name!'

'What about 'Forest Songs'?' suggested Shafiqur. 'It doesn't need to be anything too specific. The imagery will speak for itself to some extent, and so will the music. After all, many of the pieces do relate to the forest, one way or another.'

'Yes, I like that,' replied Laurita, with a smile. 'What do the rest of you think?'

Following a brief discussion, it was generally agreed that 'Forest Songs' would do nicely, and a brief preamble could be written which dedicated the collection to the forests of the Dandenong Ranges, as well as to the people who fought to save the forest from the recent fires.

Finally, as the evening was drawing to a close, Laurita made an announcement, one she had put off for as long as possible, not wanting to upset anyone, especially Shahid. 'Some of you will already know,' she said, speaking slowly and in a low voice, 'that when I first came to Melbourne it was only to be a brief stay before I left for Peru. I intended to fetch a variety of edible tubers and roots from a gene bank in Lima then bring them to Ethiopia for an experimental project, where they were to trial them in soils damaged by decades of drought and erosion. Naturally, when I was unable to complete this project because of my injury, the Federation sent another seed gatherer in my place, but now that I'm almost well enough to carry out my duties again, they need me to take on another project.' Laurita paused, glancing at Shahid, who appeared shocked and upset, having assumed she would stay, perhaps even work with him.

Yngwie also glanced at Shahid, then lowered his eyes, thinking about the future. Surely she could travel the world working for the Federation while at the same time remain in a relationship with Shahid? They seemed so ideally suited. Sighing inwardly, he nevertheless asked, 'Will you be coming back?'

'I hope to,' replied Laurita, with a brilliant smile. 'I have applied for a transfer to permanent duties here in Australia, to be based in Melbourne and to only take on work which entails short trips elsewhere. There might be the occasional overseas project, but only in emergencies, when another seed gatherer can't do the job for some reason.' She paused again, looked directly at Shahid, then said, 'I feel this could be the home I have always wanted, if you think I would be welcome.'

It suddenly dawned on Wania and Shafiqur why she had made this announcement, rather than discuss the situation with Shahid in private. She was asking for their blessing, for their approval of her relationship with their son. Laurita was also asking for Yedda's agreement and for Karla and Aurora's support. It was even possible that, as her new friends, she wanted Jonathon and Yngwie to give their approval to the plan as well. This truly was about family and friendship, not only about a personal relationship.

At almost the same moment, the same realisation struck Shahid. Returning her smile, he stood up, took her hand in his, and kissed it. When she also stood, he held her in his arms and, to the applause of everyone present, kissed her on the lips. Aurora and Yedda sat nearby, purring loudly and making sure not to listen to what the two were thinking. After all, some things were best kept private!

With only a few weeks left of his time in Melbourne, Yngwie made good use of his working 'holiday' by continuing to assist the Federation team resolve the outstanding issues with the messaging system and its associated satellites. Finally, however, the day arrived when he was given formal permission by Morag MacIain to go home.

'Well, Kaj,' said Yngwie, holding out his hand, 'it's time to say goodbye, and you may be surprised to hear this, but thank you.'

'What for?' answered Kaj, firmly shaking Yngwie's hand as they stood by the departure gates at Tullamarine airport, just outside the international flight lounge, where they and Yngwie's other friends had spent the past hour sharing a light meal and talking about the future.

'For being someone I could enjoy working with and learning from.' Yngwie grinned, then added, 'You taught me a great deal about good work practices, too. I hope we meet again one day.'

Hesitating, Kaj chuckled and said, 'To be honest, I did not think I would like you, but must admit to having grown quite fond of you, after all – and even Torleif, though I do not think he quite captured my nose and eyebrows properly in the caricature he sent me. Still, no doubt his artistic abilities will improve with practice. Now, it is almost time for you to board your flight, so I had better let everyone else say goodbye as well. Good luck, Yngwie, and stay out of trouble, eh?'

'I will, believe me!' Yngwie turned to Karla and hugged her fiercely. 'Don't be a stranger,' he said, 'and come to Norway one day. I will show you where our ancestors lived.'

Karla smiled wistfully, sad to see him go, then nodded and held his hand for a moment, before standing back as he kissed Laurita on the cheek, then Wania. Shahid put his hand on Yngwie's shoulder and gave him a quick hug, while Yedda wound herself around their legs and trilled her farewell. Sitting by Yngwie's luggage, Aurora had waited patiently for her chance and now moved forward to look up at him, her golden eyes gazing into his. Kneeling down, Yngwie stroked her head and held her paw for a moment while he silently said goodbye. Standing up, he shook Jonathon's hand, and then Shafiqur's.

'I am so very glad you, Torleif and Kaj, together with the rest of your team, succeeded in repairing the flaw in our satellite system,' said Shafiqur. 'It's a remarkable feat to find out who created it, and then, with Aurora's help, to assist the Federation in bringing the person to justice. You have more than made up for the trouble you caused and it has been a pleasure to add you to our circle of friends. You will always be welcome in our home, should you return one day.'

'Thank you, Shafiqur. I'm sure I'll come back, perhaps once I finish university. I may even apply to work here in Melbourne, if they'll have me.'

'They would be silly not to want you, young man!' replied Shafiqur, smiling broadly. 'Well, I see your flight is being called, so goodbye, and all the very best. We look forward to seeing you again.'

Yngwie picked up his luggage, and with one last backwards glance and a farewell wave, left them to board his flight home.

Two months later, on a clear, cold, winter's morning, when Shahid woke, he felt Laurita's warm body against his and was almost tempted to stay where he was and not get up to prepare for work. Yedda, snuggled up at the foot of their bed, yawned and went back to sleep, but fifteen minutes later, when Shahid had finished his prayers and put away the embroidered mat made for him by his mother, she woke up, realised it was time for breakfast, and leapt onto the floor with a loud thud. The noise woke Laurita, who stretched luxuriously, opened her eyes and mumbled, 'Is it that time already?'

Smiling, Shahid leaned over to kiss her brow, his dark eyes telling Laurita how much she meant to him. She raised her arms to put them around his neck, gently pulling him down towards her and kissing him properly. Releasing him, she stroked his cheek and said, 'I should get up too and help Wania prepare our food for the day. I know she enjoys doing so much for us, but I really *should* help. After all, she has to work today, too.'

Returning the caress, Shahid held her close for a moment longer, then left her to have a shower, while he used the guest bathing room. Yedda, meanwhile, had opened the door, which responded to her paw prints, and wandered off to the kitchen. Wania turned around when she heard her soft meow, and said, 'Hello! You're hungry, aren't you? Yes, of course you are. Here, I have something for you.'

She put Yedda's bowl, containing mashed pumpkin and soy yoghurt, onto the floor in her own special place by the kitchen sideboard. Watching her, Wania thoroughly enjoyed the sight of the cat eagerly eating the food, and afterwards, sitting back to clean her face and paws. By this time, Shahid and Laurita had arrived, holding hands and dressed for their day in the forest: a day to celebrate – the mountain ash were ready for their seeds to be harvested.

'Good morning! It's a wonderful day to be out in the forest. I almost envy you,' said Wania, holding out the coffeepot, ready to pour them each a cupful.

Laurita kissed her cheek, accepted the coffee with a smile, and sat down to eat the pancakes waiting on the table. 'Thank you so much, Wania. These are wonderful, as always,' she said, after the first mouthful. 'You'll have to teach me how to make them. I'm not much of a cook, as you know, but I'd like to learn.'

'You will, if you want to,' answered Wania, with a grin. 'It takes time, and there's no hurry. Still, you can help prepare your midsun meal, if you want. Shahid mentioned you felt I was doing too much for you.' She laughed at Laurita's embarrassment. 'Don't worry; I don't mind sharing the kitchen, or anything else. You're welcome to do as much or as little as you please.'

Turning to Shahid, Laurita grinned and said, 'Your mother is using her psychology on me.'

Shahid returned the grin, but paid attention to his own pancakes rather than enter into the discussion. He was perfectly sure his parents and Laurita could work things out without his interference, although sometimes a quiet word in their ear did no harm.

Breakfast over and their supplies for the day prepared, they said goodbye to Wania, packed the landjet, and once Yedda was safely secured as well, took off, landing soon afterwards on the access way closest to the mountain ash they were to climb. With their backpacks in place and

Yedda following close behind, they walked for several kilometres up the side of the mountain until they reached the majestic stand of gigantic trees the firefighters had managed to save. While Yedda watched, Shahid and Laurita began their arduous climb to the top of the first tree they intended to harvest. Reaching their goal, and after making sure they were safely harnessed into position, they began cutting the precious seed heads and carefully placing them into sturdy containers. Working systematically, they at first failed to notice three luminescent green lights hovering nearby, yet at the same time, keeping their distance. One of the trio moved towards them, then retreated, but finally flitted forward and sat on a small branch, just out of Shahid's reach. He turned around, saw the creature and gasped, then quickly checked to see whether Laurita had noticed. She had. Not only did she notice, the two other green lights were now perched on a branch close by.

'Shahid! What on Earth are they? They're incredible!' She reached out to touch one, but it moved away, darker areas of green, where its eyes perhaps were, seeming to watch her.

'Don't touch them!' signed Shahid urgently.

Laurita stared at him. 'Have you seen them before?'

He hesitated, and then nodded. All three lights now sat on a branch near Laurita, clustered together as if finding comfort from one another. A high-pitched keening sound startled her and she held her hands to her ears, but it stopped as suddenly as it began. Instead, they started 'whispering' and moving closer, until they were within only a few centimetres of where Laurita was suspended by her safety harness. She looked at Shahid again, but he seemed unconcerned, so she stayed still, listening to their strange voices, which changed to a low cooing sound as they lifted into the air and flitted back towards him.

'What are they?' asked Laurita again, then 'heard' Yedda ask the same question. The cat could 'see' the lights in their minds, and added, 'Are *they* seed gatherers too?' assuming that if they were in the treetops, they must have a reason for being there.

'No,' Shahid told her, 'they're not seed gatherers like us, but they care for the forest in their own way.'

His words echoed in Laurita's mind and she gaped at him in astonishment. 'You know what they are?'

Shahid didn't reply immediately. Instead, he considered what to say. 'Yes,' he answered at last, via Yedda, 'but please don't tell anyone else. There are very few left, and they worry that if we don't keep their secret there will soon be none at all. As far as I'm aware, only Jonathon, Karla, Yngwie and Søren know about them. Jonathon saw them some time ago, and they helped save Yngwie, Dandelion and Søren when they were almost trapped by the fires. Søren told Karla about them, and everyone has agreed to keep it to themselves. The rescue team who came for them also saw and heard the lights, but Jonathon says that with everything else going on at the time, they seem to have forgotten, which is just as well.'

'I promise to keep their secret,' said Laurita softly, watching them and listening to them whisper to each other. One by one, they flew back to her, circling around her head, then, with one last keening cry, they sped off into the forest and disappeared.

That night, as they lay together in their bed, Laurita said, 'Shahid, do you remember when you asked me if I would write a song just for you? Well, today, seeing those extraordinary creatures made me realise even more strongly that life still has so many mysteries. I know you have your own way of dealing with this and I have mine, but I need to say something very important, which is to do with wanting to be with you for the rest of our lives. One day, and please don't think I'm being morbid, one of us will go before the other, so I tried to write a poem that would express my feelings about you and about our love for each other. I thought about it all day and wrote the words after dinner. Would you like to hear the poem now? It's a duet, for two people who care for each other as much as we do.'

When Shahid kissed her, she sat up in bed, picked up her hand reader from the side table and began to speak, while Shahid listened, his heart overflowing with gratitude for this precious life, now his to share:

Divinely dancing minds entwine
Delicious whispered words of truth
Endearments rained in sweet refrain
The gentlest touch a blessing sent ~
Yet autumn leaves fall to the earth
One last embrace, then silent sleep
'Til morning laughter, light and mirth
Seem lost, the world a darkened place
The pattern gone, consigned to dust.

Yet summer fires, consuming flames,
Provide the chorus to this song ~
Bittersweet its binding spell
Where death brings forth abundant life
Where loss brings joy beyond all price
When from the ash an orchid blooms
And trees, once black, are turned to green
With songs of gold and velvet hue
With songs of life ~ and always you.

§

Such woven magic in your words,
As time stands still then, rhythmic, moves
Beyond the seasons, back and forth,
The ripples reaching out until
We face the time when our hands met.

The tender moment, briefly spent,
Has spanned the years and holds us still
With memories of joy and pain,
Again the fabric of our lives
Has shown its colour, true and strong.

The woven magic of our words,
With thread of silk and bright sunlight,
Will hold us fast in life's embrace,
The tears, the laughter, brief and long,
The magic spell of twilight's song.

§

## EPILOGUE

### Ninety years later...

Jimmy Goldberg was used to walking through the forests at night and usually there was nothing to alarm him...nothing he couldn't deal with, at any rate. Yet tonight there were lights where they should never be, in the topmost branches of fifty-metre-high gum trees. Lights which drifted down, bounced around and then rose again, settling in amongst the treetops. Thirty years ago, his friend Tommy Smith said he'd seen lights like these. He called them big eyes that glowed in the dark, and Jimmy hadn't believed him, his friend being too fond of practical jokes.

Jimmy now crouched by his campfire, poking at the burning wood and wondering what to do. The clearing in the forest where he sat was around one hundred metres in from the edge of the extensive farmlands covering most of the district. A dense fog blanketed the entire area, cold and damp. He shivered, drawing closer to the fire and wishing he'd fetched more fuel before the sun had set. He didn't want to go further into the forest to find more. At least, not until morning.

There was no use calling Tommy, who lived fairly close by in Newborough. The fog was so heavy no one would be able to get through to fetch him...and Jimmy certainly had no intention of trying to leave. Talking to Tommy about what happened wouldn't help either. His friend would just laugh and say, 'I told you, didn't I!' This was the last thing Jimmy wanted to hear right now. However, the thought at least gave him some comfort – the idea that Tommy would laugh and not take the situation too seriously.

Coffee, that's what he needed. Hot, strong, and fresh. Jimmy stood and walked over to his tent, where he soon found what he needed. The silence in the clearing was so profound the sound of his feet breaking the dry twigs seemed almost to echo. Kneeling down, he filled the bottom section of the old-fashioned expresso machine with water, carefully measured out the ground coffee and screwed the top back on. The fire had formed some good coals, which he raked aside for the pot to sit on. Before long, it hissed and steamed. The wonderful aroma and the homely comfort of the familiar routine calmed him, although, as Jimmy drank the strong brew, he noticed his hands were still trembling.

There had to be some rational explanation for those lights. As a seed gatherer, Jimmy had seen many strange things in his long career, but of a kind that fitted in with the normal order of things. Pale green lights that danced around his head and fled shrieking into the treetops when he stretched out a hand to touch them were not normal! Ghosts? Fairytale creatures? He didn't believe in fairytales, or ghosts.

Staring into the small flames of the last embers, Jimmy pondered a while longer and decided the best thing to do was get some sleep. He reluctantly put out the fire and walked over to his tent. The darkness, without the fire, was almost complete. Once inside, the tent felt like home, which indeed it was to a traveller like him. Settling down comfortably, with his lantern glowing brightly, he took out his hand reader and found the book he had yet to finish, *Digging up People for Coal: A History of Yallourn*, written over five hundred years ago.

As he scrolled through its pages and found the images of those long-dead people and places, he wondered how any government could have been so callous as to destroy an entire community. He read, *"The town of Yallourn was designed and structured to become one component of a smoothly-articulated machine producing fuel and power."* Only fifty years after it was built, Yallourn was demolished, and hardly a trace remained of the unique and beautiful 1920s township. The pleas of its five thousand inhabitants to save their town were, apparently, ignored.

'No wonder this place is haunted,' thought Jimmy, although he knew the reputation of these forests in the quaintly named 'Haunted Hills' didn't stem from this destruction, nor from the downfall of almost the entire Latrobe Valley two decades later when the power industry was sold to private interests and many people were driven to despair. No, the 'hauntings' were traced back to the pioneering days of the mid and late nineteenth century; drovers were said to find it difficult to prevent their cattle from stampeding when they passed through these hills.

'Still, it's ironic that one of the few traces left of Yallourn is the cemetery,' he said to himself. It even employed its own dedicated caretaker. Jimmy had once met the old man. Stooped and wizened, he had recited the history of his charges: the ancient graves, as well as the new... Enough of this! How would he ever sleep if he kept thinking about it all? Jimmy put the hand reader away and turned off the lantern.

Just as he was settling down and beginning to drift off, he heard a whispering outside the tent. It went on and on, and unable to ignore the strange sound, Jimmy swore and forced himself to peer outside. There he saw five of the light creatures, as he now thought of them, perched in a row along the dead branch of an old banksia. Other than their whispering, the night was completely silent, and except for their light, completely dark. The fog had obliterated all the stars.

Edging out from his small sanctuary, Jimmy slowly took his comlink from his pocket and set it to record. As he approached, the light creatures hopped onto another branch, still whispering to each other and seeming to stare at him, their centres a little darker than the rest of their 'bodies'. Jimmy stifled an almost hysterical giggle. 'Banksia men,' he thought, remembering the wonderful old story of Snugglepot and Cuddlepie –

although banksia men were ugly little blighters, and not at all like these extraordinary things.

He was close enough by now to reach out and touch one of them and felt an overwhelming compulsion to do so. When he did, the cold was so intense and penetrating his fingers felt as if they had been burned. Jimmy snatched his hand away, then sank to the ground as a profound sense of grief overcame him. He wept, and the whispering ceased.

Just then, his comlink, which he had dropped, rang. The sound pierced the air, almost obscene in this dark, silent place. It brought him to his senses, and after hunting around on the ground for it, he picked up the comlink and answered. It was his mother, Elvira. Meanwhile, the light creatures had disappeared, fleeing back into the forest.

'Mum! Thank the Sun! You wouldn't believe how glad I am to hear your voice. But it's late. Why are you still up?'

'Jimmy, you need to come home. Your father has died. I wish I could have told you in person, but it was so sudden. He wasn't even ill...or at least, not that we were aware of. I woke up an hour ago and there he was, next to me, dead. Oh Jimmy! What can I say?' The tears ran down Elvira's face and her voice broke as she sobbed.

One week later, as they stood together after the funeral, Jimmy turned to Tommy and said, 'Do you recall all those years ago when we were kids and you told me about those lights you saw in the forest? You know, in the Jeeralangs, not far from here.'

'Yeah, sure. Why?'

'Do you happen to remember if anyone you knew died around about the same time?'

Tommy's eyes widened as he peered at Jimmy, putting one hand to his chin and rubbing it in thought. Finally, he shook his head, although in surprise. 'Yes, as a matter of fact, someone did. Do you remember my Aunt Amy? We were very close. Well, she died two days later. She's buried here too, actually.' Tommy turned away and pointed towards the northernmost corner of the cemetery. 'Do you want to take a walk? I intended to pay her a visit today.'

Jimmy nodded, and they walked slowly over to the tall headstone several hundred metres away and located beneath the branches of an old peppermint gum. A magpie warbled as they approached and both men looked up for a moment.

'So, tell me, have you seen the lights too?'

'Yes, I have, and that same night, my father died.' Jimmy looked away to hide his tears.

'It has to be coincidence, Jimmy. I don't know what those things are, but there's no way they're connected...are they?' Suddenly uncertain, Tommy stared down at his aunt's grave, wondering. *Her* death was unexpected as well. A stroke, they said, and she was only forty-three.

'Why don't I remember about your Aunt Amy? Did you tell me at the time? I'm sorry if you did and I've forgotten.' Jimmy briefly touched Tommy on the arm.

'Yeah, I did tell you, but we were only fourteen and it was a long time ago.'

'Well, I'm still sorry. Was she your father's sister, or your mother's?'

'She was my mother's twin, which is one of the reasons we were close. They were so alike and even their voices sounded almost the same.' Tommy knelt down to pull up a few small weeds the cemetery's caretaker had overlooked. He ran his hand over the speckled grey stone and over the inscription:

> In memory of my beloved sister, Amy, daughter of Robert and Violet Wentworth. Born in the year 2474 and died in the year 2517. Deeply missed by all who knew her.

'It must have been hard on your mother, too,' said Jimmy.

'It was. Not many people have siblings these days, so she always thought herself unusually lucky to have one, and particularly a twin.' Tommy stood up, brushing some soil from his hands.

'What did your aunt do for a living?'

'Aunt Amy was a river keeper. She looked after the Latrobe River and its small tributaries. She was good at it too and loved her work. We often went out on the water together, canoeing. She'd take me to all the special spots and we'd wait for the heron to come, hunting for fish.'

'My father was a river keeper too. He looked after the Thomson.' Jimmy stared at Tommy. 'That *is* rather odd, wouldn't you say?'

'It is, yes. And you're a seed gatherer, while I'm a specialist wildlife healer.' Tommy shook his head. 'I think the cemetery's getting to us. We'll soon start believing the lights have some occult meaning.'

'Warning us someone close is about to die?' Jimmy tried to smile, yet somehow couldn't.

'I guess so. Maybe someone *they* care about as well. The old will-o'-the-wisp legends about marsh lights and suchlike...'

'Yes, exactly. I think the Welsh myths used to talk about them being warnings of death. The thing is, there aren't any marshes in the Jeeralangs, or around here... Anyway, I'll show you the recording I managed to get.' Jimmy took out his comlink, found the file, and handed the device to his friend.

Frowning, Tommy watched the recording, then scratched one eyebrow and gave back the comlink. 'Pity I didn't think of doing the same thing! Still, they're just the same as the ones I saw. I looked them up afterwards and found stories from all over the world. The Argentineans called them 'Luz Mala', meaning 'evil light'. They believed them to be wandering, malevolent ghosts.' Tommy grinned and lightly punched Jimmy on the shoulder. 'Look, we have to stop this, or everyone will think we've completely lost it. There has to be some other explanation.'

Nodding, Jimmy sighed, and they walked back the way they'd come, back to the rest of the funeral party.


'Are you sure we should be doing this?' Jimmy swore softly as icy water trickled down the back of his neck when he brushed against the leaves of an overhanging branch. He belatedly pulled up the hood of his waterproof jacket.

'Yeah, why not. The worst that can happen is we don't see them, in which case we go home to our nice cosy beds and come back again tomorrow night. If we do see them, we have the equipment to get a proper record.' Tommy poked Jimmy in the ribs. 'Scared, are you?'

'No! I've spent almost as much time as you creeping around forests in the dark. I've just got the feeling these things won't show themselves unless something awful is about to happen. It wasn't exactly fun when I was here last time, you know.' Jimmy wriggled a little to make himself more comfortable, although the steady drizzle of rain seemed determined to make life difficult. For one thing, it made visibility worse and the night darker than it would otherwise have been. When they first started out, before the rain began, there had been enough moonlight for them to easily find their way.

An owl screeched and both men jumped, then chuckled as a large wombat crashed through the forest, only metres away from where they were hiding.

'Let's hope the lights aren't easily scared off,' murmured Jimmy.

'Probably not... They've been here a long time, by all accounts. They'd be used to rampaging wombats by now.' Tommy took out his thermos and poured them both some hot tea. 'Here... Careful, don't spill it! Gee, you *are* rattled.' Tommy laughed, earning himself a glare.

They waited in silence, listening to the small noises of the night and sipping their hot tea, automated recording equipment at the ready, preset with selective motion detectors. Tommy reached for the thermos to pour himself a second cup...and found his hand was too numb to grasp it. He tried to clench his fingers and couldn't, tried to speak to Jimmy and couldn't, gazed at his friend and could barely see him. Without further warning, he collapsed, face forward, onto the cold, damp earth.

Jimmy gasped, dropped his tea and flung himself towards his friend. 'This isn't the time for one of your stupid jokes, Tommy! Stop it!' He gripped Tommy by the shoulder, turned him over and shook him. 'That's enough! This isn't funny, you idiot!'

When Tommy didn't respond, Jimmy realised that although his eyes were open, they weren't seeing him. He felt for a pulse and it was there – feeble, but there – so he took off his jacket and covered his friend with it, afterwards dragging out his comlink and calling the nearest medcentre. Surely it wouldn't take them long to respond!

Moments later, he heard the calm voice of a medtech. 'What's happened?' she asked.

'It's my friend, Tommy Smith. He collapsed without warning. His eyes are open, but he's not conscious; his skin is cold and his pulse is weak. We're in the Haunted Hills forest, near the old Yallourn site, doing some research.'

'We should be able to get someone out to you in about fifteen minutes. Keep him as warm as you can and turn him onto his side. Do you want me to stay online until they get there?'

'No, I'd rather concentrate on Tommy. I'll call back if anything else happens. Thanks.' Jimmy put the comlink back into his pocket and did as the medtech suggested, then felt for Tommy's pulse again. There was none.

'Oh no! Please, no!'

Hastily turning Tommy onto his back, Jimmy was about to make an attempt at resuscitation when the sound of whispering in the branches above distracted him. He looked up and saw the five green lights 'watching' them. One floated down to rest on Tommy's chest, and after a few moments he gave a great gasp, looked at Jimmy, and sat up. The light creature trilled, just like a cat, then rejoined its family. Content, they whispered to each other before disappearing from view.

Jimmy sat on the ground with his head in his hands, trembling, while one of the ambutechs examined Tommy, who now lay comfortably on a hoverbed.

'Keep still just a little longer, please,' said the ambutech, as Tommy fidgeted and generally made a nuisance of himself by talking too much.

'Sorry,' replied Tommy. 'But I saw it! I can't believe I saw it! Green, glowing, sitting on my chest and looking at me! Wait till I tell everyone about this!' He grinned, then tried to look contrite as the ambutech sighed and shook his head.

'Very nice for you, I'm sure... Green, glowing, and sitting on your chest... Well, you seem fine, physically at least. They'll have to do some proper brain and body scans once we get you to the medcentre, but at the moment, everything seems good. You're lucky your friend was here with you.'

The other ambutech – who had been speaking with Jimmy, crouched down on the ground beside him – stood up, saying, 'Jimmy here saw them as well, Martin. I don't think they're hallucinating or making up some story to cover up for anything. See, they even have it all on file.' The ambutech, whose name was Anastasia, showed Martin the recording equipment's viewing screen, which was now playing back the evening's events. Martin looked at it and his mouth opened in surprise. 'By the Sun, what are they?!'

'I don't know,' replied Jimmy, rubbing a hand over his face and standing up, 'but I've seen them before, not long ago, and so has Tommy.'

'Yes, yes, that's right. Thirty years ago, I saw them. Just the same, floating around in the forest, shrieking when they saw me.' Tommy tried to sit up, but fell back, suddenly weak. 'Oh damn, I don't feel too well after all.'

Martin measured his pulse and found it was racing. 'Take it easy, Tommy. You're fine. It's just a reaction to all the excitement. Alright, are we all set to go? Good, you go first, Jimmy, and Anastasia will light the way and make sure you're okay. I'll follow behind with Tommy. We'll be fine. It's not far and the forest is open enough for the hoverbed to get through without too much trouble.'

Walking carefully, no one noticed the light creatures silently following, keeping well above their heads and far enough behind not to be easily seen. Every so often, they clustered together, waited a few moments, then continued on, listening and watching. They heard Jimmy's question to Anastasia: 'Has anything like this ever happened to anyone else, that you know of?'

Anastasia shook her head. 'No, but I'm new to the area. I can ask around, if you like?'

'Yes, that'd be great. Thanks.' Jimmy kept an eye to the ground as they negotiated the last few metres leading to the forest edge. The ambulance was there, waiting for them, a reassuring sign that things would soon be back to normal.

When Anastasia turned to check whether Martin needed any help with the hoverbed, without warning, a huge branch from a nearby gum tree cracked, broke, and fell in their direction. She screamed and ran towards them. At almost the same instant, Jimmy dropped the equipment he was carrying and jumped out of the way as part of the tree fell in his path. As he did, three of the light creatures swooped down to intercept the branch that was about to strike Tommy and Martin.

Everyone watched in stunned silence as the creatures were crushed into the earth, their light flickering before it went out.

'They saved us,' whispered Tommy, while Jimmy scrambled in amongst the twigs and leaves in a frantic attempt to find them. One faint light could still be seen, and for a long moment, Jimmy held it in his hands, while the two remaining light creatures hovered above his head, wailing, their voices high and shrill. Soon, all that was left was a soft, dark, furred creature with two large green eyes that fluttered and then closed. The others dropped down to briefly touch Jimmy's cradled hands, then flew off into the night.


The first face Tommy saw when he woke was Jimmy's. 'How long have I been sleeping?' he asked.

'About two and a half hours. The practitioners say you've had a stroke. They're amazed you recovered at all and can't explain it. They'll be writing a paper for their journal, apparently. It seems you've become famous overnight – at least in medical circles.' Jimmy grinned, doing his best not to upset his friend any more than could be helped.

'A stroke! Just like Aunt Amy...and they saved me, didn't they? Why, Jimmy, why did they choose to save me, and why did three of them die to save Martin and I when the branch came down?' Tommy reached out to grasp Jimmy's hand, his face eager, his brow furrowed in concern.

'I don't know, Tommy. What's even worse is that if we hadn't gone in to find them, they wouldn't have died at all. The poor little things...' Jimmy remembered the brief warmth of the light creature's small form as he held it in his hands, and then the deep sorrow he felt while quickly burying it in the forest, close to the others who died.

Tommy released Jimmy's hand and sat up, frowning. 'What are they, Jimmy? They're not like anything I've ever heard of, and I should know!'

'I'm hoping Anastasia will find something in the medcentre's records. She promised to look into it straight away. Oh, and by the way, we haven't told the practitioners about the lights.'


Anastasia stared at the medcentre records, unable to believe what she saw. Why had no one done this search before? If they had, surely everyone would know about this by now! Over the past one hundred and seventy years, there were nine instances in the Haunted Hills forest when people had been saved from life-threatening situations by what was variously described as 'lights', 'strange green things', 'weird fluorescent balls of light', 'floating light creatures', and so on. Each of the people involved worked in professions similar to those of Jimmy and Tommy. In none of these cases, however, were any witnesses present, which is probably why no one had followed up on the sightings.

In her excitement at the discovery, Anastasia's immediate thought was to tell the practitioner in charge of Tommy's treatment, but decided instead to discuss it with Martin.

'So, what do you think,' she said, as Martin shook his head in amazement.

'I think we should leave it alone. It's best if no one knows about them. They died saving our lives and more might die if people start looking for them. Just for once, let's be satisfied not knowing the answer.'

For a long moment, Anastasia gazed at him in surprise, then silently nodded and erased all trace of her search.